THOMAS

The JADED
GENTLEMEN
series

GRACE
BURROWES

Cover Design by Wax Creative, Inc.

Print ISBN 978-1514190593

Hadrian Lord of Hope is Published by Grace Burrowes Publishing
21 Summit Avenue
Hagerstown, MD 21740
www.graceburrowes.com

Dedication:
To those who feel as if they've loved in vain.
No love is ever in vain.

CHAPTER ONE

What did it portend, when a man arrived to his newly acquired estate and found an execution in progress?

"The damned beast is done for," a squat, pot-bellied fellow declared from halfway down the barn aisle.

Thomas Jennings, Baron Sutcliffe, had an advantage of height over the crowd gathered in the stable. Nonetheless, he apparently hadn't been spotted as he'd ridden up the lane, and he didn't draw attention watching from the shadows near the door.

"The *damned beast* was rallying until some idiot fed him oats at midday, Mr. Chesterton," a woman retorted.

She stood at the front of the group, slightly above average height, a neat dark braid hanging down a ramrod-straight back. Her dress was muddy about the hem and so far from fashionable Thomas could not have accurately named the color.

"Horses in work get grain at midday," the Chesterton fellow retorted. "If you wanted special treatment for your personal mount, you should have come to me." He uncoiled a bullwhip from around his middle, an ugly length of braided leather lashed to a heavy wooden stock. "I say the horse needs to be put down and I'm the stable master here, missy."

This woman would not take kindly to being called *missy*. A blind man could have discerned that from the command in her tone.

Thomas was far from blind.

The lady stood in profile to him, her nose a trifle bold, her mouth wide and full. Not precisely a pretty woman, though her looks were memorable. She blocked the door to a stall that housed a raw-boned bay gelding. The beast stood with his head down, flanks matted with sweat. A back hoof lifted in a desultory attempt to kick at the horse's own belly.

"The horse wants walking," she said. "A few minutes on grass every hour, clean, tepid water, and no more damned oats."

Chesterton let the coils of his whip fall, the tip of the lash landing on the toes of the lady's dusty boots.

"You are prolonging that animal's suffering, Miss Tanner," Chesterton said. "What will the new owner think of your cruelty? The beast turns up colicky after you ride him to exhaustion in this heat, and you won't even give your own horse the mercy of a quick death."

"We've had two other cases of colic in your stable in the last month, Mr. Chesterton. Any fool knows a horse recovering from colic ought not to be given oats."

Thomas had certainly known that.

"If a horse can't handle his regular rations without coming down with a bellyache, then he's not recovering, is he?" Chesterton retorted.

Chesterton flicked his wrist, so the whip uncoiled behind him. With one more jerk of his wrist, and he could wrap that whip around the woman's boots, wrench her off her feet, and get to the horse.

A stable lad sidled closer to the lady, though she gave no

indication she'd noticed the advance of Chesterton's infantry.

"Chesterton, think," Miss Tanner said, more exasperation than pleading in her tone. "Baron Sutcliffe has only recently purchased Linden, and he will now receive my reports on the crops and livestock. When he learns of three dead horses in one month, every one of them a valuable adult animal in otherwise good health, what conclusion will he draw about his stable master? Give me another twelve hours with the gelding, and then you can shoot him if he's not coming around."

The offer was reasonable to the point of shrewdness.

"No baron worth a title will listen to a woman's opinion regarding his land or livestock. You'd best be packing your things, Miss Tanner, or I'll be the one *reporting* to the nancy baron what goes on at Linden."

Time to end this.

"As it happens," Thomas said, sauntering forward, "the nancy baron is here, and willing to listen to any knowledgeable opinion on most topics. Perhaps somebody might begin by explaining why a half dozen men to whom I pay regular wages are loitering about in the middle of the afternoon?"

The lady did not give up her place in front of the stall, but Chesterton coiled his whip and puffed out his chest.

"Alvinus Chesterton, your lordship. I'm Linden's stable master. Yon beast is suffering badly, and Miss Tanner is too soft-hearted to allow the horse a merciful end."

Miss Tanner's soft heart was nowhere in evidence that Thomas could divine.

He assayed a bow in the lady's direction, though manners would likely impress her not one bit.

The point was to impress the louts surrounding her. "Miss Tanner, Thomas, Baron Sutcliffe, at your service. Chesterton, if you'd see to my horse. He's endured a long, hot journey down from London and needs a thorough cooling out."

Chesterton clearly didn't like that suggestion. In any stable, the lowliest lad was usually stuck with the job of walking a sweaty horse until the animal could be safely given water and put in its stall. The stable master stomped off, bellowing for somebody named Anderson to tend to the baron's horse.

Now for the greater challenge.

"Your horse is ailing?" Thomas asked the lady.

"I own him," she said, chin tipping up a half inch. A good chin, determined without being stubborn. In contrast, her eyes were a soft, misty gray—also guarded and weary.

"Chesterton tried to tell you what to do with your own livestock?"

"He tried to shoot my horse, and would have done so except I came by to make sure Seamus was continuing to recover."

Amid the pungent, dusty, horsy scents of the stable Thomas picked up a whiff of roses coming from—her?

"Let's have a look, shall we, Miss Tanner?"

Oh, she did not want to allow a stranger into her horse's stall, but the realm's only female steward—and possibly its most stubborn of either gender—defied her new employer at her peril.

"Miss Tanner, I will not shoot the animal without your permission. You could have me charged before the king's man for such behavior, baron or not."

Thomas would have preferred "or not," though that choice had been taken from him.

Still, he refrained from physically moving the lady aside, reaching past her to open the door, or otherwise publicly disrespecting her authority as owner of the horse and de facto steward at Linden.

Standing this close to Miss Tanner, Thomas could see she was worried for her horse, though Chesterton had been about to use his bullwhip on the lady.

"The gums tell the tale," Thomas said, quietly. "Your gelding is not trying to get down and roll, and that's a good sign."

Outside the stable, Rupert's hoof beats went clip-clopping by on the lane.

"Tell the fools to walk your horse out in the shade," the lady said. "They should get his saddle off too."

Miss Tanner was trying to distract Thomas, trying to wave him off for however long it took her to inspect her sorry beast. Thomas was not willing to be distracted, not as long as Chesterton and a half dozen of his dimwitted minions lurked about.

"Rupert walked the last two miles from the village," Thomas said. "He's barely sweating and will manage well enough. I wanted to make a point to my stable master, and you, my dear, are stalling."

That chin dipped. "Chesterton could be right. I don't want to put Seamus down."

A spine of steel, nerves of iron, and a heart of honest sentiment. Interesting combination.

"Miss Tanner, the last time I saw a horse shot, I cried shamelessly. It's a sad business all around." Thomas had been twelve years old, and Grandfather's afternoon hunter had broken a foreleg in a damned rabbit hole. The twins had sworn off foxhunting, and Theresa had cried loudest of all.

Grandpapa, for the only time in Thomas's memory, had got thoroughly inebriated.

Miss Tanner pushed the stall door open, and the horse lifted his head to inspect the visitors. A horse approaching death would have ignored them or turned away.

"Seamus, this is Baron Sutcliffe," Miss Tanner informed her gelding. "His lordship says he won't shoot you."

"A ringing endorsement." Thomas let the horse sniff his glove. "Also the truth. When did you first notice a problem?"

"Last night. I came down in the evening, and Wee Nick alerted me. He and Beckman took turns with me walking Seamus for most of the night, offering him water and periodic nibbles of grass. By morning, Seamus seemed to be functioning normally, and I thought we were through the worst."

Functioning normally was doubtless a euphemism for passing manure.

"Somebody gave him oats at noon?"

"Some imbecile."

A horse who'd done without much fodder the previous night and skipped his morning ration of oats would have been ravenous for grain by noon, and bolting grain never boded well for an equine's digestion.

Thomas stroked a hand down the gelding's sweaty neck. "Part of Seamus's problem is simply the heat. Why wasn't a bucket hung in his stall?"

"I don't know. We usually water them at the trough. Nick hung a bucket last night, but in summer, the buckets need to be scrubbed regularly."

Seamus craned his neck in the lady's direction.

"Shameless old man," she murmured, scratching one hairy ear.

Uncomfortable the gelding might be, but he was not at death's door if he could flirt with his owner. Thomas lifted the horse's lip and pressed gently on healthy pink gums. A horse in the later stages of colic would have dark or even purple gums.

"He's uncomfortable," Thomas said, "but not in immediate danger. He should be on limited rations—hay and grass, not grain—and no work for several days, exactly as you intended. Was this Nick person among those watching Chesterton threaten your horse?"

Had Thomas not come along, the men might have started exchanging bets, *or worse.*

Miss Tanner scratched the horse's other ear. "Nick, Beck, and Jamie have gone into the village to get the last of the provisions for the house in preparation for your arrival. Chesterton timed this confrontation for their absence. None of those three would have allowed Seamus to be fed oats."

The lady did not want to leave her horse undefended, and

Thomas couldn't blame her, but she would have to learn to trust her employer's authority.

"Come, Miss Tanner. I've yet to see my new house, and as the closest thing I have to a land steward, you are the first among the staff with whom I must become better acquainted."

"You'll want to eat," she said, tousling the horse's dark forelock. "To change, and Mrs. Kitts is doubtless in a taking that you've tarried in the stable this long."

Thomas did want to eat, also to drink a large quantity of something cold, and to bathe—God above, did he want to bathe.

"You there!" Thomas called to a skinny older fellow pushing a barrow of straw and muck down the barn aisle. "Your name?"

"Hammersmith, my lord."

"Hammersmith, if Miss Tanner's horse shows any signs of renewed distress, or is taken from his stall for any reason by anybody save Miss Tanner, you are to alert me immediately. Not Chesterton, not the local magistrate, not Wellington himself is to handle that animal without Miss Tanner's permission."

"Aye, milord."

"And when you've dumped that barrow, please see to it Seamus has half a bucket of clean water."

"Aye, milord. At once, sir."

"*Now* will you accompany me to the manor house, Miss Tanner?"

She gave the horse's chin a deliberate, final scratching. "Yes, my lord."

* * *

Baron Sutcliffe, was entirely too big to stalk about a busy stable as quietly as a hungry tom cat. He spoke softly too, in the cultured tones of a gentleman, but Chesterton had paled at the sight of his new employer—and put away his whip.

For that alone, the baron had Loris's loyalty.

She'd been so focused on her horse she'd not noticed the

addition to the crowd until Sutcliffe had strolled through the grooms like Moses parting a Red Sea of malevolence and mischief. The baron had been a human storm front rolling toward her, heedless of anything in his path.

No, not heedless—indifferent. Sutcliffe had known Chesterton and his lackeys were milling about, and he'd seen Chesterton fondling that infernal whip.

Sutcliffe simply hadn't cared.

The baron's exquisitely tailored riding attire and public school diction sat in contrast to Loris's conviction that his lordship would have relished a display of violence. One man against a half dozen and he'd been *amused* by the odds.

"So tell me about the enmity between you and Chesterton," the baron said, lacing his arm with Loris's. He'd matched his steps to hers—not all men would.

"He's your stable master, my lord, and we loathe each other."

"Why?"

Because I have breasts and a womb and am smarter than he or any of his near relations. Because the stable is not my domain and I could run it better than he'll ever be able to. Because he's mean, and male, and no stable lad who wants his wages will gainsay such a master.

"Chesterton loathes me because I am an unnatural female," Loris said. "I loathe him because he is needlessly cruel to the beasts who depend on him. Besides which, he is bigoted, backward, and incapable of hiring competent stable help."

As soon as the words were out of Loris's mouth, she wished them back. Not fifteen minutes after meeting her new employer, she was whining. Loris didn't like that the baron held her livelihood in his titled hands, she didn't like explaining herself, and she didn't like—oh, she most sincerely *hated*—that he'd been on hand for that scene in the stable.

She would have hated more what would have happened if the baron hadn't come prowling along.

"Chesterton will not trouble you further," Sutcliffe said as they reached the steps of the manor house. "Of this, I am certain."

"You expect him to leave?"

The baron regarded her with eyes of such dark blue they might have been a portraitist's artistic exaggeration. He had a baronial nose that on another man could have shaded toward unfortunate, but on him looked proud in the best sense. Loris did not like Sutcliffe—she didn't *know* him—but she approved of that nose.

"I do not expect Chesterton to spontaneously quit my employ," the baron said. "I can't abide incompetence in any employee. Either Chesterton did not know how to care for your horse, or he deliberately jeopardized the gelding's health."

Sutcliffe held the door for her. Of course, he would not knock on the door to his own home.

And, of course—barons probably set great store by their manners—he was politely warning Loris that *her* time at Linden Hall could be drawing to a close as well.

Then what would she do? Papa had run off to God knew where, she had no useful skills to fall back on other than stewarding, no family to turn to, and not even a true friend to her name.

Rather than take issue with his lordship's fussing, Loris preceded him through the door.

Unfortunately for her, all of her fear, fatigue, and uncertainty came trundling right along with her.

* * *

No footman, butler, or porter attended the main entrance to the Linden manor house. Thomas began a list of Linden's shortcomings: an empty stable yard, an incompetent stable master, and an unattended front door.

He gestured to the right. "Let's have our discussion in the library, Miss Tanner."

As best Thomas recalled the description of the house, a library lay off that direction. Perhaps an appearance of the

Eighty-Second Regiment of Foot would have resulted in one of his staff coming at last to investigate.

Thomas had asked Miss Tanner to join him, mostly to separate the combatants in the stable and test the loyalty of the lads. If harm came to Miss Tanner's horse despite Thomas's orders, then the stable master would not be the only one sent packing.

Miss Tanner preceded Thomas to the library, at home in the Linden manor house and not the least bit self-conscious about it. The tip of her long braid kicked up with each impact of her boot heels on the carpeted corridor.

She could not know where that tempted a man to focus his gaze.

The house was exactly as its previous owner had described: lovely with an emphasis on light, and an airy graciousness created by soft colors, ample windows, high ceilings, and elegant appointments.

The help might be lacking, but the fields were in fine shape, the buildings in excellent repair, and the house itself immaculate and welcoming.

The room Miss Tanner lead him to, while not large, yet qualified as a library. A wide fieldstone hearth lined half of the outer wall, French doors graced the other half. A fine oak desk sat near the doors, positioned to take advantage of the natural light. The long, heavily cushioned couch faced the hearth, bookshelves extended behind the couch, and a sideboard stood along the inside wall.

Upon that sideboard sat a full decanter and four sparkling crystal glasses. Thomas lifted the stopper and sniffed the contents, congratulating himself on his purchase again.

Lord Greymoor had sold the place as is, where is, including fixtures and furnishings. Fortunately for Thomas, the estate was kept ready to receive its master—or his guests.

"May I offer you a drink, Miss Tanner?"

She stalked around the room, though her first instinct was

likely to sit at Thomas's desk, where she'd no doubt ensconced her tidy bottom many times before.

She left off pretending to inspect book titles and peered at him.

"A drink. Of?"

"Excellent brandy." Thomas poured himself a hefty tot. "I intend to sample it myself, but it wasn't my horse who was just given a reprieve from a firing squad."

"Perhaps a small portion," Miss Tanner said, taking a position at the French doors. She'd turned her back to her employer, which was rude, but probably no more rude than referring to an equine firing squad.

Miss Tanner was a conundrum, part lady, part employee, part something else Thomas couldn't easily label. He was helpless to resist conundrums, because a man who'd made his fortune in commerce craved sense and order in all things.

"A restorative," Thomas said, crossing the room to pass her what even a high stickler would allow was a tonic to nerves under a severe trial. He stepped back and half-leaned, half-sat on the desk.

They could tally up their respective rudenesses later. "Has Chesterton threatened you previously?"

Miss Tanner tilted her glass and took a sniff of the contents. "Must we discuss this?"

Thomas sipped his drink, studying a tallish, dark-haired woman with gray eyes and a Gypsy cast to her features. Now that he had the chance to examine her riding habit in decent light, he'd classify the color between mud and dust.

She moved, dressed, and spoke to hide the fact, but Loris Tanner was undeniably attractive.

Thomas liked women, generally. Liked their pragmatism and humor, their affection and resilience. He liked the women he took to bed, particularly the ones who found their way there, passed an enjoyable hour or three, then found their way back out of his bed—and his life—with a smile and a wave.

Loris Tanner had a kind of beauty women seldom valued and men never overlooked: earthy, dark, curvaceous, and strong.

If she were sweet and merry, he might have had a problem, but her surliness was helpful, because they'd likely be working in relatively close quarters—provided Miss Tanner was as competent as both Lord Greymoor and Greymoor's cousin, Guinevere, Lady Amery, had claimed.

"One usually imbibes a drink, Miss Tanner."

She sampled her brandy, her expression transforming from a pensive scowl to open wonder.

"What a lovely, lovely, business this is."

Thomas added an intriguing streak of hedonism to Miss Tanner's inventory of characteristics, because as she partook of the spirits, she closed her eyes and tipped her head back, as if to savor the heat sliding down her throat and warming her insides.

"You are a connoisseur?" Thomas asked, sipping his own drink. The blunt word was tippler, the vulgar word was drunk. Applied to a woman, those terms also implied a class of tragedy Thomas had observed all too often.

"My work requires I be out of doors in all kinds of weather," Miss Tanner said. "The occasional medicinal indulgence does not go amiss."

But in all the time Miss Tanner had assumed responsibility for running the estate, she hadn't sampled the owner's brandy even once.

The conundrum reared its head again. A lady decided whether a gentleman was to sit in her presence, but an employer was the one who made that offer to the employee.

Thomas's saddle-weary arse made the decision for him. "Shall we sit, Miss Tanner?"

She took the center of the sofa, back straight, hands quietly holding her drink in her lap, as if she were enduring a social call and trying not to glance at the clock.

"You had questions, my lord?"

Have Chesterton and his like kept their hands off you? "How long have you lived on this property, Miss Tanner?"

"I have lived on this property since before Lord Greymoor purchased it almost ten years ago—he was Lord Andrew Alexander then. My father was steward here until about two years ago."

Her grip on her drink had grown quite snug.

Best get the next part over with. "What happened to your father?"

"I do not know. He either left or met with foul play. Papa was ruinously fond of drink, but because his lapses were as infrequent as they were spectacular, Lord Greymoor tolerated him."

Ruinously fond. Poetic of her.

This much, Thomas had already been told, but he suspected Mr. Tanner's minor lapses had been covered up by his daughter, who'd apparently become her father's right hand despite her gender.

"I cannot abide a drunk, Miss Tanner. Particularly not in a position of responsibility."

Thomas's guest raised her glass, as if examining the beauty of sunlight passing through brandy.

"I cannot abide a drunk in any capacity whatsoever, my lord."

"We are in agreement then." Thomas also could not bear to bully this woman regarding her father's shortcomings when she'd tried so hard to atone for them. "How do you find Linden at present?"

Now she swirled her drink, a fortune teller divining her tea leaves.

"Improving," she said at length. "Prospective buyers came down last autumn, and because they were astute, and members of Lord Greymoor's family, they were able to inform him of certain changes needed to benefit the property."

Again, she was being honest, if carefully so. Guinevere Hollister Allen, Lord Greymoor's cousin, and a frighteningly competent woman, had come to look the property over with Douglas, Lord Amery, now her spouse. They had discovered Loris quietly performing the tasks of a steward in her father's absence.

"Linden is improving, how?" Thomas asked.

"We've sold many of the sheep, which were grazing the place into oblivion. We're looking at irrigation and drainage improvements, and have started on them in a modest way. We'll ship the first loads of firewood this autumn, and the ledgers are certainly in better condition than they were."

We have, *we* are, *we* shall. Miss Tanner spoke like a true steward, one who viewed a patch of ground as creating a community of the people who cared for it and depended on it.

"What changes remain to be made?" Thomas crossed to the decanter to top off his glass and gestured with the bottle to inquire if his steward would like more.

"No, thank you." Her tone suggested drink mattered little when the land was under discussion. "What this property needs is time and people who care about it. For shearing and lambing and so forth, we're using itinerant crews, as we do for planting and harvest. The local people still work some of the staff positions, but we're short-handed, and those we do have aren't as knowledgeable as they should be."

Thomas suspected much of the "we" aspect of working Linden was in Miss Tanner's mind—or her heart.

"Is the lack of staff a criticism, Miss Tanner?" Thomas resumed his seat, scooting his chair closer to the sofa. He wanted desperately to prop his feet up on the low table, and might have if his steward were male.

But his steward, or the closest employee he had to a steward, was female, and Thomas would not discommode her unnecessarily.

"Whom would I be criticizing, your lordship?"

"Me."

"I don't know you well enough to criticize or praise you, sir. What would I criticize you for?"

Oh, how Thomas longed to pull of his boots and put up his aching feet. "You might criticize me for purchasing a property without even seeing it? For buying land in a part of the country I'm unfamiliar with? For firing my stable manager without having a replacement to hand?"

"Chesterton is an ignorant bully. The horses hate him, and with good reason. He never speaks when he can yell, and he never passes up an opportunity to snap that infernal whip."

Miss Tanner's comment reminded Thomas— inappropriately, of course—of when the ladies at the Pleasure House had taken a patron into dislike. Their judgment, sometimes despite all appearances to the contrary, had invariably been sound.

"Who hired Chesterton?"

"One of Lord Greymoor's factors," Miss Tanner said, finally taking another sip of her damned drink. "If I were to criticize anybody, it would be my former employer, though he was ever a gentleman and never overtly negligent of his estate."

"And yet, he fell short in your estimation. Honest of you to admit it," Thomas remarked. The brandy spread a lassitude through him that revealed a pervasive fatigue. He was tired to the bone, and in need of a meal, a bath, and a clean bed, in that order.

"Lord Greymoor didn't take this property seriously," Miss Tanner said. "Oh, he liked to bring his Town cronies down for hunting in the autumn, or come around at planting to ride his horses over hill and dale, but he wasn't—he did not love his own land. Papa said his lordship had nobody show him how to go on with the property, and his lordship was young."

Though Miss Tanner was younger than Greymoor, she could apparently neither comprehend nor entirely forgive his lordship's lack of attachment to the estate.

"You expect me to *love* Linden, Miss Tanner?"

She set her drink aside. "What I expect matters not one bit, does it?"

Her expectations had been all that had kept Linden together for nearly two years.

"A gentleman isn't supposed to argue with a lady," Thomas said, even though arguing with this lady would be a lively undertaking.

They lapsed into a silence Thomas felt stretching into a brood. All the while, his steward sat primly, six feet and a mysterious female universe away.

Thinking of the horse? Thomas rose and stretched a hand down to her. "Thank you for your time. We'll talk more, I'm sure."

Miss Tanner looked first at his hand, then up at his face, then down at his hand again before she seemed to grasp that he was offering to assist her to rise.

She stood, dropping his hand immediately. "Shall I fetch Mrs. Kitts to you?" she asked, moving toward the door. Miss Tanner loved the land, but she did not in the least love being interrogated by the landowner.

Lady or not, Thomas was her superior. "Miss Tanner, I haven't yet excused you."

She waved a hand. "A small oversight, your lordship. You mustn't feel the need to stand on ceremony with me."

Then she was gone, leaving Thomas to put his feet up in a bemused solitude that soothed after the peculiar developments of the day. To arrive to one's own property—and he had sent notice ahead—and find nothing and no one to greet him, was a lowering comment on the state to which his life had arrived.

He appropriated a portion of his steward's drink. What did he need with a welcoming committee, for pity's sake?

A quiet tap on the door heralded the arrival of Mrs. Kitts, a round, graying little terrier of a woman who seemed to think if she smiled long and hard enough, Thomas might smile back.

"Shall I assemble your staff, Baron?"

Baron? Well, yes, Baron. Baron Sutcliffe.

"In twenty minutes, and I'll take a tray in my rooms for supper, say around half eight."

"*Very* good, my lord." Mrs. Kitts bobbed with the enthusiasm of a female one-third her age. "*Very* good."

She withdrew, apparently pleased with her assignment, with her new employer, with the state of life in general, while unease nagged at Thomas. Nobody could be that happy, not all the time, and if they were, they should have the decency not to show it.

He took the last of Miss Tanner's drink to the French doors and gazed out over the fields and pastures lying between the manor and the home wood. Lord Greymoor and Lord Amery had both told him the home wood was far too large and poorly maintained. The benefit of this neglect was a quantity of deadfall, enough that Thomas would enjoy wood fires at his own hearth where and when he pleased, and he would also have income from selling the excess if he so chose in the short run.

Loris Tanner had pointed out the potential profit to be made, and Greymoor had given her leave to start harvesting the wood last winter. She'd also drafted the plans for the irrigation and drainage system, and she'd culled the flocks to manageable numbers.

All in all, she'd proven competent as an interim steward, but to Thomas's expert eye, she was utterly inept as a woman.

Women did not interpose themselves between livestock and bullwhips. They did not march about in stifling heat as if on dispatch for Wellington. They did not accept offers of brandy in the afternoon, even on medicinal terms.

Women liked to dress up and be told they were pretty. They flirted, simpered, and manipulated, and were usually very charming with it. Women teared up prettily at the mention of distressing developments—their favorite hair ribbon going missing, for example—and they gazed at a fellow as if they might enjoy activities with him that weren't mentioned in polite circles.

Loris Tanner had been raised by her father, a drunkard by her own account, who had dragged her from one rural estate to another. She'd never had the benefit of genteel associations, and that lack showed.

Thomas would have to do something about her. He wasn't quite sure what, but doing something about Loris Tanner went onto his list of matters to be addressed—right at the top.

CHAPTER TWO

Thomas had long ago resigned himself to a life full of petty ironies and minor frustrations. Here he was, bone weary and much in need of slumber, but unable to sleep. He'd summoned Chesterton and dismissed him with two months' wages and no character other than a letter verifying the period of employment and position held.

Chesterton's gaze had narrowed on the epistle, though Thomas doubted the man could read. Thereafter had come—bless Mrs. Kitts and her staff—a bath, a good meal, and bed.

All a weary fellow could want on such a day, but sleep, fickle lady, would not join Thomas in the bed.

He tossed, he turned, and he tossed the other way. He mentally recited some of Caesar's Gallic letters in the original Latin. He composed an epistle to his former employer, David Worthington, Viscount Fairly. Next, he made a stab at the Scottish royal succession from Kenneth MacAlpin down through the Jameses, none of which brought slumber closer.

So Thomas got out of bed, pulled on his breeches and shirt, and padded barefoot down to the library for another nip of the "lovely business."

A niggling cocklebur of a thought intruded on the way to the decanter: Thomas had let his stable master go. A man of business knew that loose ends were the stuff of avoidable disaster, and Chesterton's dismissal meant nobody was in charge of the stable.

Rupert was in the stable, as was Miss Tanner's gelding.

Thomas used the flame from the sconce in the corridor to light a carrying candle and left through the French doors. Moonlight gilded the path to the stable, and the night breeze made the air nearly cool, a blessed change from the sweltering day.

Heat lightning flickered to the north, but the horses were calm, some munching hay, some dozing.

Seamus had curled up in the straw of his loose box, his gaze clear, the remains of a pile of hay near a hanging bucket. Somebody had brushed out the gelding's coat so no trace of his earlier ordeal remained.

Beside the bucket, nestled on a horse blanket, Thomas's steward lay curled into the corner.

A woman—a tired, badly dressed, inconveniently pretty woman—defended the Linden stable.

With plural pronouns, perhaps?

Thomas scooped Miss Tanner up, blanket and all, as gently as he could and cradled her against his chest. For her to share a bed with a horse was ill-advised, unsanitary, and a poor reflection on Linden's owner.

Miss Tanner muttered, "Tired," and, "soon." Possibly, "Papa."

The stable was one of Linden's best features, lavishly commodious and sturdily constructed. It would do well enough for Miss Tanner as protection from the elements. Thomas deposited his burden on the pile of hay tossed down for the morning's rations—he'd slept on worse and been grateful—though he'd likely not looked as fetching.

In the saddle room, he found a wool cooler used to keep a hot horse comfortable in the winter—clean, fortunately. He brought it back to the woman slumbering in the hay and hunkered down to tuck it around her.

"Seamus?" she murmured sleepily.

"Go to sleep, sweetheart. Seamus is well."

She subsided into her dreams, leaving Thomas nothing more to do but slip from the barn and walk back to the house.

He scrubbed his dusty feet clean, finished a hefty nightcap, and tried once more for sleep, though something would, indeed, have to be done about Miss Tanner.

* * *

Linden's new owner, His Most Exalted Imperial Handsomeness, Thomas Jennings, Baron Sutcliffe, had created a *situation*, and Loris did not intend that the situation be allowed to fester.

She strode into the barn at full daylight to find that somebody had forked the morning's ration of hay into each stall, but otherwise, the lads were lounging about, enjoying an absence of supervision.

The stalls had not been mucked. The water buckets had not been scrubbed or refilled. A lead rope was coiled in the dirt, where any unsuspecting horse could tangle a hoof in it and come to grief. The riding horses at pasture overnight had not been brought in.

Loris planted herself in the center of the aisle, between the main doors and the group of idle men, and tugged off her straw hat.

"Good morning, gentlemen."

Only the largest, referred to as Wee Nick, nodded before resuming his solitary effort to rake the barn aisle.

"Until Baron Sutcliffe finds a replacement for Mr. Chesterton," Loris said, "I will direct your activities. I expect the stalls to be mucked and rebedded with fresh straw, the water buckets scrubbed and refilled, the riding horses brought in, and the harnesses, saddles, and bridles cleaned, if you please. Should you ask it of me, I will make specific assignments; otherwise, I'll assume you can sort out who does what among yourselves. Any questions?"

A taut silence followed, during which Wee Nick quietly departed in the direction of the pastures. Loris slapped her straw hat back onto her head and turned to leave.

"I've a question," one fellow called out. Anderson was the natural successor to Chesterton in terms of the stable hierarchy: lazy, mean, and insolent. "If we don't hop to your commands, *Miss* Tanner, how will you make us, without Chesterton's bullwhip?"

Loris nearly thanked Anderson, because a direct, public confrontation would settle matters most efficiently, and she had the perfect—

"Perhaps," a deep voice drawled, "I'll equip my steward with a whip."

Sutcliffe strolled up the barn aisle, attired in snug breeches, spotless linen, gleaming boots, a silk waistcoat the same deep blue as his eyes, and a black riding jacket. The man had no business looking so well put together. He probably even smelled good, of flowers and spices and—

A memory tickled the back of Loris's mind while His Baronial Handsomeness paused at the half door to his gelding's stall.

"Dear me," his lordship murmured. "No one has tended to Rupert's housekeeping. How puzzling. The women responsible for the manor don't need a bullwhip to inspire them to do an honest day's work for an honest day's pay. My quarters were spotless."

A telling point, easily made.

"Miss Tanner?" the baron called, scratching at Rupert's withers with every appearance of casual affection.

"My lord?" Loris didn't move, though she abruptly felt compelled to stand closer to his side.

"How many men should it take to keep this stable up to appropriate standards?"

"Five or six, if they're hard workers, and we don't have any difficulties with lameness or illness."

The baron went on scratching his horse, to the gelding's obvious delight.

"Miss Tanner, you must advise me as to which of these men are expendable. I cannot abide inefficiency. Perhaps we might discuss this while you ride out with me this morning, assuming you're free to join me?"

Such manners, while Sutcliffe wielded his authority more tellingly than Chesterton had ever cracked a bullwhip.

"If you wish, my lord."

"My thanks." The baron swept the silent group with a glance that conveyed amused disdain. "In addition to your other duties, gentlemen, you will please saddle Rupert for Miss Tanner and a second horse for myself. Have the horses in the stable yard in twenty minutes, for I'd spare myself and Miss Tanner the worst of the day's heat as we make our initial inspection of the land. Miss Tanner?"

The baron offered Loris his arm, and with the stable boys gawping at that spectacle, Loris took it.

She and his lordship perambulated in silence into the stable yard, as if no one were glaring daggers at their backs. The baron escorted Loris some distance along the front paddock, to a bench in the shade of a spreading oak.

"That was completely unnecessary, my lord."

"Do not drop my arm," he replied as they sauntered along, "nor by any gesture or expression shall you imply we are in less than complete charity with each other."

"We are not in complete charity with each other, sir. You have destroyed any prayer I had of holding authority over that group of scoundrels."

"I have established your authority," the baron corrected her, *pleasantly.* "Which is more than you could have done on your own."

And yet, somehow, Loris had managed Linden *on her own* for nearly two years.

"You *shamed* them," she hissed, "comparing them to the housemaids. They'll hate me the worse for it, the housemaids will put on airs, and nothing will be done as it should."

Sutcliffe took out a handkerchief edged in lace the same shade of blue as his eyes, and batted at the bench, which was perfectly free of dust, dirt, and bird droppings.

"What would you have done if I hadn't appeared, Miss Tanner? Lectured them into mucking out the stalls?"

"Withheld their blasted pay," she retorted. "Tomorrow is their half-day, and they're paid at midday. Any man who didn't put in a full day's work wouldn't get his full pay, and I would have informed them of this fact had you not interrupted me."

The batting about with the handkerchief went on until the bench was likely cleaner than Mrs. Kitts's sideboards.

"That might have worked, Miss Tanner, but who would have done the work today?"

"Those who wanted to be paid," Loris shot back. "Never threaten a pack of jackals with an empty gun, Baron. I would have stated to all that those who didn't work to my standards would not be paid, and then left the men to sort it out."

Sutcliffe folded his handkerchief into sixths and tucked it away. "Then you would have the two or three worthy ones covering up for the slackers."

Oh, he was a quick study, and so early in the day. "*They already do*, and what care I about that, if the horses are tended to? The burden of enforcing discipline would then fall on the men doing the work, not directly on me."

Sutcliffe gestured to the bench, and even that, a simple twirling of his wrist, was grace personified.

"Interesting approach, madam, but what if the few honest ones leave in disgust?"

Blast him for putting an elegant finger on Loris's nagging

worry. "They might, though today's crisis would have been averted."

"Or merely delayed to a less opportune moment. Will you need to change into a habit if you're to ride this morning?"

"I will not." Had his lordship switched topics to avert further argument? "Why put me up on your gelding? Rupert looks quite assured of his own importance."

Like beast, like master.

The bench sat in the shade a little above the stable, and in the distance, several lads dumped wheelbarrows of soiled straw into the muck pit, horses were brought in and turned out, and water buckets emptied.

"Rupert will behave if I'm about, Miss Tanner. Please do have a seat."

Loris was tired, more tired than usual even, given the time of year. She sank onto the bench, and Sutcliffe took his time settling in beside her. Did he put himself in such close proximity to her on purpose, or in the past two years, had she lost track of proper deportment between the genders?

"I'm hardly sitting in your lap, Miss Tanner." Laughter lurked in his lordship's blue eyes, daring Loris to leave him smirking on his bench in solitude.

She stayed right where she was and pretended to study the activity in the stable yard. "Why did you inform those men I'd be up on Rupert?"

His lordship laid his arm along the back of the bench, a gentleman completely at his perishing, fragrant leisure.

"I am intimately familiar with Rupert's saddle and bridle, and with the horse himself. If the equipment has been sabotaged, if there's a burr under the saddle, I will more easily perceive it than I would were your mount unfamiliar to me."

This was worse than if he'd sought to challenge Loris's authority. "You think they would try to *hurt* me?"

"I'm not willing to take that chance, in part because your safety is my responsibility, but also because such insubordination needs to be identified and eradicated immediately."

E-rad-i-cated. Sutcliffe snapped off each syllable, like a ferret shaking a fat rat by its neck.

"You could eradicate everybody in that group but Wee Nick, old Jamie, and Beckman, and we'd be no worse off." Loris skimmed her boot along grass overdue for rain. "Chesterton didn't start his mischief yesterday until those three had taken the wagon into the village. They wouldn't have stood for his nonsense."

"Fear not. We'll decide what to do with the dead wood among the lads, and they won't plague you much longer. But a question, Miss Tanner." The baron crossed his long, booted legs, not a care in the world. "Where do you dwell?"

"Dove Cottage." Did he know she'd neglected to dwell there last night? "My house lies through the trees off the drive and is named for its gray color."

"Ah."

That was all. Merely a lordly "ah," and no explanation for the origin of the question or the significance of its answer. At some point in the night, Loris had apparently roused enough to leave Seamus's stall and cuddle up on the morning's ration of hay, where somebody had draped a clean wool cooler. She had no recollection of it, surely a sign of extreme fatigue.

Botheration.

For months, Loris had wished her father would come home. When that wish had proved fruitless, she'd wished Lord Greymoor might take a more active interest in his property. Then she'd learned Linden was for sale, and she'd wished the new owner would take the place in hand.

Loris thus found herself in an unenviable category of people: She'd got what she wished for at last, and could now regret this good fortune at her leisure.

* * *

Thomas forced himself to relax and enjoy the morning air, when he wanted to oblige his steward with the rousing set-to she craved.

Alas, the louts across the way would respect neither Miss Tanner nor Thomas for airing vocabulary at such an hour.

The day would soon be brutally hot, and Thomas had come to the stable thinking to give Rupert a chance to stretch his legs. The horse had brought him down from London, jogging through the countryside with unflagging energy. He should be subdued enough for Miss Tanner today, if perhaps a bit stiff from his night of confinement.

Miss Tanner looked fresh, composed, and tidy—certainly none the worse for dreaming away her night on a pile of hay. She'd brushed and plaited her hair, and donned another sturdy, nondescript dress. This morning, she wore a straw hat, wide-brimmed to protect her face from the sun, but as close as Thomas sat to her, he detected a sprinkling of freckles across her nose.

Also a hint of lemon about her person, lemon and something else, something edible—cinnamon or nutmeg. She'd turned to keep an eye on the stable yard, and Thomas's gaze was drawn to the side of her neck. Her dark hair was swept back into some fancy variety of braid, but in the morning's humidity, tendrils curled against the soft skin below her ear.

Would Miss Tanner enjoy being kissed there?

Surely, the heat had inspired that idle curiosity.

"The horses are ready," Miss Tanner said, shooting to her feet.

Thomas rose more lazily and again offered her his arm.

"I detest this," she muttered as they ambled back toward the stable yard. "Every time I take your arm, I feel you are informing the world I haven't the physical strength or competence even to walk across level ground."

"You are so prickly, Miss Tanner," Thomas replied. "Does it not occur to you that strolling arm in arm is a harmless way for a gentleman and a lady to enjoy proximity to one another without offending convention?"

"Offending convention?" she snorted. "It offends *me*, sir, and if you're showing me your manners for the sake of convention, we can dispense with further sacrifices of a similar nature."

Lord Fairly would like her. Lady Fairly would *adore* Loris Tanner. "You find this courtesy offensive?" Thomas asked, making no move to withdraw his arm.

"Not the courtesy."

"Then my person, perhaps?"

"Not your person, particularly, but the fiction that your assistance is required."

Which implied she also took issue with Thomas's person *generally*.

"If you should stumble, madam, would you prefer that I allow you to fall flat on your... face?"

Miss Tanner slipped her arm from his and marched over to Rupert, who waited by the ladies' mounting block.

Thomas followed her to the horse's side, one step behind. "Allow me to check the fit of his equipment, madam."

Miss Tanner comprehended the import of a raised eyebrow, because she stepped aside as Thomas moved the saddle back all of one inch, refastened the girth, loosened and then tightened the noseband on the bridle, and gave Rupert a visual inspection.

The horse was no more reticent than the lady when matters were not to his liking, and he stood placidly in the building heat.

"Rupert awaits the pleasure of your company, Miss Tanner."

Miss Tanner hopped up the steps of the mounting block and swung a leg over the horse's back. Thomas realized only then that the horse was not wearing a side-saddle, and his steward was prepared to ride astride, abetted by some manner of divided skirt.

How indelicate, though riding astride was probably more

comfortable over the long term than riding aside.

She gestured at a sizeable dapple-gray whose reins were held by an exceptionally large blond fellow.

"That gelding is Evan, your lordship. He's a steady sort, and not the most enthusiastic about the faster paces."

While Miss Tanner seemed to prefer life at a dead gallop. "We'll get along," Thomas said, swinging up and settling into the saddle. He took a minute to readjust the length of his stirrups, patted the horse, and nudged him firmly with his calves. Evan was apparently preoccupied with weighty matters known only to himself, because he stood stolidly despite Thomas's suggestion that the time had come to move.

A single, solid whack with the crop on Evan's broad hindquarters startled the horse into a trot, which earned him a pat on the neck, and had Rupert moving off in his wake.

They rode over the home farm, past two tenant farms, and back onto Linden land proper before Thomas noticed that his steward was smiling at him.

"You make Evan look like quite the blooded gentleman. He'll be full of himself now, won't you, Evan Alexander?"

"The horses acquire Greymoor's surname?" Thomas asked, letting the gelding have a loose rein.

"Why not?" Miss Tanner replied, doing likewise with Rupert. "That would make you Rupert Jennings," she informed her mount.

"Actually, it's Sir Rupert Jennings, according to a very young lady I know. Has a pleasant ring to it. Do you like children, Miss Tanner?" Thomas asked, holding a branch back to allow her and Rupert to pass.

"I do, but not those kind of children." She brought her horse to halt, and Thomas followed her gaze to a farm pond that lay through a break in the trees. The tranquility of the scene was broken by the laughter and yelling of a half dozen stark naked boys of various ages and sizes.

They took turns running the length of the dock, then

hurtling into the water, bellowing encouragement and insults at each other all the while.

The pond would feel divine, even this early in the day.

"What's wrong with that variety of children?" Thomas asked, as the smallest boy went sailing off the dock.

"They are boys. Noisy, trespassing little boys who should not be here unsupervised."

To Miss Tanner the lack of supervision was apparently a worse transgression than the lack of clothing.

"The day will soon be stifling," Thomas said, "and they are full of energy. A nice, cool pond makes for a perfect start to their morning."

"They are children, Baron. They require supervision."

"They swim like otters." Would the woman argue whether the sun rose in the east? "The older ones look out for the younger ones."

"Not always," Miss Tanner muttered darkly, just as one of the largest boys careened off the dock, landing squarely on top of the little one who'd gone ahead of him.

"Timmie!" a third child screamed. "Our Timmie! He's gone under! You've killed my brother!" Splashing, yelling, and general, wet pandemonium ensued.

"God's riding boots. Wait here," Thomas ordered, shrugging out of his jacket and tossing it to the lady. "I mean that. Please wait here."

He cantered the horse to the edge of the pond, dismounted on the fly, yanked his boots off, and executed a slicing dive from the end of the dock. The whole sequence, from Timmie's disappearance to the surface dive, took only a handful of seconds.

Timmie had sunk like a stone directly beneath the scene of the impact, and when Thomas broke the surface, he kept his right arm crooked around the child's chin and swam for the dock. The other boys were still yelling and churning up a tempest, but one of them had the presence of mind to hoist himself onto the dock and reach down for Timmie.

Thomas heaved himself up as well and knelt over Timmie, who wasn't moving, though he hadn't been in the water long. Thomas picked the child up and tipped him so his head fell below his chest, but little water drained from his mouth or nose.

"Is he dead?" one of the boys asked. "Me mum will kill me if he's dead."

"Timmie's mum will kill us all," another pointed out ominously.

"She'll kill me first," the bigger boy said. "Mister?"

Thomas beheld a circle of wet, anxious little faces. "Timmie simply got his bell rung a bit too hard. I expect he'll come coughing back to consciousness directly. Perhaps somebody could fetch his shirt?"

The boys, so casually naked around each other, exchanged glances suggesting they realized that their nudity was now displayed before a grown man, one who'd galloped out of nowhere to rescue Timmie—and the rest of them. They made a collective grab for their shirts, then returned to the dock.

"If someone could tether my horse," Thomas said, "I'll be spared a long walk to the manor."

"You're that baron fella," the largest boy remarked. "Down from London, you are. Heard me da talking about you with Timmie's da."

"I'm that baron fellow," Thomas admitted, just as Timmie began to cough and sputter. "Thomas, Baron Sutcliffe, gentlemen. Our friend is back among us."

The largest boy tousled Timmie's wet, wheat-blond hair. "You all right then, our Timmie?"

"What happened?" Timmie asked, expression dazed.

"You got your lights put out, my lad," Thomas said. "Let's get you into your shirt, lest these ruffians toss you back in the water to assist in your recovery."

"He talks funny," Timmie observed as Thomas pulled a

shirt over the boy's head.

"He's the baron from up the manor," the biggest boy explained. "He saved your life, Tims, when I jumped atop you and thumped you so hard."

Timmie regarded Thomas owlishly. "May I please sit, Mr. Baron?"

"You may sit," Thomas said, easing back to leave the child sitting unsupported on the dock, "but you must answer some questions."

Tim fumbled with the sole button on his shirt, his manner befuddled. "Questions?"

Thomas went through a litany learned in many a lowly tavern. "What day is this?"

"Tuesday."

"How many fingers am I holding up?"

"Three. Is that ring gold?"

"Yes, with a sapphire inset. Who is your king?"

"Good King George, though he's mad as a March hare, and me da says the fat Regent is spending us into the poor house."

"Whose land are you on?"

"Linden's."

"Where does your mama think you are?"

Timmie eyed another boy who resembled him in every particular.

"We took our da his lunch at the mill," the boy said. "He forgot it when he left this morning."

"And the rest of you gentlemen?"

Two should have been bringing a plow horse back from the farriers', the other two were at loose ends, their mother being confined in anticipation of the arrival of their eighth sibling.

Thomas sat crossed-legged on the dock, wondering how long his steward would remain concealed in the trees. Six little boys imitated his posture.

"Now look, you lot. You could have had a tragedy here this morning, if Tim had remained in the water and unconscious. You need to bring an older boy along, a strong swimmer, and you need to let your parents know what you're about."

"My ma won't never let me swim," one of the smaller boys groused. "My brothers wouldn't come 'cause they say I'm too little to play with."

"Tell your father, then," Thomas suggested, "who I am sure swam in this very pond when he was a lad. Your brothers are missing out on the pleasure of a fine, cool swim, and the pleasure of spending time the other older boys."

The largest lad shook his head. "They can't give us permission, our papas," he said, "because they don't have permission from you. The earl, that Greybeard fellow, he was never here, so nobody cared. But you're here."

The situation in a nutshell. "I am here. I intend to live here for the foreseeable future."

Glances were exchanged all around, assuring Thomas a place on the evening's gossip agenda in every home in the village.

"That other fellow," Timmie said, plucking at his damp shirt front. "Greybottom, he wasn't hardly ever to home."

"That's why the earl sold the land to me." What were these children trying to say?

"Me da," Timmie replied, scowling at his wrinkled fingers, "he said we'd have to go to Manchester for work if the new owner of Linden weren't to home any more often than the old. He said the earl ran a bunch of bloody, bleatin' sheep for quick money to spend up to Londontown."

Thomas sat among the boys on the dock and recalled Loris Tanner's judgment of Lord Greymoor: The earl had been an absentee owner who either hadn't taken the land seriously, or simply hadn't *known how* to take the land seriously.

Thomas was similarly ignorant, but he was willing to learn, if Miss Tanner were willing to instruct him.

"We've sold a good many of the sheep. They were hard on the land." *We* being Thomas and his steward, apparently.

Timmie nodded, not looking half so confused. "That's good. I'll tell me da."

Thomas rose, bringing the boys to their feet as well. "Tell him where you went swimming, but try to have a word with him when your mother won't overhear. You don't want to worry her."

"She'll worry me with a birching," Timmie muttered, to the hearty agreement of his confreres. "Has a fearsome arm, does Ma."

"I'll be off then, lads, but don't come here again without one of the older boys, if you please."

Thomas left amid choruses of "no, guv," and "never, yer worship."

Evan had been tied to a bush, which the horse was ingesting with remarkable dispatch for one so lazy. Not until Thomas had gathered up his boots and led the horse back through the trees did he consider the difficulty—the impossibility, rather—of riding home barefoot and sopping wet.

CHAPTER THREE

Even sopping wet, with his boots in hand, his lordship looked perfectly at his ease.

"I've allowed the drama of the moment to leave me with a problem, Miss Tanner."

"Sir?" Loris knew good and well what *his* problem was: Soaked to the skin, he'd ruin a perfectly good saddle if he rode all the way home, and because he couldn't put boots on over wet breeches, his other option was to walk the distance barefoot.

Her problem was that, attired in his London finery when dry, Thomas Jennings, Baron Sutcliffe, was an imposing figure. After a thorough dunking, his fine linen shirt clung to his muscled chest, his summer-weight breeches hugged his lower half, and—oh, drat him to Hades—his naughty smile said he knew his attributes were disconcertingly obvious.

Loris was blushing. She knew it, he knew it, and he was *enjoying* her distress—she knew that most of all.

"What shall I do with my wet self, Miss Tanner? I value good equipment as much as the next man, and somebody paid considerable coin for that saddle."

"I can carry your saddle if you ride bareback, or we can leave the saddle here under a convenient bush."

Sutcliffe's nonplussed expression gratified Loris inordinately—though fleetingly.

"Bareback is not particularly comfortable, Miss Tanner, less so when one's clothing is damp. I'm not about to leave a valuable saddle behind to tempt the youth of Sussex."

His lordship expected *her* to solve his problem—doubtless a test of some sort.

"I can ride back to the manor and retrieve dry clothes for you, sir."

He ran a hand down Rupert's glossy neck. "Rather a long way, and a long time to leave me here with nobody but Evan to entertain me."

The baron casually undid his neck cloth and waistcoat, then drew his wet shirt over his head and wrung it out. Loris turned Rupert so the baron's nudity wasn't in her direct line of sight.

Though she had peeked, and she did not care if he knew that.

Gracious days, Sutcliffe was breathtaking. Town life apparently left a fellow with sculpted muscles rippling around his frame in the most peculiar fashion. His chest, his arms, his abdomen... ye gods. As the baron squeezed sections of wet linen, his biceps had bunched and his stomach muscles...

"Miss Tanner?" From the corner of her eye, she watched as the baron went on wringing out his shirt. "I haven't all day to discuss hypotheticals while I broil in the sun. How do you propose to get me home?"

"You could stay here all day, and eventually, as hot as it is, you will dry off." While Loris would soon expire of mortification.

And curiosity.

"That course will not do," he said, giving his shirt a final, muscular twist. "I have matters to attend to, and idleness is not in my nature." He stalked around into her line of sight, his boots and waistcoat in one hand, his shirt and cravat slung over one shoulder, Evan's reins in the other hand.

Loris closed her eyes and bowed to a fate she had probably earned with all those prayers for an estate owner who'd take a personal interest in the property.

"You can ride up behind me."

"Brilliant idea," the baron replied, sauntering over to Rupert with a smile that boded ill for somebody. "Fold up the saddle pad to protect the cantle, and I'll lash my boots and clothing behind Evan's saddle."

While he used his cravat for that purpose, Loris did as he instructed and took Evan's reins so the baron could ride behind her. Even with her leaning forward over Rupert's neck, getting the baron mounted was an awkward business. The worst moment was when he swung up, and his chest fairly pushed Loris down along the horse's crest, so she was covered by him, the way a stallion—

God's riding boots, indeed.

Then his lordship was mounted behind her.

"I'll steer," the baron said, settling his bare hands over her gloved ones. "If you'll pony Evan behind us."

Loris nodded, carefully, because his lordship's bare chest was snug against her back, and she didn't want to hit his nose with her head. She relinquished Rupert's reins in exchange for Evan's, and became so much cargo, the baron in control of their mount.

"Rupert can't be very comfortable," the baron remarked as the horse ambled off, "having you crouched over his neck like that."

Loris eased more upright. "You are wet, and I prefer to remain dry. If you're willing, we can stop at my cottage, which is closer than the manor. My father's clothing should fit you."

"That will serve."

"Must you speak in my ear?"

"Must your ear be so handily located near my lips?"

Loris retreated into silence, a long silence, because the horse, though easily seventeen hands, was carrying double and thus kept to the walk by his master.

"So tell me about my employees in the stable," the baron said after they'd bumped along dusty lanes and past fields badly in need of rain. "I assume the blond giant is your Wee Nick?"

"Not my Wee Nick. Nicholas is very much his own man. I suspect he's had to be, with how Chesterton and the others treat him."

"Wee Nick is treated differently? How?"

This interrogation was another blessing resulting from Loris's wish for Linden to have an involved owner, and yet, the question was reasonable.

"For one thing, Nick is treated as if strength is his only attribute. He makes lovely birdhouses, beautiful, whimsical creations I'd adore were I a bird. Around the barn, he's expected to handle the heaviest jobs, and to do so uncomplainingly. He's expected to be good-natured about constant teasing; he's generally regarded as not too bright when in fact, he's simply quiet."

"How long has he worked here?" the baron asked, turning Rupert along a field lush with clover despite the ongoing lack of rain.

"Nick and Beckman showed up shortly after my father left and have been here since. Few remain who've worked at Linden for most of their lives."

"The boys at the pond conveyed the sense I'm on probation with the locals. They weren't impressed with Greymoor's absentee style, and I'm expected to be a similar disappointment."

Ever so gradually, while they talked, Loris relaxed. Rupert had a steady, smooth walk, even carrying double, and the morning sun dried his lordship off at least above the waist.

"Greymoor was at heart a good man," Loris said. "He didn't put on airs, and he was scrupulous about paying the trades, but he relied entirely on Papa's guidance when it came to managing Linden. His lordship's brother was here more than Lord Greymoor was the last few years."

"I believe the earl was traveling on the Continent prior to coming into his title."

"I didn't mind his lordship traveling one bit."

"Because then your papa was more able to indulge his vices?" Sutcliffe suggested.

This again. Always this. "No, Baron." Loris did not clench her teeth, and she did not drive her elbow back into her employer's ribs. "Not because my father was less accountable in the earl's absence, but rather, because when Greymoor was gone, the earl's titled friends did not impose on his hospitality down here, and make mischief to their wealthy, irresponsible hearts' content."

Behind her, the baron came subtly to attention. When he spoke, his voice was quiet and very close to her ear.

"Miss Tanner, did the earl's friends *bother* you?"

The man hadn't been born who wasn't at least occasionally a bother. "I learned to avoid them, and I suspect his lordship instructed them to leave me in peace. Then the earl went abroad, and his friends were no longer a problem."

The baron guided Rupert into the orchard that ran behind the home wood. "Miss Tanner, do you know how to disarm a man who seeks to do you mischief?"

"I know to use my knee," Loris said, coloring at the topic.

"If a man places his hands around your throat, thus,"—Sutcliffe dropped the reins on Rupert's mane and circled her neck with his hands—"what defense have you?"

"Is there one?" The baron's hands were dry and warm. The sensation of his touch on Loris's neck was both foreign and fascinating.

"You take my smallest finger on each hand," he instructed,

"like that, and you yank it back and away from my own hand. I will be forced to ease my grip."

Loris peeled his hands away from her neck.

"Is there more I should know?" Because all too often, this kind of common-sense information would have been useful, and yet Loris's own father hadn't apprised her of it.

"Of course," Sutcliffe replied, taking up the reins again. "The first thing you do when threatened by a man is scream bloody murder. Most men can't perpetrate certain kinds of mischief if an audience is likely to come pounding around the corner. And use your legs—your legs are stronger than your arms. Kick, jab, flail, and aim for his most vulnerable parts when you do."

"What else?"

"Use your sharp joints—the elbow in the ribs, the knuckle in the eye, your fingernails across his throat," the baron went on. "Use your dead weight. If he's got you about the waist, tromp on his foot hard, then sag your entire weight without warning, and throw him off balance."

Sutcliffe's voice held a banked force, as if the topic were more than theoretical to him, and yet he was a man—a large, magnificently fit man.

Loris twisted in the saddle to peer at him. "How is it you know of these maneuvers?"

"As Lord Fairly's factor, I traveled extensively and ended up in interesting situations from time to time. I've also had responsibility for females who found themselves in difficult circumstances with unruly men. The ladies needed to be forearmed."

"Did they carry weapons?" Loris asked as the orchard gave way to the wood itself. When would a lady find herself in difficult circumstances with unruly men—unless she was a makeshift land steward, and the absentee owner's stable had fallen into the hands of ruffians?

"Some of the ladies carried weapons," the baron said.

In the shade of the old woods, the temperature was cooler. Loris resisted the lure of his lordship's heat—barely.

"The ladies preferred knives," he went on, as if discussing the merits of embroidery over cut work. "From my perspective, most men can overpower a woman sufficiently to wrest a knife from her, and then she's enraged her attacker and armed him as well."

Sutcliffe had argued with somebody repeatedly over the wisdom of arming women with knives. Loris thought back to his punctilious escort of her that morning.

"What exactly did these women do that put them in such situations?"

Rupert walked along, twigs snapping beneath the weight of his iron shod hooves. A squirrel scolded from above, and a late blooming patch of wild lilies added a splash of orange to the greenery all around.

Did the baron see the beauty he owned? Did he note that the lilies bloomed later here than in the sunnier locations?

"The women I knew were prostitutes, Miss Tanner. My employer owned a brothel, among many other enterprises. I occasionally managed that establishment for him."

Gracious flowering gardens. What did one say? "I see."

Loris remained silent for long moments, while the baron steered the horse along a wagon track that cut across the wood. Sunlight beamed onto the grassy lane through the dense canopy, creating a sense of time having slowed in the quiet of the summer morning.

"What do you see, Miss Tanner?"

The baron would have been fiercely protective of those women. Loris knew this now, but wasn't sure how she felt about it.

"May we please change the subject?"

"This wood is lovely," he said. "Such a shame to disturb it to harvest the deadfall."

Sutcliffe was being considerate. Loris wished she

might study his face and tell from his eyes whether he'd accommodated her for her sake or his own.

"Greymoor never even rode through here before approving my plan to sell firewood. I don't think he could have borne to see this place disturbed if he had."

"If *you* didn't want to disturb the wood, then why did you make the proposal?"

The baron was astute. Loris respected this about him, though his intellect wasn't always convenient.

"I liked Lord Amery," she said, "the fellow who came to look at Linden last autumn, and his cousin. They would not have allowed a bunch of rackety fribbles from London onto the property for weeks of drinking and carousing."

This time, Rupert cut a path right through a patch of lilies, several of the blooms coming to a swift end as a result.

"So you were trying to impress Lord Amery with the profit to be made?" Sutcliffe asked.

"I was. He was kind to me, and struck me as a man worthy of trust."

"If Douglas Allen cannot be trusted," Sutcliffe replied, "then Judgment Day has come. He's about the most sober, responsible, boring fellow you will ever meet."

Boring was no price at all to pay for kindness and trustworthiness, and Amery's lady hadn't found him boring in the least.

"You know Lord Amery, then?" Loris asked.

"I know him fairly well, because that employer I mentioned earlier, Lord Fairly, regards Lord Amery as a close friend. They were brothers-in-law at one point, and they still have some complicated family connection through Fairly's sisters."

"How is it a man you describe as boringly proper is friends with a man who owns a brothel?"

"Men are like that. We don't make sense."

Must he sound so proud of that shortcoming? "An eternal verity, to be sure, my lord. Take the right fork up here," Loris said at a divergence of the path. "The trail winds up at my cottage, and this way, you will not be seen in your damp glory by one and all."

"Protecting my modesty, Miss Tanner? Bend down," he directed as they approached a sapling hanging low over the path.

"Protecting my own," she shot back, leaning over Rupert's neck. Behind her, the baron bent forward as well, so Loris's was momentarily pressed against his lordship's naked chest.

"Perhaps I should walk," she said when they straightened, "or you should ride Evan from here." Lest she expire from the baron's proximity before she reached the safety of her cottage.

"We're almost there, and whatever damage I've done to your cantle and Rupert's back won't be remedied by switching horses at this point. Down again." Sutcliffe didn't wait for Loris to bend, but nudged her forward, his chest to her back.

Fortunately, the trees were thinning, and soon Rupert toddled around a small pond at the foot of Loris's grassy yard.

The baron drew his gelding to a halt right at the back porch of Loris's dwelling, a tidy cottage that sat in the middle of a clearing. Blooms spilled from hanging baskets and half barrels, from beds and borders and window boxes. His lordship would probably think them frivolous and a waste of seed and soil.

Though Loris loved her flowers, and made more than pin money from them in a good year.

His lordship slid off the horse's back end, right over the beast's tail, then reached up for Loris.

"I'll wait out here with the horses, my lord."

"Off you go. You've been on that horse all morning. You might as well stretch your legs while I attend to my wardrobe."

Sutcliffe tugged Loris from the saddle, and she found herself standing beside Rupert, the baron's hands still on her waist.

And, heaven have mercy, all Loris wanted to do was close her eyes and *feel* the warm bulk of his lordship's muscles under her fingers. Thank God she still had her riding gloves on.

The baron stepped back and hung his damp shirt, waistcoat, and cravat over the porch railing.

"My father's clothes are in the trunk at the foot of his bed," Loris said. "You'll find wash water in my bedroom, and you may use my combs and brushes as well."

Sutcliffe bowed. "My thanks."

The gesture should have been ridiculous when he was clad only in damp breeches, but when he turned to go, Loris was too mesmerized by the sight of those breeches clinging intimately to the baron's fundament.

On babies, buttocks were cute. On horses, they could be muscular and impressive. On grown men, Loris had somehow failed to note they existed. But the baron's muscled flanks were a sight to behold.

For, oh ye trumpeting cherubs, his lordship was not wearing underlinen.

* * *

"You followed Chesterton into Haybrick?" Nick asked Beckman.

Beckman paused, a load of dirty straw in the barrow before him. Inside the barn, the air was close, but outside in the stable yard, the temperature would already be stifling.

"I followed him to the Cock and Bull," Beckman said, taking out a flask and tipping it up. "I tarried with my pint long enough to hear Chesterton railing against the injustice of his fate. He took a room at the inn, and was in the company of Anderson and a couple of the other disaffected stable lads when I left."

They hardly qualified as stable lads. Most of the crew Chesterton had hired had been little more than incompetent, and Nick was glad to see them go.

As were the horses, no doubt.

Nick had not been glad to see Loris Tanner ride off in the company of Baron Sutcliffe.

"Did any of the grooms mention quitting?" Nick asked.

"Yes," Beckman said, tucking his flask away and mopping at his brow with a frayed linen handkerchief. "They grumbled about barons who came strutting down from London, and about the daughter of a steward who needed to learn her place. I had the sense talk was mostly for my benefit."

Mostly, but not entirely. Nick did not need this complication now, and neither did Loris Tanner.

"Sutcliffe seems like a reasonable sort," Nick said. "I don't think he'd blame the loss of a half a stable crew on Miss Tanner."

Beckman stuffed his handkerchief in his pocket. "I'd rather they did quit, Nick. The next man I see mishandle a horse will meet the business end of my fists."

The heat was making everybody irritable, though Beckman wasn't simply expressing his temper. He was protective toward those who could not defend themselves, and Nick was painfully familiar with the same impulse.

"Where do you think Miss Tanner and the baron have got off to?" Nick asked.

Beckman hefted the barrow. "It's too hot for Sutcliffe to get any wayward notions, Nick. By the time you finish raking the aisle, she'll come trotting up the lane, a tired, befuddled baron trotting after her. For two years, most of the fellows working this estate have worn that expression, and for two years the estate has run more or less well."

On that observation, Beckman took the dirty straw out to the muck pit, leaving Nick to finish raking the aisle.

By the time he was done, even the barn was becoming as hot as a Dutch oven, and still, Miss Tanner and the baron were nowhere to be seen.

* * *

Loris ran up Rupert's stirrups, loosened his girth, and took his bridle off, doing the same for Evan so they could graze in her back yard. She cast around for something else to do, something to prevent her from dwelling on the damp, impressive baron in her house—likely naked in her house.

He'd be inspecting her personal dwelling, handling her things, and knowing him, he'd make his assessments without bothering to dress first.

Loris grabbed a watering can, filled it at the pump, gave the pansies an extra drink, then busied herself pulling off dead blooms. To remove the spent blossoms and gently untangle the plants soothed her, like currying a horse or brushing a child's hair. Tending her garden was usually an activity for the cool of the evening, a time for solitude and winding down from the day's exertions.

"I see you've decided to trust Rupert," the baron said, as he came down the stairs in stockinged feet. He retrieved his boots from the bottom step and sat to tug them on.

"Have I grown an extra nose?" he asked, standing.

"Those are my father's clothes." They had never looked like that on Micah Tanner.

"He liked a well made garment, though I gather he wasn't quite as tall as I am." Sutcliffe shrugged into his riding jacket. "Do you miss your father?"

Loris took up Evan's bridle and slipped it onto the gelding, who didn't regard a bit as a reason to stop chewing the grass in his mouth.

"For so long," Loris said, "since I was a girl, I felt responsible for my father, as if my reason for living were to look after him and take care of him. I do miss him—he had a keen sense of humor and never forgot a detail of agricultural science."

Loris was also relieved that her father had taken himself off. She tightened the horse's girth and ran the stirrups down the leathers rather than voice such a disloyal, bewildering sentiment.

Her father had never forgotten anything *when sober.*

The baron said nothing, likely busy with his own stirrups and girth.

"My father was like most of us," Loris went on. "A mixture of the admirable and the exasperating, and preoccupied with his own concerns. You note that Papa's taste in clothing was refined. So was his taste in almost everything. He'd do without rather than tolerate goods of merely average quality. He was given to dramatics, which was tiresome for a person not given to dramatics, and who managed the best she could on a modest budget."

"That's honest," Sutcliffe said, coming to stand beside Evan. "Up you go."

Loris cocked up her left leg at the knee, allowing the baron to grasp her booted ankle. He one, two, three'd her into the saddle.

One-handed.

"What do you think happened to your father?" Sutcliffe asked as he climbed aboard Evan and took up the reins. His wet clothes remained draped over Loris's porch railing, large, startlingly white, and best ignored.

Loris ought to have resented the baron's question; instead, having somebody to talk with about Papa's absence was another relief.

"I honestly do not know what has become of Papa. He could behave himself for months, but then, when he'd drink spirits, he'd binge to the point he could not recall what he had done, where he had been, or with whom. In that condition, he could have been picked up by a press gang."

"Last I heard,"—the baron nudged his horse into a walk— "few press gangs lurked in the wilds of Sussex."

"He could well be dead." Loris suspected the baron had been thinking this, and was too much of a gentleman—too kind—to be so blunt.

"How will you spend the rest of your day, Miss Tanner?"

Another abrupt, welcome change in subject, courtesy of his lordship.

"I will look in on the stable, and make sure Chesterton's

effects are delivered to the Cock and Bull. I'll send Wee Nick for that, because I'll want a receipt from the man, and Nick can read. We should also bring in Penny from the mare's pasture."

"Who is Penny, and why is she to give up her grass?" the baron asked as they turned up the long driveway.

"She is another of Greymoor's rescues," Loris said. "His lordship had a soft spot for damsels in distress. Penny is a draft mare plowed to permanent lameness. Greymoor bought her to tend the yearlings, then decided she wasn't sound enough to travel to his other properties, where he owns a stud farm. He bred her to Pettigrew's stallion and hoped to produce a nice, large, placid riding horse."

The baron's eyebrows went up, as if women were to believe baby horses came prancing forth from the middle of fairy rings.

"What do we know of Pettigrew's stud?"

Talk of assaults, fallen women, and a missing steward had not merited much of a reaction from Sutcliffe, but an unusual choice of brood mare had the baronial eyebrow arching heavenward.

"Pettigrew's stud has good conformation but a sour disposition. I would be cross too, had I his life."

"You don't approve of Pettigrew's husbandry?"

Odd word choice. The horses approached the front paddock, and again, Sutcliffe arranged his mount so Loris and Rupert had the best of the shade.

"Squire Pettigrew died some years ago," Loris said. "His widow stands the stallion, and she isn't a horsewoman. The beast is not exercised, not safely confined in a stud paddock, not allowed to consort with any other horses. It's easy to see how he would become out of sorts, but she continues to keep him bored, isolated, and without meaningful work."

Sutcliffe glanced over at Loris, as if the terms—bored, isolated, and without meaningful work—might have applied somewhere besides the horse.

"Stallions can be difficult," Sutcliffe said, as they approached the stable.

A baron could be difficult, too. "A stallion will have a personality, my lord, but the stallion is the horse as God made him, and he'll need companionship, a sense of purpose, and understanding. Not isolation and harsh handling."

Old Jamie came out to take their horses and frowned without comment at the ring of dampness at the back of Rupert's saddle.

"When you are done with your tasks here, Miss Tanner," the baron said as he assisted her to dismount, "might you attend me in the library at the manor? We have much to discuss, and can reschedule our inspection of the remaining land."

"As you wish, sir."

He bowed and sauntered off, and the damned man probably knew full well Loris was watching his retreat.

Again.

* * *

"You want to get rid of me when we've been married only a handful of weeks?" David, Viscount Fairly, asked his wife.

In the privacy of their bed chamber, he could venture such an honest inquiry. Letty sat at her vanity, the picture of domestic innocence, though Fairly knew—and liked—that she watched him in her mirror.

"Sussex is not darkest Africa," Letty said, setting aside her hair brush and rising to kiss her spouse. "Thomas has no one else to help him settle in, and he would never ask you to visit when we're so newly wed."

Thomas Jennings would never ask anybody for anything. Fairly knew himself to be cast in the same mold, and yet, he'd asked the madam of his brothel to marry him. Thank God, and a goodly complement of mutual regard—also mutual lust—she'd accepted.

"You are trying to muddle me," Fairly said as Letty bit his earlobe.

"Am I succeeding?"

He led her to the bed, a lordly acreage of pillows, quilts, fragrant sheets, and wonderful memories.

"We must talk, Letty-love." They had enjoyed many conversations in that bed, not always using words.

Letty turned so Fairly could undo her laces. With the neckline of her dress dipping low across her chemise, she undid his cravat and sleeve buttons. In a very short time, these marital courtesies had become routine, and yet, Fairly would never take them for granted.

Letty draped her dress and stays across a chair. Fairly's shirt, waistcoat, and breeches soon joined the pile, and then— the morning was warm, after all—Letty's chemise topped the lot, like icing on a sweet.

"Into bed," Fairly said, smacking Letty's bum. She'd made the mistake of telling him she liked a confidently playful application of his hand to her fundament, so Fairly was doomed to oblige her frequently.

Letty crawled across the bed to the side closest to the window. "You are going down to Sussex, David. For years, you had no one to rely on but Thomas, and he never once failed you."

"Why can't you come to Sussex with me? Amery took Gwen with him, and that turned out rather well."

Fairly climbed onto the bed and took a moment simply to enjoy the breeze across his naked flesh, his wife's hand in his, and the rock-solid sense that though they were newly wed, they'd already developed a foundation of honesty and respect.

"I could come to Sussex with you, but then I'd be the odd lady out, and you'd fret, and Thomas would fret, and that is not the point of the excursion."

Fairly kissed his wife's knuckles. The day was warm, so a lazy loving was called for, all soft kisses and sweet sighs. His cock stirred in anticipation, and Letty took him in her hand.

"I get the sense Thomas does not enjoy having a title,"

she said, her fingers glossing over Fairly like the breeze across the pristine sheets. "Your hair is golden even here, reddish golden."

"Thomas never wanted a title," Fairly replied, though he'd soon be unable to form coherent sentences. He and Letty competed with each other to see who could pretend to ignore arousal the longest.

He invariably lost, but in the interests of giving a good account on behalf of new husbands throughout the realm, Fairly turned to his side and drew his hand down Letty's midline.

"I forbid you to tickle me," Letty said, arching into his caress. "How long has Thomas been a baron?"

"Two years, that I know of. His twin cousins killed each other in a duel, so the title represents a double tragedy to him. I don't know as he has any other family, save a sister or a cousin or an aunt at the Sutcliffe family seat. I love to see the sunshine on your naked breasts."

That was the last thing Fairly said for long minutes, besides, "please," "now," "damn it, Letty," and "my love."

Letty was dozing on his chest, the breeze cooling them gently as the day advanced, when Fairly bestirred himself to recall their earlier conversation.

"Do you really think I ought to look in on Thomas, Letty-love?"

"You'll worry otherwise," she said, running her tongue from his collarbone to his ear. "You must be presumptuous and lordly, Husband. *Tell* Thomas you're making a visit. Don't hint, don't ask, don't suggest. He'll get the knack of baron-ing if you demonstrate some viscount-ing."

"I rather prefer husband-ing and lover-ing."

"I'm fond of your husband-ing and lover-ing, too, and because you are leaving for Sussex by the end of the week, perhaps you'd best bestow more of same upon me now, hmm?"

Fairly indulged his lady's suggestion to the utmost, for the least he could do was make sure she missed the hell out of him when he went a-viscounting in the wilds of Sussex.

CHAPTER FOUR

Loris waited some twenty minutes in the manor house library while her employer changed into attire of his own. She used the time to consider what she might have said or done differently during the morning's outing, what employment she might find if Sutcliffe gave her the sack, and what she had on hand for luncheon, breakfast being but a dim, fond memory.

To combat nerves, she took down the matched pair of pistols stored on the highest shelf. They might not be dueling pistols per se, but they were high-quality firearms, and had likely not been cleaned in some time. She set about rectifying that oversight, seating herself on the threshold of the French doors, spreading the necessary tools on the flagstones at her feet.

"Penny for them, Miss Tanner."

Loris yelped at the baron's voice. He lounged against his desk, a drink in his hand. How long had he been lurking at her back, and why hadn't she heard him?

"Spirits at this hour, my lord?" She arranged the guns in their handsome case and rose before his lordship could burden her with his assistance.

"Cold, sweet tea, Miss Tanner." The baron saluted her with his glass. "The Regent favors it with ice when he's feeling poorly. Would you like some?"

"No, thank you, my lord."

Standing on a small stool, Loris stretched up to slide the case onto the top of the bookshelf, from whence she'd taken it. Before she could turn around, the baron's hands closed on her waist.

"Must you be so blasted independent?" He swung her down from her perch and glowered at her. "You might have asked me to put the guns away, and then you wouldn't have needed to teeter about on that stool."

"Your concern, while appreciated, is not needed, sir."

Sutcliffe had managed a brothel. Very likely, in her wildest imaginings, Loris could not dream of the experience those hands of his had gained while roaming female bodies.

The baron stepped back and stalked across the room to the desk, upon which he propped a lordly hip.

"Will you join me, Miss Tanner?" He waved a hand at the chair facing the desk, and—because he was her *employer*— Loris took a seat.

"My thanks," he said, not seating himself on the other side of the desk, but rather remaining right where he was.

Where to look? Loris chose the shelves behind the desk, which held a variety of children's miniatures collected by Linden's former owner. Not a flower in sight, for all Linden had acres of gardens.

"For the next few weeks, Miss Tanner, I will impose significantly on your time. When does harvest fall here?"

"Not until September for the field crops. The apples are usually later than that, and the gardens don't stop producing until October, or even later, if the autumn is mild."

Did his lordship wear underlinen beneath this pair of breeches, or did he habitually do without—and if so, why?

"So for now, you can spare the time to educate me regarding my property?"

Loris was at once pleased that Sutcliffe would ask and dismayed at the prospect, but not dismayed enough to risk a glance past his thighs up to his sapphire-dark eyes.

"No task should be more important than familiarizing a landowner with his estate, sir."

"We are in agreement, then. We'll ride out in the mornings, provided the weather is fair, and you can show me more of the land. I'd also like you to introduce me to the people, of course, including the tenant farmers, the tradesmen, and the neighbors. We must see to the account books, which I've yet to locate, and the—what now? I've barely got out two consecutive sentences, Miss Tanner, and already I note an unattractive set to your chin."

Loris did look at him, resenting that he remained on his feet until she realized that even in his own home, even in *her* company, he might have been waiting for permission to be seated.

"Introductions to the neighbors are not my place, Baron."

"Why not? You live here, I am recently arrived, and somebody must squire me about until I know who goes with which estate."

Embarrassment swept up Loris's neck and heated her cheeks. "I wouldn't know how to go on."

"You wouldn't…?"

A silence, while the baron considered, and Loris blushed, and allowed her resentment to crest just short of loathing for forcing the admission from her. She did not loathe Sutcliffe, but she loathed the situation.

"Do you wish to *learn* how to go on?" his lordship asked.

What was he—former manager of a brothel—asking?

"Why should I learn how to properly serve a cup of tea," Loris said, "or make small talk of children and the weather? I will never have children, and whereas other women consider the weather a safe, dull topic, I consider it fascinating. We live and die by the weather, starve or grow rich. How mundane is that?"

Her employer regarded her for a long, uncomfortable moment. "Show me your hands."

Loris mentally fumbled around for a retort, but she was too slow, and the dratted man had her hands gently but firmly gripped in his. He raised them for a thorough inspection.

"You have the hands of a lady," he observed, "which is no small feat, considering how much of your day you spend in the saddle, in the barns, in the fields, or otherwise out of doors."

"I wear gloves," Loris replied, dread mixing with something else at the feel of his fingers wrapped around hers. "I abhor gratuitous dirt."

He leaned in and—of all the unseemly displays—took a whiff of her. "You have the fragrance of a lady, and you speak like a lady, at least in your diction and vocabulary. I suspect, Loris Tanner, you would like to be a lady in truth."

She stood and snatched her hands back before pacing the length of the room and whirling on him.

"I see no point in trying to make a silk purse out of this market sow's ear, my lord. I work, and ladies don't work. Ladies don't see what I see in the course of a day. They don't walk through manure and determine if milk is dripping from a mare's udder, or clean a gelding's sheath to spare him the ham-handed groom's attentions. *I am not a lady.*"

Sutcliffe's expression was inscrutable, when Loris had barely managed to keep her voice down. He wasn't taunting her, not on purpose, but neither did he, titled, wealthy, handsome, and male, know what impossibilities he asked of her.

He regarded her steadily, the way Loris kept her gaze on a green horse giving a saddle its first delicate sniffing over.

"Hear me out, Miss Tanner, and come sit, if you please, so I needn't shout the length of the room to discuss this with you."

Loris resumed her seat near the baron's desk, though that concession cost her, for his thighs remained uncomfortably near, and they were muscular thighs.

What was *wrong* with her?

"You are now gainfully employed as a steward on this estate," Sutcliffe began, "and if I find your services adequate, you could continue in this position for some years. But I might sell the property, I might find another steward I like better. I might be such a difficult taskmaster you're too unhappy to continue with your duties, and then, Miss Tanner, what options have you?"

"I can work elsewhere." Though not as a steward. Women did not find employment as stewards. They might own their dower estates, manage for an absent or incompetent husband, and *take a hand in things*, but no decent, proper woman admitted to stewardship of real property as her means of support even if that was the case in fact.

"Where will you work, madam? Greymoor's cousin became a manager of sorts on her grandfather's estate, simply because she had grown up there, and Greymoor was out of the country when other provisions might have been made. Were it anyone other than Guinevere Hollister who traveled down here with Amery, you would have lost your position last autumn."

Sutcliffe chose then to fall silent, which was uncharitable of him. Just as Loris considered fussing with the drape of her skirt, he resumed his lecture.

"You found the one estate in all of England where the owner would even consider permitting you to continue in your father's position, even temporarily. Do you expect to find another?"

"No," she bit out, rising. "I know how fortunate I am, and what an unusual situation I have. I never sought the position of steward here at Linden, my lord, but the crops would have rotted in the fields if I hadn't stepped into to manage in Papa's absence. None of the men were willing to do as much, and now I am the best-qualified resource for the steward's tasks, whether you call me your steward or not. You understand this."

"I do," he said, with ominous gentleness, "but my dear, I could be tossed from my horse tomorrow, and my estate might pass into the hands of some old lecher who believes women should be kept meek and silent. You need an alternative plan."

Men died. They disappeared, they were set upon by thieves, they fell ill. Loris could not imagine his lordship coming to grief from the back of a horse, but he had—damn and drat him—made a valid point.

Loris's father had been strutting about the village green one day and nowhere to be found the next.

"I cannot accept that snabbling a man with my pretty manners and empty head is a suitable alternative plan," Loris said, again indulging in the compulsion to pace. Why must she sound so forlorn, when marriage had never been a possibility for her? "I have no wish to marry. *I have no dowry.* I am fortunate I have passed the age where anyone expects me to even try to find a spouse."

"How old are you?" More of Sutcliffe's soft, handsome voice—a voice that hinted at concern and confidences. The women whom he'd known in that den of vice must have taught him the power of that voice.

"Five-and-twenty."

"Not so old as all that. If you were a man—"

"*If I were a man.*" Loris crossed her arms rather than raise a hand to her employer. "Those are the five most useless words in a woman's vocabulary. I will never be a man, nor would I wish to be."

"You don't want to be a man, and you say you don't want to be a lady. What do you want to be?"

Loris turned away from Sutcliffe to face out the doors. While she made the baron wait for her answer, the scent of lavender drifted in from the summer day. Beyond the manor's gardens, the pastures, fields, and home wood made a bucolic tableau of peace and plenty.

She hadn't been quite honest with him. While the steward's position had never been her goal, the care of all that fertile ground and healthy livestock had beckoned to her. She'd wanted to see Linden thrive, season by season, the same way a mother anticipated her child's first words and first steps.

Lord Sutcliffe was not Loris's enemy. He did not deserve her ire. He deserved her loyalty and respect.

Also the truth, to the extent she knew the truth.

"I want to be safe," she said. "I want to know that my informed judgment will not be questioned by some fat, swaggering idiot with a bullwhip, when all I seek is to keep an innocent animal from avoidable misery. I want to know that any London dandy who comes to the neighborhood will not presume on my person.

"I want to know that my manners and conversation are adequate," she went on, "that I won't become the butt of the local gentry's jokes when I open my mouth at the assemblies or in the market, that I will have something to say to the ladies my age besides inappropriate remarks about the lambing and calving."

Loris leaned a shoulder against the doorjamb, abruptly weary of the baron, the heat, and her own recitation.

"If I can't have these things, Baron Sutcliffe, then all I want is to be left alone."

* * *

In extensive travel as a man of business for a wealthy lord, Thomas had made the acquaintance of many beautiful women. Some were sufficiently attractive to marry great fortunes, others used their looks to garner wealth in different ways.

Those ladies all made the same mistake: They believed their beauty evident only when they were beheld from the front. Whether they emphasized entrancing eyes, a spectacular figure, or classically perfect features, they lacked faith in their appeal from within—or from behind.

The nape of a woman's neck could be fascinating, the flare of her hips irresistible. The curve of her spine might give a man many sleepless nights, and the line of her shoulders could say much about the burdens she carried or the self-respect that sustained her.

Loris Tanner's folly was worse than most, for she failed to note her appeal from *any* angle, while Thomas could have studied her for hours.

She bore aloneness in her very posture, back erect, shoulders set, tidy braid hanging straight down her spine. He wanted to comfort her, and yet, she'd probably snarl and snap if he so much as touched her shoulder.

Which was in part his fault. He'd been humoring her as if she were one of Fairly's professional women when restless between favorites. Worse yet, Thomas had been amusing *himself* at Miss Tanner's expense, thinking her a quaint, rural eccentric. A woman he could tease at his pleasure, one who hissed and spat and blushed, and then expounded with astonishing knowledge on agrarian topics.

She wanted, for good reasons, to be left alone, and in every movement, glance, and word choice, she enshrouded herself in solitariness.

Loris Tanner wasn't alone as a widow was alone. The widow had a past association with a man to give her status and memories. Nor was she alone as young ladies were, teetering on the brink of courtship and marriage, full of dreams, potential, and hope. She wasn't alone in the manner of a maiden aunt, deriving meaning from a tangential contribution to extended family.

Loris Tanner's aloneness was that of an orphan, of a person who deserved a different set of circumstances, but was powerless to bring them about.

Thomas knew how that felt, knew the rage and bewilderment of it.

"I can't change the nature of the London fribbles," he said, turning her by the shoulders. "I can't assure you that you will never have another surly employee, but the etiquette and polish that will earn you the respect of your peers, the women and men who consider themselves polite society around here, I can give you that."

Misty gray eyes studied a spot behind Thomas's shoulder. "Why would you?"

He'd hoped for grudging gratitude—more fool he. "Perhaps so I can marry you off, and rid myself of the only female steward in the realm, whether she admits to that title or not."

Miss Tanner's glower was magnificent. She could have quelled riots with that fiery, disdainful, righteous expression—or started them.

"I never wanted to be a steward, sir. I did the job because nobody else was on hand with the proper knowledge, and for my efforts, I am an embarrassment to you."

She had freckles across her nose, freckles of the kissable, countable variety, which she probably hated.

"You are not an embarrassment to me, Miss Tanner." A puzzle, a challenge, a conundrum, not an embarrassment. "I suspect, however, you frequently embarrass yourself."

"You would rehabilitate me? Why would you take on such a thankless project? I am no relation to you. I would know your motives, my lord."

Fair question, which Thomas would ponder another time, when it wouldn't cost him his momentum in their argument.

"By way of explanation, or perhaps analogy, let me explain to you why I no longer manage a brothel."

She took a step back, but didn't cede the verbal field entirely.

"My employer," Thomas began, "David Worthington,

Viscount Fairly, became enamored of the madam he hired for his brothel. Mind you, she was not his mistress. He sought to marry her. In the course of their courtship, it was pointed out to Fairly that running a brothel is a logical contradiction for a gentleman. If honor requires that a man protect the weak, and use his influence only for good, then exploiting women who have fallen outside the bounds of decency is the worst sort of lapse."

Miss Tanner resumed her seat before the desk, which meant Thomas could study the interesting line of her jaw when she was at the limit of her patience with her employer.

"Fine for the viscount," she said. "I suppose he was in love and willing to appease his lady with moral reform, but what has that to do with you?"

Thomas took the chair beside hers, an un-cushioned, spindle-backed and damned uncomfortable seat.

"Fairly wasn't appeasing his lady, he was appeasing his conscience."

"And you will appease yours, by rescuing me from my bumpkinhood?"

No bumpkin reasoned so nimbly, or fearlessly.

"Perhaps I will give myself a steward with drawing-room polish, or perhaps I will reform you right into the arms of some local worthy, who can promise you a life free of hog wallows and manure pits."

She looked puzzled, as if she'd miss her hog wallows and manure pits were they taken from her.

"The point, Miss Tanner, is that you should have a choice. You may choose to work out your days here, the housemaids and stable hands your only companions, or you may choose to circulate in the local society and comport yourself as something other than an oddity. Your father apparently socialized as a gentleman would, and you should enjoy a feminine version of the same privilege."

Thomas ought to have left Loris Tanner's father out of the

conversation, but common sense weighed in favor of having options, for the lord of the manor, the yeoman putting in crops, or the prostitute on the stroll. Miss Tanner would be tempted in part because her father had left her *no* options.

And yet, Thomas had dangled before her a lure he himself had long ago turned his back on: acceptance by polite society.

"You may attempt to explain a few matters of etiquette to me," Miss Tanner said, "though don't expect me to spend much time at this project. Managing your estate is a busy undertaking, Baron, and I won't have you criticizing me for slacking as a steward as well as being unable to stand up at the assemblies. The land must take precedence."

This oversight, this gap in her social skills, was no small handicap in a rural community, and yet her own father could easily have spared her the awkwardness.

"You can't dance?"

"I don't know the steps, and learning them at the expense of my neighbors doesn't seem fair."

Such a public education would be unfair—to her. "When is the next assembly?"

"We have them monthly during fair weather, the first Saturday of every month."

Miss Tanner knew the schedule, and probably made sure to have a great deal to do on those first Saturdays.

"That gives me our first goal," Thomas said. "At the August assembly, Loris Tanner, you will dance."

With him. Thomas would see that she also danced with others, but of a certainty, she would dance with him.

"We wasted only the entire morning reaching that decision," she said, popping up and moving to the French doors—and away from Thomas. "If you'll excuse me, I must pay out the wages for the stablemen and the gardeners, and then they'll take their half day."

"Then you'll join me for luncheon."

She leaned back against the doorjamb in a pose no proper

lady had ever adopted in company, though it looked confident on her.

"You're serious about this, and you'll start in on me at luncheon?"

"If I am skilled in my conversation, my dear, you will not know my campaign has commenced."

Miss Tanner shook her head and ducked out onto the terrace, while Thomas congratulated himself on his skill. His campaign had already begun, and the lady hadn't even noticed.

* * *

Having dispatched Nick and paid the help, Loris trooped up the drive to the manor house and kept a wary eye on the sky. Rain would be welcome, but hail and strong winds could ruin the year's ripening grain in the space of a twenty-minute squall.

She opened the front door to the house without knocking, and was surprised by Harry, the senior footman, in livery and at attention behind the door.

"Good day, Miss Loris. Shall I tell the baron you're here?"

Bother the baron and his Town ways. "I am expected, Harry. Himself has invited me to join him at luncheon."

Harry tugged down his jacket, which sported gold piping at the cuffs and collar.

"Allow me to announce you, Miss Loris. His lordship says we're to have our company manners on for you." Harry preceded Loris down the corridor and announced her to the self-same man she'd parted from little more than an hour earlier.

"Thank you, Harry." The baron rose from his desk. "Please let the kitchen know Miss Tanner has joined me. We'll take luncheon on the terrace in twenty minutes."

Harry departed with a smart bow—since when had Harry Oglethorpe learned to bow?

"What has you smiling?" the baron asked as he came around the desk.

"Harry. He winked at me, the old wretch." Though he'd looked years younger sashaying about in his new livery.

"Why do I know the same familiarity on my part would earn me a slapped face?" The baron stopped directly before her. "Miss Tanner."

He bowed, a careless, elegant display of manners that inspired Loris to dip him a curtsy, though she felt like a complete ninnyhammer.

"Baron Sutcliffe. Are we to practice our manners now?" She offered him her hand to make the point, and he took it in his own, and actually kissed her knuckles.

Softly, gently, lingeringly.

Gracious days and heavenly choruses. Maybe lessons in manners weren't such an awful idea.

Sutcliffe let go of her hand, and Loris snatched it away, as a horse did with its hoof when the farrier finished rasping the sole level.

"You don't allow a fellow to actually kiss your hand, my dear. It isn't the done thing."

Loris didn't bother replying—*allowing* hadn't come into it—and his lordship's lecture was only getting started.

"If the fellow is a suitor who wishes to impress you with his ardor," he went on, "then perhaps you might overlook the encroachment, but a proper gentleman would merely bow over your hand or kiss the air above it."

"Then why did you kiss my hand, and what should I do if another man is so forward?"

"You'd typically be wearing gloves, so the effect of the gesture would be lost, wouldn't it?"

Loris wanted to hide her bare hands behind her back.

Sutcliffe offered his arm. "A lady," he said, "even the very highest stickler, takes her gloves off at table. You must have a wardrobe suited for something other than riding about the countryside, however, and I must have a side-saddle made for you as well."

Not if he deducted the cost of that saddle from Loris's wages, or expected her to go without sleep to alter the only proper riding habit she owned. The bodice of that garment had grown a bit too snug many years ago.

In the spirit of good manners, Loris kept those protests to herself.

His lordship led her through the French doors to a table in the shade of the oak trees bordering the terrace. The cutlery was laid out in a confusing array of silverware, plates, glasses, and other paraphernalia.

"I will never keep this all straight," Loris said, dropping Sutcliffe's arm. "Food tastes the same whether eaten from the large fork or the small, or from the fingers. Can we not simply forget this whole idea, Baron?"

"We cannot," he replied with a pleasantness Loris was learning to dread. "Do you find it repugnant even to take my arm, Miss Tanner?"

Loris tucked her hand into the crook of his elbow, when she wanted instead to hike her skirts and pelt for the stable.

"I find it ridiculous, my lord," she said as they strolled to the table. "I have been walking unassisted for a quarter century. Why am I to hold your arm?"

"Let's wander a bit," he suggested, moving them down a graveled path into the deep shade. "Suppose we are two young people, each single, and each considering an interest in the other. How might we spend time together to ascertain whether such interest is worthwhile?"

Young people, as if five-and-twenty were old?

"What kind of interest?" Loris asked, finding his lordship's sedate pace a trial. She had ledgers to balance, a broodmare to keep an eye on, cheeses to inspect in the cheese cave, an oat crop ripening faster in some fields than others.

"I refer, Miss Tanner, to the interest men and women do, from time to time, develop in each other."

How gratifying. His lordship was becoming impatient,

despite his languid pace. "You mean an amorous interest or an intimate interest, sir?"

"They are one and the same."

"They most assuredly are not."

"I beg your pardon?" His positively bored tone should have been a warning to Loris that she'd transgressed the narrow boundaries of what was and was not proper conversation. Alas for the baron's delicate sensibilities, she had no more ability to ignore his "I beg your pardon," than a breeding bull would ignore an interloper in his pasture.

"An interest rooted in the base urges and a romantic interest are not the same at all," Loris said, her own patience fraying. "Lord Greymoor's associates evidenced an interest in any female more than one-half or less than twice their age, unless his lordship was in the immediate vicinity to impose a bit of decorum. Their attentions held nothing of romance. They were the human equivalent of the Pettigrew stud, for whom an afternoon's dallying is simply what happens between a nap at noon and oats at supper."

If that. Pettigrew's stallion at least indulged in the horsy equivalent of some cuddling after the festivities.

"Point taken," the baron conceded. "But won't you also agree, Miss Tanner, this topic is inappropriate in polite conversation?"

"Then why did you bring it up?"

The baron laughed, a hearty, happy sound that puzzled Loris.

"You are ridiculing me," she said, stepping away, "and we are not ten minutes into this endeavor. You will understand why my enthusiasm is lacking."

Sutcliffe's smile faded to a warmth in his eyes that Loris hadn't seen previously. He was a perilously handsome man even without that hint of approval in his regard.

"I apologize for my laughter, Miss Tanner, but you neatly turned the game on me. Congratulations."

And that made anything better? "I have your congratulations, but I still have no explanations for why we must toddle around linked like this." She used both hands to wing Sutcliffe's arm away from his body.

A muscular arm. Quite muscular.

"Keep your hands on my arm like that." He used that soft voice again, the one that slid over her senses like a honeysuckle breeze in the middle of a moonless night.

"Do not teach me to flirt, your lordship. I have no use for those skills and never will. Teach me which fork to use, how to make table conversation, and how one seats three viscounts at the same table, though I have never so much as seen three viscounts at once, and hope to die in that innocent state. Leave off the nonsense."

"Is it really nonsense?" Sutcliffe asked, turning them back toward the table on the terrace. "Have you met no one with whom you've wanted to take a moonlit stroll, or sit with to enjoy the evening breezes?"

Loris had met precisely one baron who made her think of moonlight and shared confidences, drat him to the nearest patch of nettles.

"I have a cat for those activities," she said, dropping his arm. "Where shall I sit?"

More nonsense. His lordship seated her—as if she hadn't been maneuvering herself into chairs for almost as long as she'd been walking—but surprised her by not immediately taking the chair to her left.

He bent low, his cheek near hers, his mouth directly beside her ear. "You regard this whole business as so much silliness. You are in error."

Loris was in *trouble*.

Sutcliffe took his seat, unfolded his serviette on his lap and gave Loris a pointed look until she did likewise.

"Why isn't this entire exercise silly?" Loris asked. "You waste your time and effort doing for me what I can easily do for myself. I wait about for you to stroll along, to hold a chair, to even choose a chair for me, when we could both be getting something productive done."

"I speak German," Sutcliffe said, pouring her a glass of lemonade from a crystal pitcher, "and French, and Spanish, fluently. Greek and Latin are givens. I am passably competent in Italian and Portuguese, and I have a smattering of Arabic, and several other languages. Why do you suppose I speak English now?"

And speak it beautifully? "So I comprehend you." Loris comprehended his words. Comprehending *him* would take years.

"Just so. English is not a better language; it is not spoken by the most people; it is not particularly euphonious. I speak public school English because in these circumstances, that is the language in which I will be understood and taken seriously."

The lemonade was chilled, an extravagance on such a hot day. "I hadn't considered etiquette a language, but I suppose it is."

"So will you stop arguing with me and pointing out how ludicrous it is for me to extend you courtesies?"

Loris *liked* crossing swords with the baron. "I lack the self-discipline to keep my tongue still over the truly ridiculous matters."

"What do you find truly ridiculous?"

"Is that a polite topic?"

"Well done."

His lordship hadn't answered the question. "You really should smile more often, my lord. You have charm, though you hide it well."

"Weapons in plain sight are easily disarmed," he replied, his smile fading.

Loris was spared having to decipher that comment by the arrival of the food. Patiently, Sutcliffe coached and reminded and otherwise instructed regarding table manners and cutlery, making the whole business matter-of-fact and far less humiliating than Loris had feared it would be.

"These manners turn good food into tedium," Loris said as the empty plates were removed, though the cold roast chicken had been delicious tedium. "We make an avoidable mess for the servants to clean up. Soap, water, time, fancy dishes—they all cost money."

"True, but refined table manners are like vocabulary, Miss Tanner. Use the wrong word in a sentence, and you can offend or amuse your audience, or otherwise subvert your intended meaning. Pick up the wrong fork, and you give every other woman at the table a weapon against you."

"I cannot call Mrs. Pettigrew out for a slur to my honor, and challenge her to forks at dawn, Baron. Besides, if you drill a land steward on her manners long enough, she will be bored cross-eyed." Also overwhelmed. "May we agree the pedagogic portion of the meal is complete and discuss estate matters?"

Wherein Loris would be the professor and his lordship the student.

Sutcliffe traced his finger around the rim of his wine glass. He'd served a cool, crisp, fruity white wine that Loris had wanted to savor in solitude on her back porch.

"You are a difficult pupil, Miss Tanner."

"Finally, a compliment. Thank you. Now, do you want to know what's afoot in your stable?"

"I gather you have bad news."

Had Sutcliffe not been on hand, the news would have been bad indeed. "Nick says the grooms are likely to walk with their pay, most of them at least. They are no great loss, but finding replacements will take time."

"Nick knows this how?" Sutcliffe asked, twirling the empty wine glass by its stem.

"He listens," Loris said, as the delicate glass spun in the baron's fingers. "He's thought to be not too bright, so he overhears things."

"Does Nick seek to curry favor with you with this overhearing?" Sutcliffe's question was chillingly casual.

"Nick isn't in the habit of confiding in me, if that's what you're asking. I sent him into the village with Chesterton's effects, and he wanted to know if he should cast about for more stable help while there."

"Help that *he* would supervise?"

Oh, for pity's sake. "I doubt Nicholas Haddonfield aspires to anything loftier than peace and quiet at the end of his day, a good night's sleep, and the occasional pint at the Cock and Bull. Why are you so suspicious?"

"My nature, I suppose." Sutcliffe left off toying with his wine glass, like a large, hungry tom cat stopped flicking its tail when the poor mouse peeked out from its hole. "You've said Nick has worked here for some time, and he's certainly physically powerful. Why wouldn't he seek other kinds of power as well?"

Loris helped herself to the last of the baron's lemonade. "Do you enjoy the burden of being Baron Sutcliffe? Knowing someday you must curtail your freedom with a suitable bride, produce the heir, manage the retainers, that sort of thing?"

"What makes you think I'd shirk that duty?"

Surely, the time had come to resume a discussion of manners?

"Not shirk. You're procrastinating, though," Loris said, gently, for the baronial tail had resumed flicking at a great rate. "You have an inherited title, my lord, and with that title comes a patch of land. You comprehend the basics about managing an estate, but you know little of loving one. You don't like to be told what to do, where to do it, or when, otherwise you would be on *that* patch of ground, and not going out of your way to familiarize yourself with *this* one."

Sutcliffe rose and extended his hand to her. "You have odd notions about land and the people who own it."

Loris stood, all too relieved to have the meal concluded. "I will take my leave of you, and I hope I have not given offense."

"More than your insight, Miss Tanner, is necessary to offend such a one as I. May we discuss estate business further at a later time?"

"The discussion of estate business never concludes for long, your lordship." And Sutcliffe hadn't told Loris what to do about the stable. "Shall I await you tomorrow morning in the stable?"

"You shall."

"Then we can spend some time at the home farm, and the following day is market day. If need be, we might find more stable help there. Perhaps you'd like to join me on that excursion as well?"

"I would. Until tomorrow, Miss Tanner, and thank you for sharing your company with me over luncheon."

"Oh, very pretty, Baron." Loris beamed at him in sheer relief. "My thanks for your company as well."

She curtsied, glad to be able to make a dignified retreat. That last salvo, about enjoying her company, had been teasing on his part, or more lecturing, but her reply had been in earnest.

Loris enjoyed the baron's company, even when he was being preachy and protective, and that would not do *at all*.

CHAPTER FIVE

"The fellows at the Cock and Bull say Sutcliffe is a big swell and dressed to the teeth in London finery," Giles Pettigrew said. "He sounds like another incarnation of Greymoor."

Who hadn't been a bad sort, though in recent years, he'd been too busy frolicking on the Continent to notice that a woman had been attempting to steward Linden's acres. Thank heavens that same woman knew better than to let a member of the aristocracy turn her head.

"Pass the salt, Giles," Claudia Pettigrew drawled. "Mrs. Chipchase says Sutcliffe is here to stay."

How Giles hated it when Mama adopted that rosy, smug tone of voice, and yet, she was entitled to her amusements. He passed the salt, after he'd spooned a bit onto his beef.

"How could a housekeeper know the mind of a baron only recently arrived?" Giles asked.

Mama considered her wine, a red that tended more to heartiness than delicacy. Alas, the cellars had shown the lack of a man's discerning influence since Giles had come down from university last summer.

"Mrs. Chipchase is cousin to the miller's wife," Mama said, dragging the salt spoon about in the cellar, "and she knows half the small holders in the shire. The baron came across some boys swimming in a Linden pond, and told them he'd be residing on the estate for the foreseeable future. Don't underestimate the talk of women, Giles. Ours is a pretty neighborhood, and country life appeals to many a titled man."

Giles nearly snatched Mama's wine away from her, for she had the dreamy, dangerous look she wore when she was scheming over a fellow. She stood that wretched stallion in part so the gentlemen of the shire had specific business to transact with her, regardless of the indecency of the situation.

Mama was pretty, having passed on to Giles blond hair, blue eyes, and fashionable height. She was also vain and did not fare well without the notice of gentlemen. Giles understood this, and so he interfered only a little in managing the stallion, a little dealing with the trades, a little in estate matters.

He'd apparently have to interfere with the wine order, too.

When he came into his funds, upon marriage or upon attaining the age of five-and-twenty, he'd interfere a very great deal wherever the hell he pleased.

"Sutcliffe hasn't had the title long," Mama said, "and the ladies with whom I correspond say he's a fine, mature specimen with an interesting past. You will pay a call on him. Welcome him to the neighborhood, offer to acquaint him with the good families in the area."

The beef was tough, the potatoes undercooked. Cook had probably been tippling again, or feuding with Mrs. Chipchase. Everywhere, Giles was surrounded by women in want of guidance.

"We could pay a call together," Giles suggested, though Loris Tanner did not approve of Mama, which was an irony indeed. Mama was a lady, while Loris was…

Loris was the woman Giles would marry. He understood restless women, understood that they'd do outlandish things to get noticed. He understood, most of all, that they needed and even appreciated a firm hand managing them, and Loris had no papa, no brother, no cousin, no husband, to look after her properly.

Miss Tanner needed a husband, badly, for Sutcliffe would likely dislodge her from her informal position as self-appointed steward. Giles could advance his suit without having to apply that firm hand in any obvious way, and Miss Tanner would be grateful for his offer.

Giles had been considering this plan for the past two years—since Micah Tanner's disappearance—though the look in Mama's eyes suggested the time had come to hurry things along a bit.

"You can call on Sutcliffe informally," Mama said, draining half her wine glass at a go. "Invite him to dinner, talk horses with him. Then you introduce us in the churchyard, and the baron can call upon me."

In the churchyard, where every woman for ten miles around would see Mama staking her claim. Giles knew the pattern, and the ladies in the neighborhood did too.

"An excellent plan," Giles said, for Mama did not like Loris either—Mama never liked anybody for very long—and would doubtless argue for Sutcliffe to find a more suitable steward once she'd got her hooks into the baron.

Ironic, that Mama's interest in Sutcliffe might be the very impetus for Giles's funds to finally come under his own control.

* * *

"Was market really so boring as all that, my lord?"

Miss Tanner posed her question from Evan's broad back, where she looked as much at ease riding aside as she did astride. Her habit was years out of fashion, but fetching nonetheless, and exquisitely well-fitted in all the right places.

"Market," Thomas replied, "was a thrilling exhibition of all that is right and dear about rural England."

"Fresh vegetables are all that is right with England?"

Had Thomas's observation tempted her to smile? She'd smiled at some neighbor, a tall, blond, fellow, near a stall selling sweets.

"You would be surprised, Miss Tanner, what a want of fresh vegetables can do to a man, if it goes on long enough."

She turned her face to the sun, letting her straw hat slip down her back, something no well-bred lady would dare do for fear of freckles.

"You have suffered this hardship, my lord?"

Did nothing deter this woman? "Occasionally. Not like the sailors in the royal navy, of course."

"One wonders why anyone would join that organization."

"Hence the press gangs," Thomas pointed out. "But tell me, Miss Tanner, why did you disappear when the Pettigrews introduced themselves?"

"I've told you, I do not respect Mrs. Pettigrew's horsemanship."

Miss Tanner was incapable of sexual innuendo, which left only the literal sense of her words.

"Out with the rest of it, Miss Tanner, or I'll gossip in the churchyard until I've learned what I seek to know."

She fiddled with her reins, twitched her skirts, and adjusted her grip on her whip.

"My father courted Mrs. Pettigrew, or something like it. He strove mightily to impress her, to spend time with her, and to please her."

A litany of mortal sins, based on Miss Tanner's tone. "Did Mrs. Pettigrew look with favor on his suit?" Thomas asked as they left the hubbub of the village behind them. "Your father was a gentleman, albeit a lowly one."

"She teased him," Miss Tanner said, as if flirtation between consenting adults were a felony offense. "Claudia Pettigrew is a viscount's daughter, though she had no brothers, so the title went to a cousin. I don't move in elevated circles, but I am sure she toyed with a *lowly* steward."

"Toyed with him? How is a grown man toyed with by a mere widow?"

"That mere widow," Miss Tanner bit out, "fancies herself something of a... Well, she doesn't always behave as a lady ought."

The lane was deserted, and Thomas was intrigued. "You mean she's a slut? She sleeps around, is free with her favors?"

"That is hardly polite, but you have the right of it. She made her plays for Greymoor, but I doubt he found her worthy of his attentions on more than a handful of occasions. I suspect she admitted my father to her bed when it suited her."

What father would allow even an adult daughter to entertain those suspicions? And yet, where Loris Tanner was concerned, allowing was likely not a consideration.

"Your father was a grown man, and without a woman's companionship."

"Therefore," she concluded, "he must needs drop his breeches on somebody's bedroom floor, for not to do so would cause his reason to flee, and his man-parts to shrivel up?"

Man-parts. An addition to Thomas's polyglot vocabulary. "What grudge do you bear against those who enjoy themselves as adults will?"

Who enjoyed themselves as Thomas had not in far too long?

"Mrs. Pettigrew accused my father of rape, and while Squire Belmont, as magistrate, took his time apprehending the suspect, my father departed."

Thomas mentally struck the good widow off the list of neighbors whose acquaintance he would encourage.

"My dear, I'm sorry." For in driving off the father, Mrs. Pettigrew had left the daughter without a chaperone or protector. Thomas hoped his apology stretched far enough to cover his needling, too, though this tale was one he needed to hear from his steward.

"With Papa's drinking," Miss Tanner went on, "and his memory problems, his word against the word of the widow would have meant nothing. She might have seen him hanged for her entertainment, my lord, a high price to pay for trying to love her."

This conversation had started out focused on vegetables, and now, somehow, Miss Tanner had brought it 'round to *love*, as women invariably did.

"Your father paid a high price for being a fool and a drunkard, you mean. Or merely a drunkard."

Miss Tanner swiped the back of her right glove against her cheek. Like any woman riding to the left, she carried her side-saddle whip in her right hand. The tip of the whip tickled Thomas's chin as the lady scrubbed at her cheeks.

"Could no one contradict Mrs. Pettigrew's accusations?" Thomas asked. Had no one pointed out to Tanner that he was choosing drink over his own daughter's welfare?

"The matter never reached an investigation," Miss Tanner said, lowering her whip. "I think Mr. Belmont wanted Papa to have time to flee. Matthew is a decent sort, and a neighbor to both Papa and Mrs. Pettigrew. Papa took only a few clothes, funds, and personal effects."

What else could a man take with him? "Such as?"

"A Bible, a miniature of Mama and me, some letters." Miss Tanner used her left hand to wipe at her cheeks this time. "His favorite flask."

Bastard. To take the flask but leave the daughter. Thomas knew the fury and confusion Loris must have endured, for time and again, his sister Theresa had made comparable choices. Choosing the figurative flask over her own good name, and her younger brother's respect.

"What do you know of your mother?" Thomas inquired, because in all the hours he'd spent with Miss Tanner, this topic had never come up.

"I know what the woman in that painting looked like. She had my dark hair and my eyes, but other than that, I know nothing."

Another reason to be glad Tanner was gone, for what sort of man gives a daughter nothing of her own mother?

"Not even her name?"

"When he referred to her at all, Papa would say only that my mama was lovely, and he'd loved her dearly. I assume from the past tense she is deceased."

Thomas nudged his horse through the turn to the Linden drive. "You don't know what has become of either of your parents, then. Do you have any memories of your mother?"

Miss Tanner was an orphan in truth, albeit an adult orphan. Thomas had that in common with her, though he would rather have shared a preference for Mozart or syllabub.

"No clear memories," she said, turning her horse as well. "I have vague impressions. An old lullaby I think she used to sing to me, a perfume scented with honeysuckle."

"Why do you think that?" Thomas shouldn't have asked, though he could not have said why. He ought to have asked how the draft mare was doing, or if Miss Tanner thought the clouds hanging over the Downs promised rain.

"When the honeysuckle blooms," she said, "I miss my mama terribly and am easily moved to tears." She kicked her horse into a canter, and Thomas let her get a few lengths ahead of him before urging Rupert to the faster gait.

* * *

"You could have waited for me inside," the baron said, ambling along the gallery flanking Linden's western façade.

Why must he always be scolding her? "It is cooler out here," Loris countered, "or less hot."

"This weather worries you?" he asked, winging his arm.

Loris accepted Sutcliffe's escort—she chose her battles with him—and he led her not back into the house, but around to the rear terrace. Lunch awaited them, but this time, no shaded table sat laden with intricate place settings of crystal, china, and silver.

"A picnic. Well done, sir." What a relief, to approve of something Sutcliffe had done.

"We've about exhausted the intricacies of the dining table."

In the past few days, they'd exhausted Loris's patience and her store of small talk, too. She was now equipped to preside at formal and informal meals, serve tea, and exchange pleasantries in the churchyard.

None of which was easy, though Sutcliffe had equipped her with a set of simple, orderly rules that helped a great deal.

"Now, if I could only acquire some polite conversation and skill on the dance floor," Loris said, taking a moment to enjoy the scent of the lavender border. Maybe her mama had also been fond of lavender, for the scent soothed wonderfully.

"Rome wasn't built in a day."

"*Such* original flattery, my lord. The next assembly is only three weeks away, and I've yet to learn the first step. What have you to say about that?"

"I've given it some thought," he said, guiding her to the blanket spread in the shade of the oak. "Traditionally, the lady sorts out the hamper, Miss Tanner, while the gentleman takes his ease philosophizing at the clouds."

"The important work must always be entrusted to the gentleman." Loris folded down onto her knees near the hamper set on one corner of the blanket. The baron, true to his word, reclined several feet away, legs crossed, and arms folded behind his head.

"You behold," he said, "a gentleman hard at his labors."

Loris peered into the hamper, though his lordship recumbent made a handsome picture. If he attended services this Sunday, he'd cause many a head to turn in the churchyard.

"I behold cold chicken," Loris said, "slices of cheese, ripe peaches, and buttered bread, along with a flagon of wine and some lemonade."

"Wine for me, if you please," the baron murmured, eyes closed.

Hard at work, indeed. Considerate of him, though, to include a picnic on Loris's curriculum.

"Is my company so dull that I've put you to sleep?" Loris asked as she withdrew linen serviettes, plates, and mugs. These midday meals at the manor were fortifying, on several levels. The food was good, the company interesting, and the strain on Loris's own larder was eased by the baron's fare.

Then too, Loris was not accustomed to a pause in the middle of the day, a time to rest, talk, and regroup. If the baron declared her manners sufficiently polished, she'd miss these meals.

Miss—perfidious admission—spending time with Sutcliffe. They were within sight of the manor; gardeners and groundsmen were right around the corner of the house, and yet, Loris enjoyed a sense of privacy with Sutcliffe too.

"Your company is lovely," the baron murmured without opening his eyes, "but I've yet to get the knack of sleeping on these hot nights. I've weighty matters to consider."

Loris fixed him a plate and poured wine into one of the glasses. Now, when she'd rather while away an hour discussing clouds or nothing in particular, his lordship would stick to business.

"What think you of putting the stable into Nick Haddonfield's hands?" his lordship asked.

Loris gently laid the plate on his chest. He opened his eyes, his expression bemused.

"Nicholas is indeed a weighty matter," she said. "Best not to consider him on an empty stomach."

"Is *Nicholas* of any special significance to you?" Sutcliffe asked, lifting the plate and rising to a sitting position on abdominal strength alone. He crossed his legs and balanced the plate on one thigh, as a boy might have.

He was no boy, though he understood boys better than

Loris ever would.

"Nick is a friend," Loris said, arranging her own plate, "to the extent he will permit friendship. He is quiet, though, and likes his privacy."

"Would he make an adequate stable master?"

Far more than adequate. "The horses love him. He is capable, he works hard, and he won't go bearing tales in the village behind your back."

"But?"

"I doubt he'll want the attention such a position would bring him." Loris took a sip of ambrosially cold lemonade. Sutcliffe had laid in a store of ice, of all the extravagances, and she heartily approved. "Nick gets along well enough with others, but I doubt he seeks a promotion."

His lordship bit a strip of chicken in half. "Lacks ambition, does he?"

Loris picked up a slice of cheese, their own cave-aged cheddar. "Nick lacks for nothing, but he's content as things are."

Contentment. No wonder Loris had had trouble identifying this aspect of Nick's personality, because she'd had little experience with it herself.

"Can't Haddonfield be content as a stable master?"

"You should ask him." Or Sutcliffe should get back to studying clouds so Loris could study *him*.

"You don't want to do the asking? Will you eat that cheese or wave it about to attract squirrels?"

Loris ate the other half of her cheese. "Lord Greymoor, being partial to horses, traditionally managed the stable directly. I can talk to Nick if you like."

"I like," the baron replied. "Your Nick would accept the post from you more easily than from me."

"Why would you say such a thing?" Loris went for a slice of chicken this time, the scent of tarragon and lemon making her mouth water.

"Call it baronial intuition." Sutcliffe plucked the chicken from Loris's hand and took a bite. "There, you see? The food is for eating, not directing the choir."

He passed the rest of the chicken back to her, and Loris tore off a bite, eyeing him warily. His sense of humor took getting used to, but at least he wasn't lecturing her about forks.

"How's that mare doing?" he asked, polishing off his own slice of chicken.

"Penny?" Loris replied between bites. "She's restless. Nick and I were discussing the need to set up a foal watch for the next few nights."

"Foal watch?" Sutcliffe used a silver knife to pit a peach. He popped a slice into his mouth and closed his eyes. "Good God, these are heavenly."

Loris watched him consume his food, fascinated with the way his throat worked when he swallowed, the bunch and play of muscles in his jaw when he chewed, the lean strength in his fingers on the knife. He was, in a sense even a steward could appreciate, a *prime specimen*.

In a sense a woman could appreciate, Sutcliffe was a decent man, too.

"What does foal watch consist of here at Linden, Miss Tanner?"

"We take turns keeping an eye on the mare throughout the night. She's due to foal any time, and being a mare, she'll likely choose the dead of night to give birth."

"So you'll stay up all night to witness one of nature's routine processes?" he asked, taking another bite of peach.

"You've never seen a foal born, if that's how you view it," Loris retorted. "When things go right, it's wondrous. When things go wrong, you haven't much time at all to sort matters out and help the mare."

"Are you worried for her?" Sutcliffe sliced the remainder of the peach into sections and arranged them on a plate. Everything he did was so casually competent, Loris was tempted to throw her chicken at him, but the food was simply too delicious to waste.

Then too, she was an adult, and Sutcliffe was her employer. There was that.

"I am worried about this mare," Loris replied. "For all we know, Penny hasn't had a foal before, and an older maiden mare can have difficulties. It's also late in the year for the birthing, and if we hadn't had so much rain this spring, the grass could be burning out by now."

The grass was burning out, and that was worrisome, but at least they'd got the hay off.

"We've grass aplenty, for now," the baron said, "and the stud was not as big as the mare, so the foal is likely to be of a manageable size for her. Have a bite of peach. They're considered a delicacy."

Loris took a sip of cold white wine. Discussing equine reproduction was less awkward when undertaken while sharing a blanket.

Fancy that.

"Penny will likely be fine," she said, "but one worries. Horses can get the whole business done in twenty minutes, though everything can also go so horribly wrong."

"What can go wrong?"

"Stillbirth, a leg back, arrested labor, red bag, trauma to the mare, infection, a broken pelvis, broken leg, hemorrhage…" Loris's recitation was interrupted by the sensation of a cold, sweet peach slice held to her lips.

"Eat," Sutcliffe prompted softly, leaning across the blanket, arm extended. "Don't ruin it by fretting for the horse as you do, and please don't scold me for my forward behavior either. Such talk puts a man's digestion off."

Tentatively, Loris bit off half the peach section. "Scrumptious," she murmured. "Sinfully, utterly, oh…"

Sutcliffe held the other half of the slice against her lips as he regarded her with an odd gravity. Loris took the second bite, her lips grazing his fingers. He fed her another slice the same way, starting a peculiar heat in her middle that owed nothing to the summer weather or the meal.

"More?" he asked.

"No, thank you, though the fruit is lovely."

"Lovely," he agreed. "Absolutely lovely."

Loris busied herself with repacking the hamper, and Sutcliffe subsided once again onto his back, the fraught moment passing amid the clatter of cups and plates.

"We're to have company," the baron said, eyes once again closed.

"Oh?" *We* were to have company?

"David, Viscount Fairly, is threatening to grace us with his presence."

"He was here before. A largish fellow, blond hair, fine manners."

"And mismatched eyes," Sutcliffe added. "One blue, one green. That's him."

The viscount would keep Sutcliffe occupied then, this would be the first, last and only picnic for Loris.

Surely, a good thing. "You worked for him," she said. "You speak as if he's a friend."

"He is, of some sort, but what his purpose is I do not know."

Ignorance of any degree was a rare admission for Sutcliffe. "Lord Fairly's purpose last autumn was to ensure Miss Hollister and Viscount Amery were getting on well enough, but not too well."

"How do you know this?" he asked, opening one eye. "You were never introduced to the man."

Harry had ventured an opinion, as had Mrs. Kitts. "I kept an eye on things from a discreet distance, and Miss Hollister— Lady Amery—has corresponded with me."

"You women and the things you tell one another."

Then his lordship dozed off, right there on the blanket.

Loris quietly put away the detritus of their picnic and clasped her arms around her bent knees. In slumber, the baron was sinfully handsome, but the fatigue he kept at arm's length claimed his features, and something else shaped his countenance, something more subtle.

The baron was lonely. In sleep he looked wistful, as if longing for something lost in his past. The dark lashes fanned against his cheek were both boyishly innocent and naughty. Loris watched him for a few more minutes, reluctant to leave him alone.

To leave him unguarded. Why he should need guarding was beyond her, a fine, grouchy specimen of titled manhood like him. Loris eased over onto her side, pushed the hamper off the blanket with her toe, and closed her eyes.

She certainly wouldn't sleep here on the same blanket as her employer, but her own dreams had been troubled of late, and resting one's eyes was sometimes a good idea.

She drifted off amid a pleasant fantasy involving a handsome dragon feeding her peach-flavored kisses.

CHAPTER SIX

Thomas dreamed of plush, pink lips sweet and glistening with the nectar of ripe peaches. He came awake, half-aroused, half-amused at his dreams, a bee droning near his ear.

Not eighteen inches from where he lay, Loris Tanner was also enjoying a nap. She had curled on her side, her features more patrician in repose than when animated. Thomas permitted himself several long minutes to simply appreciate her, at peace for a change, not charging about, firing off questions at him, or expounding knowledgeably on the difference between spring and autumn lambing.

Thomas brushed a finger down the curve of her jaw. Her skin was as silky soft as it looked—softer even. Thomas missed that, the feel of a woman's skin. As her eyes fluttered open, he drew his hand back.

"*Wachet auf, liebchen*," he murmured.

She blinked. "What did you just say?"

"Wake up," he translated, *dearling*.

"I was merely resting my—drat!" Her hand flew to her left eye, and she sat up abruptly.

Miss Tanner rubbed at her eye, then tried to hold it open, then rubbed it again as tears wetted her cheek.

"I've something in my eye," she said. "Something that shouldn't be there."

"Let me see." Thomas scooted closer on the blanket, but couldn't see a thing, because the lady was looking down, then holding the irritated eye closed, then rubbing at it. He caught her hands in his and held them in her lap.

"Close your eyes and stop fussing," Thomas instructed, sitting hip to hip with her, but facing the opposite direction. He drew his knees up and shifted Miss Tanner by the shoulders so her back rested against his knees.

"Don't fight me," he instructed. "If you keep rubbing, you could do serious damage."

"Blast and bother, it hurts."

Thomas framed Miss Tanner's face with his hands. "Relax, and let me be in charge for a moment. The eye is delicate, and you could impair your vision permanently with your rubbing and poking."

She closed her eyes, her cheeks damp, the left eye already a trifle irritated. This close, Thomas couldn't help but once again take note of Miss Tanner's lovely complexion, the freckles telling a tale of refinement thwarted by practicality.

He leaned closer and gently eased her eyelid up with his thumb. The next maneuver was one Fairly, a physician, had learned from an old ship's surgeon. Thomas eased the mote from Miss Tanner's eye, brushed a kiss to her forehead, and sat up.

He handed the lady his handkerchief, then touched a finger to his tongue and extended his hand toward her. A tiny sliver lay on his fingertip.

"And you used your——?" Miss Tanner goggled at him with damp-eyed consternation.

"My tongue," he said, taking the handkerchief from her to dab at her cheek, then handing it back again. "I saw Fairly do it with little Rose when she was about to pitch a screaming fit at the horrible, awful, mean cocklebur in her eye. Not particularly sanitary, but neither is rubbing your eye."

"I thank you." Her tone was more dubious than grateful, though Thomas was glad to have helped her. Never had he thought to envision Miss Tanner as a damsel in distress.

She'd deal with him severely if she knew he'd thought of her thus.

"Some lemonade?" He held out a mug to her, knowing she'd be self-conscious about her teary appearance.

"Thank you."

Two consecutive thank-yous. Time for some small talk, or a judicious soupçon of charm.

"You are welcome. My apologies for drifting off. I sometimes don't realize how tired I am until I am forced to pause, and I go out like a snuffed candle."

"You will sleep better soon, sir. You simply aren't at home here yet."

Thomas accepted his handkerchief from Miss Tanner and tossed it in the picnic hamper, though he'd rather she'd kept it.

"Are you at home here, Miss Tanner?"

"I've lived here a good ten years, Baron. That's longer than any other two places I've lived put together, and for the most part, I've been happy here."

No, she had not been happy. "For the most part?"

"My father has had a problem with spirits for as long as I can remember. Then he left, and I stepped into his shoes without telling Lord Greymoor, without even really intending to do anything but keep things together until Papa came back. I love working with the land, the beasts, and the crops. I have not always loved what my life has become."

She'd loved drudgery, for which she'd not been compensated until recently.

"That is a fair summation of my own situation," Thomas said. "I derived a sense of value managing the viscount's business, making sure the reports were accurate, solving problems or anticipating them if I could. I was always tending to business, and somewhere along the way, I stopped tending to Thomas Jennings."

"Thomas? Your name suits you."

Such a smile she had, all benevolence and pleasure, like a girl with her new pony. Thomas had been in her company for most of every day at Linden, and this was the first he'd seen of *that* smile.

It would not be the last, by God. "I strike you as a Thomas? Why is that?"

"Thomas is a fine, old name, and biblical." Miss Tanner opened the hamper and extracted another slice of cheese, extending it to him first, like some oblique form of communion. "Thomas is a solid, dependable, honest name. You are a Thomas sort of fellow. And of course, St. Thomas Aquinas was a learned, worthy man as well."

"This is exceptionally fine cheese, and you've offered a hearty endorsement of a fellow you've only recently met, Miss Tanner." She'd given Thomas more compliments than he'd heard in his entire lifetime combined—solid, honest, dependable, learned, *worthy*.

Miss Tanner divided the next slice of cheese in half, passing Thomas his share.

"I haven't known you long, that's true," she said, munching on her cheese, then leaning back on her hands. "In that week, I've seen you inspect every acre of land for which you're directly responsible, and ask many intelligent questions. You'll get to the tenant farms in their turn. You've asked about every neighbor on every side, and you went out of your way to meet half of them this morning, at market, on their own turf. You got rid of Chesterton, and you'll give Nick the running of the stable. I've seen the measure of you."

While Thomas was only beginning to learn her. "All that, in a handful of days?"

Miss Tanner rose quickly, before Thomas could assist her, but he was on his feet with the same speed.

"When you are responsible for all this," she said, waving an arm, "the dairy, the sheep, the horses, the pasture, the crops, the marketing, the equipment, the wood, the home farm, the tenants, the game, you cannot manage by precise formulas. You must trust your instinct and accept you won't always be right."

She alluded to a courage Thomas didn't entirely understand, but this instruction from her was much needed if he was to become a proper owner of the estate.

"What if you're not right about me?" Thomas asked, studying the pastures and wood in the distance. Beautiful scenery, but in the past week, he'd learned to see it as a responsibility, too. "What if I'm a wastrel, rakehell, miscreant who won't face his responsibilities?"

Thomas's own grandfather had summarized him thus at one point, just prior to sending him away. Theresa had known better than to second those accusations, at least.

Miss Tanner slid her fingers through his, though she too, gazed out across the fields, as if a joining of hands was a matter of complete happenstance.

"At the very least, Baron, you are both men, the rakehell, perhaps, but also the responsible fellow who will care for his land and people to the best of his ability. A rakehell can mature into the other, but it is very unlikely the careful, reliable man will entirely degenerate into the rake."

Miss Tanner slipped her hand from Thomas's, though she could not possibly know what a comfort her faith in him was.

"May I ask a favor of you, Miss Tanner?"

"You may ask."

Asking was the only privilege a gentleman could claim where the ladies were concerned. Before he lost his nerve, Thomas charged onward.

"If I gave you leave to use my name, would you? When we

are private, that is." "Why would you allow me this familiarity? I certainly never called Greymoor by his name, nor did my father."

Thomas asked this of her, because he wanted to call her Loris, wanted her to have one fellow in the entire shire who didn't refer to her as Miss Tanner. The good ones would call her thus out of respect, most would infuse their address with veiled disdain.

She was canny though, his Loris. She'd sniff out prevarication, so Thomas settled on a version of the truth.

"I never expected to hold a title. I didn't want it, I *don't* want it, in fact. I am not, to myself, Baron Sutcliffe. I have no idea who that fellow might be. I have always been Thomas Jennings, and for my adult life, Thomas Jennings has been the factor of David Worthington, now Viscount Fairly. It grows wearisome to be only *the baron*, or *his lordship*, or Sutcliffe, and never, ever just plain Thomas."

Miss Tanner used the toe of one worn boot to flip the lid of the hamper closed.

"My father has been gone more than two years," she said, "and when I talk to myself, which I do frequently, I am Loris Evelina Tanner. Since my father left, no one, not Mrs. Kitts, not Nick, not the boot boy, has called me anything but Miss Tanner. That sounds so starchy, and so *old*."

So safe, too. Thomas didn't mention that.

"Shall I call you Loris, then? You are most assuredly not old." Though she could be very starchy.

"When we are private."

"We are private now." Though within full view of the house, because Thomas valued propriety where she was concerned.

"I will take my leave of you, *Thomas*."

She smiled at him, an extravagant beneficence that far eclipsed mere permission to use her name.

And he smiled right back. "Until next we meet, *Loris*."

* * *

"His lordship won't like this," Nick said. "Come have a look, Miss Tanner."

Loris bent over Nick's shoulder and peered at Rupert's hoof, upturned between Nick's big hands.

"He's sprung a shoe," Loris observed, for the iron shoe was twisted at an odd angle to the bottom of the foot. "Can you get it off the rest of the way?"

Nick rose, setting the hoof down gently. "I can, but Rupert didn't spring that shoe while dozing in his stall all on his lonesome, Miss Tanner. Look at the marks here and here."

Deep scrapes were etched on the outside of the hoof wall. "Perhaps we should discuss this elsewhere, Nicholas?"

"Give me a minute to get the dratted thing off." Nick dealt with the shoe, told Jamie to see to soaking the horse's foot, and followed Loris out of the barn and up the garden path toward the manor house.

"Is this a good time to tell you the baron wants to put you in charge of the stable?" Loris asked.

"Was that your idea?" Wee Nick was clearly displeased by this impending honor, but he was too good a fellow to curse before a female.

"I told him you were content with your station, but his choices are limited—you, old Jamie, or Beckman." For Loris would not tempt fate by managing the stable herself, not even if the baron equipped her with two bullwhips.

"For the present," Nick said, snapping off a white rose, and passing it to Loris. "I will manage the stable, but tell the baron he needs to find someone better suited to the job."

Balderdash. "You will do a better job than Chesterton. If you don't want to take orders from me, then you can answer to the baron." From who, Nick had arguably just stolen a rose.

"I would much rather take orders from you than from his almighty baron-ship. I like my peace and quiet, and I like the horses. Managing people, especially stable lads, is a thankless and tedious job."

Not balderdash at all. "For which you should be handsomely compensated," Loris reminded him, laying the rose on the edge of a bird bath, the stem submerged.

They walked the rest of the way to the manor house in silence. Nick at least didn't expect Loris to take his arm and mince along like some helpless granny. Around Nick, Loris never felt the fluttery, useless feelings the baron engendered. She wasn't tempted to watch Nick walking away, wasn't curious about what his fingers would taste like with peach juice on them.

Loris asked Harry to find the baron for them, and then led Nick to the library.

"I forget what a lovely house this is," Nick said.

"You're not up here very often?"

"I try not to be," Nick replied, going to the French doors and leaning on the jamb. He was so tall that even slouching, the hair of his crown fluttered against the top of the doorway.

"Every window looks out on a pretty view," he said, "and you've made sure every breeze brings in the scent of flowers. I see the little Vermeer is no longer hanging in the stairway, though. Still, to live here would be a fine thing."

"Interesting sentiment," said the baron from the doorway, "for a man who's reluctant to accept a higher station."

His lordship moved entirely too quietly.

"Reluctant," Nick replied, turning slowly, "to accept greater pay for even greater trouble and strife. Telling someone else to muck the stall I am perfectly capable of mucking myself doesn't elevate my station, Baron."

The men exchanged feral smiles, as if the carping and sniping was all jolly good fun. They'd probably enjoy wrestling in the dirt like boys and comparing the size of their biceps.

Nick was the larger specimen. Sutcliffe was likely faster and more devious.

The baron propped himself against his desk. "I assume this isn't a social call. What may I do for you? Drink, Haddonfield?

Miss Tanner?"

The baron threw down a challenge, a taunt from the reluctant nobleman to the reluctant stable master.

"Nothing for me," Loris murmured, but the baron was already pouring three servings of brandy. His hospitality to his employees was unusual, both for its graciousness and for its peculiarity.

Brandy at two of the clock—for Loris's nerves, perhaps?

"We have a potential problem in the stable," Nick said, sipping his brandy delicately. "Damn, but this is good. My compliments—apologies for my language, Miss Tanner."

"The Marquis of Heathgate keeps the estate supplied," Sutcliffe said, "or he did for his brother, Greymoor. We'll see how I stand in his favor. What is this problem?"

Nick ignored the mention of the titles, though Loris could go for months without hearing even the word *marquis*.

"Miss Tanner," Nick said, "will you explain for his lordship?"

"Rupert managed to spring a shoe while standing in his very well-bedded stall," Loris said. "Nick is certain the shoe was on tight when your horse was unsaddled after our outing earlier today, but the stable was untended for portions of the day. We suspect mischief."

The baron studied his drink, from which he'd yet to sip.

Ten years behind schedule, adolescence had apparently decided to plague Loris, for she could not stop gawking at the breadth of his shoulders or the angle of his jaw.

Sensations stole up from memory, of the baron steadying her face between his hands, his breath across her brow. She took a sip of brandy, for her nerves, indeed.

"Anybody who would hurt an animal on the sly," the baron growled, "would hurt a woman, a child, another animal were the opportunity to present itself. What precautions can you suggest?"

"We can make sure the barn is not left untended," Nick

said, "and because the draft mare is due to foal, we'll have a rotation of people in the barn at night. Miss Tanner has asked me to make up a schedule."

The very Miss Tanner not six feet distant from either of the men in the room.

The baron swirled his drink and brought it to his nose. "Did Miss Tanner tell you to include her in that rotation?"

"She did," Nick replied. "She is the steward, and unless you want the stable run under your immediate direction, I take my orders from her."

Oh, Nicholas. He was really very dear, but his gallantry was misplaced, for Thomas—his lordship—was the last man to disrespect Loris's station.

"Then you are accepting the post of stable master?"

"You need the help," Nick said, "and you have no alternatives to hand whom I would trust to take proper care of the horses, save Miss Tanner, and she is far, far too busy. For now, I'll see to the stable."

Nick should have been an earl, at least. In one sentence, he'd tossed out a half-dozen implied criticisms, hints, innuendos, and other concealed barbs. The baron was helpless, working Loris too hard, untrustworthy, a poor manager, and on probation with his stable master, for starters.

"Mr. Haddonfield," Sutcliffe said, "you are a treasure, and I am blessed indeed that you'll condescend to take my stable in hand."

Loris watched more of that predatory smiling and took a swallow of fine drink, only to find the glass had somehow become empty.

"We should ask some questions," she said, lest somebody start snorting and pawing. "Ask the help if they noticed anything, send someone to make a few inquiries at the Cock and Bull to see what Chesterton has been up to. We might rig an alarm for the mare's stall. Nick, whom shall we send into town?"

"Yes, *Nick*," the baron said, "who can hang about at the tavern without drawing attention to themselves while Miss Tanner and I question the staff here?"

Nick set his unfinished drink on the sideboard. "I am known to enjoy the occasional pint or three, and I never draw much notice because I keep to myself. If it doesn't storm this evening, I'll stop at the Cock and Bull and see what I can find out."

"We'll need a list," Loris said. "Anybody who was in the stable between when the horses came in, and when you found the sprung shoe."

"Just how did you find the sprung shoe?" the baron drawled.

Gracious, sweltering days. If Sutcliffe had dashed his drink in Nick's face, the accusation couldn't have been clearer.

"I toss more hay to the horses in the stalls at midday and in the late afternoon," Nick said, "to keep them from getting bored and out of sorts. When I opened Rupert's door, he gave me an odd look, and was standing with one knee bent. I noticed the shoe then and found Miss Tanner shortly thereafter. We came immediately here after discussing the matter between ourselves."

"Which I appreciate," the baron replied. He took Loris's empty glass and returned it to the sideboard. "Who is in the stable now?"

"Old Jamie," Nick said, "and I've told him there's trouble afoot."

"I wouldn't tell anybody else," his lordship said. "Let's ask our questions first and compare answers."

"As you wish," Nick replied. "Until tomorrow, and thank you for the excellent brandy."

No "my lord," no "your lordship," not even a begrudging, "Baron."

"You're welcome." The smile was back, ferociously gracious, faintly amused, and entirely too handsome.

Then that smile was turned on Loris. "Miss Tanner, if I might have a moment?"

"Of course. I'll see you at the stable, Nick."

Nick took his leave without waiting for the baron to excuse him, though he tossed a bow in Loris's direction, something he'd never done before.

The heat was making them all daft.

"You don't trust Nick?" Loris asked when that good fellow had departed.

"I trust that Nick isn't responsible for tampering with Rupert's shoe. But you saw him, Miss Tanner, and you must know he's not being entirely honest."

Loris knew no such thing. "I saw him sip your good brandy and accurately report his suspicions. I saw him take a civil leave of me and willingly accept my authority when many others would not."

"Loris, my dear, settle your feathers."

Loris. Why must he call her Loris now—and Loris *my dear*? Because she'd given him permission to, that's why.

"Explain yourself," she said, opening one of the French doors in hopes a breeze might come along, bearing her common sense back to her.

"Think, madam. What stable hand has an ability to tell excellent brandy from the merely good? What stable hand speaks with that much sophistication? What stable hand takes on a titled lord in conversation, and more than holds his own?"

"I haven't your experience of the world, my lord, to know a stable hand from an earl's son. Nick is good with the horses and comfortable in the stable."

The brandy sent lassitude through Loris's limbs, adding weight to the fatigue resulting from a hot, sleepless night. She appropriated a pillow from the couch and lowered herself to the cool stones of the raised hearth—unmannerly of her, of course, but she'd smack the baron with the pillow if he lectured her on etiquette now.

"The Earl of Greymoor is the best stable hand you will ever meet," Sutcliffe said, "simply because he eats, sleeps, and breathes his horses. That's why I believe Haddonfield had nothing to do with this sprung horseshoe—he would never hurt a horse, not intentionally."

So what was all the posturing and pawing about? "Nick noticed the Vermeer that used to hang in the stairway is gone," Loris said.

The baron opened the second French door, and a lavender-scented zephyr riffled the lace of his cravat.

Must he be so attractive?

"Greymoor gave the Vermeer to Fairly, before he sold the place to me," the baron said. "Fairly passed it along to his wife. I didn't care for it."

While Loris had adored the image of a mother and toddler in a prosaic moment of a sunny day.

"That image was peaceful," she said. *Comforting.* "The very scene to draw the eye as one ascended or descended the stairs."

"The painting was *sweet.* Better suited to Fairly's tastes." His lordship studied the view from the French doors, a view he'd had hours and hours to appreciate. "Does Haddonfield harbor feelings for you?"

Loris left off fiddling with one of the pillow's gold tassels.

Men and their queer starts. "If he did, *which he does not,* that would be none of your business, Baron. Nick is a good man and protective by nature, but he has never given me the slightest hint he seeks anything more than cordial relations between us."

"Would you know, Miss Tanner, if a man sought more than that from you?" The lavender or the oaks or something must be fascinating to his lordship, for he didn't turn to ask even *that* question.

"You mean, would I know if Nick had the kind of prurient interest Greymoor's guests did?" Loris scoffed. "Those intentions can be spotted miles away." Though alas for her, she hadn't always been so alert to them.

The baron turned, propping his shoulders against the door jamb. The sunlight gilded red highlights in his hair, the breeze teased the dark curls fringing his brow.

He and Loris were private now. Why was he no longer calling her Loris? Or *my dear*?

"I mean, Miss Tanner, does Haddonfield hold honorable intentions toward you, or at least respectful intentions?"

What did any of this have to do with a sprung shoe on the baron's gelding?

"Nick is willing to take direction from me, shows me the requisite courtesies, and does a good job. What difference does it make if his intentions are honorable or respectful?"

His lordship scooted one shoulder, as if scratching an itch, then crossed the room to join Loris on the hearth stones.

"A man and woman may deal with one another respectfully, to the mutual pleasure of both, though neither seeks a liaison ending in marriage," he said, his tone maddeningly pedagogic.

She should whack him for his little tutorial in wickedness, though his lordship also had a well hidden streak of protectiveness.

"You think Nick seeks those sorts of dealings with me?"

"Could he?"

Loris felt the baron's heat, felt the slightest rustle of his breath against the side of her neck. He smelled good, of meadows and grass, of soap and flowers.

Not of the stable, as she must.

"I've seen on more occasions than I wanted to, what mischief grown men can get up to," Loris said. "The male mind is beyond my fathoming. I deal with your kind only because my work necessitates it."

"Your safety will as well," the baron said, tucking a strand of her hair over her ear.

"I beg your pardon?" Loris made no effort to hide her disgruntlement. The heat and humidity undid her coiffure, but the baron scrambled her wits without even trying.

"If you think I'll allow you to spend hours alone in that barn in the dead of night, madam, you are very much mistaken."

"I am, for the present, your steward," Loris began patiently, "and we have little knowledgeable help, and it only makes sense—"

The baron held up a hand, and his smile became again that feral, happily predatory grin.

"You may take your shift at night, Miss Tanner, only if you have my company for your protection."

Bother. Bother him, bother his smile, bother his reasonableness, even.

"I don't like it," she said, wishing she hadn't let him teach her all about cutlery and small talk. This condition of his was both gentlemanly and not quite proper. Prior to spending time with Sutcliffe, Loris would not have allowed either problem to come to her notice, much less bother her.

"You are concerned for my safety," Loris said, and she'd long since given up being concerned for her standing beyond the Linden estate itself, so what mattered the appearance of impropriety now? "You may accompany me if you insist, but foal watch is boring, and it's hard to stay awake."

"In your company, Miss Tanner, remaining awake will be no problem. Now, allow me to escort you to your cottage, where we will see what can be done to ensure you'll also be safe when asleep in your own bed."

Sutcliffe wouldn't back down, compromise, or give up, no matter how pleasantly he beamed at her.

"Very well, Baron. If you insist, I will permit this, though I like it not." Nor would Loris venture to call him Thomas.

"The alternative, madam," he said, taking her elbow and leading her to the door, "would be to move you up here to the manor house until we get to the bottom of the situation in the stable. Neither your reputation nor your slumber would benefit from that."

What slumber? "I wouldn't do it. One sprung shoe cannot cause us to panic, my lord. That is very likely the goal of Chesterton's actions anyway." Though he'd probably delegated the actual mischief to Anderson or Hammersmith. Only Nick, Jamie, and Beckman remained in the stable, and they'd have their hands full.

"I do not panic, Miss Tanner, but your safety must come before any other concern."

Loris panicked often, but from a young age she'd learned not to show it. "Weren't you planning to call me Loris?" she asked, wrapping her fingers more snugly around the baron's arm.

"I was, Loris."

Sutcliffe placed his hand over hers where it rested on his arm, and escorted her to her cottage at a ridiculously sedate pace.

Doubtless, in deference to the heat.

CHAPTER SEVEN

"I am without a personal mount for the nonce, so where does one acquire horseflesh around here?" Thomas put the question to his steward as she led him through the woods.

He was the escort, true, but Loris Tanner knew every path.

"Claudia Pettigrew has some good horses," Miss Tanner replied, "and her lads aren't too bad about backing them. Mr. Dale has comparable stock, but you'll have to deal with the widow if you want to breed Penny back to her stud. Mrs. Pettigrew might bargain more generously if you're also buying from her."

"So you and the widow are cordial?" Thomas asked, relishing the cool of the shade.

"We are civil." That single sentence brought the temperature in the wood down yet further. "She is never outright rude to me, nor I to her, but in her conversation, she always manages some deprecating innuendo, and I lack the sophistication or desire to adequately parry her barbs."

"Give me a good, honest fistfight any day," Thomas said, "and spare me from the weapons of women."

Thomas had forgotten how lovely an old wood was in summer. He and Miss Tanner had ridden for a short way through the wood, but at the time, he'd been steering the horse and the conversation, and trying not to take too much notice of the lady.

Now, he liked the look of her here, sunlight slanting down, the scent of greenery around them, no sound but for a bird chirruping overhead.

"You deride the weapons of women," Miss Tanner said, gesturing Thomas down a fern-bordered path. "Were you and Nick employing the weapons of men? With that 'excellent brandy' and 'you are a treasure' nonsense? You were rearing and squealing like a pair of stud colts."

Stud colts. An impressive and decidedly un-genteel image.

"We were squaring off over the right to protect you."

"The *right to protect me*?" Loris sputtered, coming to a halt. "The right… you neither have the right to protect me. I am a woman grown, and I've been without the protection of a man of any sort for the past two years, and before that…."

Thomas held back an oak branch for her. "Before that, Miss Tanner?"

"Before that, I was more often the one protecting my father than the other way around," she said, resuming her march on her own.

"Protecting how?"

They were approaching her cottage, an architectural confection sitting snug and flowery in the clearing in the woods. Here, the surrounding trees kept the worst of the heat away, and quiet pervaded the air.

"It doesn't signify." She stopped as they broke from the trees, but remained in the shade, a bright smile slapped on her mouth, while wariness lingered in her eyes. "Would you like some cider or lemonade?"

"You're dodging, sweetheart," Thomas said, brushing a wisp of hair from her temple with a single finger.

She batted his hand away. "Don't do that."

"Don't do what?"

"Don't be so... forward, so familiar." She turned away, crossing her arms. "So *kind*."

Thomas had seen that posture from her before, when a stable full of men had been ready to hurt her and destroy what she held dear. He stepped closer so she could feel him right behind her.

The next words would also hurt her, but her solitariness did her a far worse injury, and had been paining her for far too long.

"You want me to desist," Thomas said, "because if I am kind, and you come to trust me, then you might admit to me what a relief it is to be away from your dear papa. To not have to worry over when he'll disappear again, leaving you to once more cope with his lapses, his absences, his worthless apologies and protestations of reform. You won't have to acknowledge the pity and contempt you bore from your neighbors, and you won't have to admit the man who should have protected and cherished you broke your heart, again, and again, and again."

Thomas could recite that litany because his sister had taught him a version of the same sorrow.

Miss Tanner hunched in on herself, as if gale force winds buffeted her from behind. Then her shoulders hitched and a sound escaped, one expressing no dignity and much grief.

Thomas turned her gently and took her into his arms. Nobody would see her here, momentarily discommoded by a bumbling baron. He tucked a handkerchief into her hand and wished he were back in London, where no one expected subtlety from him, and he was simply Fairly's man of business.

Loris Tanner had built a fortress of self-reliance and privacy, and Thomas had tunneled beneath her defenses with honesty, when she was prepared to outlast sieges of contempt or withstand the mortar fire of indifference. The citadel of her composure did not crumble slowly, but rather, collapsed in a heap.

Another woman, a London lady, might have sniffled, waved her handkerchief about, and dabbed at her eyes.

Loris Tanner carried on like a tired child, like a woman should carry on only when safe in the confines of her own home, in guaranteed and protracted solitude. She wasn't merely whimpering or tearing up, she was *crying*.

Thomas kept an arm around her shaking shoulders and walked her to the front porch, where he lowered her to the bottom step. He took the higher step, sat with a leg on either side of her, and anchored her to his chest.

Tears meant to manipulate were familiar to him, and he was adept at cajoling, teasing, and placating the women who used them. He was equally comfortable cutting the tears off with a swift, unsympathetic word, or a mocking glance.

These tears did not want placating, they wanted *comforting*.

So Thomas held Loris, stroked her hair, and rubbed her back in slow, caressing circles, while she locked her arms around him as if she might drown were she to let him go.

"I will never look you in the eye again," she said after long, unhappy moments. Her face was tucked against Thomas's chest, and her voice was husky, though her arms had loosened their grip about his waist. "You are an awful man, Thomas Jennings, to provoke me so."

That she could scold him was reassuring.

"I am a beast," he acknowledged, resting his chin on her crown. "You may keep the handkerchief."

He cast around for something to say to distract her from gathering her emotional bricks and beams while still in his arms. She would want a personal admission from him, something genuine.

I'm sorry came to mind, though he wasn't sorry to have been the shoulder she cried on. A storm of such proportions had to have been building for years.

"Fairly came upon me in the middle of a bout of tears,

once," he said. "I thought I'd have to knock his teeth down his throat so great was my humiliation."

Loris squirmed free to peer at him. "*You* were crying?"

Her eyes were shiny and puffy, her nose reddish. Some vagrant instinct in Thomas more usually devoted to balancing ledgers wanted to kiss that nose, to kiss any part of her, better.

"I was feeling sorry for myself," he said. "I'd missed the funerals of twin cousins, fellows I'd grown up with. They'd occasionally tolerated me of a summer rambling around my grandfather's estate, though I hadn't seen them for years. They were scapegrace ne'er-do-wells, the pair of them, but for them to be gone—I felt very much betrayed, alone, and frightened. Then too, we'd parted on bad terms, and I was angry they'd died without mending the breach."

Betrayed, alone, frightened. He was probably describing Loris's emotional reality as well as his own past, and yet, with his sister, who'd lost the same pair of cousins, the breach had yet to be mended.

Loris sat forward, and Thomas let her go that far.

"I used to think when Papa would go off on his sprees, the worst part was people telling me they'd seen him stumbling out of the Cock, or over in Haybrick or Trieshock, buying a round for the house. I knew he'd be back in a couple of days, tossed out of the back of a farmer's wagon, stinking, insensate, and filthy. I dreaded his homecomings, the stench of him, the tears, the apologies, and the careful questions he'd ask, trying to reconstruct his latest debauch."

God's bullwhip. If the man hadn't decamped, Thomas would have tossed him from the property—though, Loris, loyal daughter that she was, would probably have gone with her papa given the chance.

Her father hadn't given her that option—*yet.* "How long had this been going on?"

"Years. But now my confusion is worse. Now I vacillate between dreading that he will appear again in the same condition, or worse, never appear at all."

Thomas lowered himself to the bottom step, to take a place immediately beside her.

"Have you considered what you'll do if he returns?" he asked, snapping off a dead pansy from among its cousins. Tanner should return, by God. What man could leave his only child with no provision and not worry over her fate? Had Greymoor made any search for his missing steward?

Had the magistrate? Anybody?

"If Papa comes back," Loris said, tossing another wilted flower aside, "Claudia Pettigrew will lay information against him. Her pride will demand that much."

The worst item on Loris Tanner's endless list of dreads was likely that her father would be executed for the crime of rape, which was… awful.

No wonder she'd cried her heart out. "You think your father might be guilty?"

"He was never a violent drunk," Loris replied, dabbing at her throat with Thomas's handkerchief. The gesture was dainty, weary, and—damn it all to hell—alluring. "Papa was jovial and gregarious—nobody thought to send him home when there was so much fun to be had. But when Papa was far gone, even he didn't know what mischief he got up to. A daughter is not the best predictor of such behaviors in her own father."

"I suppose not." Nor would Loris grasp the fundamental contradiction of rape accusations and severe inebriation.

Though blind drunkenness hardly constituted a defense to rape.

A thoughtful silence arose, one softened by the scents of the forest and flowers around them. Thomas should dredge up an apology for making her cry, except clearly, she'd *needed* to cry.

While he had needed to be with her when she did.

"What did you do instead of knocking the viscount's teeth

down his throat?" Loris asked. "When he found you grieving?"

Grieving. A genteel, if accurate, description of one of the most unbecoming moments of Thomas's adult life.

"Fairly was the soul of kindness. He patted my back, handed me a generous tot, and fussed and pothered until I could be safely sent up to bed. He has never mentioned it since." Though Thomas reflected on that memory frequently, for—as mortified as he'd been—it was a dear memory.

"A good friend."

Never quite that. "A good man."

"Will you let me pretend this embarrassing lapse of dignity has not occurred, my lord?"

Thomas ignored her dodging back into use of his title. "Now, that will be difficult. For Fairly, you see, had no need to recall the pleasure of patting my back, nor lending me his handkerchief. In your case, I am most unwilling to part with similar recollections."

"You are teasing me." Loris wasn't upset, but neither did she sound pleased.So Thomas tried harder. "You are the best-smelling female of any species I've had the pleasure to stand downwind of. Why would I part with the memory of your embrace?"

Ah, a small smile. Sunshine in the dense woods, honeysuckle gracing the humid breeze.

"I make my scents as a hobby," Loris said, pinching off yet another of the wilted pansies. "You have such a variety of flowers on your estate, Baron. I like to capture their fragrance for my own pleasure."

Thomas bumped her shoulder with his. He would rather have bumped her cheek with his lips—merely as a gesture of comfort, of course—but the moment was too fragile for such a risk.

"Today you are wearing you mother's honeysuckle scent," he said. "The day I met you, you wore roses, and I've also caught a hint of lemon and spices from you. That one is particularly riveting, but I like the lily of the valley fragrance too."

"Your wood is carpeted with lily of the valley. You could perfume London from one end to the other if you wanted to."

"Perhaps we will." For Thomas could hardly manage such a task without his steward, could he? "That will have to wait until spring. For now, I will inspect your premises with a view to your safety."

* * *

The baron had stomped around Loris's cottage muttering about hinges and braces, as if the small dwelling were a castle in need of fortification. Between admiring her embroidery and sniffing at the bouquet of orange lilies on the sideboard, he'd quizzed her too.

Had anybody tried to locate her errant papa? Not that she knew of.

Had she? No, for how would she have attempted that?

What had Micah Tanner's drunken revelries typically involved?

Loris had answered honestly, though the memories nearly reduced her again to tears: relieving himself in the Haybrick village fountain, riding his horse into church on Easter morning, making up treasonous songs about the Regent's dietary habits.

Sutcliffe had stopped asking questions after that. By the time the baron had marched off in the direction of the stable, Loris's cider was sitting badly in her belly, and her vision had become unreliable.

When she ought to have been studying the hardware around her door and attending carefully to the baron's lecture on lock picking—how had he learned about lock picking?—she'd instead been fixated on his hands, which conveyed strength and competence, but also an unnerving masculine elegance.

And those hands on her person had been... devastatingly gentle. They had asked nothing, borne no hurry or judgment.

Loris knew a man's hands could be beguilingly tender—Viscount Hedgedale's hands had been seduction itself, *at first*—but she hadn't realized that a man could be a source of comfort.

Loris went after the flowers potted along her porch railing, yanking wilted blooms into a pile of fading color.

"I understand selfish men," she muttered to the flowers. "I understand men who are too proud to take orders from me. I understand men who look after their own interests first and last. I do not understand this man."

She tossed a lovely little pansy that had not yet begun to wilt onto the pile of spent flowers and sat back when she realized what she'd done.

"Apologies," she said, retrieving the flower and carrying it inside. "I am muddled, because I do not understand the baron, and yet I want to."

She rinsed out the mugs in the sink and filled the one the baron had used for his cider with water, then dropped the pansy into it and put it on her bedroom windowsill.

"I want very much to understand Baron Sutcliffe, and that is surely my worst folly yet."

* * *

Thomas left Loris beheading pansies on her shady front porch, and took himself by the stable to confer with Nick. His quarry wasn't hard to spot, for Nick towered over Jamie as they stood in the stable yard conversing.

"Gentlemen, have we sufficient privacy we won't be overheard?" Thomas asked.

"We do," Nick replied, and he was right. The open air was often the safest place to discuss any delicate matter, though the sun was brutal and not a breeze stirred.

"Miss Tanner has mentioned the possibility her horse was purposely fed a full ration oats as he was recovering from a colic," Thomas began. "What do we know about that ration of oats and the person who fed it to the horse?"

Jamie spat in the dirt, an eloquent comment on any who'd mistreat a horse.

"I toss hay morning and noon and late afternoon," Nick said, scraping a booted toe in the dirt, "and feed oats in the early morning after the horses have had their hay. Chesterton tossed hay in the morning and fed the oats at midday. He didn't feed hay at noon, just hay in the morning, oats at noon. In this heat, feeding that way was ludicrous."

"Miss Tanner didn't question him about these peculiar practices?" Thomas asked.

"She took him on proper," Jamie said. "Any damned fool knows you throw hay first and only then do you offer grain if a beast is in work. She told Chesterton to feed her horse according to her preferences, and she'd hold him accountable for trouble with the rest."

Hold him accountable how? Thomas had wanted to hang a bullwhip over every entrance to Loris's cottage, but she would have thought him daft.

"And yet, despite her clear instructions, her horse is the one who suffered a colic," Thomas finished. "Let me guess: Her altercation with Chesterton over this matter was very public and quite loud."

"She weren't loud," Jamie retorted. "Miss Tanner ain't never loud, but Chesterton was sowing the whole discussion broadcast in a high wind. Him, they might'a heard down at the Cock, the way he was takin' on."

Nick remained silent.

"We have someone either hell-bent on striking at Miss Tanner," Thomas said, "or we have somebody trying to incriminate Chesterton by striking at Miss Tanner. We also need to replace the lost stock, the sooner the better. I'm told Mrs. Pettigrew might be able to oblige."

"Or," Nick countered, "we have a couple of incidents of pure bad luck. Horses colic, and they spring shoes in every stable."

Was Nick being reasonable, or was he protecting somebody? His former co-workers in the stable? Himself? He looked like a particularly healthy exponent of a fine rural Saxon heritage, but his blue-eyed gaze was fixed on the barn's cupola, and his boots, while dusty, looked to be Hoby's work.

"In all the time Greymoor owned this place," Thomas asked, "did you ever have several horses colic in one month, much less fatally?"

"As far as I know, this summer is the first time we've put any horses down," Nick said. "Why don't I walk you back to the manor, Baron? We can discuss replacement of the horses lost in Chesterton's care, and Jamie can keep an eye on the stable."

A fine idea, when Thomas was getting nowhere interrogating them together. Come to that, where was the groom named Beckman, the third and final member of the staff whom Loris regarded as trustworthy?

Thomas and his stable master crossed the yard without Nick offering another word. When they reached the fountain in the middle of the circular driveway, Nick scooped up a handful of pebbles and perched on the fountain's rim.

The sun was hot, but the sound of the splashing water was soothing, and here, not even Jamie would overhear them.

"A gentleman," Nick observed, tossing a pebble into the water, "doesn't kiss and tell." He tossed another two pebbles, the rings rippling across the water. "I am a stable lad, not a gentleman."

"Right." A stable lad who recognized Vermeer, spoke with public school diction, and wore a pair of boots from the finest boot makers in London.

"You, are having too much fun playing baron to be as careful as you ought," Nick said, "so I will be blunt. You mention buying horses from Mrs. Pettigrew and breeding Penny back to her stallion. Claudia Pettigrew is a troubled woman."

She was, by reputation, a spoiled bitch, though Thomas knew better than to judge anybody by reputation alone.

"Mrs. Pettigrew will reel you in with the typical innuendo and flirtation," Nick went on as the fountain splashed merrily along, "and you will trip happily to her bed, thinking to romp an afternoon away. She doesn't want you to touch her for the sake of your pleasure or hers. She wants you to touch her so she can hate you. I can't think of another way to put it, but I have it on the best authority that the woman deals in intimate hatred."

This was not about ill-treated horses—or was it?

Men did kiss and tell. Hell, Thomas had managed a bordello for Lord Fairly. Men would brag about their conquests, their stamina, the responses they wrung from their partners, and the ease with which their quarry succumbed to their blandishments.

"And yet, I've been advised to breed Penny to the widow's stallion," Thomas said, "and look over her available riding stock." He'd at least pretend to do the latter, because Claudia Pettigrew had authored Loris's latest misfortunes, and yet, that matter had never been investigated either.

The rest of the pebbles went into the fountain in a shower. "You think you know what you're doing," Nick said, rising and dusting his palms together, "because you've navigated the social cesspool that is London society, but Baron, the woman is rumored to have poisoned old Squire Pettigrew. She's cold, and the direction of her malevolence is unpredictable. Clearing Micah Tanner's name would go a long way toward impressing Miss Tanner, but Loris won't understand why you're getting to know the widow better."

Even Fairly would have had had trouble parsing Thomas's motivations in this case, and yet Nick Haddonfield had divined them in a moment.

"Haddonfield, you are too damned smart, too quiet, too big, too handsome, too well-spoken. If I didn't find you altogether too likeable as well, you'd be tossed out on your ear."

"I have my charms," Nick said, resuming their progress toward the manor, "and one of them is a nature that will demand an accounting if you trifle with Loris Tanner's feelings."

Oh, delightful. Chivalry from the stable, long after it might have done Loris any good.

"Haddonfield," Thomas said, "you do not overstep, because you seek to protect a lady's virtue, but she has already informed me quite explicitly we are neither of us entitled to protect her. She will make her own decisions, and she has no desire to marry when her own father demonstrated, and I quote, 'the folly grown men can get up to.' Mind that in defending her interests, you are not also trampling her privacy and her independence."

Nick paused to let Thomas pass through the French doors into the library first.

"A pretty little speech, Baron, but Loris Tanner is an innocent, and the momentary pleasure of romping with you will be little consolation to her when her heart is broken and her hard-won self-respect is shattered by your casual dismissal of her after the fact."

An indignant retort about Haddonfield minding his own business, or not jumping to dirty little conclusions, was called for, but Haddonfield was only articulating what any man of conscience would say. Loris Tanner was not only innocent, she was lovely in her innocence, and vulnerable in her isolation.

More to the point, as Thomas's employee, on his estate, she should consider herself under his protection.

"Please take yourself off to the Cock and Bull this evening, Haddonfield, and be as dumb as you credibly can be."

Haddonfield executed an elaborate court bow. "I shall be a veritable dunce. As my baron commands, so shall it be."

Thomas snorted at that foolishness and wondered again

who Nicholas Haddonfield was, and why he was masquerading as the Linden stable master.

CHAPTER EIGHT

"The prospect of company has become something more than a threat," Thomas said. "We are to entertain Viscount Fairly in the near future."

Thomas invoked the use of the baronial *we* while sitting beside his steward on her porch swing, having escorted her there when their shift with Penny had ended.

"I can't tell in this dark if you are looking forward to Lord Fairly's company, Baron, or dreading it."

"Both," Thomas said, putting the swing in motion.

Based on the setting moon, he placed the hour at about four of the clock. Loris had lasted for most of their two-hour watch, but then succumbed to the lure of slumber just before Beckman had come to relieve them. Tall, blond, muscular, and taciturn, he put Thomas in mind of a younger version of Nick.

But then, rural populations, like the aristocracy, tended to inbreeding.

"Shall I put the kettle on, sir?"

"No tea for me." Loris would hare away to her hearth and leave him out here among the bats and owls. "Bear me company for a bit?"

As her employer, Thomas could demand, command, order, imply, and summon, but he tried to keep his imperiousness within the confines of what she owed him as his employee. At four in the morning, she owed him not one damned thing.

"It's too hot to sleep."

"That it is," Thomas said, closing his eyes and leaning his head against the back of the swing. "Fairly threatened in his last correspondence to pay a call, and when I didn't wave him off, I knew he might invite himself down. He is not a man who sits still for long, in any case."

"You have spoken of him as if he were a friend. You certainly respect him. Are you concerned you won't know how to interact with him as a peer, rather than an employee?"

Thomas shifted his arm so it rested along the back of the swing, nearly touching Loris's shoulders. Linden was cursed with employees more astute than was convenient for a tired, new owner. Thomas, having long been an astute employee himself, understood their motivation: Look after the employer, or the employment could come to a quick, unhappy ending.

"That's your problem," Loris concluded. "Fairly is no longer your employer, and he'd be your friend if you'll allow it."

Frightening notion. Fairly took his few friendships very much to heart. "That is a problem, how?"

"You have no discernible taproots, Thomas."

Loris's use of his name in the darkness was a caress to Thomas's weary soul. Because his eyes were closed, he felt rather than saw her lean her own head back against the swing, encountering his arm and letting her head rest against his forearm.

"Am I a tree, to have taproots?"

"We all have taproots. My father is a taproot for me. He is what makes me so determined to do well with Linden, to avoid ever being any man's dependent, but he is also where I learned all I know and love of the land. I cannot divine your taproots."

"Maybe you can't see them." Or maybe Thomas had systematically hacked himself free of them.

"Roots grow underground, of course. If you watch, you can usually tell where they lie. The horses are a taproot for Nick. Pride in the appearance of Linden holds Mrs. Kitts in place. I cannot tell what anchors you."

Were Thomas's breeding organs not beginning to throb insistently, he might be able to focus on this business of taproots.

His tired body had chosen now, though, to betray his gentlemanly intentions where Loris was concerned. The whole idea of something sunk deep and tenaciously into rich, dark soil lent itself to naughtiness, and Loris deserved better than that.

"I had best be going," Thomas said, though he didn't move. "The sun won't be up for another hour, and one can at least try to sleep."

"You should hang a hammock on your balcony. The back of the house usually catches a breeze, and that's preferable to indoors on nights like this."

Nights like this… in the past week, the heat had become so concentrated the nights no longer cooled off appreciably. The air bore a sultry, pent-up feeling that compounded with Thomas's wayward imagination to conjure thoughts neither decent nor restful.

"Loris…."

"Yes?"

Kick me off this porch now, but kiss me first. "Both of us need not keep watch in the stable. I can sleep in of a morning, whereas you cannot. Why don't you let me take the watch and call you if Penny needs assistance?"

"Have you ever birthed a foal?"

"I have, and because Fairly is a physician, when he was

on hand, the experience was appallingly educational. I know enough to summon assistance when I see a little hoof waving at me from beneath Penny's tail."

And clearly, a woman who could argue practicalities like this was not falling prey to wayward thoughts, which realization should have dashed cold water on Thomas's imagination.

"That is spectacularly indelicate," Loris said. "Maybe tomorrow night I will let you take the watch, provided Penny doesn't foal today. She's very, very close."

If God were merciful, Beckman was foaling the mare out at that moment, for Thomas's self-control was trying hard to slip from his grasp.

"I'll be off then." Thomas pushed to his feet. "Get yourself inside and drop the crossbars, if you please." He reached a hand down but, in an effort to clasp Loris by the upper arm, inadvertently grazed her breast. Still, he hauled her to her feet, bringing her body almost flush against his.

A pause, while she gained her balance, and he brushed his lips across her forehead. Once, lightly, before stepping back.

"Good night, sweetheart," he whispered. Then he was down the steps, and feeling his way along the darkened path winding through the trees.

* * *

"You couldn't sleep?" Beckman asked.

Nick slid down the wall beside Beck, though even now, at the coolest hour of the night, when the horses dozed in their stalls or napped in the pastures, the barn was barely comfortable.

"I will be glad when the situation here has resolved itself," Nick said. "Penny seems fine."

Beck was a first-rate horseman. He paid attention to the animals, took their welfare seriously, and took pride in his work. That last had been a long time coming, particularly with Chesterton running the operation. Beckman had learned a lot from Jamie, and was big enough that the other lads hadn't tangled with him when he'd ignored or subverted one of Chesterton's orders.

Which he'd done nearly as often as Nick and Jamie had.

"Penny will drop that foal in her own good time," Beck said, moving a wisp of hay from one side of his mouth to the other. "When I started my shift, Miss Tanner was fast asleep on the baron's shoulder."

Well, of course. Damn Sutcliffe to the muck pit.

"He owns the estate, Beckman, and she's a grown woman."

The light was trickling into the sky to the east. Whoever said the darkest hour came just before dawn had never worried his way through an English summer night.

"You could charm her," Beck suggested.

Beckman had a sense of humor, though it was subtle. Nick cuffed him on the shoulder in case the comment was serious.

"Charm her, and then what? Once the harvest is in, I'm moving on."

"I like it here," Beck said, which Nick hadn't seen coming. "I thought shoveling horse shit all day, going days without a proper bath, living like this would surely drive me to Bedlam, but Chesterton needed constant watching, and the animals appreciate good care."

Nick had waited nearly two years to hear these words, and while they comforted, they also underscored the fact that before long, neither he nor Beckman would be on hand to protect Loris Tanner from miscreant stable masters—or from handsome barons.

"Get some sleep," Nick said. "I'm the stable master now, so you have to do as I say."

"Such wit, Nicholas. Or perhaps the heat is making your delusional." Beck tossed aside his wisp of hay, rose, and sauntered off into the gloom.

While Nick remained where he was, prepared to worry his way through an English summer day. Sutcliffe was right to be concerned about the stable, for even bad luck couldn't explain all the sickness and injury that had plagued the Linden horses.

Had Nick been able to locate Micah Tanner, he might have worried less, but apparently no one had succeeded at that task.

Sutcliffe would get around to trying though, and then who would protect Loris Tanner from what the baron might find?

* * *

Loris Tanner came striding around the corner of the manor house, her hair tidily braided, her appearance neat, nondescript, and utterly practical.

"How can you move with such energy in this heat?" Thomas asked, rising to hold a chair for her.

"I didn't come to sharee on your breakfast," she said. "We have matters to discuss."

Good morning to you, too, madam. "Don't we always have matters to discuss, and won't our discussion be more pleasant if you're seated?"

She sat, back not touching the chair, hands folded in her lap, a picture of maidenly submissiveness, but Thomas knew better. Loris Tanner was keeping her powder dry, and woe unto him who couldn't dodge her shot.

"May I offer you some sustenance? Toast? A cup of tea? I've ordered the kitchen to keep some on ice, as long as the weather is so beastly."

Her head came up. "That is quite a luxury."

More like a necessity. "I own a warehouse full of ice, and what I haven't set aside for my own use is making me quite a tidy sum in this heat. Now, let me fetch you a cold drink, and then you can tell me what has put that thunderous frown on your face."

Her tired face, damn it, and even a trifle pale.

Loris Tanner didn't rail and carry on as most other women would, but she quivered with upset silently nonetheless. Her very stillness indicated how agitated she was.

Thomas set a cold glass of sweetened tea before her on a linen serviette. "I like it with sugar and mint, but tell me what you think of it."

Loris sipped the drink, then set the glass down, her expression surprised. "That is wondrous lovely."

Wondrous lovely, indeed. "In India, they've been drinking spiced tea with ice for centuries. You didn't sleep well, my dear. Not that anybody could in this heat."

She stood, turned her back, and muttered something unintelligible, so Thomas rose as well and stepped up behind her until he was close enough to catch the scent of lemons and spices from her hair.

His favorite of her repertoire of fragrances. "I beg your pardon, madam?"

"You mustn't kiss me," she said, barely above a whisper.

Thomas stood near enough that he could have tipped his head and visited the offense on her again, this time on the nape of her neck. While his senses inebriated themselves on Loris's scent, his mind grappled with her words.

"I mustn't kiss you. I wasn't aware you had suffered my kisses to any great degree, but then, it is hot, and a man's recollections can be addled."

Loris turned and tapped her forehead twice with her finger. "You've stolen kisses from me, here. It won't serve, and you will desist." She might have been scolding an unruly puppy, so stern was her tone. Thomas stood his ground, and so did Loris, which left them toe-to-toe in the morning shade.

"I am not to kiss you here." Thomas brushed a finger against Loris's brow. "Then where would you like me to kiss you? Here?" He drew a finger down her cheek. "Or here?" The same finger touched her lips fleetingly.

Kisses her forehead had been gestures of utmost restraint and respect, and she was in a taking over *that?*

"You are mocking me," Loris hissed, still glaring up at him from close range.

Thomas would not dare. "I am paying you a compliment. Let us sit, so we might be civilized with each other." He took her bare hand in his and led her back to the table, where she sat, just as poker-straight and indignant as before.

He took a fortifying sip of very cold tea, which he probably ought to have dumped in his lap.

What would Fairly think, to see the "ever-competent Jennings" trying to explain himself to the ever-more-competent Miss Tanner?

"I gather you don't object so much to kissing—which is harmless enough in itself—as you do to the implication I might not stop with kissing?" Thomas began. "You admit you've attempted liberties?" she shot back, color rising in her cheeks.

"A few brotherly pecks on the forehead do not a seduction make," Thomas responded gently, though such forwardness might a seduction portend. "What have you against kissing?"

"I am not a Puritan. I have been kissed. Kissing is all well and good between those whose affections are pledged, and those who can trust each other to exercise restraint."

A countrywoman's attitude, tolerant and sensible, though Loris's tone was colder than Thomas's tea.

"Do you think, Loris Tanner, I would force myself on you?"

She raised troubled eyes to his, and Thomas saw not insult in their depths, but abused trust. Whoever had kissed her had failed either to exercise restraint, or to pledge his affections, the rotter.

"I would not force myself on you," Thomas assured her frostily. "I *need* not, and I would not. An unwilling woman holds no appeal whatsoever. Never has, never will. Do you believe me?"

She reached for his glass of cold tea, though her own sat at her elbow. "If I were to believe any man, it would be you."

In other words, Loris did not believe herself safe *even* with him. She had dozed at his side in the damned barn, and because of a brush of his lips to her forehead, she'd filled in all her tunnels, lit her Greek fire, and loaded her cannon.

Thomas stood, tugged Loris to her feet, then pulled her over to the deepest shade on the terrace.

"No squawking, if you please, madam. This requires privacy."

* * *

Loris braced herself, expecting to find the baron's mouth mashed to hers, her body trapped in a suffocating clinch. Then his lordship's hands would start roaming and squeezing.

He might progress to odd noises and even more awkward endearments.

In the past, if Loris simply held still, she could outlast unwanted amorous advances, and her indifference had been deterrent enough. With the viscount, she'd capitulated to his assurances that "kissing is the prelude to much greater pleasure."

Pleasure for him, possibly, though befuddlement and consternation had been Loris's reaction.

She turned her head, hoping to avoid the inevitable, though the baron's hand cradled her nape. To her surprise, he held her loosely, stroking his hand down the length of her braid, resting his chin against her temple. A breeze sprang up, fragrant with lavender, a scent that had Loris relaxing despite her situation.

She was tired, and Sutcliffe's embrace was comfortable. Comforting, even.

"Put your arms around me," Sutcliffe said, his voice blending with the soft breeze and the slow, rhythmic caress of his hand on her back. Loris complied, despite the clamoring of common sense to the contrary.

Thomas Jennings was the first man in her acquaintance whom it was truly, bone-meltingly lovely to be near. She vowed to stop him if he really misbehaved—knee to the vulnerable location if needs must—but for the moment, she leaned against him.

He exhaled, stirring the hair behind her ear.

To be held in such an undemanding way was sweet and restful. Loris closed her eyes, took in the scents of flowers and expensive shaving soap, and rode the slight rise and fall of Thomas's chest as he breathed.

He kissed her brow—no offense in that.

Lazily, he expanded the range of his wanderings to include her eyelids, her cheekbones, the line of her jaw, the turn of her neck. By the time he was exploring the tender spot below her ear, Loris was angling her chin to accommodate him, and her body was tucked snugly into his.

Gracious lovely days, she ought to say something, but this was no assault, and yet these intimacies were doubtless more than the lesson Sutcliffe had intended. A demonstration, perhaps, of gentlemanly restraint.

The baron hadn't kissed Loris's mouth. She wished he would—kiss her mouth and be done with it.

"You deserve to be kissed," he said, "not trifled with, but pleasured, the way a lady is entitled to be pleasured even in the passing gesture of a kiss," he murmured against her throat.

Despite the heat of the morning, a shivery sensation skittered up Loris's spine.

Sutcliffe grazed his lips along her neck and cradled her jaw against a callused palm. He pressed the softest of kisses to Loris's slightly parted lips, then withdrew, leaving her every opportunity to step back, slap his face, and pretend he had taken advantage of her.

Which Loris could not do, drat him. She sighed in defeat, not even opening her eyes lest she find the baron mocked her.

She knew less than she'd thought about kissing, much less, and Sutcliffe knew too much. Loris couldn't even resent him for that, because his instruction was… lovely, and heartbreaking.

He was right: This was a woman's due, this unhurried, attentive exploration of her pleasures and preferences. Grief assailed Loris, grief for a girl who'd been too unworldly to recognize disrespect when it leered and groped at her, a girl who'd been weary of lies and yet unable to hear them when it mattered most.

Damn them all, the liars and viscounts, the drunks and debauchers.

On that thought, she took possession of the baron's mouth, kissing him in earnest, escalating the soft, sipping play of his lips on hers to firmer contact. He met her challenge, his tongue tracing her lips—a question, an invitation, never a demand. When Loris joined him in a tentative exploration, Thomas welcomed her, teased her into bolder maneuvers, then retreated into more delicacy and invitation.

He shifted his hips—yes, he was aroused; no, she was not horrified—and swept a hand over her breast in a passing caress.

"And now, madam, the restraint I promised you. The restraint any gentleman should promise you." The baron eased his mouth away and returned to a simple embrace, his hand on Loris's back in languid caresses.

Heat lightning quaked through Loris's insides, the aftermath of a storm that left the air more close than before the cloudburst. This demonstration had altered forever her horizons and her sense of herself.

Also her sense of *him*.

Sutcliffe was too good at this. He ought to give kissing lessons and write treatises on the topic.

"You," he whispered against her hair, "are a Congreve rocket with a lit fuse."

His lordship sounded gratifyingly winded, and nearly as dazed as Loris felt. Poetry abruptly made sense to her. All the callow, giddy looks exchanged in the churchyard shifted from silly to enviable.

"Sweetheart?" Thomas murmured, trying to tip her chin. "Loris?"

This careful, coaxing swain was his swaggering lordship?

Pleasure of an entirely different sort chased off Loris's

upset. She'd done this to him, left him winded and whispering. She'd surprised him and turned a demonstration of gentlemanly restraint into a trial of his lordship's self-control.

"You have lit a fuse of your own," Loris said, glossing a hand over his falls. He probably hadn't bargained on arousal, and yet kissing her had done this to him. How… interesting.

How…. lovely.

"A lit fuse? Why, yes. I rather do."

They stood in each other's embrace, his lordship's gaze amused and—if Loris wasn't mistaken—proud? Not of himself, precisely.

Of them?

Of her?

"Shall we sit, madam?"

The sophisticated, articulate, handsome baron needed to compose himself. Loris wrapped her arms around him in a fierce little hug, then stepped back and resumed her seat at the table. His lordship took the seat at her right elbow and reached for his iced tea.

He sipped, then held the glass against his left cheek, then his right, then his forehead. Perhaps his lordship was coming down with an ague?

"You were about to make a point, with the kissing," Loris said. And the caressing, and the cuddling, and the whispering.

"A point? Perhaps I wanted to see you smile, precisely as you're smiling now, and see your gray eyes take on pussy-willow softness, though I have never before in my life likened any part of a woman to pussy willow. I am gratified, however, to see you at rest, quiet for once, and perhaps considering"—he paused, the glass just at his lips—"that your opinion of kissing needs revision."

Loris's opinion of *him* certainly did, and that was… that was a problem, the very problem she'd intended to discuss with him.

The discussion had abruptly grown more necessary, also

more difficult.

"When you do the kissing, my lord, it's lovely. Thus, my dilemma." The baron set Loris's own drink in front of her, but she didn't dare pause to savor it. "The *problem* is that you can rob me of my reason, and that is worse than merely robbing me of my dignity. I have never—you kiss too well. I am not willing to marry, and you are not asking me to be your baroness. I see no point in further dallying."

A minor tragedy, that. Loris had dallied with the viscount, out of curiosity, loneliness, boredom, and ignorance. Wisdom precluded her from dallying with Sutcliffe. She liked Sutcliffe, she liked kissing him. Some day in the distant future, she might, in small ways, even trust him.

But to have that distant day, she must be sensible now, drat the luck.

The baron held her drink to her mouth. The cold, sweet tea was ambrosial, a pleasure that made a hot summer morning a delight rather than a torment.

"Then dallying must have a point?" he mused. "I have never encountered a dalliance that had any other object but pleasure, comfort, and companionship. Best of all, a woman can dally without surrendering her independence."

Loris took another sip of her drink, needing the fortification, and the time to absorb that his lordship might very well, possibly, perhaps *be propositioning her.*

"You would content yourself with my clumsy attentions, when half the women in southern England would jump at the chance to share your bed?"

Dark lashes lowered over blue eyes now slumberous, for which nonsense, Loris nearly kicked his lordship's shin.

"You are not storming off in a cloud of injured dignity, Loris. Why do you think I'd have such an easy time of it, finding a woman to share my bed?"

She was tempted to lecture him about appropriate topics of conversation, but they needed to have this discussion.

"You are handsome,"—Loris ticked off on her fingers— "wealthy, titled, *experienced*, and not seeking a bride. The widows would kill for a shot at you."

"Your rural analogies are quite graphic," Thomas said, running a finger around his cravat. "I have no interest in putting on airs for some predatory female who will come to call on Tuesday afternoons, and expect me to drop my breeches and service her on demand."

So that's how it was done? Why Tuesdays?

"I am immediately to hand," Loris said, "and too ignorant to make inconvenient demands on you. Moreover, you have to know I would neither put on airs, nor expect you to escort me about as if I mattered to you. Forgive me if I am too flattered to accept such a proposition."

Thomas laid a hand over hers, his fingers cool from holding the icy beverage.

"You mischaracterize my sentiments, madam. We will be in each other's company often enough that we must have honesty between us regarding any mutual interest. I'm not ashamed that I find you attractive, nor should you be ashamed to admit a reciprocal appreciation. I imply no proposition, only a mutual regard."

That kind of mutual regard from Sutcliffe could bring Loris pleasure—also heartache, scandal, and awkwardness. And yet, what had propriety gained her, except loneliness and hard work in the shadow of her father's misdeeds?

A calf bawled for its mama out across the fields, the sound a reminder to Loris of realities even a wealthy baron could not alter. He had taught her how to navigate the cutlery at a fancy table, and he would teach her how to dance. Sutcliffe could even teach her the glorious subtleties of a shared kiss.

But Loris could not allow him to teach her to pathetically depend on a man's notice, or to lose sight of the livelihood that stood between her and the poorhouse.

"I am glad we understand each other, Baron, for I wasn't

propositioning you either. You will excuse me, for I have work to do."

Loris stood, wishing Sutcliffe would argue, flirt, tease, or even grab her by the wrist and prevent her flight.

"I mean you no insult, Loris," he said, remaining in his seat. "And be assured nothing that happens between us can jeopardize your livelihood, short of gross incompetence, and you're simply not capable of that."

"You mean me no compliment, either." She bent and kissed his cheek. "Enjoy your breakfast."

With a lingering pat to the bulge behind his falls, she left him and ducked onto the path through the trees.

* * *

"You have the beautiful estate, the wealth, and the title," Fairly observed. "So when will you take a wife?"

His handsome, blond lordship had ridden into the Linden stable yard at mid-morning having traveled down from Town by moonlight. Thomas had ordered the table on the terrace set once more, for a breeze stirred at the back of the house, and the view was lovely.

"You are usually more subtle, Fairly," Thomas said, pushing a plate of peach slices across the table. "I assume you will dash off a report to your viscountess before the sun sets, and lament that since I left your employ, no suitable woman has snatched me up."

Nor had any unsuitable women snatched Thomas up. He could still feel Loris's hand, boldly patting the evidence of neglected manly humors.

"Better to marry than burn," Fairly quoted sanctimoniously. "And in the country, a man hasn't as many options as he does in Town."

Perhaps not, but *a man* could think in the country, could take time to see and smell and enjoy what and who was immediately before him.

"You mean," Thomas said, "the country lacks a surfeit of

bored, randy society women who will let a fellow tumble them without developing expectations of him?"

Though the ladies did harbor expectations—the straying wives, the bored widows, the soiled doves. They all had expectations, of disappointment, of financial support, of pointless dramatics.

"The ladies in the provinces are not usually of such easy virtue," Fairly said, munching a juicy peach slice into oblivion. "And the ones on your own estate are, of course, not available."

Merciful devils. Fairly was quoting scripture *and* preaching. Thomas waved a fly away from the peaches.

"Of course, Fairly. Absolutely unavailable." The fly was persistent enough that Thomas draped a serviette over the fruit.

"Thomas, you aren't bothering Miss Tanner already, are you?"

Miss Tanner was certainly bothering Thomas. She and Fairly had met in the stable yard, according to his lordship. Thomas hadn't been on hand to offer introductions, which had slowed Fairly down for about the time Loris would have spent on a shallow curtsy.

While Thomas had been in his room, naked on the bed, dozing in the aftermath of a bout of self-gratification.

"Miss Tanner won't have me," Thomas said, because Fairly's intrusion on private matters needed to end, as did, apparently, the flirtation with Miss Tanner.

Blond brows drew down in consternation. "She won't have you in her bed as a lover, or as her spouse? How did you ascertain either, when you've been here only a short while?"

"She won't have me as either." Thomas slid a fork beneath the linen covering the peaches and appropriated a slice. "She has made it quite plain she won't marry—she has her reasons—and I'm not looking for a wife, so there's an end to it." Though when Thomas announced his lack of interest in a wife, and had he been in earnest or in jest?

In any case, there *should have been* an end to it. A combination of lust, protectiveness, and inconvenient curiosity argued otherwise.

Fairly sat back, his wrought iron chair scraping against the terrace. "Are you prepared to be a gentleman about this, Sutcliffe?"

The form of address was new, and grated like the metal chair against the flagstone terrace. Always before, Fairly had used "Jennings," "Mr. Jennings," or in situations of extreme irony, "my dear Thomas."

"I will be a gentleman," Thomas said, though he might be a persistent gentleman.

Loris *interested* him. Attraction to a pretty woman was simple animal spirits—of which, Thomas had an ample supply—but Loris... She challenged, she questioned, she kissed with shy enthusiasm, then she patted Thomas's falls and flounced off to check on the brood mare or consult with the beekeeper.

"Why not simply marry her?" Fairly drawled, swirling his chilled tea. "She's comely and of breeding age. She'd manage your estate and your household as well. Marriage to her makes a kind of sense."

"She will not have me," Thomas said again. "Though I dare say, it's worth a try to propose. If not, there are widows about the neighborhood somewhere, I'm sure of it."

Fairly set his glass down and tipped his chair onto the back legs. "Not the Pettigrew woman? Greymoor's description of her was unnerving."

In the manner of the British aristocracy, Fairly laid claim to family ties that included Linden's former owner, Lord Greymoor, who was married to Fairly's younger sister. In the past, Thomas had marveled at Fairly's network of family and acquaintances.

In the past, Thomas had also claimed only tenuous ties to the aristocracy.

"You are the second man to warn me off Mrs. Pettigrew,"

Thomas said. "My stable master told me very articulately that Mrs. Pettigrew hates men, and allows them liberties so she can hate us all the more."

Fairly, who had owned a brothel and whose judgment of the fairer sex was nigh faultless, let out a low whistle.

"Greymoor said she's a woman who gets colder the deeper you thrust, and then she mutters about having been ill used. Not a woman I'd tangle with."

Greymoor was a gentleman and he did not gossip. That he'd use such vulgar language about a woman with whom he'd dallied turned Thomas's stomach on behalf of all concerned.

Fairly was yawning discreetly before the food was gone, so Thomas summoned Harry to show the viscount to a bedroom where a tepid bath would be waiting. Thomas remained on the terrace, moving his chair to remain in the shade, the better to ruminate.

Marry Loris Tanner?

Part of him leapt—literally—at the idea. To have her in his bed, on his desk, in his hay mow… the possibilities were endless, and endlessly pleasurable to contemplate. Loris would be assured lifelong security, Thomas would have his heirs, and a well-run estate.

But marriage itself, an irrevocable, lifetime commitment to one woman, and one woman only… That had the feel of a trap, of domestication. Marriage was forever, and Thomas was by no means old. He had time to produce heirs.

Though nobody had endless time. Thomas was the last of his line, and should he die without issue, the Sutcliffe estate would revert to the crown, leaving his sister homeless and without income. The last thing Thomas wanted was to be responsible for Theresa's welfare, but neither did he wish her in the gutter.

He hadn't seen his only sibling for nearly nine years, had thought of her only fleetingly until coming to Sutcliffe.

Marry Loris Tanner? Court her, woo her, win her hand…?

Thomas was not particularly eager to become a father, but the prospect of securing Loris Tanner's trust, at the very least, was intriguing.

The lady spoke of independence, but her kiss had been full of possibilities.

Thomas downed the last of a glass of lemonade, rose, and headed for the stable, intent on issuing his steward an invitation to dine that evening at the manor.

CHAPTER NINE

The baron had been polite, friendly, and insistent that Loris join him and his guest for dinner. Chesterton's bullwhip hadn't intimidated her half so much as Sutcliffe's invitation, but she presented herself promptly at the appointed hour anyway.

Loris wore her finest summer dress, one she treasured too highly to wear even to church. Her hair was swept back into a chignon at the nape of her neck, the absence of her braid swinging against her back making her feel exposed.

Harry welcomed her into the house. "Their lordships are in the parlor, and I'm to announce ye, lord love us." He clicked his heels and winked.

"Miss Loris Tanner, your lordships," he brayed merrily.

"Thank you, Harry," the baron said. "Miss Tanner." He took her hand and bowed over it. "Madam, may I make known to you David, Viscount Fairly. Fairly, Miss Tanner is my most excellent steward. My apologies to you both for not being on hand to make introductions earlier today."

The viscount bowed over Loris's hand. "I declare myself enchanted. Sutcliffe, shoo, that may I monopolize the lady's company while you, mine host, fetch us our drinks."

Lord Fairly seized Loris by the arm and turned her toward the open French doors, smiling down at her with such conspiratorial friendliness she forgot to be nervous.

"Sutcliffe on a mission to be hospitable," the viscount stage-whispered, "is a formidable prospect. You must promise to stay at my side, Miss Tanner, and take him firmly in hand when he gets too obstreperous."

The viscount was a beautiful man, his features so perfectly proportioned and finely honed, Loris wished she'd at some point had drawing lessons. Mismatched eyes, one blue, one green, should have rendered his features discordant, but they only made his appearance uniquely lovely.

To behold Thomas—Lord Sutcliffe, in this company—a more rugged, reliable sort of handsome, was reassuring.

"Lemonade, Miss Tanner, with a splash of white wine." The baron held out a tall, glass garnished with late strawberries and a sprig of mint.

"That means,"—the viscount leaned down to murmur—"at some point the glass held some lemonade. Imbibe carefully, lest we make you tipsy."

Loris was already tipsy. She was to share a meal with a baron and a viscount; the one was hospitable, the other charming.

"And your drink." Sutcliffe handed the viscount another glass of the same concoction. "Mixed for a gentleman's palate."

The baron suggested they enjoy the evening air, for dinner was still at least twenty minutes away. The viscount stayed at Loris's side, regaling her with humorous incidents from his travels with Thomas, then switching to a series of anecdotes involving his young nieces and nephews.

As her drink disappeared, Loris was aware of two things. First, Thomas was content to simply watch her. He contributed to the conversation, but mostly he sipped his drink, and let the viscount do the bulk of the entertaining. Second, she was in the social presence of true gentlemen for the first time in her life.

Oh, the neighborhood included considerate men, fellows who held doors, who stood when she entered the room, but Thomas and his friend had a polish to their manners, a bred-in-the-bone consideration that enthralled her. She'd seen glimpses of it in Thomas before, in his insistence on her safety, his deference to her gender, his unwillingness to forgo most courtesies regardless of her station or occupation.

But this gathering was purely social, and aided and abetted by the viscount, Loris was enjoying herself.

"Would you care for another drink, Miss Tanner?" Thomas asked.

"Perhaps half that much?"

Harry stepped onto the terrace and announced dinner, and Loris found herself escorted around the side of the house by the viscount.

And so the evening went, with the men carrying the greater burden of conversation, and the meal progressing from one light, spicy course to the next, until the sun was all but set, and a breeze gently fluttered the drape of the tablecloth.

"I don't know when I've eaten as much delicious food at one meal," Loris said, sitting back. "Or enjoyed as much pleasant company."

"A benediction," the viscount said, smiling.

His lordship's smile spoke of sincere pleasure to be in Loris's company. She had no doubt that when he chose to, the viscount could use that smile to devastating effect.

Thomas rose and extended his hand to Loris. "I propose some exercise to counteract the soporific effects of our meal."

"Are you to stroll with the lady in the gardens while I enjoy my own company?" Lord Fairly asked.

"Mustn't pout," Thomas remarked pleasantly. "Though now that you are a contented old married fellow, we know Miss Tanner would be safe on your arm."

"Safe and bored to tears are two different things, young

Thomas."

"I am nearly the same age as you," Thomas replied, "but I will not escort Miss Tanner through the gardens. I will busy myself at the keyboard, while you teach her the rudiments of the Roger de Coverly."

"Dancing. Ever a worthy pastime, don't you agree, Miss Tanner?"

Well, drat. An ambush. Loris had suspected this was Thomas's agenda, but had lost track of her caution between one glass of "mostly lemonade" and the next.

"I hardly know what to make of dancing," Loris said as they moved into the house. "I have never learned, though the baron has made it a goal to teach me both some country dances and the waltz before the assembly early next month."

"A gathering of the locals?" Fairly asked. "I shall make a point to be here."

Thomas opened both doors and windows in the music room, then opened the lid of the gleaming Broadwood piano.

"I shall play, and you, Fairly, will be the dancing master. If he stomps on your feet, Miss Tanner, yell and I will summon the physician."

"Who would be yours truly," Fairly reminded them. "After a fashion."

Without further ado, Fairly took Loris by both hands and stepped her through the patterns of the dance. She made wrong turns, bumped into him, and nearly lost her balance more than once, only to find the viscount unerringly righting her, turning her by the shoulders, or twirling her by the hand, though they had to imagine the other dancers who'd complete the set.

Thomas accompanied them with a casual skill that suggested musical talent buried under the accented downbeats and frequents stops and starts.

"I must rest," the viscount declared when Loris had the rudiments reliably under control. "And a drink, Sutcliffe, if you don't mind. I daresay Miss Tanner could use one too."

Their host left them alone, and Loris fell prey to a sudden awkwardness, one the viscount must have sensed.

"I am utterly harmless, Miss Tanner," he assured her, leading her to a settee along the wall. "Your expression suggests you might have been thinking otherwise."

Fairly had never been harmless, of that she was certain. "I am unused to the company of gentlemen, my lord. I do not converse fluently in your dialect, but neither do I distrust you."

"Then my evening is a success. You are a quick study at the dance."

"Thank you. You make learning easy."

Drawn along by the viscount, Loris found herself comparing upbringings with him, surprised to find his earliest memories were of winters in a Scottish croft.

"Don't you two know how to light candles?" Sutcliffe asked.

Loris advanced on the baron and took the tray from his hands, leaving him free to light the candelabra on the piano and a branch of candles on the mantel.

The viscount took his proffered glass and strode over to the piano. "As the ranking title in the room, I am handing out a proclamation: By decree of the Viscount Fairly, benevolent, protective ruler of this keyboard, Baron Sutcliffe will now instruct Miss Tanner regarding the waltz. You might find it cooler out on the terrace, and my horrendous banging will certainly be audible halfway across the shire."

"Miss Tanner?" Thomas extended a bare hand. "May I have the honor of this dance?"

Loris popped a curtsy. "You needn't look like your toes have been scheduled for their execution, my lord."

He raised a hand to lead her out. "I do not believe that is the prescribed response." Neither was, *I wondered if you'd ever ask.*

Loris placed her fingers over the back of his hand and

processed with him to the center of the floor.

"The pleasure, my lord," she recited, "will be entirely mine, though it's a shame not to simply listen to such lovely music. His lordship plays well."

"He's been getting pointers from Lord Val Windham, who is truly gifted. Your hand on my shoulder if you please, and my hand here."

He explained the need to keep a consistent distance between them, both for the sake of propriety and for the sake of their synchrony as dancers. When Fairly swept into the opening bars of the waltz, Loris stumbled at the feeling of being pulled off her feet.

"I lead, you follow. It isn't complicated, Miss Tanner."

The varlet was laughing at her, despite his polite tones. "Does it need to be so fast?"

"I heard that," Fairly called from the piano bench, slowing the tempo considerably. "The answer is no. The waltz can be enjoyed in a variety of tempi."

Thomas reestablished their position, but then folded Loris's hand against his chest and pulled her in closer.

"Try it this way. One can't use this position in public, but it might give you the feel of the dance more easily."

The feel of the *dance?* What Loris felt was Thomas's body, the warm, strong length of him pressed against her, guiding her as they moved around the room. She felt the pull and glide of his muscles beneath her hand, the rise and fall of his chest against her knuckles. She felt the scent of his soap wafting to her awareness, and the cadence of his breath where he rested his chin against her temple.

Fairly's playing had become languorous, a delicate twining of melody and rhythm, both soothing and haunting, even as it moved them around the floor. In one smooth turn, Thomas propelled Loris out onto the terrace, where the air was indeed cooler, and scented with lavender.

Her first impression was disorientation, from the warm and

reasonably well-lit music room, out into the cooler darkness of the summer night. Losing Papa had been like that, a complete shift of realities, no warning, no chance to prepare.

That sense of a life off balance still haunted her, and always might.

Dancing with the baron, though, Loris floated in a sense of safety. Thomas cradled her against his chest, she rested her head on his shoulder, the darkness, music, and summer air combining to scatter reality like so many stars in the night sky.

Thomas was aroused. Not flagrantly, but enough that Loris could feel the swell of him against her belly. She was pleased that he was affected thus, though she did nothing to indicate her awareness, nor her pleasure in it.

Because that desire would go nowhere. Stewarding Linden, Loris held on to propriety by her fingernails, and gentlemanly restraint from the baron would have to be matched by feminine common sense on her part.

When Loris could not have been more relaxed without losing her footing, the music faded. Inside the music room, the branch of candles was lifted from the piano bench and borne from the room, leaving the terrace in shadows.

Loris moved as if to step back, but Thomas's arms kept her right where she was. "I should go, Baron."

"You should not, not yet. Tomorrow is soon enough to resume marching around and giving orders, Loris Tanner. Tonight you will allow yourself some time for pleasure."

She was already drunk with unanticipated delights. No wonder the assemblies were always well attended.

"You will provide the pleasure, Baron?"

"I hope I already have, though I wonder what Fairly said in my absence." Thomas had turned Loris against his side, and slipped an arm around her back to walk with her toward a pergola at the foot of the gardens.

"The viscount is protective of you, my lord." Protectiveness from a friend ought to be acknowledged and cherished.

"If I am protective of you, madam, my reception is not so cordial."

Loris could not afford—oh, bother what she could afford. "Hush. The night is too pleasant to ruin with your chatter."

Her senses opened up, to the stillness of the evening air, the scent of honeysuckle, the songs of crickets, and a lone nightingale tootling to his true love in the home wood. Her heart opened up as well, to the knowledge that Thomas was about to kiss her—really kiss her—and she welcomed that, even as she knew this kiss could not change anything between them.

When they arrived at the pergola, Thomas simply held Loris for long moments, his hands roaming the bones of her back, her hips, the turn of her waist, the nape of her neck.

"When you wear your hair up," he said, nuzzling her temple, "I can hardly keep my attention from you. The way you curve and turn is grace personified." He punctuated his words with kisses to her shoulder, soft, warm, damp kisses that left Loris boneless in his arms.

"We need to be seated," he murmured. "Come."

They were inside the pergola in a few steps, the side toward the house covered with a thick growth of honeysuckle. The setting was as private as one—or two—could be out of doors by moonlight. Thomas seated himself first, leaving Loris standing between his legs.

"Straddle me," he urged, tugging at her hand.

"We shouldn't."

She shouldn't, shouldn't wish for what could not be, shouldn't long to set propriety aside and let pleasure have even a moment. The summer night was lovely, though, and in Thomas's arms, Loris had felt lovely too.

With the smallest nudge from the baron's charm, common sense would lose the fight to those lovely feelings, at least this once.

Maybe the time had come for Loris to permit that defeat.

"What we shouldn't do, Loris Tanner, is waste the peace and privacy we have to enjoy each another's company for the next little while. You may trust me to guard your virtue, if you want it guarded, but I would pleasure you as well."

The baron was a brilliant negotiator, making it clear that Loris's choices were not being taken from her. Only ignorance and loneliness were under discussion, and those she wanted to banish.

"Come here,"—he tugged on her hand again—"and be with me."

Loris put her hands on the baron's shoulders and awkwardly straddled his thighs. She hovered there, not knowing what to do with herself until Thomas put his hands on her hips and urged her onto his lap.

"Give me your weight and let me hold you." His voice held none of the brusque desperation that Hedgedale's had. If Loris needed all night to find her way to the pleasure Thomas offered, then he'd investigate that night with her.

She heeded the urging of his hand on the back of her head and rested her forehead against his shoulder. His arms settled around her, and when she was cuddled in his embrace, he commenced a kissing war against her last reservations.

Don't think, his kisses whispered. *Kiss me back, relax, trust me…* All of the entreaties Loris had heard from others, but with none of the sly groping, no hint of force lurking in either the words or the caresses.

Thomas did not inflict his kisses, he offered them, then waited, inviting Loris to offer hers in return. What had been a matter of enduring a bewildering unpleasantness with others became another waltz entirely with him, a slow, graceful twirl away from cares and worries, and into endless ease.

Everything in Loris was enthralled. Her list of duties for the next day went drifting away on a breeze, and her misgivings about involving herself with her employer soon followed. If she got up and walked away, intent on being only Linden's steward for the rest of her days, Thomas would never by so much as a lifted eyebrow allude to her decision.

Loris was cherished *and* desired, safe *and* poised on the brink of folly. Part of her observed these paradoxes from the bows of the honeysuckle, a silent mental nightingale that would regret or rejoice over the night's adventures later.

The rest of her realized that Sutcliffe was deftly, systematically, undoing the falls of his breeches, leaving Loris momentarily hovering above his thighs.

"Thomas? I do want you to guard my virtue, do you understand?" He must do the guarding, for she no longer could.

"I understand, Loris, and I will not betray your trust. Stop fretting, and prepare to enjoy yourself—to enjoy *me*."

Loris trusted Thomas in this regard, trusted the utter resolution in his voice, trusted the gentleman in him. Still, she held herself a little above him, abruptly as much at sea as if this were some new, intricate dance, and she'd had too much wine.

"Kiss me," Thomas said, humor in his voice, "and for God's sake stop *thinking*."

He put his hands on either side of her face, threaded his fingers through her hair, and touched his lips to hers. He stilled her by means of kisses, soft, little kisses that greeted each of her features in turn, then grazed along her jaw to the tender skin of her neck.

Loris liked having her neck kissed. When Thomas nuzzled the spot where her shoulder and neck joined, her entire body relaxed. She drifted closer to his lap, only to find a part of him had drifted skyward.

The night air seeped from Loris's nape down between her shoulder blades to the top of her chemise. The caress of a breeze on her skin and the little touches of Thomas's fingers as he freed her from her dress were pleasant, almost as pleasant the whispery sigh of his hand across the fabric covering her breasts.

Thank God it was too hot for stays and bindings and voluminous underlinen.

Thomas's mouth settled on Loris's, just as his breeding organs met her most intimate parts.

"That's just me," he whispered, "and simply another part of us kissing. I will not be inside you. Your weight feels good to me, though. Very good, so stop being shy."

Loris allowed more of her weight to rest on him, and that contact gratified in ways she could not have described.

"Better," Thomas murmured. "More would be better still."

He declared an intermission of sorts, to deal with clothing. Loris was soon wearing only her chemise, while Thomas's shirt hung over the pergola railing, fluttering in the moonlight like a white flag of surrender. His jacket, Loris's best summer dress, his waistcoat and cravat, all ended up on the opposite bench, so much tidily folded propriety stowed six feet away.

"Lovely," Thomas said, resting his forehead against Loris's throat when they were again entwined on the bench. "A moment, please."

A summer-night version of silence descended. The breeze stirred green leaves, livestock shifted and grazed in the pastures at the bottom of the hill, the faint kiss of water over rocks came from the stream that ran behind the stable. Moonlight blanketed the gardens in benevolent shadows, and the scents of a thousand flowers perfumed the moment.

For a procession of instants, Loris was wealthy. She held command over Thomas's endless patience, his erotic wisdom, his very body, and while tomorrow would come, complete with awkwardness and regret, for the next hour, Loris could own a fortune in satisfaction and pleasure.

"Move on me, sweetheart," Thomas said, gently palming Loris's breast. "You'll feel better if you move, and God knows, so will I."

He abandoned her breast long enough to grasp her hips

and show her what he meant. Soon, Loris was sliding her wet sex along the rigid length of his arousal, a slow, push and retreat of her hips toward some goal she could not have pursued without him.

"Like this." Thomas held Loris still and ground himself against her in three slow, glorious thrusts of power, heat, and arousal. "That hard, at least. You do it."

Loris complied, convinced by Thomas's example and the pleasure blossoming where their flesh met.

"Like that," Loris said, her mouth searching for Thomas's even as her hands roamed his chest. The sharp edge of frustration melted into the knowledge that whatever she needed to find satisfaction, Thomas would provide for her.

Loris moved against him, abandoning the last of her caution, because in this, she utterly, absolutely trusted Thomas Jennings. The novelty of that, the sheer relief of it, was as wondrous and seductive as all his kisses and caresses put together.

* * *

Was this how a titled gentleman introduced his steward to an evening of fine manners and genteel company?

That remonstration clamored at Thomas from the edges of an agony of self-restraint. Desire rode him with whips and spurs, while regard for the lady kept a tight grip on the curb reins.

Loris deserved better. She deserved promises in addition to her pleasure. She deserved… Thomas wasn't sure what else, wooing, probably, though she'd settle for satisfaction, and that much he could give her.

He wanted to possess her, wholly and repeatedly; wanted to drive her over the edge while he thrust inside her, but honor forbade that course. Instead, he wrapped one arm around her waist and found a naked breast with his free hand.

He'd neglected her breasts, neglected to touch her intimately, neglected *so much*.

"Come with me," he murmured, applying a slight pressure to her ruched nipple. "Let go for me, Loris. Let go for yourself…"

"Thomas." An innocent's question lay behind the simple utterance of his name.He grasped that question, understood it, gloried in it, and lifted his hips to increase Loris's arousal. At the same time, he fastened his mouth over hers, a plundering kiss that urged her to plunder his treasures as well.

And by God, she did.

"*Thomas.*"

Wonder became demand, as he bucked against her, until she was keening, clinging, and riding him for long, fraught moments.

"Gracious, everlasting, eternal… wondrous days," Loris sighed, folding down to pant against Thomas's shoulder. The utter amazement in her voice had him smiling, despite his arousal. He stroked her back in slow caresses, and let her literally catch her breath before beginning to move beneath her in lazy rolls of his hips.

They were both damp with sweat, and Thomas liked that. Liked that Loris had demanded exertions of him, liked that the breeze on his back, chest, and face was a greater pleasure than had Loris been a sedate lover.

She raised herself off his chest and frowned at him. "You didn't…?"

Did she wish he had?

"I'm about to," Thomas assured her. "You could again, too." Though much more self-denial, and Thomas would expire of his damned gentlemanly restraint.

Loris cuddled down to his chest. "I dare not."

"Dare to," Thomas challenged, sliding a hand between their bodies. He could address this one of his many oversights, if she allowed him to. "You have to relax, sweetheart, and not be in a hurry. Trust me to bring it to you, hmm?"

He resumed kissing her, sweet, hot, unhurried kisses that

soothed as they aroused. Between their bodies, his fingers and thumb insinuated themselves into the damp creases of her flesh.

Thomas set up a rhythm and pleasured Loris thoroughly, learning when to ease off, when to bear down, until she was poised again on the brink of satisfaction. He'd enjoyed pleasing her, enjoyed the challenge of learning her responses and showing her the path to pleasure.

He was in such trouble.

"Now, love. Let go for me now."

Before the words had left his lips, Loris was shaking with the force of her release. Thomas moved in counterpoint to her, taking only three strokes to bring on his own satisfaction, a silent crescendo of gratification that left him wrung out, relaxed, and oddly at a loss.

He kissed Loris's temple. "You dared. Admit it. I was right."

Right, and entirely undone.

Loris's fingers drifted over his mouth, silencing his smugness, but tracing the line of his smile as well.

"Pleased with yourself?" she murmured.

"Exceedingly." Also appalled and enthralled. "Are you pleased with yourself?" Thomas asked, smoothing Loris's hair back from her forehead. More to the point, was she pleased with him?

"I am dumbstruck. Not at myself, but at *this*. I am five-and-twenty years old, I have been with a man, I manage all manner of breeding stock, and I understand reproduction, but this…"

Loris had been with a selfish lout, and Thomas would collect those details later.

"We can hope reproduction won't play into it." A bit of that at-a-loss feeling ebbed as Thomas found solid ground for both the lover and the gentleman. "If we were to conceive a child, I'd expect you to marry me."

The hand Loris had been winnowing through his hair paused.

"Would that be so bad? To be my baroness? To raise our children here at Linden?"

Children whom Thomas had been assuring himself not eight hours ago need not concern him yet.

Loris sighed, her breath breezing over his shoulder. "We must ensure every measure is taken to prevent conception."

Her statement bore concessions she couldn't possibly realize, implying that she would become Thomas's lover in the fullest sense. Her capitulation had the male animal rejoicing, while the gentleman's consternation turned to caution. Even a land steward might not grasp all the subtleties of human copulation.

"Short of abstinence, sweetheart, no measures are foolproof. If you conceive, will you marry me?"

That felt right, to make the offer honor demanded, despite short acquaintance, despite the circumstances.

Loris could say no, in which case Thomas would not touch her intimately again; or she could say yes, and take precautions, and have her cake, so to speak. What Thomas hoped Loris Tanner would never do was promise him marriage and then break her word.

"Marriage is a serious business," she said as a bat went squeaking past the pergola. "Would you take it seriously?"

In a conditional sense, Thomas was *proposing* to her, and she was right: Marriage to Loris Tanner should not be entered into lightly.

"I would take marriage to you seriously," he said, resting his cheek against hers. "I would expect the same commitment in return."

"I will think on this." She resumed her caresses to Thomas's hair, and what few wits he'd gathered went flittering off into the night. "I am not... I am not myself right now, and while I understand the honor you do me, I would not make you the best baroness."

She was muddled. Thank a merciful deity, she was muddled,

too.

"You'd decline marriage out of consideration for me?" Loris's concern for Thomas's station was touching, also aggravating as hell when no part of him relished having a title.

The bat made another pass, swift as thought. Loris climbed off Thomas, leaving the cool night air to shock him in intimate places.

"I can bring knowledge to the marriage regarding this estate," she said, settling beside him and tucking her chemise over her knees. "I've little to offer in the way of polish and connections, and absolutely nothing to offer in the way of wealth."

How honest she was, and how Thomas treasured her for that.

"I needn't wed an heiress." An heiress was the last burden a sensible man took on willingly. "I won't press you for reassurances, only because you flatter me when you say you are not yourself after our lovemaking."

Some part of Thomas needed flattering. He'd ordered Loris to join him and Fairly for dinner, intent on flourishing his manners.

Hah.

"How did I go from lecturing you against kisses on my forehead," Loris said, reaching for Thomas's coat and draping it over her shoulders, "to making those *noises*, and begging you, and clutching at you…? I do not understand myself." She let her head drop to his shoulder, at least physically comfortable with intimacy, though her mind or her heart or some other confounded female part of her clung to its reservations.

"You succumbed to my charm, and to the seduction of waltzing in my arms, and perhaps, Loris, to the simple pleasure of being a healthy young woman blessed with an abundance of passion."

"What did you succumb to?" she murmured against his shoulder, taking a pinch of his skin between her teeth.

"Answer carefully."

Thomas mentally kicked himself. Of course Loris would want to hear the words of appreciation, praise, and gratitude.

"I succumbed,"—he nipped her earlobe—"to a pair of luminous silver eyes that see into my soul. I succumbed to a smile that blesses as it teases. I succumbed to a mind that doesn't stop until a problem is solved and has no fear whatsoever of speaking any relevant truth. I am abundantly glad I succumbed, too, and look forward to succumbing often in the near future."

"You flatter," she concluded, though Thomas had, in fact, bared his soul. "I can accept that you like me well enough. You would not bed somebody you disliked."

"I don't. I didn't, and whichever hopeless clod-pole you surrendered your virginity to had better hope his path never crosses mine. He was inept, Loris, to neglect your pleasure."

"If the experiences get any more pleasant, Baron, I will surely expire."

Loris was finding her balance, and that helped Thomas find his.

"You mustn't flatter me so shamelessly." Thomas sifted his fingers through her unbound hair—when had it come down?—and let it cascade the length of her bowed back. "Your hair is glorious."

Her everything was glorious.

"I should cut it. Long hair is not practical given what I do all day, but I can't bring myself to take the shears to it."

Shears, as if she were one of Thomas's ewes. "You are forbidden to cut your hair."

Her smile was wicked in the moonlight, and she wore Thomas's coat far more carelessly than he ever had.

"Take that tone with me, Baron, and I will crop every lock short."

Ah. *Point taken.* "Sweetheart, I adore your hair, and would hate to see it cut for something as mundane as practicality. You deserve to indulge as many vanities as you please."

"Better, Sutcliffe. I would like to stay here with you all night, but I confess to some fatigue—for which you are partly responsible—and the foaling shift in the barn will come all too soon."

Well, hell. Had Thomas expected Loris to join him in his bed?

"I'll take that shift, my dear. You were robbed of an early bedtime by your demanding employer, who now insists on imposing his company on you right up to your doorstep."

Thomas could feel Loris weighing her weariness against the need to reprove him for presumption, for the same lassitude dragged at him.

"I do not want to leave your embrace, Sutcliffe. This is your fault."

Generous of her, to offer that small, hopelessly appreciated reassurance.

"I do not want to let you go." The feel of Loris drowsing trustingly on his shoulder and the contentment following shared pleasure made the thought of standing, much less walking, repellent.

"Up I go." Loris hoisted herself to her feet and rubbed her derriere as she arched her back. "I comprehend why beds are the recommended location for these sorts of activities."

"Beds have their uses." Thomas stood and used the coat to pull the lady closer. "So do haylofts, couches, desks, lawns, attics…" He'd fall asleep making a list, a long, lovely list. "Let me do you up, lest my wayward thoughts create havoc with your need for sleep, but I want you to promise me something, Loris Tanner: Please don't be starchy and dismissive toward me tomorrow."

Thomas paused to sort out clothing, and search again for the words that would convey his meaning without surrendering the last of his dignity.

"The moment we part," he said, "you'll commence fretting

and regretting, and there's no need for it. I don't expect you to sit in my lap at breakfast, understand, but neither will I have you pretending tonight didn't happen."

He was ordering her not to be *rude* to him?

"There is bound to be some awkwardness," Loris muttered, passing Thomas his coat.

"There is bound to be some *shyness*." He resisted the urge to sniff at his coat in hopes it bore Loris's scent. "That isn't the same thing at all. Shyness is endearing."

She fell silent and let him button this, hook that, and tie the other, then she did the same for him. They walked along the garden paths, hand in hand, while Thomas regretted the presence of both staff and guest—damn Fairly's meddling—at the manor house.

"We arrive to your bower, princess," Thomas said, at the foot of her cottage steps. "So I must bid you farewell."

Loris went into his arms, sparing Thomas his first experience with begging.

"What is the worst that could happen?" he murmured into her hair.

"I could get a babe, and we could be forced to endure one another's company for miserable decades."

"That can't happen." *Not yet.* "What is the worst that could happen based on matters as they stand now?"

Loris was quiet for long moments, though Thomas could feel her casting about for an honest response.

"We could be embarrassed with each other," she said.

"Not embarrassed. *Shy*, which is endearing. And we will be. But friends can tolerate some shyness on occasion, yes?"

Thomas had never been friends with a woman, despite having been in proximity to any number of friendly women. As a boy long ago, he'd adored his older sister, though.

Loris stepped back and twitched at the cravat Thomas had fashioned into the loosest of bows.

"Friends accept one another," she said.

Thomas sketched a bow. "Then I will see you on the morrow, and wish you the sweetest dreams—of me."

For he would certainly dream of her.

CHAPTER TEN

Loris hid in the only manner she knew how to hide: She worked from dawn to well after sunset, despite heat, despite dust, despite fatigue that weighted her every step. In addition to all of her other duties, she took it upon herself to check every gate on the Linden home farm several times a day, because somebody—a small boy, or one of Chesterton's disgruntled minions, perhaps—was randomly unlatching gates and leaving livestock to roam at large.

No more invitations to dinner came from the manor house, which was a mercy. Loris and the baron had discussed *marriage*, and they barely knew each other.

She knew his taste, though, knew the exact flavor of his kisses, knew the marvel of his muscular shoulder against her lips.

That knowledge kept Loris disoriented, almost dizzy as she steered a wagon down one of the farm lanes. A well-run estate managed its water resources, so neither flood nor drought jeopardized the crops, and Loris had started the home farm crew on the task of creating an irrigation pond.

Hard work, but for the men in the water, not as uncomfortable as working the fields under a broiling sun.

The wagon bumped along, noise and dust a fitting counterpoint to Loris's thoughts. She could not get Sutcliffe out of her mind or out of her dreams. She almost wished he'd confront her, but Penny had dropped her foal with Beckman in attendance and thus Loris had no more privacy with her employer.

Rather than intrude on Thomas's time, in the days since nearly ravishing him in the pergola, Loris had stayed busy.

Her reprieve ended as she pulled the wagon up to the bank of the stream running between a pasture and a hayfield. Tall oaks provided shade, and that was another mercy, for the labor was difficult when the river footing was soft and the rocks large.

Here, the stream was closer to a small river, running wide and slow when high, or over half-exposed rocks and boulders when rain had been scarce.

Rain had been very scarce, so now was the time to harvest the rocks from the river and deepen the channel.

The men had cuffed their breeches at the knee, though most were damp to the thigh. Muscles bunched and corded with their labor, bare backs glistened with sweat. So happy were they, trading insults, wrestling rocks, taunting and splashing each other, that they didn't notice Loris bringing the wagon to a halt on the lane.

If she weren't half-dead from the heat, this sight would have sent her into a near swoon. For among the men, Nick, the baron, and the viscount worked side by side.

Nick was like a plow horse, bulky with muscle and grand. The viscount was sinewy, also very pale.

While Thomas…. The sight of him half-naked, wet, exerting himself in an elemental fashion almost toppled Loris from the wagon. She'd nibbled on those shoulders, she'd clung to them and learned their contour by repeated, lingering touch. Moonlight did not do those shoulders justice. Thomas had apparently been in the sun without his shirt previously, for his skin was dusky compared to Nick's and Fairly's.

Thomas was… worth dreaming over, for he had strength in perfect proportion to his size, neither bulky nor too lean. He whipped damp hair from his eyes while making some comment about Nick's ugly face causing the fish flee.

Loris felt the instant Thomas's gaze lit on her, and a hot morning became oppressive.

"Gentlemen," he said, wading to the bank, "we have company."

This was Loris's fourth trip to the riverbank since sun-up. The men would fill the wagon bed with rocks, and she'd haul the load across the fields, to a stone wall under construction between two pastures.

The previous three trips, the baron hadn't been among the men. This time, ever man left the water and reached for his shirt. Sutcliffe tossed a shirt to Nick, another to Fairly, then shrugged into his own.

"Miss Tanner, good morning."

Why did his breeches have to be wet and his feet bare as he prowled up to the wagon? Even his feet—wet, pale, sizeable—fascinated Loris.

"My lord, good morning. If you'd stand aside, I'll back the wagon down the bank."

"Nick will handle the team. You will please spare me a moment of your time, Miss Tanner."

Nick's head emerged from his shirt, and doing up buttons appeared to challenge his considerable intelligence. Fairly was similarly afflicted with bewilderment over how to turn back his cuffs.

"As you wish, my lord, but only a moment. I'm overdue to check gates." Loris set the brake and wrapped the reins. She prepared to hop down, though simply standing left her knees weak and her ears ringing.

The baron's fault, of course. He seemed angry with her, when the very sight of him made Loris want to grin stupidly.

"For God's sake," Sutcliffe growled. "You're weaving on your feet. Get down this instant."

He scooped her out of the wagon, but did not allow her to stand. Instead, he carried her to the shade of the largest oak and set her on a blanket.

"Fairly, get over here!" he barked, rising. "You lot, take a break. Nick give the team a drink."

"My lord," Loris began, organizing her skirts to at least allow her to stand. "What in the world are you going on——?"

She nearly toppled off her knees, assailed by vertigo and an abruptly pounding heart.

More affliction, though she couldn't entirely blame the baron, not when she'd been hot and exhausted for the past three days.

"She's not well," Sutcliffe said, as Lord Fairly's feet came into view. "For half the week, she's been haring around in this heat, never where I'm told I can find her, and now this."

The baron's voice sounded distant and irritated. Loris leaned back against the tree and focused on the cool sound of the water splashing past, for she couldn't find the words to argue with him.

"I'm a physician," Fairly said, hunkering beside Loris and taking her straw hat from her head. "Let's humor Sutcliffe, shall we, madam? The heat is beastly, and you do seem a bit pale."

Thomas stuffed his shirt-tails into his breeches. "She's quiet too, and that's unnatural for her. Miss Tanner does not hesitate to air her opinions."

"Miss Tanner can hear you," Loris muttered. She'd meant to fire off her remonstration the way she'd skip a rock across a pond. One crisp snap of her arm, and a good half-dozen bounces later the rock would sink or smack up against the opposite shore.

Fairly took her wrist, his grasp cool. "Your heart's a bit fast, Miss Tanner. Sutcliffe, the lady could use a drink."

"Nick, fetch Miss Tanner some water!"

Nick left the horses knee-deep in the stream and brought over a flask.

"She's pale," Nick accused. "Baron, I do not like her pallor. I told you your steward has been working too hard."

"You will both excuse us," Fairly said, standing and putting his hands on his hips. "If I'm to serve as a physician in this instance, and I can already tell you somebody ought to, then I must have privacy with Miss Tanner. You will both take your overbearing, unhelpful selves—"

"Thomas?" Loris said.

He was on his knees beside her in an instant.

"I'm fine. You needn't worry."

"She's not fine," both Fairly and Nick said in unison.

"You're arguing with us," Thomas said. "That's reassuring, but will you please allow Fairly to take a look at you? He's quite competent, and if he's at all inconsiderate or presuming, I'll kill him."

"So will I," Nick said.

Fairly unbuttoned Nick's top shirt button, which was in the wrong button hole, then rebuttoned it correctly.

"Miss Tanner, my fate is in your hands," Fairly said, patting Nick's shoulder. "Your devoted servants are worried about you, as am I, in case anybody wants the opinion of the only medical man on the scene."

So that's why Thomas's brows formed nearly a single line over his eyes? Fairly and Nick looked worried, while Thomas... his gaze was steady, but behind his regard, Loris sensed a panic he might not even admit to himself.

"Nicholas, perhaps you'd keep an eye on the horses," Loris suggested.

"Yes, Nicholas," Thomas added, snatching the flask from Nick's hand. "Water the horses, or something. Keep the men away, and have Beckman fetch my horse and Fairly's."

"Your servant," Nick said with an ironic bow. He managed to look lordly even barefoot, half-sopping, his shirt-tails hanging out. "Miss Tanner, please listen to Lord Fairly. If Sutcliffe bothers you, I'll kill him."

"My thanks." These offers of murder on her behalf were all quite touching, but Loris was more interested in the contents of the flask.

"Is that water?" Fairly asked, plucking the container from Thomas's grasp. He uncapped the flask and sniffed. "Smells like water, and it should be cool because Haddonfield kept it in the stream. Small sips, Miss Tanner."

Loris had drained her own flask hours ago and hadn't realized how thirsty she'd become.

"You're parched," Thomas said, brushing her hair back from her forehead. "Fairly, finish your interrogation, then I'm taking Miss Tanner to the house, where she will rest for the remainder of the day, and for once take an order without arguing."

His palm was cool as he cupped Loris's cheek. She really ought to argue with him, because he needed her to argue with him, not because she in any way took issue with his proximity or his generosity.

"Sutcliffe," Fairly said, his fingers going to the buttons at Loris's wrists. "I know you're concerned, but I need to ask Miss Tanner a few questions, and your hovering doesn't help."

"I'm not going anywhere," came from Thomas just as Loris murmured, "He can stay."

The relief in Thomas's gaze was more potent than all the summer heat and still air combined.

"I am outvoted," Fairly said. "Marriage has accustomed me to this indignity. Miss Tanner, have you been bustling about in the heat a great deal lately?"

"From morning to moonrise," Thomas said, unbuttoning Loris's other cuff. "She's racing about, as if the demons of hell were snatching at her hems."

"I've been busy," Loris said, as each man rolled back one of her cuffs.

Thomas produced a handkerchief and dampened it with the water from the flask, then pressed the cool cloth to her wrist.

Heaven, in that simple gesture of consideration.

"Have you been getting enough fluids?" Fairly asked.

"I have my ale, water occasionally. Tea twice a day."

"You need more water, lemonade, cider, nothing approaching spirits of any sort," Fairly said. "My guess is you are tired lately, even making allowances for your activity level."

"Any damned fool can see she's exhausted," Thomas muttered, re-wetting the cloth and pressing it to Loris's forehead. The relief was nearly erotic in its intensity.

"I attend my duties," Loris said as cool water dripped from her temples. "Summer is a busy time at Linden."

"You have shadows under your eyes," Thomas growled, though his touch on her cheeks with the cool cloth was deft and sweet. "You're pale, you haven't your usual spark. People will say I've worked you to flinders, when in fact I haven't even been able to track you down, much less order you to slow your pace."

"You're babbling, Sutcliffe," Fairly muttered, as he again took Loris's wrist.

"His lordship has been working in the heat as well," Loris said, for Fairly ought not castigate a man for being concerned. "I will admit to some fatigue, and I am quite thirsty, now that you ask."

"Fairly, refill the flask," Thomas said, shoving the little container at the physician.

Fairly went off on his assignment, while Thomas undid the bow at Loris's throat.

"You've been avoiding me. You infernal, stubborn woman, why would you avoid me? If you don't want me pestering you, all you need say is that you're not interested. I'm not a brute, I don't force myself on anybody, and if it hasn't become apparent, your well-being matters to me. I would never take—"

"I didn't know what to do," Loris said. "I'm not used to that. I'm sorry. I dreaded seeing you again, feared you'd regret the time spent with me in the pergola. I longed to see you again, and that will not do. My father longed for his drink, you see. I'm muddled, and there's work to do."

Thomas sat back, snatched her hat, and waved it slowly before her like a fan. The resulting breeze was worth more than rubies.

"You're not making sense, love."

"Because of you," Loris said, closing her eyes. "I can't think, I can't sit still, I can't stop thinking, and I have no energy. This is all your fault. I've missed you."

Now she was babbling, though having some time to rest against the tree, and having been given some water, Loris realized she was not on her mettle. Her thoughts were in disarray, and she wanted nothing so much as to tear off her clothes and plunge into the stream.

"Confusion is a symptom of heat exhaustion," Fairly said, putting the cool flask into Loris's hand. "You need rest, fluids, cool, and quiet. Your strength will come back more slowly than you'd like, and you must not become overheated again in the near future. Sutcliffe, I suggest you take Miss Tanner to the manor, order her a cool bath, and set the housekeeper to plying her with lemonade for the next week."

"The next week?" Loris squeaked. "I can't sit on my backside swilling lemonade for the next week. Somebody must find the boys unlatching our gates and deliver them to Squire Belmont for a stern lecture. We ought to marl the fallow pastures, because the hay is off and rain due any day, and now would be an excellent time to see to it. The cheeses should be turned in the cheese cave, the maiden ewes need to be moved, the—"

Thomas wet the cloth and this time placed it right over Loris's mouth. Even that felt heavenly.

"You'll make me a list." He moved the cloth to Loris's throat. "Fairly will vouch for me. I take orders exceedingly well. Utterly trustworthy, that's me."

His voice was a little too brisk.

"Trustworthy, to the life," Fairly added, with equal good cheer. "I've given Thomas responsibility for the viscountess's well-being on occasion, not simply my own life, so surely, you must permit him to step and fetch for you, Miss Tanner. Otherwise, he'll plague you with his company, and I know you've done nothing to deserve such a penance."

Thomas balled up the wet handkerchief and fired it at Fairly's chest. "Cease with the character assassination, my lord. If you behave, I'll write to your viscountess and tell her you're in a decline for lack of her company."

Fairly's brows rose. "You'd do that for me?"

Beckman led Rupert and a white mare up to the lane. He too had found his shirt, though he was smiling faintly, and Beckman was not a fellow Loris had seen smiling often.

"We're for the manor house," Thomas said, scooping Loris up and rising with her as if she weighed no more than a fluffy sheep. "Bring her hat, Fairly."

Such was the lassitude into which Loris had fallen that she let Thomas carry her to Fairly's horse and deposit her into the saddle. Fairly passed Loris the straw hat, and then Beckman handed her the reins.

"Keep to the shade," Fairly said. "A cool bath, fluids, rest, and a few days ordering Sutcliffe about will restore you to fighting shape."

"And entertain the rest of us," Beckman muttered as the baron swung aboard Rupert.

When Beckman smiled, he bore a resemblance to Nick that Loris hadn't noticed before, or perhaps all grown men shared a certain look when they were being adorable.

"To the manor," Loris said. "Baron, if you'd lead on?"

Thomas gave Rupert the office to toddle forth, and soon Loris was in the shade of the home wood, contemplating a cool bath, rest, good food—and a proximity to the baron for which she was utterly unprepared.

* * *

"I know your stable master from somewhere," Fairly said, as he and Thomas enjoyed a bottle of wine on the back terrace. "When his hair was wet, earlier today, I got one of those flashes, memory that might be from reality or might be from a dream. When last I saw him, his hair wasn't as light, but then, he's in the sun a lot, and perhaps in winter his hair darkens. My recollection of him was from a ballroom, in evening attire."

Crickets were singing, and lavender scented the breeze. The sun hadn't quite set, and the air was at least moving.

"Loris doesn't know much about Nick," Thomas said. "He showed up shortly after her father disappeared. Any task thrown at Nick, he handles with uncomplaining competence. Witness, he and Beckman are off inspecting the gate latches Loris swears somebody is systematically opening. More wine?"

"Loris?" Fairly asked, ever so casually.

"Miss Tanner."

"She called you Thomas earlier. Heat exhaustion can cause mental confusion, but I don't think the lady was confused about what to call you."

Thomas was confused, but also at peace, to know Loris was dozing up in an airy bedroom in a corner of his manor house. He kept to himself that Nicholas Haddonfield's little flask had born a coat of arms that Thomas was sure he'd seen before.

"The lady works too hard," Thomas said. "I'll see that she doesn't imperil her well-being again."

"Speaking of threats, what do you hear of this Chesterton fellow?" Fairly asked, putting his booted feet up on a wrought iron chair.

Thomas had shared meals with Loris at this table, and he wished she'd agreed to join him and Fairly for dinner again. Not to polish her manners, not to bring her employer up to date on estate matters, simply to be with him at the end of a long, tiring day.

"Nick told you about Chesterton?" Thomas asked.

"Your stable is short-handed, and the Linden stable is the last place I'd expect Greymoor to have skimped on staff. I pried, I poked, I casually observed. You know how it's done."

Thomas finished the last of his wine, a fruity white Loris would have enjoyed.

"You're lecturing me for keeping a detail of my present situation from your notice," Thomas said. "Chesterton will soon leave the area in search of coin. I'm not your responsibility anymore, Fairly, though your concern is appreciated."

The title had done that, eased Thomas away from Fairly's tendency to mother-hen all in his ambit. The change was awkward, but overdue.

"Very baron-ly of you, my dear Thomas, establishing the picket lines, flexing your authority under your own roof. I'm impressed. Well done and all that, but it won't wash. You are my friend, have been for ages, and friends worry over one another. Pass the strawberries."

Thomas took two, then passed over the rest of the bowl. What a comforting way Fairly had with a scold.

"Chesterton is at the local lodging house, hoping for work," Thomas said, twisting off the strawberry stem and firing it into the lavender bed. "All but two of his former employees have moved on, either drifting into Town, or looking to sign on somewhere as the harvest work approaches."

Fairly bit into a strawberry. "Somebody is unlocking your gates, you say?"

"Loris—Miss Tanner—says. Local boys without enough supervision, Chesterton's friends, or my own staff protesting my ownership or Miss Tanner's authority."

Fairly remained quiet for so long, Thomas wondered if he'd fallen asleep. The viscount was by no means an indolent man, but Thomas had been surprised when Fairly had suggested they strip off boots and shirts to assist with the crew in the river.

The water had felt divine, and the physical exertion sheer glory, for worrying over Loris had nearly tied Thomas in knots. Fairly's suggestion had also allowed Thomas his first opportunity to work side by side with the men who labored on his land, to take their measure, and let them take his.

Which was probably exactly what the viscount—who owned many estates—had intended.

"I've been meaning to raise a topic that I expect will be sensitive," Fairly said.

Darkness was gathering. If Fairly had waited this late in the day to raise a topic, the matter was sensitive indeed.

"We've never had secrets from each other, Fairly." Mostly because Fairly was exactly what he appeared to be: brilliant at trade, reluctant at viscount-ing, and besotted with his wife.

"I have never had secrets from you," Fairly said, taking another strawberry from the bowl. "You had a title for more than a year before I knew anything of it, but Letty says I mustn't chide you for that."

Bless Letty. "I've no interest in voting my seat."

"Nor have you even *visited* your family seat. Not in all the time I've known you, which is nearly ten years, Thomas."

Fairly had been merciful in one regard. He'd waited until the sun had fled to raise this topic. Thomas could clench and unclench his fists silently, could mentally steel himself to risk Fairly's disapproval—also Letty's.

"Sutcliffe Keep has sat on a Sussex hillside for centuries," Thomas said. "Absent a lot of expensive ordnance, I couldn't blast it into the sea if I wanted to."

And he did want to, though Theresa would then be

homeless.

"I have letters, Thomas," Fairly said, softly, gently. "They came to the Pleasure House after your remove to Linden, and they came from Sutcliffe Keep. Whoever she is, she's persistent."

Determined. Theresa was determined, in all her undertakings, whether they led to her ruin or sent her flying on her pony over a stile Thomas's older cousins had been reluctant to attempt on full-grown horses.

"I am persistent too," Thomas said, though what he truly was, was tired and missing his land steward. "The lady is adequately provided for, and I will ignore her letters as I have all of her previous correspondence. This does not concern you, Fairly."

If Thomas had to choose—loss of privacy over this issue, or loss of the viscount's friendship—he knew not which pain he'd select. Theresa's decisions had driven every possible friend from her side, every hope of a decent match.

Perhaps driving friends away was family inclination.

"You concern me," Fairly said. "Worse, you concern my viscountess, and thus I must intrude where gentlemanly discretion would urge me to hold my peace. I know this much, Thomas, whoever she is, she won't go away. Family doesn't. They own you, and you own them. It might take decades, but that bond must be acknowledged."

Fairly spoke from sad, difficult experience, and he meant well.

"I do not deny the bond, Fairly, but neither can I deny her betrayal."

As the absolute darkness before moonrise descended, the sky came alive with occasional flashes of heat lightning. Perhaps at long, long last, badly needed rain would bless them.

Fairly rose, helping himself to one last strawberry.

"Before I retire, I need only burden you with one more sentiment. Whoever she is, a mad aunt, a tippling mama, a cousin who bore your child out of wedlock, she can do nothing to alter the regard Letty and I have for you. There's family, Thomas, and then there's family. Good night."

On that extraordinary speech, Fairly ruffled Thomas's hair and disappeared into the library, making not a sound.

Thomas remained on the terrace, choosing a strawberry by feel from those remaining in the bowl. He selected a smallish specimen, for they were often more delectable than the larger berries.

Summer sweetness graced his palate, and the wind stirred the trees, creating a delightful breeze. No light came from Loris's window, so Thomas had no excuse to leave the darkness.

Theresa had betrayed her younger brother, seen him all but banished from Sutcliffe when he was little more than a boy, and sent him off to university while she sank into as much vice as a country existence afforded a young woman of good family.

The sheer bewilderment of her choices still stunned Thomas every time he tried to examine the past he shared with only that one, disgraced sister.

Tonight, however, a question nudged aside the intractable sense of having been betrayed by the only person who'd mattered to him.

Loris Tanner had been repeatedly betrayed by her father, publicly humiliated by him, her welfare threatened over and over by Micah Tanner's choices, and yet never once had Loris voiced disloyalty to him. Loris acknowledged her father's failings, but she yet saw his strengths, and would rejoice at his well-being if he came riding up the Linden Lane tomorrow.

Thomas could not imagine rejoicing at the sight of his sister, but for the first time, he acknowledged that neither did he wish Theresa ill. He didn't open her letters, but he was reassured by them all the same.

She managed a legible, steady hand, she kept track of his direction, and she continued to post her correspondence from

Sutcliffe, all of which was—damn her, and damn Thomas too—very reassuring.

* * *

Loris slept intermittently for nearly eighteen hours, then rose from her guest bed, dressed in clean clothes brought over from her cottage, slipped down the maids' stairs, and swiped two sandwich halves from a stack on the kitchen counter.

She escaped the manor without encountering either the baron or the viscount, and took the path through the gardens to the stable. Penny and her filly were enjoying the hospitality of the foaling stall, and nothing started a lady's afternoon off quite as nicely as paying a visit to a healthy baby horse. Then too, Seamus had had a mishap in the pasture, according to Nick, and Loris wanted to look in on her gelding.

The foal was asleep, her mother curled beside her in the straw. The sight sent a queer pang through Loris's heart, as if the last bite of her sandwich half had got stuck in her throat.

"We should take Penny off to the stud in the next few days."

Nick's voice startled Loris, so lost had she been in thoughts of lavender-scented sheets and a tea tray graced with a single rose.

And a baron who'd prowled through her dreams.

"You could talk his lordship out of breeding Penny back," Loris replied as Nick stretched out a hand to the mare. "I know you disapprove of breeding in the foal heat. Sutcliffe would listen to you."

Mares, by some unkind quirk of nature, came into season within two weeks of giving birth. When Loris's father had explained that to her, she'd cringed at the very thought.

"Penny can take care of herself," Nick said, dropping his hand when Penny didn't rise to greet him. "The baron is going over to Pettigrew's this afternoon, ostensibly to try out riding horses. I suspect he'll discuss breeding Penny while he's there."

Discuss it with Claudia Pettigrew.

Perhaps this explained the flowery porcelain tea service and slim volume of Wordsworth sent up to Loris's guest room not an hour earlier. She was supposed to drowse away her afternoon on a shady balcony, while Thomas…

While Thomas did anything he pleased, because he was the owner of Linden, and entirely his own man.

"You can ask the baron what his intentions are," Nick said. "We'd all like the answer to that question."

Nick's tone was ironic, and unlike him. Since Thomas's arrival, the quiet, deferential, outsized stableman had become a noticing, articulate fellow who smelled faintly of privilege and secrets.

Where was Nick when the gates were being unlatched? Who had been in the stable with Nick when Rupert's shoe had been sprung?

Loris's musings were interrupted by the baron striding into the stable, Viscount Fairly at his side. They were in riding attire, a magnificent testament to London tailoring, though already, the toes of their boots were dusty.

"Miss Tanner." The viscount greeted her first, raising her bare hand in his gloved one. "You look quite on the mend."

Loris bobbed a curtsy, which felt damned silly in the stable. "My thanks, your lordship. I am feeling much restored." Also irritated, that Thomas would undertake this horse-shopping mission without consulting her.

"Miss Tanner, I see you've eschewed my hospitality already," Thomas said. "Why am I not surprised?" He took his turn bowing over Loris's hand—more damned silliness.

Thomas's gaze was concerned, amused, possessive, cool… so many things, and all of them sent spring lambs gamboling up and down Loris's spine.

She retrieved her hand. "I understand you'll try out riding horses this afternoon at Pettigrew's."

Thomas squeezed off a glare at an innocently smiling Nick. "My stable lacks depth, Miss Tanner, and I must discuss

Penny's situation with Mrs. Pettigrew."

The viscount left off scratching the mare's ears, for she'd bestirred herself to greet him, when she'd ignored the man who brought her oats every day.

"I find it odd," Fairly said, "that the widow herself contracts the stud services. An awkward choice, if her son is on hand."

Awkward for Giles, too, whom Loris liked, despite their parents' entanglement. She imputed her liking to a sense of tacit sympathy from Giles, which was more than others in his position would have felt for her.

"Giles does most of the training, now that he's down from university," Loris said, as the foal tottered to standing. "Giles is accounted a pleasant young man by all who know him."

The baron produced a lump of sugar from a pocket and passed the treat to Fairly.

"How about by you, Miss Tanner?" Thomas asked. "What does my steward think of Mr. Giles Pettigrew?"

Was this jealousy? Curiosity? An employer's honest question of a steward?

"He's simply a neighbor," Loris replied, "but he does ride well, and he's always been decent to me, when not serving as his mama's whipping boy."

Giles had even asked if Loris would stand up with him at the spring assembly, though she'd declined of course. Claudia Pettigrew would have seen her ruined for that presumption.

"Serving as the widow's whipping boy sounds like an unpleasant fate," Thomas said.

"There are worse fates," Loris replied, "and one of them might result from choosing a horse for me without consulting me first." For while Seamus had been enjoying an afternoon's leisure in a pasture, he'd got to playing with another gelding, and taken a smart rap to his chin.

He stood, hip cocked, dozing in a stall across from Penny and Treasure. His chin was both cut and bruised, he'd be some weeks recovering before he could take the bit again.

Nick was down the aisle, grooming Rupert. Jamie tended to the viscount's mare in her stall. Fairly pretended to visit with Penny and the filly, who'd been named Treasure.

Loris would have had more privacy in the common of the local posting inn. Sutcliffe stepped closer, pulled off his gloves, and lowered his voice.

"You would look the proverbial gift horse in the mouth, madam?"

Or the gift baron, with his lovely manor house and lovelier kisses? Loris had considered that question, when she hadn't been reading poetry and swilling two pots of fine gunpowder tea scented with jasmine flowers.

"Seamus will come right soon enough. I would not accept such a gift horse, my lord. Not one chosen without consulting me." *Not from that woman.*

Thomas reached beneath Loris's chin and tied the trailing ribbons of her straw hat. His fingers brushing her jaw were deft, businesslike, and... muddling.

"Perhaps, Miss Tanner, we might discuss this while the horses are being saddled. Stroll with me?" He offered his arm, which Loris accepted, all the while telling herself she would not make a habit of such silliness.

"Absence does not appear to have made your heart grow fonder, my dear," Thomas observed as they sauntered out into the morning sun. "Did you think I'd scold you for leaving my house?"

Loris had hoped he might, a little. "I cannot remain under your roof, sir. You disturb my dreams enough as it is."

Such a naughty smile he had. "So you express shyness by arguing with me before others and thinking ill of me."

"I could never think ill of you, though I would like, for fifteen minutes, to think of something *other* than you. Have I mentioned the hare population? Your farmers are up in arms over the damage, and I've yet to discuss this with you."

The baron seated her on the shady bench under the oak.

"Bother the hares. I would have liked to have paid you a call last evening, bringing you my especial brand of comfort and consolation in the midst of your suffering."

His expression was concerned, his manner entirely solicitous. His eyes danced with mirth.

Gracious days and starry nights, Thomas was *flirting*.

And Loris hadn't the first inkling how to flirt back.

CHAPTER ELEVEN

"I am merely a bit tired, my lord." Loris was also besotted, which his lordship seemed to grasp well enough without her telling him. "Hares can destroy a substantial portion of the root crops that feed a family through the winter."

Though hares were game, and thus must be preserved for the landowner's exclusive sporting diversion. A clever woman might have mined that legal reality for an analogy of some sort—a clever, flirtatious woman.

Which Loris was not.

"Miss Tanner, surely you know I will earn the contumely of every landowner for three counties if I allow my farmers to shoot hares indiscriminately. Did you have any luncheon? No guest of mine is allowed to go hungry. I have in my pocket a sandwich made with our own excellent cheddar. I saw you fleeing across the garden and saved you some sustenance."

A sandwich in his pocket?

"I have half a sandwich in my pocket, sir, and I was not your guest. Will you please attend to the topic at hand?"

Thomas ranged an arm around the back of the bench. "I

attend every word that comes out of your mouth, my dear. Tell the farmers to set snares for the blasted hares and to fence off the vegetables. I don't care for the taste of game, nor will I invite a pack of wastrels from Town to blast away at pheasant who've grown tame eating corn from my figurative hand."

His farmers would thank him for the next forty years for this generosity. They might even put a stop to whoever was unfastening random gates.

"So we're not to leave corn out for the flying game?"

Thomas's fingers brushed against the top of Loris's arm. "I'd rather you didn't, not unless we're enduring a severe winter, in which case my tenants will probably need the grain for their livestock."

"Are the farmers allowed to bring down the flying game, sir?" This had to be done discreetly, away from the tenancies bordering Sutcliffe itself, for the law did not favor such lenience.

"The only flying game I'm interested in at the moment, Miss Tanner, is fluttering about beside me on this bench. I left you in peace and quiet only because Fairly ordered you to rest, and my intentions toward you are not the least bit restful."

Jamie led out the viscount's gray mare. Thomas's gelding would be led out any minute, and this moment of conversation—flirtation, mutual torment, whatever—would be over.

"Please do not buy a horse for me today, my lord."

"I wouldn't buy a horse for you without your approval," he replied. "I need to set up Penny's breeding, and we're short a few good horses, so I'm making my trip serve two purposes. Then too, I want to take a closer look at the woman who is responsible for costing you your father's company."

This again. Loris adored Thomas's protectiveness, but abhorred his meddling.

"My father's fondness for excessive drink cost me his company," she said, scuffing her heel across the parched grass.

"As much as I'd like to blame the widow entirely, she could not have accused my father of a crime had he not made one witless choice after another. Sooner than later, he was due to come to grief."

"He was." Thomas's fingers made soothing circles on Loris's nape, and all the starch in her, all the common sense and voracious hares of self-doubt went leaping into the hedges. "May I visit you when we return?"

Loris had drowsed the night away before an open window and sipped tea half the morning on a breezy balcony. All the while, she'd considered Thomas's overtures and how she ought to respond to them.

She *ought* not to have responded at all, of course. Propriety, the nagging fear of her father's excesses, all manner of voices had clamored for her to renounce the pleasures Thomas offered.

Except... The Baron Sutcliffe was not Viscount Hedgedale, lying his way beneath her skirts. Thomas wasn't a wastrel down from Town, amusing himself by shooting at tame birds too stupid to know their safety was at risk.

Thomas offered pleasure, but he also tendered companionship, for which Loris had been starved for far too many winters. He was an ally, of which she'd had none. He was a friend, and he was somebody who would someday value Linden as she did.

"You may visit me later," Loris said, rising, "but please don't expect much. We have matters to discuss, Baron, and I will not be put off by your charm."

"I am duly warned."

Loris accompanied him back to the stable, not happy with his plans, but glad to have the afternoon to herself.

Damned if she wasn't already thinking of taking a nap.

"Given him his scolding for the day, Miss Tanner?" Fairly teased. "I don't see any handprints on Sutcliffe's backside or his handsome face, so I assume he behaved."

"I must set an example for your sorry self, Fairly," the baron replied. "Miss Tanner, good day, and thank you for bearing me company."

Nick was dragooned into accompanying the baron and the viscount when they trotted out of the stable yard, though he let them know he was none too happy about it.

"They ride well," Beckman observed, coming up behind her.

"Most men of means do, though Nicholas does too. My sense was, given the option, he'd rather have stayed here mucking stalls with you."

If Nick was quiet, Beckman was nearly silent. He was a hard worker, and the horses liked him, but Loris could not recall a conversation with him prior to the baron's arrival.

"What of you, Miss Tanner? Are you longing for options other than those before you?"

Nothing in his tone was flirtatious or disrespectful. The riders disappeared around the bend at the foot of the drive, and a quiet descended, along with a return of Loris's fatigue.

"I am content with my situation, Beckman. What of you?" *Have you been leaving gates open or tampering with horseshoes lately?*

Dust danced over the lane, settling only slowly. The sky was white with heat, and Loris wanted to fan herself with her straw hat. She had the sense if she moved even that much, Beckman would simply return to the shade of the stable rather than answer her question.

"Giles Pettigrew wagers excessively," he said. "The man cannot walk past a cock-fight without losing significant sums, and you have more options than you think. Nicholas would agree with me."

He stalked away, his walk putting Loris in mind of Nicholas.

Less and less did Nick play a convincing version of a slow, taciturn stableman, content to mend harness, muck stalls, and poultice swollen joints. He wasn't the placid, obedient simpleton he'd so easily portrayed. Beckman also noticed more than which horse had a swollen hock, which bucket needed extra caulk.

Since the baron's arrival, much had changed, particularly in the stable. Loris didn't grasp exactly what had shifted, but she knew better than to turn her back on a situation she could neither control nor understand.

* * *

Mrs. Pettigrew was blond, blue-eyed, attired in the first stare of equestrian fashion, and well into the transition from voluptuous to matronly. She batted her eyes, she pressed her bosom against Thomas's arm, she smiled at everything he said.

She stopped short of caressing his cheek with her riding crop, thank God.

In London, such behavior would have been mere flirtation. Thomas had endured worse, though the ladies at the Pleasure House had had more refined manners, at least below stairs.

The Pettigrew heir, Giles, seemed oblivious to his mother's conduct, but then, what choice did a son—or a younger brother—have?

"Baron Sutcliffe rides beautifully," Mrs. Pettigrew purred, loudly enough for Thomas to hear her, though Fairly, her audience, stood right next to her on the arena rail.

"Sutcliffe is one of those fellows who does everything well. What think you, Baron?" Fairly called out cheerily. "Have you found something you can ride?"

Thomas drew rein and patted the horse he'd been trying out. "This fellow has adequate gaits, but I can consider only the first gelding for purchase."

The widow released Fairly's arm, to which she'd affixed herself like a lonely barnacle.

"Only the one, my lord?" she asked. "I would think a man with your talent would need to keep a full stable of attractive options."

How... tedious.

"I do like variety," Thomas assured her as he climbed off

the horse, "but I've also spent enough time in the saddle that I seek a certain fire in my mounts. Your horses are almost too well trained, if you take my meaning."

In other words, they were ridden with less than adequate *tact*, made into servants who took orders rather than partners in equitation.

"We have some greener stock, my lord," Mrs. Pettigrew said. "Giles won't offer the youngsters to most customers, because a tantrum or spook can unseat the unprepared. Would you care to inspect the younger stock?"

Nothing would unseat Loris. She practically lived in the saddle, from what Thomas had observed.

"By all means," Thomas said. "Fairly, would you like to try a few?"

Fairly beamed a smile at the widow such as cherubs aimed at their celestial pudding.

"I will check on my mare and stretch my legs, if you'll excuse me, Mrs. Pettigrew."

"Make yourself at home, my lord, while I entertain the baron with some of our more spirited rides."

And to think Thomas had passed over an afternoon wrestling rocks in the Linden stream for this outing.

The viscount wandered off as Thomas escorted the widow around the corner of the barn, where he half-expected her to fling him behind the nearest hedge and have her wicked way with him.

Gave a man pause, to take the air on the arm of a female predator. Uncomfortable pause. Thomas had met Claudia Pettigrew's ilk before, though, and if he felt anything for her, it was grudging, tired pity.

"You remind me of another capable female, Mrs. Pettigrew," Thomas said. Nick was in conversation with a stable boy near the mounting block, and was under orders to keep Thomas in sight at all times. "The steward at Linden is a lady. I believe you might know her?"

A hitch in Mrs. Pettigrew's gait suggested Thomas's conversation gambit wasn't the flirtation she'd been hoping for.

Life was just full of disappointments.

"Miss Tanner? Our paths have crossed on occasion," Mrs. Pettigrew said. "She's not the most feminine of personages, poor thing. We never see her at the assemblies, probably because she can't dance, or lacks suitable attire. I'm told she's frightfully competent with lambing, calving, and foaling. I take a keen interest in the management of my late husband's property, though, so I can't judge Miss Tanner for flouting convention, can I?"

And yet, judge Loris, she did.

"Has it been difficult, managing Squire Pettigrew's stud farm? Your neighbors seem like an agreeable lot, and the land is certainly suited to raising horses."

"The business does well enough," the widow said as they approached the training arena. "I miss profoundly the guiding hand of a devoted companion. And yes, our neighbors are quite agreeable. Tell me, how fares your predecessor? Greymoor owned Linden for nearly a decade, and in that time, we became quite congenial."

The hell they had.

"Greymoor and I have had few direct dealings. I bought the property sight unseen, on the strength of Fairly's recommendation. He's quite the canny businessman, though one doesn't bruit that about. If I am discontent here, I will simply sell the place in a few years."

Linden wasn't entailed and wasn't the family seat. Thomas could do what he pleased with the entire estate... in theory.

"We would miss such a pleasant fellow in our midst," Mrs. Pettigrew said. "Surely you wouldn't tire of our company so quickly?"

A small part of Thomas winced for his hostess, for any woman whose dignity didn't inform her the time had come to give up playing the coquette. Loneliness and adult appetites were one thing, and if Mrs. Pettigrew had propositioned him on the strength of honest, friendly lust, he would have been politely flattered.

But Claudia Pettigrew, regardless of her age, appearance, or standing, didn't know Thomas, and didn't care to know him. She didn't want his company, she wanted control of a wealthy, titled, attractive conquest. Thomas recognized the type, because the very same mentality afflicted most of the male clientele who'd frequented Fairly's brothel.

Rather than bludgeon the woman with a pointed rejection, Thomas turned his attention to the young man working with the youngster in the arena before them.

"Your son rides well."

Young Giles sat with easy grace, letting the gelding dance and carry on under him. Gradually, the horse became more interested in what Giles asked, and less interested in expending his energy on fruitless displays.

Amid effusive reassurances that the horse was a good fellow and a brilliant study, Giles stepped down from his mount, whom the grooms were only too happy to lead away.

"Did you see him, Mama?" Giles asked. "D'Artagnan will come 'round now. He simply needed to figure things out for himself. Giles Pettigrew, sir. Mama, introduce me to this fine gentleman."

Mrs. Pettigrew obliged with the civilities, though she shifted to stand upwind of her son.

"Are you looking for anything in particular, Baron?" Giles asked when the hot weather had been discussed adequately. "Perhaps you need some dependable mounts for guests? Lord Greymoor entertained sizeable groups from time to time. I have several possibilities, if you're after guest horses."

Thomas felt resentment rolling off his hostess, for Giles had what Mrs. Pettigrew lacked: a true love of horses and the true horseman's willingness to talk his craft with anybody, particularly those similarly afflicted.

After about two minutes, Mrs. Pettigrew turned a blazing smile on Thomas. "I will leave you two gentlemen to discuss horses, while I find our missing viscount."

Who was, fortunately, adept at not being found unless he wanted to be.

"Madam." Thomas bowed without taking Mrs. Pettigrew's hand.

"Baron." She strolled off, walking like a woman who knew—or hoped—her retreat was being thoroughly perused.

Giles, when mounted, was graceful, poised and athletic. Off the horse, he hadn't yet grown into his frame, and perhaps he never would. He reminded Thomas of a gamboling puppy, paws and ears flapping in every direction.

"You have good stock, and your property is attractive," Thomas observed, though signs of wear were evident as well. The occasional gate sagged on its hinges, not a single pot of salvia graced the stable yard, the barn aisles were unraked. "But so far, I haven't seen a horse I'd consider for Miss Tanner, which was one reason for calling upon you."

Giles put his boot up on the bottom step of the mounting block and swatted the dust from the toes with a limp handkerchief. The exercise was pointless, dust being the order of the day, but Thomas had the sense Giles needed a moment to compose himself.

"Come with me to the barn, Baron, and I'll introduce you to Aquitaine and Saxony."

They were four-year-olds, a colt and a filly, with differing temperaments. Aquitaine, called Ace, was big, bay, and full of himself. Saxony, called Saucy, was a chestnut of equally impressive bone and size, but sweet, flirty, and easygoing.

"Saucy would make a good mount for Miss Tanner," Giles said, "but Claudia does not approve of Miss Tanner, and might not be amenable to selling her Saucy."

Claudia, not Mama. Gone was the beamish boy, and in his

place, an unhappy young man who was not yet in control of his life.

"Does not approve of Miss Tanner?" Thomas pressed, bending to inspect the mare's feet and pasterns. "Because she is my steward?"

Thomas might have glossed over the reality:

Because Miss Tanner has *tried to hold the reins* in her father's absence.

Because Miss Tanner *has done what she could* for Linden, given *the limitations of her gender.*

But the truth was, Loris Tanner was a better steward than her father had ever been, and Thomas... proud of her. Damned proud, and also protective.

Fairly's words came to mind: *I pried, I poked, I casually observed. You know how it's done.* Though little prying was necessary: Claudia Pettigrew could not approve of a prettier, younger woman, much less one who'd found an honorable, if unorthodox, path to self-sufficiency.

"Perhaps," Giles said, "the problem is that Miss Tanner tries to be a good steward."

And she succeeded. "You know this how?" Thomas straightened and walked around to stand right against the mare's tail, so he could sight down her spine.

"Because I *know* Loris Tanner," Giles said, quite on his dignity. "You mustn't judge Miss Tanner, Baron, for she's only a woman. When sober, her father was very skilled at his trade, and she learned a great deal from him. She's doing the best she can, though I'm sure you'll find another better suited to the position in due course."

No, Thomas would not. He might find another competent steward, but Loris loved the estate she called home. Thomas still did not understand entirely why.

"You believe Tanner's daughter is as skilled as he was?" Thomas walked to the horse's head and pried open the mare's teeth, only to have her pull her lips back, swish her tail, and stick her nose in the air.

"That's hardly a fair question, Baron," Giles said, mopping his brow with the dusty handkerchief and leaving a streak of dirt over one blond brow. "Miss Tanner hasn't her father's years of experience. I don't know what you've heard, but Miss Tanner doesn't deserve the talk that's spread about her. She works very hard, far harder than a lady ought. I'm confident she'll make the right man a fine wife, and eventually, this queer start at Linden will be behind her. Talk always dies down, over time, particularly if a woman makes a superior match."

Talk died down if overly helpful neighbors stopped discussing a woman behind her back.

"Let's put these two under saddle," Thomas said, rather than respond to Giles's outburst. The colt ignored the filly, which was odd, but perhaps they enjoyed the equine version of sibling indifference.

While the grooms dealt with Ace and Saucy, Thomas took a draught of lemonade from his flask.

Time for more prying, poking, and casually observing. "I'm told Mrs. Pettigrew has definite ideas about her breeding stallion's care."

Giles's gaze strayed to the far side of the arena, where Nick was visiting with a lone black horse housed in a small shed. No trees shaded the building, and the heat inside would be brutal.

"Papa is rolling in his grave," Giles spat, "to think his precious Johnny is never let out, never allowed to romp, never given a pasture-mate for company."

The stallion made a half-hearted attempt to nip at Nick, who dodged easily. "Johnny?"

"Jonathan Swift," Giles said, rolling back the cuff of his sleeve and pulling on riding gloves. "Haddonfield mentioned you might bring us your draft mare to breed. I sneak Johnny what attention I can and insist on riding him from time to time, but the lads will peach on me to Claudia if I change his routine at all. She's not stupid."

The last was said with more than a little petulance, yet another warning regarding Mrs. Claudia Pettigrew.

* * *

Thomas Jennings, who'd strolled frequently—and without any visible interest—among a house full of the loveliest sexually available women in London, apparently missed his steward.

David, Viscount Fairly, noticed what others did not in part because he missed his viscountess with a low, grinding ache.

Thomas glanced frequently in the direction of Linden, discreetly consulted his pocket watch on three occasions, and declined all offers of refreshment and hospitality. The situation gave a viscount cause to hope, when for nearly a decade, Thomas Jennings had been a monument to male independence.

He was not indifferent to the fairer sex—Thomas was as protective as a mama bear with one cub when a woman's welfare was imperiled—but he'd always been in command of himself, whether in a barroom, a brothel, or a ballroom.

Until now.

After a hot, humid eternity of flirtation from the widow and enthusiasm from Giles Pettigrew, Thomas climbed onto Rupert's back, and Fairly could almost hear Nick Haddonfield's echoing sigh of relief.

"You abandoned me," Thomas complained as their horses ambled along in the direction of Linden. "That woman all but crawled into my pockets, and where are my trusted friend and my stable master? Out chatting up the lads and flirting with the mares."

"Two of the lads," Fairly said, "used to work for you. They were all too happy to find any sort of employment, much less at a place where their immediate superior does not chide them with a bullwhip. They say Chesterton is still in the area, and talking all manner of nonsense against you and Miss Tanner."

Dark brows lowered gratifyingly. Had Fairly been a betting

man, he'd have predicted that Thomas's bachelorhood would be among the goods harvested before winter.

As would Miss Tanner's spinsterhood.

"Giles mentioned the talk," Thomas said. "Nicholas, anything to report?"

More gratification, to see that the fellow who'd spent years delivering reports knew how to ask for them as well.

"That stud is growing mean," Nick said. "I've half a mind to steal him and put him in hands that will treat him properly. He's a decent fellow at heart, and deserves better. Some of the staff imply Mrs. Pettigrew poisoned her spouse, you know. Arsenic's easy enough to get hold of."

"My, the things a man learns about his neighbors after he's purchased a property," Thomas mused. "Horse thievery is a hanging offense, Nicholas."

Nick dropped his reins on the mare's neck and stretched up in the saddle, while Fairly was plagued again with a nagging sense of having seen Nick before.

"A hanging offense, indeed—if I'm caught." Nick settled back and took up his reins. "You will excuse me please, gentlemen. I left Jamie and Beckman to handle all of the afternoon chores, and I'm sure I'm needed in the stable."

He touched his hat brim and cantered off, his mare kicking up a trail of dust.

"Don't say it," Thomas muttered as the hoof beats faded. "A plain stable master does not joke about hanging felonies, much less contemplate them seriously. Nick showed up shortly after Micah Tanner disappeared, and the coincidence bothers me."

"Loris Tanner bothers you more," Fairly observed.

Casually. Letty would have expected some finesse from her husband, after all. She treasured Thomas and had great hopes for him.

"Loris Tanner bothers me without ceasing. She's haunted by her father's disappearance, and I can't abide that."

"Your own family isn't haunted by yours?" Fairly asked with the cavalier unconcern of a true friend whose affairs were in order and whose reflexes were lightning fast.

Fortunately for Fairly, the afternoon was apparently too hot for brawling in the dirt.

"Miss Tanner doesn't even know her mother's name, Fairly. Did her father wander off, willingly leaving her in that state of ignorance?"

Fairly tipped up a flask, and gave himself a moment to choose his words.

"Tanner left his daughter in ignorance regarding her mother for the first two decades of Miss Tanner's life, didn't he? Some people live as if they have all the time in the world to resolve familial problems, when in fact, in a single day, two cousins can meet their maker, and everything changes. A title befalls one, wealth, responsibility…"

This was meddling, but Fairly was haunted, too, by the memory of his ever-competent Thomas clinging to composure by a thread, staring at his brandy, and looking like the world's largest, most bereaved orphan.

Thomas had likely forgotten those few bad moments, but Fairly never would.

"None of us lives forever, Thomas."

"I will allow you to remain on your horse, Fairly, because you miss your wife and that turns you into an idiot. Moreover, Letty would take it amiss did I pummel you to flinders, though you deserve pummeling, and I'm just the fellow to tend to it. I will resolve matters at Sutcliffe in my own time, on my own terms. For now, pass me your flask. I'm parched, my own flask is empty, and I'm plagued by mysteries on all sides."

Fairly obediently passed over his flask, which had exactly half a swallow of tepid water left.

"What mysteries?"

"Where is Micah Tanner?" Thomas asked softly as the late afternoon shadows lengthened. "Is he guilty of rape? If not, why allow Loris to remain at Linden, working too hard, enduring mean talk and a meaner stable master? Who is Nick Haddonfield, and why do you think you know him? Why does Chesterton linger in the area when nobody will offer him work? Who is unlatching gates all over my property? Who sprung Rupert's shoe?"

The sun was sinking, but the land was so thoroughly baked that heat lingered in the air, thick and stupefying. Fairly thought longingly of a cool bath, and of his wife, while Thomas tried to solve mysteries years in the making.

"You forgot the greatest mystery of all," Fairly said, stuffing his flask back in the pocket. "What will you do if Loris Tanner refuses your proposal of marriage?"

Thomas used his riding crop to tap Fairly's mare gently on the quarters, and she took off at a trot toward her temporary home.

A lesser man might have used that same crop on his nosy, meddlesome former employer, but Thomas was a gentleman.

And he and Fairly were friends, after all.

CHAPTER TWELVE

"That went well," Giles said, opening a window to let some air into the library.

"You stink, and you've brought your dirt into my house," Claudia retorted, though she didn't look up from whatever she was reading. She sat at Papa's desk if she sat anywhere in this room. A tray bearing a bottle of wine and a half-empty glass at her elbow.

Giles helped himself to a sip of her wine, though he preferred ale. "Everybody stinks in this heat. I've given the lads orders that Johnny is to be let out into the small paddock for two hours in the evening until the heat breaks."

The stallion was tough. He'd endure the heat without that indulgence, but Claudia needed to face the fact that her reign was coming to an end. Then too, an unfit stallion was more likely to suffer injury when a mare took exception to his advances.

Claudia rose, skirts swishing. "You are not yet five-and-twenty, Giles, and this is my home."

In not quite two years' time, her home would be the dower

cottage, unless Giles could find some intrepid soul to marry her. That would require dispensing with the allegations she'd made against Micah Tanner, though, which was proving to be a complicated and time consuming process.

"Your point, Claudia?"

"You have no authority on this property for another two years, and even then, my boy, you will find cooperation with me in your best interests."

Not quite. The instant Giles married, Claudia's authority vanished. Perhaps she'd forgotten this aspect of Papa's final arrangements, or perhaps she'd hoped to keep it from her son.

Giles took another taste of too-sweet wine. "I work myself to death here. I am cordial to all who seek to do business with you. I manage the stable help when your temper would have them in open revolt. In what manner do I fail to cooperate with you?"

"I'm thinking of hiring Chesterton," Claudia said, closing the window Giles had just opened. "Unlike you, he doesn't tolerate laziness or insolence, not from a horse, not from the lads."

"It's stifling in here. Open the damned window."

Claudia turned her back to the window and crossed her arms. The late afternoon sun slanting through the panes was merciless, revealing a softening under her chin, face powder, and lines of bitterness bracketing a thin mouth.

"The dust comes in through the window," she said. "If you want open windows, perhaps you should dwell elsewhere."

Giles's father had explained to him that Claudia simply lacked maternal feeling. Her sole asset as a young woman had been beauty, along with a modest dowry. Her parents had accepted an offer of marriage for her from an older rural squire because that squire had owned nearly seventeen thousand acres of rentable land.

Rents had dropped, the land had tired, much of it had been sold, and the squire had retreated to the pleasures of his hounds and horses before retreating from the worldly sphere entirely.

How Giles missed his father, and how he raged at the old fellow now.

"This is, in point of fact, my house," Giles said. "It will never be your house, and you are the party who had best learn some cooperation before I turn five-and-twenty, Mama."

Her smile was smug, but in her eyes, Giles saw a rare and terrifying flash of uncertainty.

In one of her tempers, she'd taken a knife to the portrait done of her and Papa shortly after their wedding. Giles had personally hung his favorite portrait of the late squire in his London rooms, and made sure Claudia never had a key to the premises.

"What have you done, Claudia?" Giles set down his wine and opened another window, then another. She followed after him, closing them, one by one. "You've done something stupid, and you'd best tell me."

"I'm your mother, and you will not insult me."

Insult her? Giles wanted to slap her. She insulted him at every turn and was ruining his birthright. He settled for opening the French doors and inserting his person into the doorway.

"You're my mother, and I will commend you to the care of the excellent physicians who deal with hysterical women if you don't confess your latest folly. Have you spent too much at the milliners again? Are you perhaps with child? You'd best tell me. I'm the only family you have, and the only one who can clean up your messes."

She stopped by the desk, her fingers curling around the neck of the wine bottle. Giles and his mother had never had a physical altercation, but he was reaching the end of his tether with her.

"You're a boy," she sneered. "No physician would listen to your lies."

Giles remained where he was. If Claudia came at him with the wine bottle, he'd have all the evidence he needed to get her out of his house once and for all.

"I'm my father's heir. I attained my majority more than two years ago, you are driving what's left of this estate into the ground, and my patience has run out."

"The estate is mortgaged," Claudia said. "Your land is in hock, Giles, and the proceeds of the transaction are where I alone have access to them."

If she'd razed the house, poisoned the livestock, and salted the wells, she could not have dealt Giles a nastier surprise.

"You did this nearly two years ago," Giles said. "You must have forged my signature once I came of age, colluded with the old men Papa trusted to keep an eye on you."

Her smile was nearly shy and a touch proud.

Not colluded, then, bartered her favors before they were mutton dressed up as lamb.

This was the result of allowing women to overstep the bounds of what God intended them to deal with. Small children, a household staff, a kitchen garden, maids, laundry, the occasional sickroom. A woman who exceeded the ambit of her domestic abilities inevitably came to grief.

"How much?" Giles asked.

Claudia named a goodly sum, enough to put the estate back into excellent condition, enough to pay off the debts Giles juggled through the ledgers between sales of horses, rents, and acquisitions.

"May I at least assume you mortgaged tenancies?" Giles pressed. "Or did you give the damned bankers title to the very roof over our heads?"

Claudia poured herself another glass of wine, her hands trembling minutely. "Mr. Easton said the house was the most valuable part of the property, so I could keep more acres unencumbered if I put the mortgage on the manor house and its grounds."

Oh, splendid. Claudia was too arrogant to realize that if she was intent on defrauding her own son, a banker would have no qualms about turning a profit on her scheme.

"What you have done," Giles said, "is put into the hands of a lot of plundering cits the part of the estate that earns most of its revenue. You could not have made a stupider choice, Mama, but we can fix this. The bankers lied to you, which is what you deserve for breaking your word to Papa. You would have been far better off mortgaging tenancies, but all you have to do is give me the money, and we'll clear the mortgage."

She downed half the wine at one go. "No."

Well, of course. Claudia's party piece was the grand tantrum. Papa used to snatch Giles up and take him out for a hack when Claudia went on a tear. On two occasions, Papa had taken Giles into London for a week's stay, claiming the servants would need that long to set the house to rights.

London was expensive, and Claudia had been allowed to get away with too much for too long.

"How would you like to swing for committing fraud?" Giles mused. "I never signed mortgage documents, and you do not have the authority to affix my signature to anything."

His questions flummoxed her, or half a bottle of wine had, but she rallied. "Even if you brought charges against me, you'd be years sorting out the bank, and you haven't the means for that. I know where the money is, and I'm not telling you."

The day had reached that sweet hour, when the sun had sunk so low that the heat was easing. The gardens behind the house were in their full summer glory because an army of gardeners kept every bed watered and trimmed. In the long, soft shadows, the late roses in particular were magnificent.

Giles wanted to rip out every one with his bare hands.

"Where is the money, Mama?"

She would not have turned the cash over to the very bankers whom she'd embroiled in her scheme, nor would she have entrusted the money to the solicitors complicit with her intriguing. Cash, or bank drafts, were sitting somewhere Claudia could get her hands on them, and that was… the worst folly of all.

"You'll never find that money," she said, finishing her wine. "If you look until you're an old man, you won't find that money, so no more talk about criminal charges, physicians, or kicking me out of my own home, Giles. You're the horse master here, nothing more, and if I hire Chesterton, I might not even need you for that."

She would not be hiring Chesterton—they simply hadn't the money. "Have you made any payments on the mortgage, or are we two years in arrears already and about to lose our home, hmm?"

"What payments? The banker takes a note, I get the money. That's how it works. When I want the note back, I give him back the money plus a little extra. It's not complicated."

God help them, Mama had trusted Mr. Easton's explanation, never dreaming she might have found somebody more unscrupulous than she was. What were a few gambling debts compared to folly of that magnitude?

Though of course, by mortgaging the property, Mama had anticipated Giles's own scheme for paying off the worst of those debts.

Giles did something Papa had told him never to do. He turned to face the setting sun and stared directly into its rays. The brilliance felt good, as if heat and light could destroy the memory of this entire conversation.

When he closed his eyes, yellow and purple laced the dark field of his vision, and as if his father had whispered in his ear, Giles had the solution: Marriage was the way out of this conundrum. He'd had plans in train to bring that eventuality about, to bring him a biddable, grateful wife with no airs above her station, no expectations beyond what her husband allowed her.

Those plans, among others, would simply have to be

accelerated.

He turned from the sunset, left the French doors wide open, and walked past his mother.

"I'll see you at dinner, Mama, and I'll tell you what Sutcliffe had to say about the horses. He's rich, he has beautiful a stable, and he's our neighbor. Maybe you'll let me sell him the best of the young stock, because God knows, the banker with whom you whored your body and soul will soon foreclose if we don't generate some revenue."

Giles took small comfort from the fear the word *foreclose* put into Claudia's gaze, but only small comfort. He wasn't even bullying her. Because of Claudia's damned stupidity, they could lose everything by the end of the year.

Unless he married, sooner rather than later.

* * *

Loris was coming in from checking on the yeld ewes when Nicholas cantered up the drive on Buttercup, an enormous golden mare that belonged to Nick personally. She was part plow stock, but a handsome specimen nonetheless.

Not a poor man's horse, though Nick treasured her the way a poor man treasured his only mount.

Jamie came out to tend to the mare, while Loris took up the bench under the oak. Fatigue dragged at her, a function of the heat and of a long afternoon.

Nick walked over, bringing with him the scents of horse and dust. "Stop fretting. The baron is not far behind me, but I wanted to leave him and Fairly some privacy. Also to put as much distance between me and Mrs. Pettigrew as possible."

Loris *was* fretting, and she hadn't quite admitted that to herself. "We'll need to move the yeld ewes soon. The grass is nearly gone, and we can run them behind the yearling dairy heifers if we move the heifers closer to the creek."

Nick sat back, the bench groaning beneath his weight. "Sutcliffe is not your father, Loris Tanner. He'll not promise to be home for dinner, but go left into the village instead of right toward home, then turn up missing for three days."

No, but Thomas might kiss Loris sweetly on the cheek, and then disappear up to London, possibly never to be seen again. Though did a man intent on disappearing offer marriage as a conclusion to a dalliance?

"Sutcliffe is not answerable to me," Loris said, just as Papa had been answerable to no one.

"Ask Sutcliffe to whom he answers," Nick said, crossing dusty boots at the ankle. "I suspect his view of the situation is different from yours. I can move the heifers tomorrow, if you like."

Fairly's gray mare turned up the drive at a canter, her coat lathered and dusty.

Where was Thomas? Was he hurt? Was that why Fairly cantered his horse in this heat? Had Thomas accepted an invitation to dinner with the Pettigrews?

Loris was halfway off the bench when Nick's voice stopped her.

"Loris, your baron is fine. He's on his way home, and he's entirely smitten with you. The widow attempted to work her wiles on him, and he nearly yawned in her face. Cease worrying over Sutcliffe, because I have news that might pose a real cause for concern."

"The heifers can stay where they are for another week or so," Loris said, resuming her seat, "especially if we get some rain. If you have news, Nicholas, then please share it. I have two more gates to check before my rounds are concluded, and I want to see how the swine are managing before the sun sets too."

Where was Thomas?

"Your father has much to answer for," Nick muttered, "but you should know that Jamie has heard rumors of a man answering to Micah Tanner's description in Brighton."

Between one moment and the next, little changed around Loris. Jamie led Nick's mare into the stable, the sun sank infinitesimally closer to the horizon, and Loris's heart sank with it.

"Do you know Papa has come back?"

"I am repeating rumor only. Would you be relieved to know he's alive?"

"Yes." Furious too, because Papa could have written to her, could have sent word to her indirectly, could have eased her fears for him in any one of a hundred ways, but instead, he skulked in the undergrowth, risking discovery and ensuring drama.

Damn him and his drinking.

Rupert plodded around the turn at the foot of the drive. In the heat, walking the horse the last stretch before the stable was simply prudent horsemanship. Fairly's mare would require walking out, while Rupert could be put up in short order.

Relief edged past Loris's upset, because, as Nick said, Thomas was not her father. Thomas was rational, reliable, prudent... Thomas kept the promises Micah Tanner routinely broke.

"If your father asked you to leave with him, Loris, would you go?" Nick asked.

Thomas waved to her, the gesture weary. Loris waved back when she wanted to run to him and wrap her arms around him.

That impulse spoke volumes.

"If my father asked me to leave with him," Loris said, "I'd resent the request very much. Two years ago, he left me here without significant coin, without warning, without explanation, and crops ripening in the fields. He could have taken me with him, he could have sent for me. I am very angry with my father, Nicholas."

Loris had been angry for years in fact, but was only now realizing it. Not only disappointed, not only worried, not only resigned—but enraged, too.

"Good, because you should be angry with him," Nick

said, rising. "But still, you haven't said you'll refuse your papa's summons should he invite you to leave Linden behind."

"Take the baron's horse, Nicholas," Loris said. "And I'd appreciate it if you'd keep any more such rumors to yourself."

Nick executed a perfect, wrist-twirling court bow. "You may trust my discretion."

He sauntered off to the stable yard, leaving Loris alone on the bench, relieved that Thomas was home, troubled by Nick's rumors, and unwilling to trust him or his discretion.

* * *

The evening was once again filled with false harbingers of a break in the weather. The breeze gusted promisingly, lightning flashed from cloud to cloud, thunder rumbled, though not a drop fell.

The same sense of unspent energy had characterized Thomas's conversation with Loris when he'd returned from Pettigrew's. Loris had babbled on about yeld ewes, and hogs needing mud, and heifers in calf grazing nearly as close to the root as sheep did, and all the while, she'd gazed at the sky, at the pastures, at the rocks exposed by the low water in the creek.

When Thomas had ridden up the drive, Nick Haddonfield had been bedeviling her in the shade of the oak.

Had Haddonfield said something to distract her?

Was it the weather? Something else?

Someone else?

After Thomas endured an excellent, interminable meal with Fairly, he commended his guest to the comforts of the library, dunked himself in his second bath of the day, and headed through the trees to Loris's cottage.

He found her on her back porch, half a cup of cool peppermint tea at her elbow, the last of the day's light her only illumination.

"Is madam receiving callers?" Thomas asked, lowering himself beside her on the steps. The wood was hard but still held a hint of the day's warmth. Around them, the gusting wind heaved and tossed the entire canopy of the woods, like a celestial housemaid trying to shake the wrinkles from a quilt.

"I'm receiving you," Loris said, leaning into him. "I hate this weather. It teases, it promises, it threatens, but it will not rain."

Thomas laid an arm across her shoulders. "In London, the rain is a mere nuisance, or a passing inconvenience. Here, people watch the weather as a mother watches a colicky newborn."

Loris had bathed too, for the breeze caught her lilac scent and lobbed it at Thomas's imagination. Would Loris smell of lilacs everywhere? Earlier, she'd smelled of dust and grass and sheep.

Good smells, more evidence Thomas was not in London.

"Do you miss your Town life?" Loris asked.

Her feet were bare. How comfortable that must be. Thomas considered her question, but retrieved his arm to pull off his boots.

"I do not miss London, but London was familiar. I miss knowing every crook and corner of my life, knowing every publican and merchant with whom I must deal. Here, I am unknown, but I'm also ignorant. I don't like that."

Loris shifted off the steps and set Thomas's boots aside, then knelt in front of him to peel down his stockings. The moment was domestic, but also… intimate.

"The weather is fickle," she said, "but predictably fickle. We can dam, we can irrigate, we can dig deep wells, fill our ponds and cisterns. The farmer is not entirely at the mercy of the rain. What is this?"

She traced a scar across the top of Thomas's foot, the touch peculiar and delicate.

"My cousins were supposedly teaching me to fence. They were older than I, and amusing themselves at my expense."

"They *stabbed* you?"

"They referred to it as pinking and claimed it was simply part of the sport. My sister nearly pinked them through their wastrel hearts, she was so upset with them." Then Theresa had explained about sparring with tipped foils, and tetanus, and how whiskey and sugar could cleanse a wound.

And she'd cried as she'd tended gullible little brother.

"Some people find sport in the most bothersome ways," Loris said, leaning forward to press her brow to Thomas's knee. "Will you make love with me tonight?"

Lightning and then thunder punctuated the question, and gave Thomas the count of six to form an answer.

He ran a hand over her braid. "You're sure, Loris?"

Her answer was to kneel up between Thomas's knees and kiss him. Weariness, estate matters, the conundrum that was Nick Haddonfield, and the worry that came from open gates and sprung horseshoes all flew from Thomas's mind as Loris wrapped her arms around him.

"I'm out of patience," she said against his mouth. "I'm not—what is the point of waiting?"

Thomas kissed her back, widening the distance between his knees so she could wedge herself closer, though something had driven her to make this request, something Thomas mistrusted.

"What of talk, Loris? What of seeking a broader acquaintance with each other? What of needing time to assess our suitability?"

Thomas tossed out questions without expecting answers. He simply needed time to catch his breath, to brace himself against the desire Loris was fanning from a spark to a steady, hungry flame.

"I know you," she said, unknotting his cravat. "I know you will come home when you say you will. I know the widow leaves you cold. I know you care about Linden."

No, actually, Thomas did not *care* about Linden. The property was an estate, a purchase, a patch of profitable ground that came with headaches and pretty views. He did, however, care about Loris Tanner, and *she* cared about Linden.

"Dear lady, slow down. We have all night, and many nights. We've no need to rush."

She apparently had a need to rush, rolling up Thomas's cravat and stashing it in the top of one of his boots. Her mouth was back on his in the next instant, and then the risers of the steps were a hard pressure against Thomas's back.

While Loris went after his shirt buttons, cuffs, and falls, Thomas held a silent debate with himself. Something or someone had wrested Loris's natural restraint from her grasp, something as desperate as passion, but not as attractive.

"Are you afraid you'll lose your nerve?" Thomas asked, when Loris had his clothing in complete disarray. "You can change your—"

"I don't want to lose *you*," Loris said, and then she was gone, leaving Thomas like so much plundered laundry on the wooden steps. In the next flash of lightning, she was illuminated against the night sky, standing in the grass three feet away, her fingers plucking at her bodice laces.

"Allow me," Thomas said, rising and stilling her hands. He had her bodice undone in a moment and drew the dress over her head. She wore neither corset nor jumps, but stood barefoot in only a summer-length shift.

Honeysuckle and the tang of lightning scented the night air, and when Thomas tossed his breeches, waistcoat, and shirt aside, the breeze was cool against his skin.

"We should go in," Thomas said, because the thunder was coming closer, and inside, with no storm to harry them, he'd have a chance of untangling what drove Loris to take this final step in the lovers' journey.

Loris's answer was to draw her shift over her head, a flash of pale cotton revealing a paler swatch of woman in the dark garden. Then she was wrapped around him, shockingly warm, her mouth hot on his.

Her kiss tasted of determination, of too many long, hot days and cold winter nights spent in solitude, of passion too long focused on wringing sustenance from the land.

That Loris sought intimate union was beyond doubt. Some overly cautious part of Thomas wondered why now, but the rest of him was swept into desire and pleasure.

The wind picked up just as Thomas laid Loris in the cool grass and came down over her.

"Is this what you want, Loris? Here? Like this? A pagan rite for two, all of heaven looking on?"

"I want you," Loris said, wrapping one leg around his flank.

Thomas braced himself on one forearm and glided a palm down her midline. She was slim and sturdy, both, and she moved beneath his hand like water beneath moonlight.

"You're trying to rush me," Thomas said, combing his fingers through her damp curls. "This is not the time to rush, Loris."

"I'm trying to love you," she said, arching into his hand. "Do that again."

A cold drop hit Thomas's shoulder as he glossed two fingers over the seat of Loris's pleasure.

"Lightning," she whispered. "Inside me. More, Thomas."

He brewed a tempest for her, until she was writhing beneath him in the grass, her fingers manacled around his wrists. When she would have kissed him, Thomas used his mouth on her breasts instead.

Another cold drop landed on the back of his neck. "Do we go inside?" Thomas asked, bracing himself on straight arms.

"Love me," Loris growled. "All I want—*please*, Thomas."

Some men enjoyed making women beg. Thomas was not one of them. He took himself in hand and stroked his cock against Loris's sex, slowly, until she quieted. As he began a slow, careful joining, Loris's sigh fanned across his chest and tension seemed to drain from her.

As if that, the first increment of a lover's union, was all

she sought.

On a hard gust, the rain started, needles of damp so fine as to be more mist than rain, but Thomas's course was set.

Love her, he would. Slowly, inexorably, until they were moving as one, and the scent of wet flowers and thirsty earth filled the garden.

Loris welcomed him with the same ardor the garden welcomed the rain, the same driving, mindless passion. A limb cracked in the woods nearby, but Thomas could not have stopped if the very cottage itself had been struck by lightning.

While the sky raged above, Thomas made slow, sweet love to the woman who loved the land. The air cooled, the rain coalesced into a steady, wind-driven downpour, but for Thomas, all was heat and pleasure.

Thunder shook the earth, as if the storm inside them was immediately above them too, and Loris began to thrash. She bowed up, pressing her teeth to Thomas's shoulder as pleasure overcame her, and lightning turned the world momentarily brilliant.

Boundaries blurred for a progression of instants, as if Thomas made love with the storm itself, as if Loris were some pagan goddess, one with the power to command the elements and transcend time.

The last of Thomas's self-discipline slipped from his grasp, and sheer animal ecstasy shuddered through him. He could no more have denied himself satisfaction than the earth could have refused the rain.

For long moments, he simply held Loris, used his body to shelter her from an increasingly intrusive cold. She was a pool of warmth beneath him and around him and made no move to leave his embrace despite the chill, despite the certain knowledge that their clothes, strewn about on the grass, were getting soaked.

Loris patted his backside.

"Don't move," Thomas said, shifting up the few inches

necessary to unjoin them. He scooped her up against his chest and carried her into the cottage, not stopping until he could lay her on the bed and fold the quilt around her.

"I'm fetching our clothes and lighting a fire," he said. "Stay right where you are."

"You'll come back?"

Thomas sat on the edge of the bed, felled by an insight. *I know you will come home when you say you will.* For most of Loris's life, the man responsible for her welfare had not come home when he'd promised he would.

"I'll come back," Thomas said. "You dry off and get warm."

She kissed his knuckles, and Thomas made himself leave the bed and return to the cold, wet garden. He gathered up their damp clothes and brought them inside, lit a fire in the hearth from the single candle burning in the window, and spread the clothing around on chairs near the fire to dry.

He'd come to see Loris this evening intent on talking, on sorting out her restless, unhappy mood, on consoling himself for an afternoon wasted with neighbors given to tedious drama.

He'd spend the night, mostly in hopes of accomplishing in the morning what he'd failed to achieve in the evening. He made sure the fire was blazing cozily, set his boots on the mantel rather than before the heat of the flames, used a kitchen towel to scrub himself dry, and rejoined Loris in the bedroom.

She was beneath the covers, apparently asleep. When Thomas climbed in beside her, he was grateful for her heat and FOR the way she wrapped herself around him in sleepy welcome.

Loris's embrace was lovely, and yet, Thomas knew that when he awoke in the morning, his first conscious thought would be: *What the hell had happened?*

CHAPTER THIRTEEN

Thomas awoke in his own bed, though he'd dreamed of Sutcliffe Keep and of his grandfather. Not nightmares, precisely, but unhappy recollections and family history, like the list of begats that opened a book of the Old Testament.

Rather than try to sleep despite bright morning sun, Thomas rose and took himself down to the library. As luck would have it, his gaze landed on the unopened letter Fairly had brought down from London. Typically, Thomas would have tossed it into the fire within moments of reading the direction, but the weather had been so hot, no fires had been lit.

The summer Thomas had left Sutcliffe Keep had been blazingly hot. The summer he'd been banished. Theresa had told him to go, told him to leave her in peace, to stop nattering at her like a worried granny.

Told him that if she wanted to drink, whore, and game herself to death, that was none of his concern.

So Thomas had made her none of his concern, ever again, but now she was writing to him, writing every two months or so, if she could find him. Writing to say what?

He ran a fingertip over the tidy address.

Loris had endured two years without a word from her father, and Thomas knew the burden that had put on her. She worried for Micah Tanner, she bore invisible wounds that could not heal because Micah Tanner had left without a word to her. He suspected those wounds had been what had driven her into Thomas's arms last night.

Loris wanted a man who'd keep his word, the most basic requirement of gentlemanly honor. A man who didn't turn his back on his obligations, despite all temptation and human failings to the contrary.

Thomas might well have created a new life with Loris in the midst of a coupling he found unnerving in hindsight. A child, innocent and deserving of every advantage in life.

Including legitimacy.

Thomas took Theresa's letter out into the cool early morning light and slit the seal.

* * *

Despite the violence of the storm, despite the inches of rain that had fallen the previous night, the weather had not broken.

Loris had wanted a day to ponder, to plot and plan, and even marvel a little, for Thomas Jennings's lovemaking was worth marveling over. Had he been with her when she'd awoken, she'd have made love with him again, this time in a bed, for pity's sake, with sunshine illuminating his every feature and expression.

Instead, she was riding into Trieshock, between Nick and Thomas, trying to pretend that she hadn't sunk her teeth into Thomas's shoulders and her fingernails into his muscular fundament.

Trying to pretend she didn't dread the next time somebody saw a man who resembled Micah Tanner.

Nick had discommoded her with those confidences, had

discommoded her right into Thomas's arms, and Loris's only regret was that she hadn't found her way there sooner, and hadn't awoken in the same happy location.

And as for Papa... Loris wished him well. She simply wished him well, and left it at that.

"You're both quiet," Nick said. "The rain made the heat worse, and I didn't think it could get worse."

"Some limbs came down in the home wood," Thomas replied. And then, one heartbeat too late, "I could see them from my balcony. Oak, which we can use."

He'd doubtless seen the storm damage when he'd left Loris's bed at daybreak.

The men argued in desultory fashion about lumber that had been set aside to rebuild the dairy barn, and about whether to offer to buy Mrs. Pettigrew's poor stud.

Loris let their talk wash around her, though even the sound of Thomas's voice tickled her awareness.

So *that* was lovemaking. That indescribable intimacy, that shared pleasure, that tenderness without limit. For a span of time, making love with Thomas, then curled in his arms in the bed, no worries had touched Loris, no anxieties, no fears.

No awful questions about what to do if Papa returned, or sent for Loris to join him in Brighton—one of Britain's busiest ports.

Nicholas had knocked on her door and conveyed Thomas's invitation to make this provisioning trip with him, and Loris had abandoned her plans to stay home and marvel in solitude.

Rumors were not worth panicking over. Papa's looks were common—some height, graying hair, blue eyes. Many men answered to such a description.

Evan shuffled to a halt, for Thomas and Nick had argued right to the door of the Trieshock livery.

"I'll not be long at the apothecary," she told them, swinging out of the saddle.

"We'll not be long," Thomas said, handing Rupert's reins

to a groom. "Haddonfield, we'll meet you here in an hour. I'd like to be back at Linden before the worst of the day's heat."

Nick strode off to the dry goods mercantile, where he'd place a substantial order, while Loris wanted to replenish a list of medicinal stores that a winter outbreak of influenza had depleted.

Thomas took her arm uninvited and directed her toward the village square. "Well, Miss Tanner?"

Well, Loris loved the scent of him, the feel of him, the mischief that lurked in his polite address.

"Sir?"

"I hadn't the heart to waken you, you were sleeping so soundly. You've been working too hard, and I'll not have your health on my conscience."

They were to acknowledge last night's intimacy, then. "I did wonder what one says. Afterward. None of your lectures on manners or deportment covered this topic. You seem well rested yourself."

Thomas tipped his hat to a pair of beldames clad head to toe in black. What a cruel custom, in this heat, and on this lovely, lovely day. Loris wanted badly to kiss her escort right there in the street.

"Where is this apothecary?" Thomas asked. "I'm having impure thoughts and might need to dunk myself in a horse trough if I must continue striding about in proximity to your person."

Thomas was wearing his usual exquisitely tailored riding breeches, poor man.

"Don't you dare look," he muttered, just as Loris might have assayed a surreptitious peek at his falls.

"I'm having impure thoughts, too sir. Of you, in the rain, in my bed."

Another pair of ladies went by, a mother and daughter from the looks of them. Thomas again tipped his hat, while Loris felt an urge to… laugh.

"I will have my revenge," Thomas said when the ladies were past. "When you least expect it, I'll remind you what it feels like to have my mouth on your breasts, my fingers slick with your desire."

"*Thomas.*"

His expression was utterly composed, but for the devilment in his eyes. "My dear?"

"The apothecary. This is it. I might need some time here."

He lowered his lashes, and Loris felt the sweep of them against her naked breasts, a tactile caress of memory.

"You may have all the time you need, Miss Tanner. A woman ought never to be rushed when she's about her pleasures, and surely shopping qualifies. I'll be lounging beneath that tree, in the cool of the morning shade until you're ready for me."

"You are naughty," Loris said, and that was a marvel too—a lovely marvel.

She was glad to have business to transact in the apothecary, also glad Thomas had taken himself and his bold innuendo across the street. Loris purchased a quantity of pennyroyal tea, though she didn't particularly care for it, then went down the medicinal list: willow bark tea, feverfew, valerian, comfrey, mallow… She could have harvested many of these from Linden, but simply hadn't the time.

"Do you need any ginger, Miss Tanner?" the little fellow behind the counter asked.

Ginger, for the bilious stomach that Papa's overindulging in spirits caused.

"Thank you, no, Mr. Breadalbane. This is the lot of it, for now."

Mr. Breadalbane pushed half-glasses up a narrow nose. "Mr. Tanner was looking much better when I saw him last week, much more the thing. Will you be taking this with you, or shall I hold it until you can send somebody?"

Loris kept a faint smile on her face and closed her reticule with a stout tug on the strings.

"I can take it with me. We've been without for too long, and I don't want to tempt fate."

She wanted to cry, to wreck the apothecary, to smash every jar and crock on the premises. A braver woman could have asked Mr. Breadalbane where he'd seen Micah Tanner, but Loris hadn't the courage.

She already knew what she needed to know.

For the first time in memory, she'd awoken happy, eager to see what the day held, resolute in her determination not to let a mere rumor snatch joy from her grasp. So, of course, Papa must destroy her new-found hope and toss any chance she had of happiness down the nearest well.

The door pushed open, the bell tinkling merrily.

"Miss Tanner," Thomas said. "If you're finished here, I'll escort you to the livery."

Breadalbane fussed and muttered and peered over his glasses, but he eventually wrapped up Loris's purchases and passed them to Thomas.

"I see you bought pennyroyal tea," Thomas remarked, no hint of teasing in his tone.

He'd managed a brothel. No point dissembling, and yet, Loris did. "Pennyroyal settles a bilious stomach, and the heat can put my digestion off."

Thomas was silent for a few paces. "You might want to find another remedy for digestive upsets. Pennyroyal can bring on menses, even after conception."

And thus did Loris resume lying to protect her father. Had Micah Tanner not come back into the area, she'd become Thomas Jennings's lover, maybe his fiancée, possibly even his baroness.

But Micah Tanner's daughter knew better than to hope, ever. Loris had forgotten that lesson, and like the morning's heat, it pressed in on her now from all sides and made even breathing a chore.

"Miss Tanner, are you well?"

"A little tired." Loris was exhausted by years of worry, years of self-reliance and unacknowledged rage. "I'll be glad to get back to Linden."

She'd almost said she'd be glad to get home, but thinking of Linden as home had become a presumption, for without even letting her know he was alive, Papa had put her in an impossible situation.

Loris could either lie to Thomas about her father's return, and allow a man accused of rape to continue to dodge the law, or she could betray her father, and very likely see him hanged.

CHAPTER FOURTEEN

Women were prone to moods. Men were too, but Thomas could usually trace a man's moods to an obvious motivation. Fairly had been downcast because no letter from his wife had come in the morning post. Nick was quiet because Chesterton was still in the area, and nobody knew how he supported himself.

Thomas had started the day in a thoughtful frame of mind that had brightened at the sight of Loris's shy smile in the stable. He'd wanted to kiss her, with Beckman and Jamie looking on, but refrained because Loris was owed utmost respect.

Now more than ever.

"Damned if we're not in for another storm," Nick said, scowling at the sky. "We'll doubtless broil all afternoon first. At this rate the chickens will stop laying, and the cows stop giving milk."

Loris said nothing, her silence reminiscent of the young woman Thomas had met on his first day at Linden—self-contained, full of repressed emotion, and pent-up energy.

She was again a storm about to break. Not an hour earlier, Loris had been flirting with Thomas on the village street.

"Settle, you," Thomas murmured to his horse, who also appeared to be in a mood. Rupert tossed his head, and Nick's mare did likewise.

"They don't like the heat either," Nick said. "Or maybe the rain will come sooner rather than later."

For another half mile the horses plodded on, occasionally whisking a tail, or snatching at the bit.

"They weren't acting like this on the way to Trieshock," Loris said, the first words she'd offered in nearly three miles. "Something isn't... I smell smoke."

As soon as she said the words, Thomas's nose confirmed them. Nick's gaze slewed around, but it was Loris who instinctively sensed where the threat came from.

"That way." She moved her chin toward Linden. "The breeze is coming from that direction."

She gave Evan a stout kick, and he took off at a pounding canter. When Thomas turned Rupert up the Linden drive, dread turned into sick certainty, for smoke billowed from the roof of his beautiful stable.

"Loris, stop!" he yelled, bringing Rupert to a rearing halt. "Jamie, stop her!"

Jamie put himself between Loris and the stable when she might have leapt from the saddle and charged into a growing conflagration. Loris swung down, and Evan trotted off across the lane, tail up, eyes rolling.

As Thomas vaulted from Rupert's back, Beckman emerged from the stable, soot-streaked and sweaty.

"They're almost all out," he panted. "I couldn't get Penny or Treasure, but the rest were either at grass, or Jaime and I got them out."

Nick loomed up at Thomas's side. "Penny and Treasure are in there?"

"They're livestock," Thomas snapped. "Do you know how

fast a stable fire spreads?" This was one licking out from under the eaves, smoke billowing on each gust of breeze.

"They're trapped in there," Nick retorted. "Terrified and helpless. I have to try."

He disappeared into the smoke, shrugging off Loris's attempt to stop him.

"Don't you dare," Thomas spat at Beckman. "One fool is one too many. We'll not save the stable, but get a bucket line going and maybe we can stop the fire from spreading. The ground is wet, and the cisterns full. Loris!"

She already had a bucket in each hand. "The wind will carry sparks away from the manor," she said, "but we should wet down the roof of the carriage house. Thomas, Nicholas is in there."

"Penny will not come out," Jamie said. "Her stall is her safe place, her haven. She doesn't understand what's happening, and our Nick will end up dead if he tries to convince her to leave her baby."

Fairly came jogging across the garden. "I was reading on the terrace and smelled smoke. Is everybody out?"

"Nick's in there," Loris said. "He went after Penny and Treasure, but Penny won't leave her baby, and Nick won't leave his horses."

"Fill that bucket," Thomas said.

"Fill them both," Fairly shot back, shrugging out of his jacket. Thomas did likewise, until he was in boots, breeches, and shirt. Loris soaked every inch of him, then did the same for Fairly. The entire process took only moments, but still, Nick hadn't come out.

"Stay low," Thomas told the viscount. "The smoke rises, so the better air is near the ground." He spared an instant to hug Loris, then wrapped a sodden cravat over his mouth and dashed into the stable.

"Nick! Where are you?"

"Penny won't budge," Nick shouted back. "Damned mare

is terrified."

Thomas was terrified too, because flames shot forth like serpents' tongues from the hay mow.

"Get the hell out, Haddonfield," Thomas yelled. "You can't save them."

"You get out," Nick said. "I can almost—" Coughing followed. Thomas was close enough to Penny's stall to see Nick, bent over at the waist, the mare crowded against the back wall.

The filly was tucked against her mother's side and quivering in terror.

"Let's push the filly out the door," Thomas yelled. "Maybe Penny will follow."

Nick nodded, though he was coughing continuously. Thomas passed him the wet cravat, got behind the filly, and pushed. Fairly snatched the filly's halter, Nick added his efforts to Thomas's, and by main strength they pushed nigh twenty stone of terrified baby horse into the barn aisle.

"Keep as low as you can," Thomas said to Nick. "Better air. Penny's coming."

Between the fear of the fire and fear of losing sight of her baby, the mare had apparently decided to stick with her foal. Penny snorted, she pawed, she nearly knocked Thomas off his feet, and just when he thought the damned horse would be the death of them all, Loris loomed out of the smoke and grabbed Penny's halter.

"Penny, settle down. Treasure is coming with us, and we'll be away from this dreadful smoke." Loris's voice was as calm and soothing as cool water on a hot day, as comforting as a lullaby.

The big horse lunged forward, Treasure following on a panicked squeal. Daylight loomed mere yards away, when an enormous crash sounded from above, and sparks flew in all directions.

* * *

Penny mostly dragged Loris out of the barn, Treasure capering at her mother's side. When Jamie jogged over to take hold of Penny, Loris was aware of two things.

First, her shoulder was on fire from within. Penny's panic had wrenched something the wrong way 'round, and pain screamed down Loris's arm and across her back.

Second, Fairly had given the filly a slap on the rump and turned back into the smoke and flames.

And neither he, nor Nick, nor Thomas had emerged.

Loris snatched a bucket from the nearest man—the housemaids, the footmen, everybody was on hand now—and doused herself from head to toe.

"You can't go in there," Beckman said, his voice a rasping growl as he blocked Loris's path to the stable. "If I let you go in there, they'd all three take turns killing me."

"Assuming any of them survives," Loris said, dodging around him. "And they'll kill me if I let you go back in there."

She dropped to her knees and crawled to the open door, though more crashes and billows of smoke came from within. The heat was brutal, the thought of losing Thomas more painful still.

"Thomas!" she bellowed. "Follow my voice! The door is this way. Can you hear me?"

"Again!" came from the inferno within. "Where are you?"

"This way," she shouted. "Come this way, toward me. Stay low and keep coming! You're almost out, keep coming!"

Coughing sounded close to the door, then Thomas and Fairly loomed out of the smoke, both men bent low, each with one of Nick's arms draped over his shoulder, an insensate Nick dragged between them.

"He's alive," Thomas gasped. "Took a bad rap on the noggin."

They eased Nick to the ground, and Fairly hunched over him, hands braced on his knees.

Loris flew into Thomas's embrace and held on tight with

her one good arm. She was furious that his beautiful stable was going up in smoke, but grateful to her bones simply to hold him.

"You would have gone in after us," he whispered, arms lashed around her. "You would have risked death—"

"I could not lose you," she replied, nose mashed to his soaked collar. "I could not stand by and lose you like this."

The bitter tang of smoke clung to Thomas's wet clothing; here and there holes had been charred in the fabric, and a few feet away, Nick, now on his hands and knees, coughed viciously. A pandemonium of passed buckets, shouts, and loose horses was underscored by a distant rumble of thunder, but in Loris's heart, all was well.

Thomas was safe, Nicholas, Fairly, Beck, Jamie… all safe. The horses, safe. Not a life lost, not a keepsake or memento taken without warning.

Thomas's arms remained about her as he barked at two of the dairymen to get Nick into the shade. He sent Harry to the manor to fetch Fairly's medical kit. A half-dozen small boys appeared from the direction of the pond, and Thomas set four of them to bringing trays of ale and cider down from the manor's kitchen.

Two others, he dispatched through the woods to retrieve the magistrate. When Matthew Belmont's name was mentioned, all of Loris's relief fell away, to be replaced by a nagging, corrosive dread.

Papa was in the area, she was almost sure of it.

"I'm fine," she told Thomas, though she might never be fine again. "You can let me go."

He peered down at her, his face grimy, his blue eyes more brilliant than ever. "Are you ready to let go of me?"

What an awful, portentous question. Loris had been clutching him with the arm that hadn't been injured, and nobody had spared them so much as a glance. She took a step back.

"I'll have Cook start sandwiches," she said, rubbing at her wrenched shoulder, "and Nicholas should be taken up to the house."

"You're hurt," Thomas said, as if she'd not spoken. "Damn it. Fairly, get over here!"

The viscount came at a trot from Nick's side. "You bellowed?" Even the viscount's voice was roughened by smoke.

"Loris is injured, and I will kill whoever set this fire. See to her, and I'll have Nick brought up to the house. Beckman looks the worse for wear as well."

"Beckman breathed too much smoke," Fairly said, "as you have. I'll want to see to your burns, Thomas, so appoint Jamie to manage the buckets and come along like a good fellow."

Yes, please, Loris wanted to say. Come away from this awful destruction that my own father might have wrought.

"The magistrate will soon be here," Thomas said. "Rain might obliterate critical evidence at any moment, and Jamie is wild to look after Penny and Treasure. My place is here." He brushed a cool, smoky kiss to Loris's cheek. "I'll join you at the house when I've finished with Belmont. You and Nicholas are my guests until we determine how the fire started."

In other words, Thomas already suspected arson.

"Give me a few more minutes with Nicholas and Beckman," Fairly said. "I want to have a look at the shoulder, Miss Tanner, so away with you. Sutcliffe will fret about you if you're underfoot, and he's a prodigiously good fretter where the ladies are concerned."

Loris accepted her dismissal with a meekness she didn't feel. The fire might have been started by moldy hay, a spark from Jamie's pipe, a lantern allowed to burn too low.

But it hadn't been. She knew in her bones this fire hadn't been an accident.

* * *

People saw what they expected to see. A drunk learned

this early, and Micah Tanner was no exception. He'd learned to impersonate a sober fellow when a good quantity of spirits sloshed through his veins.

Then one day, he'd realized that even with a good quantity of spirits sloshing through his veins, he was mostly still sober. He'd set out to find exactly how much gin was required to render him drunk, and the answer had been a miserable, stinking lot.

He led his horse into the Trieshock livery stable, and because the hostlers were all busy, he saw to taking off the gelding's saddle and bridle himself.

"I'll be free in a minute, Mr. Henry," one of the lads said as he led a team of wheelers past.

"Almost done," Tanner replied. "There's work enough for all in this heat."

He offered the groom the smile of a fellow used to hard labor in all weather, and hoisted the saddle and pad from the horse's back. The groom had expected to see a down-on-his-luck older fellow, possibly a schoolmaster between posts, maybe a tenant farmer from up north visiting a relative in the area. They'd exchanged a few words about the weather, about the monstrous Pavilion over in Brighton, about what a mess the Corsican had made of France.

Micah Tanner, the dapper, jovial, outgoing land agent from Linden, would not have seen to his own horse, would not have tarried in the heat for any reason when a drink was to be had elsewhere, would probably not even have risked his very neck to collect one headstrong, independent daughter before leaving England forever.

Micah was not proud of that fellow.

Manfred Henry, however, was a different creature entirely. In the two years since Tanner had acquired his new identity, he'd learned to put the drink aside before inebriation beckoned, to listen more than he talked, to make do with serviceable clothing and a serviceable horse, and to work.

He could repair harness, for example, and did so in exchange for his horse's keep. He could shear sheep, pick grapes, teach at the dame schools, cut thatch, and drive sheep and cattle. All manner of skills he'd only observed or dabbled in had become necessary for his continued well-being.

Something else was necessary too. Loris must rejoin her Papa, no matter the risk or inconvenience to him. The time had come to set matters to rights, for Tanner did not like what he'd heard regarding the situation at Linden.

"Sorry, Mr. Henry," the stable boy said, jogging down the stable aisle. "That Mr. Chesterton wants his horse again, and Mr. Timms says this time we'll have our coin of him, because he has a satchel with him."

"Good riddance," Tanner muttered, low enough that only the lad would overhear. "I don't envy the man's horse."

The poor thing had been cantered right up to the stable yard in a heaving lather just as Tanner had set out earlier in the day.

"I don't envy Chesterton, if he tries to cheat old Timms," the groom replied. "Brighton won't be far enough if Timms is of a mind to track him down."

Many a ship left from Brighton, though, and soon, Micah Tanner and the daughter he'd missed for too long would be on one of them.

* * *

Thomas was an experienced man of business, a titled lord, and a hard worker. He knew how to push himself, how to take command of chaos, how to force his mind to attend to details when exhaustion or emotion tried to distract him.

He did not know how to sit on the shady bench, stay out of the way, and merely watch as others threw bucket after bucket on the smoking, steaming wreck of the stable.

Thomas was just about to start throwing buckets himself when a blond fellow on a gray mare cantered up the drive. The mare had the fit, lean, tireless quality of an experienced hunter; the man on her back bore the same air and his seat was excellent.

"You're Sutcliffe?" he asked, swinging down. "Matthew Belmont. Apologies for making your acquaintance under such circumstances, but I wanted to see the situation for myself before the heavens opened up."

Brisk, businesslike, but not presuming, and not a fool either, thank God. Every time Thomas pictured Loris, poised to fly into the stable and rescue him, he felt sick all over again. Belmont would get to the bottom of this fire, and then Thomas could sleep at night.

"Mr. Belmont, my thanks for your prompt arrival. Sutcliffe, at your service, though somewhat the worse for the day's events."

"Any casualties?" Belmont asked, loosening his mare's girth and slipping off her bridle.

"Not a one, not a horse, not a cat, not a stable lad," Thomas replied, "and that bothers me."

Belmont hung the bridle over the back of the bench, and the mare, apparently accustomed to this routine, began to graze in the oak's shade.

"You're bothered by a backhanded miracle, Sutcliffe?" Belmont asked, stripping off his gloves. "Let's have a look while you explain yourself, lest we're caught in another much-needed downpour."

Belmont led Thomas on an inspection of the ruins. The magistrate was rangy and weathered, probably five years Thomas's senior. Thomas recalled him greeting Loris at market, and Loris had seemed genuinely pleased with the squire's company.

Matthew Belmont was not a young man, not hot-headed.

Not married, either, and though he looked like he'd seen many a winter gale or blistering summer day, Belmont was attractive in the way of the blond, blue-eyed gentry who'd been working the Sussex land for centuries.

"I'm not sure there's much to see," Thomas said. "My stable is a complete loss. The horses Beck and Jamie didn't get out, Nick, Fairly, and I were able to save. No serious injuries, I hope, though Miss Tanner's shoulder will pain her for a while, and Nick took a blow to the head."

"A hard head," Belmont said, peering at the blackened timbers pointing skyward. "Your fire started near the roof; otherwise, the remains of the barn would be top heavy, not bottom heavy."

Thomas needed to be up at the manor, making certain that Loris's shoulder injury was minor, and yet he also needed to be here, where answers might be found.

"How can you tell where a fire starts?"

They'd walked around the entire ruin and now stood upwind of the stable, and yet the scent of smoke was thick in the air.

"When a fire starts low," Belmont said, shading his eyes, "the roof often survives as part of the burned shell. We wet the buildings down from the outside and leave the fire to consume the center. But you have no roof left, and your main cross-beams have fallen in, though two of your walls are standing."

"You conclude from that the fire started high?"

"Not only that," the squire went on, starting on another circuit of the barn's foundation. "The prevailing wind here—such as it's been of late—is from the south, which means the fire, had it started externally, might have left the south wall standing, unless the flames originated at or outside the south wall. Your south wall is partly standing, and yet your east and north walls are not. The conflagration was not wind-driven—the flames were not pushed from south to north—therefore, the fire was initially confined to the inside of your barn."

Across the garden, a flash of blue suggested Loris was on her way back to Thomas's side. She was in clean clothes, her hair brushed and braided. Thomas's worry subsided a grudging inch, for surely, if her shoulder were badly injured, Fairly would not have allowed her from the house?

"So the issue becomes, how did somebody gain access to the barn," Thomas said, "assuming one of my own staff didn't set the fire."

Belmont wiped his brow with his sleeve. "Excellent question, and how did that person gain access to your hayloft, specifically?"

Thomas brought to mind the image of his stable as it had been at the start of the day, an elegant, serviceable establishment that maximized the comfort of its inhabitants and the efficiency of its operations.

"The hayloft had three points of access," Thomas said, "not counting the hay port door itself. You could climb to it from the ladder beside the hay port out front, use the ladder inside the barn, or using the third ladder, also outside, enter onto the back of the mow."

Loris had caught sight of them, but Thomas made himself complete his explanation, because rain threatened, and he didn't want Loris unduly alarmed.

"Come along, Mr. Belmont. Halfway down this side of the barn, we might well find—Mr. Belmont, please be still and take note of the ground."

For there, in the rain-soft earth, right beneath where the second external ladder to the hay mow should have been, were boot prints, some complete, some partial.

"You have an instinct for investigation," Belmont said, hunkering.

"Bloody hell," Thomas muttered. "This ladder would have been the only point of entry into the hay mow not visible from the stable yard or the house itself, though we had no cause to use it. One of us ought to sketch those boot prints."

They were unique, the heel of the right boot having a nick in the outline and both heels worn at the back. The boots weren't new, and they could well be either the owner's only pair or his favorites.

"As it happens," Belmont said, tracing a finger around one heel print, "I brought the requisite pencil and paper in my saddle bags, and am fairly competent with a free-hand drawing."

"These prints are too small to be Nick's, Beckman's, mine or yours," Thomas replied, as thunder grumbled again to the south. No closer, but not moving away either. "But Jamie is quite diminutive, and he has experience with stable fires. These might even be the boots of a woman."

Belmont rose, and he was almost as tall as Thomas. "You suspect Miss Tanner? If I understand the sequence of events, she wasn't even on the property."

Thank God.

"I do not suspect Miss Tanner," Thomas said, quietly, because Loris was coming around the side of the foundation. Jamie intercepted her, and Thomas wanted to howl.

"Capable woman, Miss Tanner," the squire observed, though his tone was so dry, he might have been offering an insult rather than a compliment.

"Was it you who warned Miss Tanner's father off, before he disappeared two years ago?" And had Belmont done so out of consideration for the daughter, or for Tanner?

Belmont kicked a charred hunk of wood back to the smoking foundation of the stable.

"To warn a suspect of impending charges would have been unethical in the extreme, my lord."

Belmont had integrity. His gentlemanly honor was evident in his bearing, his gaze, his immediate response to the call of duty.

"I'm told the charges were serious," Thomas said, keeping his voice down.

"You were told the charge *would have been* rape, if I had ever charged Micah Tanner. Tanner should have realized that the law can't convict a man of a crime based on one person's word against another's, though I doubt Tanner was thinking clearly. He should have stayed and weathered the scandal. Greymoor would hardly have cut him loose over it with harvest approaching."

"Why do you say that?"

Loris had a hand on Jamie's shoulder—her right hand, while the left remained lax at her side.

I will kill any who put her at risk of harm.

"Greymoor had unfortunate history with Mrs. Pettigrew," the squire said. "She came to me seeking to lay information against him, claiming he'd used her ill the previous evening. She was unaware Greymoor and I were sharing a meal here at Linden at the exact hour the crime was supposed to have occurred, and then played cards until very late. In Tanner's case, my investigation was simply delayed because my youngest developed a fever."

Thomas started walking, because clearly, Jamie would detain Loris all day.

"Does Mrs. Pettigrew know you caught her in a lie?" Bearing false witness was also a sin.

"She knows only that Greymoor had a credible alibi, not that I would have testified on his lordship's behalf. Tanner, by contrast, fled, and thus created a presumption of guilt. He also left his daughter to deal with yet another of his follies."

Loris and Jamie moved off in the direction of the carriage house.

"You don't think highly of Mr. Tanner," Thomas said, leading the squire in the same direction.

"Tanner was tremendously likeable, which I, as an old stick of a widower, envied. But no, I cannot respect a man who treated his daughter as Tanner did his."

"She is quite capable, nonetheless."

"Frighteningly so," the squire said—wistfully? "I offered for her, when Tanner took off. She thanked me kindly, told me she would always treasure my friendship, and would I please get the hell off the property so she could check on a cow having difficulty calving."

"Miss Tanner!" Thomas called, waving needlessly. "The squire might have some questions for you."

Thomas had questions for her: Did her shoulder hurt? Would she fight him about biding at the manor house? Had she any idea who might have set the fire, for Thomas had a few theories.

"She thinks you take a dim view of female stewards," Thomas said, as Loris approached them at a brisk clip.

"I take a dim view of women left to fend for themselves by errant menfolk," the squire retorted, "as should any gentleman."

Beckman paused by the cistern, three empty buckets grasped in each hand, and engaged Loris in conversation.

"Having been turned down by Miss Tanner," Thomas said, "were you tempted to offer for Mrs. Pettigrew?"

Belmont sent another sizeable piece of charred wood flying back to the smoldering heap that was Thomas's stable.

"Lord Sutcliffe, I do not mean to speak ill of a neighbor, but that woman accused two otherwise respected men of rape in less than two years. She works her son without mercy in her stable, but won't yield to his sensible advice, and finally, she treats old Pettigrew's stallion like some demon beast, which is exactly what Johnny will become if something isn't done. Mrs. Pettigrew labors under the mistaken belief that life owes her."

Loris patted Beckman's arm, and that good fellow's ears turned red.

"What could life owe Claudia Pettigrew?" Thomas owed Loris, owed her for knowing he was lost in the damned stable, and had nearly dragged Nick and Fairly both into the saddle room.

"I'm not sure what causes the widow's discontent," the squire said. "Perhaps she wants greater wealth or lost youth, but she is formidable in her frustrations and temper. I have been trying to buy that stallion from her for years, but she will not let him go."

"Why not? He's apparently not young, he's bred much of the stock in this area, and he's also become difficult."

"She knows I want the horse," Belmont said. "Claudia Pettigrew will probably shoot old Johnny before she lets someone else treat him better than she does."

Thomas stifled the urge to run to Loris's side, pitch both Beckman and Belmont into the cistern, and carry the lady off to the safety and privacy of the manor. The last time he'd been this frantic to protect a woman—

Memory rose up, of his sister telling him he'd be better off away from Sutcliffe, and to stop hiding behind her skirts. Yes, Thomas had wanted the comfort of the familiar, and the reassurance of being near his only sibling, but he'd also needed desperately to protect her from what she was becoming.

"I almost feel sorry for Mrs. Pettigrew," Thomas said, for Loris was safe, and he was no longer a callow youth. "She's regarded as a malcontent, when in fact she could be simply a determined woman trying to manage as best her dignity and circumstances allow."

Belmont shook his head. "You can spout that gentlemanly cant all day, Baron, and I commend you for the sentiment, but rape charges are as serious as the grave. Guard your back, hmm?"

Yes, Thomas would guard his back. He'd guard his steward, too.

CHAPTER FIFTEEN

Matthew Belmont had the knack of appearing handsome and well turned out even in casual riding attire. Loris had seen him any number of times in his hunting pinks, and particularly on his gray mare, he made an impressive picture.

Though Matthew would be probably be surprised to learn what an attractive impression he made—surprised, and embarrassed.

By contrast, Thomas looked as bedraggled and out of sorts as Loris felt. His hair was still damp and sporting a few cinders, his clothing clung to him, his boots were filthy with ash and dust, and his face was streaked with grime.

Loris wanted to drag Thomas into her arms and make passionate love to him, then bathe every inch of him and make love to him all over again—for perhaps the last time.

"Matthew, greetings. Have you concluded your investigation?" She offered him a kiss to his cheek, a maneuver guaranteed to put the squire to the blush.

He bowed over her hand as if they'd met in Linden's formal parlor, the same way he greeted her when their paths crossed on market days, despite half the shire looking on.

"Miss Tanner."

The magistrate was shy. Loris adored this about Matthew, but could not afford to overlook the fact that both he and Thomas were astute men. If they'd found evidence of arson, she wanted to know of it.

"You were probably intending to talk with every person on this estate and not even greet me," Loris chided. "For shame, Matthew. Baron, the squire is not usually so wanting in manners."

Thomas remained unnervingly quiet, while Loris resisted the urge to chatter.

"You've caught me out, Miss Tanner," Belmont replied. "I meant to save you for last and linger shamelessly enough to get myself invited to luncheon, but will now have to depart with my tail between my legs."

Loris could manage small talk, but why wouldn't Thomas say anything?

"How are the boys?" she asked. "And don't think the baron will allow you to dodge his company at luncheon so easily, will you, my lord?"

"Of course not," Thomas said, gesturing toward the house. "Let's inform Cook we'll have one more at table."

While both men accompanied Loris to the garden, and thunder rumbled, she tried again to probe whether evidence of arson had been uncovered.

And was met with Belmont's inquiries about the upcoming assembly, and Loris's plans to attend.

"Miss Tanner will be attending," Thomas volunteered, the lout. "She will accompany me and Lord Fairly, and has been practicing the waltz in anticipation of this gathering. Belmont, didn't you want to do some sketching?"

"Sketching?" Matthew, usually so self-contained and capable, looked momentarily bewildered. "Right, sketching. I'm sure you'll need a few minutes to tidy up, Baron, and that should suffice for my sketching. I'll be along shortly."

Matthew strode off toward the carriage house, and Loris abruptly found herself pulled behind a wilting lilac bush.

"You," Thomas said, enfolding her in his arms. "Tell me you're hale and well and willing to accept my hospitality."

Because his clothing was damp, cold bloomed along Loris's belly and chest. She bundled close anyway, despite the shrieking protest from her shoulder.

"I'm hale and well, and willing to bide at the manor for a short time. This fire was arson, wasn't it?"

Thomas's cheek rested against her temple. Everywhere, he smelled of smoke, ashes, and loss.

"If you're so hale and well, then why is your left arm at your side, Loris Tanner? Did Fairly dose you with laudanum?"

She slid from Thomas's embrace, but stayed close enough to brush his hair back with her right hand.

"You don't need to protect me from the truth, sir. We never stored more than a week's hay in the stable's loft, and we were using the remains of the crop from last year, which was well cured and not the least damp."

He closed his eyes, so Loris repeated the stroke of her hand over his brow.

"Belmont won't say arson," Thomas murmured, "but Jamie never smokes in the stable, and not a single lamp would have been lit at mid-morning. I have an enemy who will commit felonies on my own property in the broad light of day."

Somebody had an enemy, or an inebriated father.

"You need a bath," Loris said. "You'd leave me making polite chit-chat with Matthew and Lord Fairly, when I want to question the children who showed up within minutes of the fire being discovered."

Thomas opened his eyes. "The boys?"

Had they seen anything? Seen anyone? Any of those boys would recognize Micah Tanner easily.

"Matthew is very thorough," Loris said, "but even he might

overlook children. Shall we see to your bath?"

Thomas closed the small distance between them, his embrace gentle. "How bad is your shoulder?"

"It hurts. Penny gave it a bad wrench, but I brought a great quantity of willow bark tea back from the apothecary with me, and that should suf—"

Thomas's mouth stole over hers. He was filthy and bristling with emotions Loris couldn't fathom, and she might soon be parted from him, but his kiss was the exact, perfect antidote to every worry and heartache, every twinge and pang, and had it not been agony to lift her left arm, Loris would have—

"Halloo, all!" sounded from around the lilac bush. "I say, is that you, Miss Tanner?"

Thomas pulled away, muttering something in French that Loris suspected he'd best not translate.

"Hello, Giles," she said, stepping back onto the path. "The baron and I are headed up to the house. I assume you saw the stable."

Thomas sauntered around the lilac bush and stood close enough to Loris's back that she could smell the fire on him.

"Pettigrew, hello. You will pardon my dirt."

"Word of the fire reached us at the Cock and Bull," Giles said. "The lads are calling it a miracle, though it's a dashed stinking miracle, if you ask me. Nobody was hurt, if the gossip is correct?"

"Nobody was seriously hurt," Loris said, which meant whoever set the fire couldn't be charged with murder, attempted murder, or heinous felonies other than arson. "We are soon to sit down with Mr. Belmont and Lord Fairly at lunch. Can you join us?"

She ought not to have extended that offer, but turning Giles away when he'd come out of neighborly concern would have been rude.

"Please do join us," Thomas said, taking Loris's right arm. "Another friendly face is always welcome at my table."

"I don't want to be merely friendly," Giles said, falling in step beside them. "I'd like to be useful. If you have a place to store oats, I'll send over a wagonload. The pasture is thin in this damned heat—begging your pardon, Miss Tanner—and we have enough oats to last us handily."

Loris felt the surprise go through Thomas, but before he could reject a neighborly overture, she answered for him.

"Oats would be much appreciated, Giles. Thank you. We keep most of our supply at the home farm, but will appreciate any you can spare."

"My thanks, Pettigrew," Thomas said as they approached the back terrace. "Miss Tanner will see you inside, and I'll excuse myself. Give me thirty minutes and I'll join you at lunch."

He bowed, and would have left Loris the burden of entertaining Giles for those thirty minutes, but Giles spoke up.

"I say, do we know how the fire started? Was somebody having a pipe upwind, perhaps? Or maybe some rotten hay escaped notice in the heat?"

"No," Thomas said. "No rotten hay, no stray sparks. If you'll pardon me."

Loris might have missed it, except she was gazing straight at Giles, lest he catch her admiring Thomas's retreat. Something in Thomas's reply had not met with Giles's approval, and for a moment, Giles Pettigrew had borne a very close resemblance to his mother.

* * *

Good God, a fire.

Giles made polite chit-chat while dining with a man who'd lost a stable so beautiful, Giles had longed for the day when his own might resemble it.

Sutcliffe said little over a meal of chicken flavored with lemon and basil, simmered green beans, and potatoes mashed with bacon. Excellent food, and of all people, Loris Tanner carried the conversation, letting talk of the fire have its due, then steering the topic back to the harvest, the irrigation projects, or Giles's own equine prospects.

In a pretty blue frock only a few years out of fashion, Miss Tanner presided over a casual meal easily, as if she'd been entertaining gentry and even titled guests for years.

Giles hadn't anticipated such poise from her, but attributed her skill to the necessity of the moment and the viscount's flagrant charm.

"I have a suggestion," Giles said, when servings of trifle had been brought to the table. "Your equine stock can temporarily manage in the pastures, or at your home farm. However—"

"I'm happy to foster some for you," Squire Belmont said, as his exceedingly clean plate was replaced with an exceedingly large serving of trifle. "I have plenty of room and a very competent staff in the stable."

Well, damn. Giles could not make the same offer, not without Claudia's prior agreement.

"Matthew, that is very generous," Miss Tanner said, touching Belmont's sleeve.

The squire, a man who'd solved murders and might very well solve a case of arson, smiled at her like one of his young offspring besotted with a tavern maid.

"It's no trouble," Belmont said. "Sutcliffe would do the same for me, I'm sure."

"Of course we would," the baron replied.

"Certainly," Giles said. "We're quite neighborly here, which is why a barn raising is in order. We can't replace Linden's stable, but we can build something serviceable before the weather turns nasty."

The weather already had turned nasty, for a raging thunderstorm had settled into a steady downpour as they'd started their meal.

"That is most kind of you," Miss Tanner said, shooting the baron a look as she picked up her dessert spoon.

Here was the trouble with being Claudia Pettigrew's son—

one of the many troubles. Giles could not fathom that look, not the one from Miss Tanner to the baron, not the slight smile he favored her with in response.

Was Miss Tanner being a presuming steward? An indulged houseguest? A trusted retainer? All Giles could conclude was that Miss Tanner had privileges with the baron such as her father had never enjoyed with the baron's predecessor.

That was not good news.

"Don't you care for trifle, Mr. Pettigrew?" Lord Fairly asked.

"Trifle's a right treat," Giles replied. "And a barn raising will see Linden's equine stock safe and snug come winter. My own papa organized more than one, and as your new neighbors, Baron, we'd welcome the opportunity to offer assistance."

Giles had no idea what the good folk of the shire would welcome, but a few kegs of ale would probably inspire the tenant farmers to donate a day of labor.

"I attended two of these up in Oxfordshire last year," Belmont said. "My brother is something of an expert at building simple structures, an amateur architect. I have a few sets of plans and can help with the lumber estimates."

"You'll need nails," Miss Tanner said, a spoonful of rich dessert poised before her mouth. "Glue, dowels, ropes, teams."

"Food and drink," the viscount added, and just like that, Giles's gracious, brilliant and sincerely well-motivated suggestion was carried off by a table of experts, which hadn't been at all what he'd intended.

His *life* wasn't what he'd intended either.

"Miss Tanner," Giles interjected over Belmont's description of roofing options, "rebuilding the stable is surely talk for the men."

That observation met with silence, perhaps embarrassed on the part of the other fellows, for they'd dived into the topic of stable construction without any thought for polite conversation.

Hardly the way to impress a woman who'd apparently been longing for the role of hostess.

Giles cleared his throat. "What I meant was, a more agreeable topic for feminine ears might be the upcoming assembly. I hope you will consider attending this one, and as my special guest."

He offered her a gentle smile, an encouraging smile, because Loris Tanner was not a genteel lady exactly, but she'd make an adequate wife for a man intent on a quick wedding. Giles had studied on the matter, and offering for her, while generous on his part, was still his best option.

And a better option than she could aspire to, if she were honest,

"Afraid that won't be possible," Sutcliffe said, trailing his spoon through raspberries and cream. "Miss Tanner will attend with the viscount and me. She's agreed to keep watch over us, lest we make a bad impression on the neighbors."

Miss Tanner was absorbed with another spoonful of dessert, suggesting the baron's pronouncement might be news to her.

Presuming man, but the titled ones were like that, and they did like good horseflesh.

"Then perhaps Miss Tanner will save me a dance?" Giles suggested.

"I'd be happy to," she said, setting her dessert bowl aside. "When shall we hold this barn raising?"

She liked Giles's idea of a barn raising, and she'd save him a dance. He took that for progress and rose from the table shortly thereafter. The baron escorted him to Linden's front door, Belmont trailing with Miss Tanner on his arm, while the viscount disappeared to the library, where he professed to be intent on penning a letter to his wife.

Miss Tanner took her leave of Giles with a kiss to his cheek—a heartening novelty in their dealings thus far—and then a kiss and an embrace for Belmont, after which, she decamped for the library as well.

Perhaps women preferred grown men who blushed, though Claudia's regard for the squire was paltry indeed.

"My thanks again, Pettigrew," Sutcliffe said. "For the oats, for the suggestion of a barn raising, for simply coming by."

"Least I can do," Giles replied, tapping his hat onto his head. "Squire, shall we ride together as far as your lane?"

"Certainly," Belmont said. "Sutcliffe, if you're free for dinner tonight, perhaps we'll talk more then?"

"I'll look forward to it."

Giles preceded the squire out onto the front porch, while Sutcliffe detained Belmont at the threshold.

"Belmont, do your artistic abilities extend to creating a likeness of Micah Tanner?"

Sutcliffe had posed his question quietly, but as Giles made a production of pulling on his gloves and pretending to ignore what he'd overheard, sunshine burst from behind the clouds otherwise enshrouding his day.

Micah Tanner had bedeviled many of Giles's waking moments of late. If Sutcliffe wanted the man found, that was all to the good.

"I'll bring you a few drawings this evening," Belmont said, "and some plans for a simple, serviceable stable."

The rain had eased off to a drizzle, but as Giles traipsed through the Linden gardens with Belmont at his side, he caught the first real glimmer of the disruption a stable fire could bring, irrespective of the devastation to property.

"I say, Belmont. Without a stable, and with the heavens having opened up, where exactly do you suppose the lads have stashed our horses?"

* * *

"You'll not waste a waltz on the handsome Mr. Pettigrew," Thomas growled when he caught up with Loris outside the library door. Fairly was on the other side of that door, and he had the hearing of a cat, so Thomas bent closer. "Pettigrew fancies you. Don't deny it."

Loris studied Thomas as if he'd spoken in Urdu, which he hadn't attempted for several years.

"Have you suffered a blow to the head, sir? Giles and I have known each other for ten years, and he was extending me simple courtesy on a trying day."

Pettigrew's neighborly concern had seemed genuine when he'd been offering a load of oats.

And then he'd tendered a load of something else entirely. "I managed a brothel," was what came out of Thomas's mouth. "I know when a man is interested in a woman, and that boy was sniffing about your skirts. He watched you eat your trifle like he'd make a dessert of you."

Any other woman would have been pleased. She would have simpered and twirled a curl around her finger, and prettily gloated to have made a conquest.

Loris patted Thomas's chest. "You're upset. We're all upset. I'm ordering toddies in the library, you can light the fire, and then we'll plan your barn raising. Nick will probably be down soon, and we must keep him occupied lest he go out in this rain and assure himself down to the last stable mouser that all the animals are in good repair."

Thomas did not want to plan a barn raising. "I could hire crews easily enough, and then I'd not be fretting over whether the miscreant was among the neighbors so eagerly assisting with reconstruction of my stable."

Loris kissed him on the mouth, a sneak attack that made focusing on her next words difficult.

"Let's find Chesterton, shall we, Baron? Let's interview the children, let's hear what Matthew has to say this evening, when he's had a chance to look over his notes and think the situation through."

"You call him Matthew," Thomas muttered, kissing her more thoroughly. Kissing Loris was good for him. Her touch both distracted him from his worries and restored his balance.

And she'd be sleeping right down the hall from him tonight.

"Most of the ladies call him Matthew," Loris said, brushing Thomas's hair back from his forehead. "He's a shrewd man, an excellent steward to his acres, and a conscientious father, but he likes to pretend he's the harmless widower, drifting toward middle-aged contentment."

"Belmont isn't remotely approaching middle age," Thomas said, angling his head into Loris's caresses. "And he's not harmless. Knows all about fires and other felonies."

And discontented widows, too.

"You're worried," Loris replied, leaning into Thomas, though she didn't wrap her arms around him. Her shoulder had to be paining her, so Thomas's embrace was careful.

"I'm furious," Thomas replied. "If a man is offended by something I've said or done, then all he need do is air his grievance, and I can resolve it, or at least address the charges. A fire is…"

"Diabolical. We envision hell as an inferno, the worst possible fate. Thomas, I know."

Loris had stared into that inferno and been ready to retrieve Thomas from it. All over again, his knees went weak, and his stomach churned at the thought of such selfless loyalty.

"You'll stay here until we know who set that fire, Loris. I'll not sleep unless I know you're safe."

She wanted to argue. Thomas could feel resistance vibrating through her, but hadn't she realized how easily she'd managed a meal with company? How right the role of lady of the manor was for her?

"Let's get through the next day," she said, stepping back. "We've a barn raising to plan. Fortunately, you already have a store of lumber here at Linden because we were about to repair your dairy barn."

"I'd forgotten that." Thomas had forgotten his name, watching Loris discreetly signal the footman over lunch, listening to her gently steer conversation this way and that.

Fairly had been charmed, Belmont impressed, Pettigrew besotted.

While Thomas had been enthralled. Loris had listened to all his maunderings about etiquette, paid attention to him, and wrung from his words whatever useful information they'd had.

She was his baroness, she simply didn't know it yet.

"Toddies sound heavenly," he said. "You'll join us. The medicinal tot is in order, and Fairly will agree with me."

Or Thomas would make him agree.

Loris stroked a hand over Thomas's bum as she departed for the kitchen, and that too, made a part of his world come right.

"Get in here," Fairly said, grabbing Thomas by the wrist and yanking him into the library. "You can't stare after her like that, not in public."

"Were you eavesdropping, Fairly?"

His lordship took a sniff of daisies clustered in a crystal bowl on the mantel. Daisies stank, thus the maneuver was purely dilatory.

"I might have overhead a few words," Fairly said. "Fire is a very bad business, Thomas, and I know a woman bearing up when I see one. Your Loris holds herself responsible for the fire."

"That makes two of us holding ourselves responsible," Thomas said, lighting a spill from the lamp on the desk. "That fire was deliberately set, Fairly."

The hearth had already been laid with kindling and small logs, for with the arrival of the storm, the temperature had dropped.

"You have an enemy," Fairly said, lounging against one end of the mantel. "A deadly enemy."

The tinder caught, and flames licked upward. Thomas threw the spill on the fire and replaced the screen.

Here again was what Belmont had called a backhanded miracle. "Not necessarily deadly. Not a soul was in the barn, and if Penny and Treasure were napping in their bed of straw, then from the hayloft, the premises would have seemed deserted. Loss of a building is a degree of harm worse than a sprung shoe or colicky animal, but it's not loss of life."

Fairly shoved away from the mantel. "Thomas, you're splitting hairs. Setting a fire is but a short step from murder. Somebody is always on hand in a well-run stable, the work is endless, the animals valuable. What are you saying?"

Thomas threw himself onto the sofa, glad for Fairly's presence, resentful of his pragmatism.

"I'm saying the situation might be more complicated than it first appears. Somebody is always *supposed* to be on hand in a well-run stable, but I'm short-handed. Very short-handed. Somebody who can sound the alarm, and get out the one or two animals who might be in stalls in the middle of the day—"

"In the heat of the day, most of the valuable stock will be out of the sun, *in their stalls*," Fairly began in his most severe tones.

"I know that," Thomas said, tossing a pillow onto the floor. "You know that, but somebody who's only done a poor job of looking after horseflesh wouldn't take that into account. Who would you blame, Fairly, for the loss of a valuable building on one of your estates? Who would you blame for a rash of colic, a sprung shoe, a shortage of competent help, and other trouble?"

Fairly came down beside Thomas. "One doesn't like to place blame without evidence, but my properties are all in the hands of professional stewards. They aren't merely rent agents. Those fellows are my eyes and ears. You're suggesting the purpose of all this ill will is to discredit Miss Tanner."

The smallest of the dry logs caught, and white smoke eddied up the chimney in a steady stream.

"I don't want to believe Loris is the target," Thomas replied, "but I haven't been in the area long enough to develop enemies. She, by contrast, could be reaping the ill will her father's bad behavior sowed, or the malevolence of the displaced Chesterton and his minions."

Fairly slouched down and crossed his boots at the ankle—dusty boots, the toes white with ash.

"Why wait until now to begin this campaign against Miss Tanner?" he asked. "She's been managing here for nearly two years, albeit her post was informal."

Fairly also still smelled faintly of smoke, though he'd changed his clothing and doubtless washed since helping Thomas drag Nick to safety.

"Maybe somebody's unhappy because Miss Tanner's post is no longer informal? How do I find a man who disappeared two years ago, Fairly?"

Thomas's question was greeted with a short silence as a log popped and sparks flew up, and then, "Christ in the manger."

"Not Him," Thomas said, though divine intervention had probably sent the rain onto the burning stable. "Loris's father. She's plagued by his disappearance, bedeviled by the idea he could be charged with rape if he's spotted in the area. Tanner had some means, he had the requisite skills to brew this sort of trouble, he's worked all over England, and he drank enough to go for long periods without recalling his actions."

"What sort of father puts his own daughter at risk of disgrace, much less death?" Fairly asked.

"Tanner disgraced his daughter time and again. People lost to drink have no conscience," Thomas replied. "My own sister, as dear and decent a girl as you'd ever meet, became—"

A soft tap on the door heralded Loris's return, Harry at her side and bearing a tray.

"Toddies for you fellows. I'm having a pot of chocolate."

Thomas mustered a smile, took the tray, dismissed Harry, and closed the door behind him.

"Well done, madam. Fairly is in want of fortification, only because I've not yet told him I sent a messenger before lunch with a summons for Lady Fairly."

"You did what?" Fairly asked, bolting upright.

"Sent for your Letty," Thomas said, passing his lordship a drink. "We must have a chaperone at Linden if Miss Tanner is to accept my hospitality beyond the most exigent circumstances, and after today's developments, I couldn't pry your lordship loose from the property without a trebuchet and a Highland regiment."

Couldn't pry Fairly loose from Thomas's side, which was deuced inconvenient—also comforting.

"When will she—never mind," Fairly said, setting his drink on the mantel and pacing away from the sofa. "You sent for my Letty. Well done, Thomas, even if we do have an arsonist loose in the shire. Letty knew you'd need friends about, else I would never have left my bride so soon after the nuptials. I'm babbling."

Loris took the place Fairly had vacated. "You're being a devoted spouse, but if we're truly to organize a barn raising, maybe you wouldn't mind finding pencil and paper in that desk? We've lists to make, and—"

Nicholas Haddonfield came sauntering into the library, looking freshly bathed and tidy. His hair was damp, and somebody had given it a significant trim, probably cutting off locks singed by falling cinders.

"Fairly has forbidden me to leave the premises for the next twenty-four hours," Nick groused, "as if a little tap on the head ever slowed a Haddonfield down for long. Ah, somebody brought me a toddy," he said, helping himself to Thomas's portion. "I'm sure a toddy is good for head injuries. Why is Lord Fairly seated at the baronial desk like headmaster preparing to lecture his scholars?"

Nick took Thomas's favorite reading chair, Thomas pilfered the occasional sip of Loris's chocolate, and much argument ensued, about the benefits of a tin roof versus thatch, about how many stalls were absolutely necessary if the stable was to function through the winter—for more extensive construction could be undertaken next spring.

Thomas commented here and there, but in truth, Nick, Fairly, and Loris would see that his best interests were served in the decisions made. At some point, Loris's hand had stolen into Thomas's, and his unease acquired another dimension.

He'd protect Loris, from her own father if necessary. The best way to do that was to marry her, and he was more than willing to take that step.

But was Loris willing to become his baroness?

CHAPTER SIXTEEN

Letty might be at Linden as early as the next day, and Fairly could barely contain his relief. Her daily letters had become the tenuous skein connecting him to his own sanity, for Letty's reports were all that made rustication in Sussex bearable.

That and watching Thomas Jennings, Baron Sutcliffe, fall arse over tea kettle in love with his pretty land steward.

"The baron didn't say much about the construction of his new stable, though he at least cleaned his dinner plate," Nicholas Haddonfield observed, sniffing at a stopper from Thomas's brandy decanter. The glass was in the shape of a hawk, wings extended as if to attack. "A nightcap, my lord?"

There stood another intriguing aspect of this summer's frolic. "No more for me, thank you," Fairly said. "Aren't you tired, Haddonfield?"

Nick held the decanter up to a lit sconce, the brandy catching the fire's light and sending it dancing.

"I am unsettled," he replied. "All I gleaned from dinner is that Belmont strongly suspects arson, can't prove a thing, and has sketched a boot print that might incriminate somebody, or might be simply a sorry coincidence. Any stable boy looking to tryst with a dairy maid might entice her up the outside ladder to the hayloft."

Based on the quantity of spirits that went into the stable master's glass, this bothered him exceedingly.

"Shall we play cards?" Fairly asked, though he was exhausted. "I'm not quite ready for sleep myself."

The night was blessedly cool, but also damp with the day's rain. Fairly would dream of Letty, of course, and also dream of the moment in the stable when only Loris Tanner's voice had stood between three fit, mostly hale men and an awful death.

"You've recognized me," Nick said, returning the stopper to its perch atop the decanter. "When did you figure it out?"

They were to indulge in some wagering then, though not with cards. Fairly threw another log onto the fire, mostly to give himself a moment to think.

"Unlike Thomas," Fairly said, "who lurked on the periphery of polite society, I am related by marriage to an earl, a marquis, and a viscount. I must do the pretty, though with Letty, I'll live very quietly indeed. You, however, are an earl's heir, and the tallest titled man in the realm. We've been in several of the same ballrooms."

Nick took a delicate sip of brandy, a man who knew how to savor luxuries. "A Scot by the name of MacHugh might be as tall as I am, and he's in line for an earldom too. Where does Sutcliffe get this stuff?"

"From my brother-in-law, the marquis. So what are you doing here, Reston? It is Reston, isn't it? Viscount Reston?"

By the firelight, Nick abruptly looked like the most disgusted titled man in the realm.

"Reston it is, for my sins. Beckman is our spare, and there's half a regiment of siblings that come after him. Will you tell Sutcliffe?"

"I consider Thomas Jennings a friend, Reston." Fairly

began a circuit of the library, having sat for half the evening over dinner and the other half over plans to rebuild the stable. "I was shipwrecked in India, barely made it to shore. The locals were not dealing with me kindly—my peculiar eyes, you know—and out of the sea crawls Thomas, nothing but a knife and a facility for languages to his credit. Within minutes, I became an honored guest of the nearest raja."

The more suspicious had decided Thomas was a spirit from the depths, with his glittering blue eyes and sun-darkened complexion.

Nicholas stood with an elbow braced on the mantel, his posture the epitome of the elegant lord. For dinner, he'd worn a country gentleman's finery, and Fairly's suspicions as to his identity had coalesced into certain recognition.

To the manor—and an earldom's courtesy title—born. Nick knew down to the last decorative item of cutlery what each piece of silverware was for. His table manners bordered on dainty, and his conversation was witty without straying into the ribald.

"Sutcliffe was your bodyguard?" Nick asked.

"Bodyguard, general factor, man of business, conscience. He saved my Letty, too, would not allow me to ignore her situation when others would have turned a blind eye. Sutcliffe is protective as hell of those he cares for, and I cannot support a dishonest silence where he's concerned, Reston."

"Haddonfield, please. At least for now."

The library was elegantly appointed, in keeping with the taste and Continental connections of the previous owner. Fairly took up an intricately carved ivory letter opener that would have sufficed to cut out a man's heart.

"Why?" Fairly asked, balancing the letter opener point down on the tip of his finger. "Why hide? Why muck stalls and wallow in the stink of horses and hard work when you might be chasing chambermaids about at any house party?"

"I am the Bellefonte earldom's heir," Nick said, in the same tones a man might admit to suffering a wasting disease. "Heirs marry appropriately, they beget progeny, they are… dutiful."

A well-trained physician learned to diagnose all parts of a patient, not merely the sore knee or persistent megrims that clamored most loudly for attention.

"I recognized you," Fairly said, putting the letter opener on the desk, "and Thomas could too. I don't get the sense you prefer men, so what is the difficulty with fulfilling your duty?"

Nick stared out at the damp evening. Not a star shone in the sky, not a single pale glimmer betrayed the location of the moon above the clouds.

"I'm doing penance," he said. "Also keeping an eye on Beckman, who's had some difficult years, and has found peace ruralizing as stable help. My father agreed to allow me time to rusticate because somebody needed to look after Beckman."

Why would Haddonfield have turned his back to deliver that part of his confession?

"Beckman appears to enjoy excellent health, but for having breathed too much smoke and having been stomped on a time or two by a panicked horse."

"Beckman was prone to… over-imbibing and other vices," Nick said, his tone flat. "He seems better now, but he's seemed better before, though never for this long. Polite society would ridicule him for it, but the hard work, the horses, the care of the livestock agree with him."

Or perhaps his older brother's company steadied Beckman.

Fairly wanted to see Nick Haddonfield's face, wanted to assess what was being admitted against what was being kept secret, so he crossed the room to stand beside a man who'd soon outrank him.

"The life of a stable master agrees with you, too," Fairly said.

"Sutcliffe isn't the only person with a protective streak, my lord. I'm not hiding here. My brother's situation calls for discretion, thus I'm not bruiting about a courtesy title for which I have no use."

Nick loathed that title, he *was* hiding, *and* he was looking after the man who'd guarantee the earldom's succession if Nick could not—or would not.

"I recognized you when you joined us earlier today," Fairly said. "Your hair was damp and therefore appeared darker. You've also trimmed off your curls and had combed every hair into place."

Nick finished his drink and set the glass on the mantel. "I will inform Sutcliffe of my circumstances soon. I promise you that. The time allotted by my father for this repairing lease is coming to a close. I'll be gone after harvest."

Misery rolled off Nick in waves, also resignation.

"And Beckman?"

"He'll likely depart with me, but I will not leave Miss Tanner without a stable master before the harvest is safely in."

Miss Tanner, not the baron, not Linden. Interesting.

"I can give you time to unburden yourself to the baron," Fairly said, "but you'd better tell him the rest of it, too, Haddonfield. You chose to rusticate on this estate for reasons you're not admitting, and I dislike secrets."

Thomas positively loathed secrets and intrigue of any sort.

Nick rested his forehead on the panes of the French doors. He put Fairly in mind of Penny, the great draft mare, whose every sigh and fly kick was of monumental proportions. Such a man could never truly hide, and that must be wearying.

"I mean Sutcliffe no harm," Nick said, "but I will deal harshly with anybody who seeks to harm Miss Tanner, as will Beckman. She's been more than fair to us, and life has been unfair to her."

More half-truths, but probably as much as Nick could admit.

"My earliest years were spent in Scotland," Fairly mused. "For centuries, Englishmen have been popping up all over the world, claiming to mean no harm, to come in peace, and yet, great harm often ensues, though not to the Englishmen. Find a time to clear the air with Sutcliffe soon, or I will take the matter into my own hands."

Nick nodded. Fairly gently squeezed a meaty shoulder and took himself from the library. He'd warn Thomas, of course, but first he'd discuss the entire situation, in detail, with his darling Letty.

* * *

"You needn't worry that I've come to ravish you."

That reassurance, a rumbling baritone from Loris's balcony, put her in mind of thunder, rumbling off in the darkness.

"Thomas, get in here," she said, rising off her vanity stool. "You'll catch your death standing about in the damp night air." Much less leaping from one wet balcony to the next.

He sidled through her French doors, the night sky made animate, complete with moisture clinging to the ends of his hair. No coat, no cravat, his waistcoat half-unbuttoned.

And he was all the more attractive for his dishabille.

"You should be asleep, madam. Does your shoulder pain you?"

Loris's shoulder was a temple to misery, the discomfort radiating across her back, down her arm, and even into her hand and head.

"I'm fine. How did you—?"

Thomas kissed her, cool lips, hot man, cherishing embrace. Loris leaned on him, unable to be brisk and pragmatic after the day they'd had.

"You still smell like smoke," she said. "Faint, but tangible."

"I took a walk after Belmont left, went down to the stable to make sure the fire is out. Live coals yet lurk beneath the ashes, despite the rain, despite the passing of time. Belmont said those coals might smolder for days, even with more rain."

Some fires could never be completely extinguished. Loris wondered if her father's need for drink was such a fire.

Or if her desire for Thomas Jennings was another.

"You were quiet at dinner, sir." Thomas had been quiet all day, though the menfolk—Fairly, Nicholas, Belmont, Giles Pettigrew—probably hadn't noticed.

"Let's get you in bed," Thomas said, drawing back. "Today became a day for reflection and planning, though I've never had much use for idle chatter. How well do you know Nicholas Haddonfield?"

"He's been on the property nearly two years," Loris said. "What prompts your question?"

Thomas led her back to the vanity and indicated that she should sit. "You might have rung for a maid. Trying to bring order to your hair one-handed was doomed."

Also painful, in Loris's present condition. "Nicholas could not have started the fire. He was with us."

"Beckman?" Thomas asked, untying the ribbon from the bottom of the braid Loris had barely managed to fashion.

"Beckman risked his life getting out horses trapped by the fire. I have no reason to believe he'd be that devious, Thomas."

"And Beckman was with Jamie, cleaning the coach harness in the shade by the carriage house when he went into the saddle room to get some rags. Beck's the one who discovered the fire. He might have set it, then pretended to discover it, but I agree. He'd have to have worked very quickly, and he went to great lengths and dangerous lengths to cover his tracks if he did."

Thomas was going over and over the facts, as Loris had been, trying to discover some new insight or glimmer of information that hadn't appeared in the previous four dozen examinations.

He was also putting her to sleep.

"You are very good at brushing a woman's hair," Loris murmured, eyes closing.

"I used to brush my sister's hair, long, long ago. She's my elder, and made it seem a great privilege to wield the brush."

As a boy, Thomas would have been serious and too big for

his age, not a frivolous child.

"I saw the letter, Thomas. You should answer her." Today's letter had come to Linden, suggesting somebody had provided this sister Thomas's current direction.

Of all days for Thomas to be hounded with familial correspondence...

For a few minutes, he worked in silence, rebraiding Loris's hair. As far back as she could recall, her father had never dealt with her hair. She'd learned to braid by working on her pony's tail, braids being a safety measure in the hunt field.

"I'm considering answering Theresa's letter," Thomas said, tying off the end of the braid. "There's much to say, and nothing to say." He scooped Loris up and carried her to the bed. He'd carried other women, for he knew how to settle her on the bed gently, without jostling her shoulder.

"Why wouldn't you write to your sister, Thomas?" Loris asked, scooting to the edge of the bed to unbelt her robe.

This closeness at the end of the day, Thomas's assistance at the vanity, his relative state of undress, should have been awkward, but instead, his presence comforted. Couples spoke this way, of everything and nothing. Couples ended the day together.

Loris doubted she and Thomas would ever be such a couple, and that made her want even more whatever memories she could purloin now.

"Let me do that," Thomas growled, coming around the bed. He knelt before Loris and untied the belt to her robe, then paused with his forehead pressed to her knee. "I expect I'll have nightmares tonight."

Loris ran a hand through his damp hair. "We all will, though we're all safe and mostly sound. Tell me about your sister."

Thomas rose on a sigh and just like that, finished unbuttoning his waistcoat. "Theresa reminds me of you in many ways. She even looks a little like you—tall, dark-haired, though her eyes are brown rather than gray. As a boy, I thought she was the font of all wisdom, nearly an adult, but much more full of mischief."

His waistcoat ended up draped over the low back of the vanity stool. Next he sat on a cedar chest to pull off his boots and stockings. He tugged his shirt over his head, the voluminous linen billowing in the candlelight.

Loris wanted to tell Thomas to slow down so she could savor the gradual revealing of his nudity, but she feared to interrupt his recitation.

"This appetite for mischief you speak of, Thomas. It did not follow you into adulthood."

He paused, his hands on his falls, lashes lowered. "I beg to differ."

Loris balled up her robe and fired it at him one-handed. "That's pleasure. Pleasure and mischief are related, but not always the same. Those boys frolicking in your pond where up to mischief. What do you suppose they were doing on your property today?"

Two sets of buttons came undone while Loris waited for Thomas's answer. In all her rounds of the property, checking gates, measuring water levels, monitoring the corn crops, assessing how long to leave livestock in this pasture, or let that pasture fallow, she hadn't seen the boys at the pond again.

Though they'd apparently been near the manor this morning.

"I do not like that frown," Thomas said, stepping out of his breeches as if he'd disrobed before Loris a thousand other times. "You are not a great admirer of little boys, I fear. This does not bode well for our sons."

More casual nudity, this time of the heart. Thomas was not teasing, and Loris's reaction was as much pain as pleasure, for she was unlikely to be the mother of Thomas's children.

"Those boys hadn't been swimming, Thomas. None of them had wet hair or wet anything."

He folded the last of his clothes over the vanity stool.

"Then the boys hadn't been swimming *yet*. The heat and humidity earlier today were awful."

Thomas turned to bank the fire and blow out the lamp on the vanity, but in his great self-possession, he paused for a moment first, scratching his chest and yawning.

"Are you certain you won't ravish me?" Loris asked. "Not even one small ravishment?" Not even if she begged?

Thomas set aside the fireplace poker, pushed the screen against the stones of the hearth, and crossed to the bed. His stride was fluid and relaxed, as if a state of thorough arousal was of no moment whatsoever.

"I'm not the ravishing kind," he said. "I might make slow, sweet, tender love on occasion, or pleasure a lady witless, or devote my every attention to her most secret longings, but never ravish."

"Then I suppose I'll just have to ravish you."

One corner of his mouth twitched, a glimmer of a hint of a ghost of a shadow of a smile.

"With one good arm, you'd ravish me?" he asked, climbing onto the bed.

"I'm the inventive sort," Loris said, gritting her teeth against the bounce and jostle of a large man making himself comfortable beside her. She pivoted, swinging a leg over Thomas's hips.

"Miss Tanner, you shock me."

"Hold me," Loris said, curling down against Thomas's chest. "I'll have a few nightmares of my own, you know. All three of you disappeared into that inferno, Beckman was ready to plant me a facer rather than let me go in after you, and I was ready to do the same to him."

"A bad moment for all," Thomas said, wrapping his arms around her. "You kept your head and called us to safety. I had lost my way, you know."

What little calm Loris had assembled as the day had gone along deserted her. "*Lost* your way?"

"I was using the last of my strength to drag Nicholas into the saddle room, and I was certain I was taking him to safety. We would have died in there, while I figured out the error I'd made. I could not see a thing, and Fairly was weakening with each step."

Tears were useless, Loris had learned that as a child, but she cried anyway. The thought of losing Thomas was worth tears, especially when he might have perished with Nicholas and Fairly too.

She was still likely to lose Thomas, and that was also worth crying over.

"I could not have borne for today to be the end of you," Loris said, when she'd wet his chest and thoroughly wrinkled a handkerchief. "I would have gone after you, and Beckman and Jamie would have been on my heels."

Thomas's hand on her hair was as gentle as a nightingale's song. "With your injured shoulder, Beckman unable to take a single deep breath, and Jamie three times your age and no bigger than a minute, you would have come after three men, each of whom outweighs you by five stone. What of your responsibility to Linden, Loris Tanner? Who would have tended my acres and looked after my farms if you'd perished today?"

Loris tossed the handkerchief in the direction of the nightstand. Thomas was still quite aroused, but seemed in no hurry to do anything about it.

While Loris was frantic to make love with him. "Your tenants are all experienced farmers. They'd manage without me."

But Loris would not have managed without Thomas. She'd chosen an awful time to develop a sentimental attachment, and yet reason, prudence, self-restraint, all of her old friends had deserted her.

She missed them even less than she missed her father.

Loris made love to Thomas then, conscious all the while

that he was being careful with her, mindful of her injury, and simply mindful. His caresses were deliberate, his pleasuring of her measured and relentless.

"I like this," Loris whispered, as Thomas closed his hands gently over her breasts. She hadn't taken off her nightgown, hadn't had time to when joining their bodies was so much more urgent.

Thomas made the slide of fabric over tender skin a wicked education.

"You like being in charge," he countered, closing his teeth lightly over a silk-clad nipple and arching into Loris's heat. "Like being the one to say how fast, how hard, how—sweet saints."

Loris experimented with inner muscles, with speed and depth, but in the end, she surrendered every pretense of self-restraint and let Thomas have all the passion she was capable of—kisses, sighs, groans, caresses, and her body, undulating in counterpoint to his with an abandon that shocked her.

Truly, she ravished him, taking for herself as much as she could endure and inflicting the same on Thomas, until they were both spent, and she was panting on his chest.

For a moment, Loris made herself face the notion that, like her father, she could be utterly selfish. Instead of explaining her worries to Thomas, she'd taken advantage of him and allowed the excuse of emotion to overrule the demands of common sense.

Selfishness was seductive in a way she hadn't known. A bit of her anger at her father slipped away, but only a bit.

Thomas's hands on her back were slow and warm, and sleep beckoned even before he'd slipped from her body.

"Marry me, Loris Tanner. Promise me you'll be my wife, my baroness, my love."

This was ravishment of a different order, of Loris's heart, her hopes and dreams, and while she might keep secrets from Thomas—about Micah Tanner, about his possible role in all the difficulties at Linden—she would not lie to Thomas about marriage.

"You've had an awful day," she said, kissing his cheek. "You're disconcerted and not yourself. Propose to me another time, Thomas, and we'll have a sensible discussion."

His caresses paused, then resumed. "You are slow to trust. I understand that. I will ask again, because a woman doesn't make love as you just did, without a thought to preventing conception, without a thought for anything save the passion of the moment, unless she's in the arms of a man she cares for and knows she can rely on."

Without a thought to preventing conception.

God in heaven, Thomas was right. He'd tried to withdraw, but Loris had not allowed him to.

She cast about for dismay, for self-recrimination, for any steadying shadow of a proper reaction to her folly, and found only a backward pride that she'd allowed herself this occasion of honest pleasure with Thomas.

A steward learned not to worry about the harvest until the crop was in jeopardy, or perhaps Loris had simply chosen an unfortunate time to adopt her father's heedlessness.

"In this, I trust you," she said. "I shouldn't, part of me doesn't want to, and it's probably not wise, but you're right. If you give your word, you'll keep it. If you say you'll come home for supper, then home you'll be." *If I conceive a child, and you learn of it, you'll insist on marrying me.*

How had this happened?

"I'm as surprised as you are," Thomas whispered, patting Loris's hip. "I never expected I'd fall in love with my land steward, you know. Pass me that handkerchief, please."

I never expected to fall in love... Pass me the handkerchief.

Thomas was being kind, slipping an earth-shaking declaration into the conversation between mundane intimacies. Loris let him deal with the inelegant realities following lovemaking, while she...

"My shoulder doesn't hurt as much."

"Fairly says affection is powerful medicine," Thomas replied, tossing the handkerchief toward the vanity. "Lady Fairly agrees. I am becoming convinced of the same conclusion. Shall you sleep upon me, Loris Tanner?"

He'd have her become Loris, Baroness Sutcliffe, steward of Linden, even though she was first and foremost the daughter of a cowardly sot who was also a possible rapist-turned-arsonist.

"I will sleep beside you, sir, provided you absent yourself before you're noticed," Loris said, shifting off of Thomas and tucking herself along his side. Thomas was warm, though he took up rather a lot of room.

"I'll scamper right back across the roof, and the dew-fall will make it only slightly damp," Thomas said.

Loris kissed his shoulder. "You climbed across *the roof* to get to my balcony? With the rain making everything slippery and no moon worth the name? Thomas, do not tempt fate, please. Better my reputation be dragged through the mud than you fall from the roof."

Tears threatened all over again, because whatever else was true—about Micah Tanner, arsonists, and other ne'er-do-wells—Loris could not be responsible for bringing harm to Thomas.

She would harm him, though. If she heeded a summons from her feckless father, she'd hurt Thomas terribly.

"Settle, madam. I've been traipsing across roofs since I was a boy. Sutcliffe Keep is mostly an old castle, with all manner of peculiar architecture. As a child I learned to climb up the very walls, and my sister did too."

"No wonder you grasp my situation without having it explained to you," Loris said, smoothing a hand over his flat belly. "You were left to raise yourself and did the best you could. One grows self-reliant, despite one's fears."

Thomas trapped her hand in his before she could explore

in a more southerly direction.

"That's why I might well answer Theresa's letter."

Theresa, Thomas's only family, who had disappointed him bitterly. Truly, his situation was not that different from Loris's, though she might well become another disappointment to him.

"You'll answer her letter because she climbed stone walls with you?" Loris asked.

"Because I see in your situation what it can do to a woman when she's abandoned by her only family and left to wonder, month after month, then year after year, how her errant family member goes on. Is he alive? Is he safe? Does he think of me? Why does he stay away if he's free to come back?"

Loris was glad for the darkness then, glad Thomas could not see the pain his words brought her. Whatever she'd expected him to say, it hadn't been... that.

"I wonder less and less, Thomas." How she hated to lie to him.

"Theresa has written to me, time and again, and yet she doesn't hear back from me. I'm not that little boy anymore, not that callow youth, bewildered at her choices or her selfishness. She was only a few years older than I, and yet, I attributed to her perfect adult judgment, perfect wisdom."

As Loris had wanted to attribute the same qualities to her father, who had been—and still was—an adult. If he was alive.

"You should write to her," Loris said. "You should invite her to visit, in fact."

Micah Tanner could not remain in Sussex any longer than necessary to collect his daughter and leave England. Loris had no delusions about that. Thomas would need family around him if Micah's plans bore fruit, and one estranged sister was better than nothing and no one.

"I might invite her to visit," Thomas said. "I want her to meet my intended."

"I am not your intended." *Though you are my beloved.*

Thomas shifted, gently pushing Loris to her right side. "Of course, you're not. We're merely sharing a bed, in a house with seventeen bedrooms, because it makes less work for the housemaids."

"You're laughing at me, Baron." Thomas was also wrapping himself around her, a blanket of warmth and reassurance Loris needed badly and deserved not at all.

"I admire you endlessly, and desire you almost as often. Do you ever think your father might come back here, Loris?"

The question was devastatingly casual.

"I pray he does not, Thomas, for he left under a cloud of scandal, and to return might mean to stick his neck in a noose."

Thomas wrapped an arm around Loris's waist. "I'll find him for you. You can have no peace until you know his fate, I understand that. Trust me, and I'll get to the bottom of his situation, and then you'll become my baroness."

Thomas's breathing became even, and when Loris sensed it was safe to do so, she used the edge of the sheet to wipe the tears from her cheeks.

* * *

Sailors were sustained in significant measure by their rations of grog. Thomas had known that, and had, from time to time enjoyed a tot of rum. When he and Fairly had boarded a vessel for the short voyage from Ceylon to the Indian mainland, the merest whiff of rum from the person of the English captain had, nonetheless, left Thomas uneasy.

With the whiff of rum troubling him, Thomas had noticed that ropes on the deck hadn't been tidily coiled. They'd been piled in heaps. The mainsail had been much and haphazardly mended. From a distance the ship had looked seaworthy enough, but Thomas's instincts had said otherwise.

They had sailed to within sight of land across the Gulf of Mannar, when a squall had erupted. As the storm had buffeted the ship, Thomas and Fairly had struggled alongside the crew to keep the vessel afloat. The entire time Thomas had battled the sea to get to shore, his sustaining emotion had been not fear for his life, but rage.

A sober crew, a sober captain, could have saved the ship. Thomas ought to have known better, ought to have seen the signs. He'd slogged his way to shore, furious with himself, with the captain, with the storm, and determined to locate Fairly, whom he'd last seen clinging to a floating spar.

The same sense of being surrounded by portents of doom dogged Thomas in the days leading up to the barn raising.

After rain drenched the remains the stable, hot weather blazed anew, tempers flared, and even the presence of the Viscountess Fairly didn't seem to quell a growing tension between Nick Haddonfield and the viscount.

A commotion outside the library at mid-morning heralded the arrival of Thomas's intended along with his stable master. Like everybody else, they seemed to be at daggers drawn, and the four small boys between them apparently sensed the tension.

"Baron, my apologies for disturbing you," Loris began. "Your cheese cave was beset by thieves, though, and justice must be done."

A scrawny lot of thieves. Thomas recognized Timmie, the smallest, though even in the few weeks since Thomas had last seen the boy, he'd grown. He was less a little boy, and more of a... problem.

"The children will apologize," Nicholas said, arms crossed, which only accentuated his height. "And their parents will be notified. That should be an end to it."

"We didn't take anything, sir," Timmie said. "We play in the cave because it's cool, and we're not supposed to go swimming without one of the older boys."

Thomas had been totaling sums of supplies needed for the barn raising, everything from nails to kegs of ale to sheets of tin to the flowers Loris insisted ought to be planted around any stable yard. He mentally added a sum to put a gate over the mouth of the cave.

"Caves are dangerous," Loris snapped, skirts swishing as she paced to the empty hearth. "Bats can attack, little boys can get lost. Caves are dark and damp, and crawling with bugs and poisonous snakes."

The boys, who would probably go their entire lives without seeing a poisonous snake, were clearly fascinated.

"Adders are shy," Thomas said, coming around the side of his desk, "but if cornered, they'll bite, and their venom is noxious in the extreme. Miss Tanner is right to be concerned for you."

For that's what this was—concern that only masqueraded as outrage.

"If the cave is full of snakes, why do you put the cheese there?" Timmie asked.

"The snakes guard the cheese," Thomas improvised, while Nick endured a coughing fit and Loris looked like she wanted to smack every male in the library with the fireplace poker. "Nobody in their right mind goes into a cheese cave without proper protection."

One upset land steward probably sent all the snakes sprinting for their best hiding places.

"If the cave is dark, how do the snakes see you coming?" Timmie asked.

Bright lad. His mental nimbleness probably earned him frequent thrashing, for the same trait had seen Thomas's little backside well acquainted with the birch rod.

"The snakes feel your footsteps," Nick supplied. "They can hear your racket as you practice swearing with your friends."

Several pairs of eyes took to studying the carpets, small bare feet shuffled about.

"We're sorry, Miss Tanner," Timmie said, clearly the fellow most used to dealing with upset females. "We won't go in the cave again."

"And we won't use foul language again," another fellow volunteered. "Not around a lady, anyway."

"And we won't eat any more peaches from the baron's—"

Timmie's elbow found its way to the third boy's ribs.

"Well, peaches are the best," the taller boy said, "and nobody else grows them. Pa says they're from Cathay, and Ma likes them, too."

"Thieves," Loris muttered. "Trespassers. For all we know, they set fires in their idle moments, too."

The silence in the library became deadly serious. Timmie took to staring at his own dusty toes.

"Mr. Haddonfield," Thomas said, "perhaps you'll escort Miss Tanner to the stable. She'll want to assess the progress of the fellows clearing away the debris."

Thomas himself had made that inspection not an hour earlier, surprised at how easily an entire building could be wiped off the property.

Loris preceded Nick from the room at a forced march, and in truth, Thomas could not blame her for being angry.

Or worried about children whose parents paid insufficient heed to their safety.

"You lot," Thomas said, leaning back against his desk. "If you want to be able to sit down at any point in the next week, you will be dead honest with me. I need to know what you saw the day of the fire, and then I have jobs for you. Important jobs that you must not shirk."

The three larger boys looked to Timmie, who met Thomas's gaze squarely. "We didn't take any cheese, Baron, and we don't lie. Well, Harry tells a fib or two, but only to his ma and never on Sunday. What do you want to know, and what jobs do you have for us?"

CHAPTER SEVENTEEN

By night, Loris clung to Thomas until he slipped from her bed before dawn, and then she clung to her endless list of duties. Jamie mentioned to her quietly that he might have seen a fellow in Trieshock who'd borne a resemblance to Micah Tanner, but concluded that Micah Tanner would never have ridden such a modest gelding, or worn such an old pair of boots.

And thus, when Thomas and Nick planned another outing to Trieshock to fetch the last of the supplies needed for the barn raising, Loris accompanied them.

"You're quiet this morning," Thomas observed as they rode along. This early in the day, the hedgerows provided some shade, but soon the air would be heavy with humidity and heat. Another storm was brewing. Loris only hoped it held off until the barn raising was finished the next day.

"Tomorrow will be busy," she said. "I have much to think about. Will Lord Fairly and his lady depart once your new stable is built?"

Loris liked Fairly, but he missed nothing, and for all he

doted on his viscountess, Fairly was also very protective of Thomas.

Fifteen yards ahead, Nick drew his horse to a halt in the shade of an enormous oak.

"Lady Fairly intends to accompany us to the assembly," Thomas said. "Rather, she intends to accompany you. You have an ally, Loris, another ally."

Another person who would be disappointed if they learned Loris had abandoned her post, and the baron, to take her father in hand. The reality was, Thomas would manage without Loris. He had friends, he had wealth, he had excellent judgment. Micah Tanner had only one daughter to keep him from folly, and her efforts hadn't been safeguard enough.

"What I have is a list of dry goods," Loris replied, "and you and Nicholas will be half the morning at the brewer's. Did you ever write to your sister?"

Thomas drew Rupert to a halt next to Buttercup. The morning would be long, and horses needed the occasional chance to blow.

"I have a letter for Theresa with me," Thomas said, "and I have a number of letters to post for Fairly as well. Nicholas, I don't suppose you have any mail to add to the stack?"

Nicholas had reverted to the man Loris had met two years ago. Reticent, unreadable, and hard working. He'd overseen the clearing away of the burned remains of the stable, dirty, back-breaking work that Nick took on without complaint.

Loris was comforted to think she might not be the only person at Linden guarding secrets and regrets.

Even that thin consolation evaporated into the morning's heat when Loris handed her reins off to a stable boy at the livery, and was slipped a note in return. She had to wait until Thomas and Nicholas had sauntered off to the brewery to unfold the scrap of paper, and what she read had her nearly fainting with frustration.

Passage to the New World awaits us in Brighton. Pack all of your belongings, attract no notice. Be ready to leave soon.

The note needed no signature, for Loris knew her father's bold scrawl. His handwriting hadn't changed, nor had his expectation that regardless of the inconvenience to her, regardless of her needs, regardless of obligations she might have to anybody else, his daughter would leap to his side, ready as ever to protect him from his own folly as best she could.

Before Loris had met Thomas, a man who respected her and offered her only honorable sentiments, she would have rejoiced to receive such a note. Her gratitude and relief would have lightened her every step, and she'd have lathered her horse getting home to pack.

Now, she stuffed the note in her pocket, and tucked away a good deal of resentment along with it.

* * *

"We're supposed to taste the ale before we buy it," Nicholas said as he and Thomas left the Trieshock brewery. "Then we taste it again when we get the barrels back to Linden. This is how it's done. I thought you were once a respected man of business, Sutcliffe."

Thomas had been a man of business, and now he was a man who meant business.

"Stop dawdling, Nicholas. I intend to get back to the livery before Miss Tanner does, because I want to show you something. She was determined to hover at our elbow earlier, and I can only hope what I need to show you is still there."

Nick's steps slowed even more. "Whatever it is, wouldn't you rather show Fairly?"

"Fairly is enjoying the company of his lady wife, which in this heat, says volumes about the extent of their marital devotion. Come along, Nicholas."

"They go to the pond," Nick said. "At night. It's... inconvenient, when a fellow thinks to finish off his day with a swim."

"They don't spend the entire night at the pond. I've seen them wandering up to the house by moonrise. Any balcony along the back side of the building has a view of the path. Their progress is anything but purposeful."

Thomas would never regard a certain sturdy oak in quite the same light. When Fairly had kissed his wife against the tree's trunk—kissed her, *at least*—the very boughs had shaken in a celebration of spouses reunited.

"I've heard the gossip," Nick said. "Even here in Sussex. Her ladyship once managed Fairly's brothel. One marvels that the woman could have any enthusiasm left for the male of the species."

A memory rose from the dust at Thomas's feet, of a very tall gentleman flirting gently with the ladies at the Pleasure House. He'd been blond—not as blond as Nick Haddonfield—an earl's heir, and well regarded by the women, though Thomas had no recollection of any woman taking the fellow abovestairs. Dressed to the teeth, genial, generous, self-possessed....

Bellefonte's heir. Thomas had preferred to spend his evenings at the Pleasure House in the office, with the ledgers and receipts, rather than in the parlors, unless the ladies summoned him forward to enforce good manners among the patrons. He'd seen Nick only the once on the premises, in the smoky shadows of late evening, but even across a dimly lit room, a man of Nick's proportions made an impression.

"Fairly's related by marriage to a marquis, an earl, a viscount," Thomas said, picking up the reins of the conversation. "He does business with any number of dukes, princes, and lower angels. He and his viscountess will not participate in greater society, but neither will they be cut. Letty will be happy with her viscount."

Thomas and Nick had reached the livery, which enjoyed a good deal of shade. Horses hitched out front dozed or swished at flies. A pair of stable boys sat scrubbing bridles beneath the tree.

"In here," Thomas said, leading Nick back to the stall where Rupert stood munching hay. "Look at this." He pointed to a boot print below the wooden water bucket hung in the corner. Anywhere else in the stall, a horse or a stable boy would have obliterated the print in the course of a normal day.

"This print is the same as the one you and Belmont saw?" Nick asked, going down on one knee.

Thomas unfolded the sketch he carried with him everywhere. "This track isn't fresh. The edges are not as crisp, there's dust collecting along the grooves, but it's either the same or an uncanny match."

Nick peered at the print and laid the sketch beside it. "That's a match, Baron. If that boot belongs to your culprit, your culprit was here."

"Yes, but when?" The print could be two days old or two weeks old. It could mean nothing, or it might lead to the identity of the arsonist.

"Shouldn't Belmont be informed?" Nick asked, straightening.

"I'll tell him. He's bringing over his best draft team to help tomorrow."

"Tell him today, before half the shire is thronging your stable yard. You'll want lookouts watching the ground for this same boot print."

"The boys you found pilfering cheese have been assigned that task." Among others. "What are you staring at, Nicholas?"

For Haddonfield was peering over Thomas's shoulder, but when Thomas turned, all he saw were the usual elements of a busy stable yard on a summer morning—milling horses, gossiping men, dust drifting in the air behind a passing carriage, a barefoot boy eating a piece of bread in the branches of the oak.

"I thought I saw Miss Tanner," Nick said, rubbing his chin,

"whom you must also inform of the day's developments."

Nick was lying—he'd seen something unexpected—though he had a point.

"I'll discuss what we've seen with her. If Chesterton is our miscreant, Miss Tanner needs to keep an eye out for him." Nobody had seen Chesterton since the fire, which might be coincidence—and it might not.

"Shall I fetch the horses?" Nick asked.

"Are you in a hurry, Haddonfield? First you drag your feet, now you want to be away from this place? Have you seen one of your London creditors, perhaps? I can't imagine any other explanation for why an earl's heir would be rusticating with a muck fork in his hands."

The heat had snatched those words from Thomas, for he hadn't meant to confront Haddonfield here, now, in a bustling livery stable with Loris due to come upon them at any moment.

Nick raised a hand, catching the eye of a groom. That single movement—elegant, casual, confident—banished the last of Thomas's doubts about his stable master's identity. Nicholas Haddonfield *expected* to be obeyed. He expected that his smallest gesture would merit compliance, and not simply as a result of his height and brawn.

"You had a hand in running Fairly's brothel," Nick said. "Is that where you saw me?"

Relief trickled through the irritation Thomas felt with his stable master, and with himself. Secrets were distasteful, but a man was entitled to reasonable privacy.

"You don't deny you're an earl's heir, pretending to be a rural stable master?"

"Why should I?" Nick asked, keeping his voice down. "Working for a living has not been outlawed, though finding decent employment has become damned difficult. I'll be on my way once the harvest is in, as will Beckman."

"Your brother?"

Nick nodded. A stable boy led Rupert past; another led

Evan out.

"Why rusticate at all, Haddonfield—or should I use a courtesy title?" Thomas moved off in the direction of the stable yard, Nick following. For the balance of this conversation, they needed quiet, and to be able to spot Loris before she could hear them.

"The courtesy title is Viscount Reston," Nick said as they gained a corner of the shady stable yard. "If you use it, I will knock you into the dirt, and then Miss Tanner will be wroth with me."

"I would have to return your felicitations," Thomas said, "and then Fairly would be amused at our mutual expense. Does he know?"

Apparently, when Nick Haddonfield lied, he rubbed his chin. "His lordship might have seen me at the same establishment, correct?"

A question for a question. Fairly knew, or Nick suspected he knew.

"Her ladyship would have seen you, but why hide, Haddonfield? Will Belmont have to take you up in the king's name when he learns who your father is?"

The small boy leapt down from the tree and scampered off, darting through the passersby to head straight for… Loris. She exchanged a few words with the child, shook her head, and hurried on.

"My crime," Nick said, "is being an unmarried heir to a title, and having a very determined father. Many share my fate, but I refuse to submit to it. The earl agreed I could have two years to rusticate with Beckman, who has benefited from some time in the country."

"Oh, right. With the muscle he's sporting, your baby brother can next seek employment as a pugilist. You're both simply hiding from the matchmakers?"

Fairly had dodged a few of those, and even Thomas had felt their hot breath on the back of his bachelorhood once word of the barony had got out.

"Hiding from the matchmakers," Nick said, "and in Beck's case, from bad memories and the folly they can tempt a man to. Miss Tanner approaches, and I'd appreciate it if you'd not disclose my antecedents to her."

"She'll not pester you for your hand in marriage, Haddonfield, not if you're next in line for the crown itself. Find the time to tell her the truth, though, for she's been lied to, misled, put in difficult positions, and otherwise disrespected enough."

Nonetheless, Loris should know by now that anybody seeking to further imperil her welfare would answer to Linden's present owner. On that thought, Thomas went to greet his intended, and left Viscount Muck Fork standing under the tree.

* * *

The new stable was a simple wooden rectangle with a tin roof, and most of the interior work yet to be done. As Loris had in the position of steward, the new stable met the demands of necessity, but was hardly an ideal exponent of its class.

"I have not been this tired since... I have never been this tired," Thomas said, taking the place beside her on Linden's back terrace. The sun had dropped, the moon would soon be up, and a nightingale offered a melody to its mate, though the season for courting was long past.

"I spent most of my day tripping over children," Loris said, as Thomas's arm came around her shoulders. She'd also tripped over Giles Pettigrew at least twice an hour. "By noon, half the men were tipsy, and shortly thereafter, the women were dipping into the sangria."

"And yet, the stable stands plumb," Thomas murmured.

He'd bathed, and his hair curled damply at his nape. Loris had purposely avoided him throughout the day, but she'd seen him, shirt sleeves rolled back, shirt open at the throat, sawdust in his hair, and a tankard of ale in his hand.

She'd fallen in love all over again, with a man willing to work hard, get his hands dirty, exchange a wink with the ladies, and thank each man individually for his help. In one day, Thomas Jennings had done more to secure the esteem of his tenants than many landowners did in a decade.

"Your stable stands plumb, while I can barely stand at all," Loris said. "The viscountess deserves a medal. She kept everybody fed without Cook having a single tantrum."

"Letty was raised in a vicarage," Thomas replied, taking Loris's hand. "She knows about soothing ruffled feathers. Do you truly dislike children, Loris?"

Thomas had given his little cheese thieves assignments, and they'd been underfoot at every turn.

"I suspect the problem is that I do not like my own childhood."

Since yesterday, Loris's adulthood had taken a turn for the worse too. Bad enough Papa had sent her a note, then he'd expected her to have a reply ready to transmit through some grimy boy who'd accosted Loris near the livery. All she'd been able to do was confirm receipt of Papa's summons.

"I've asked my sister to visit," Thomas said, kissing Loris's knuckles. "She'll probably have an apoplexy when she gets my letter."

Loris let her head rest on Thomas's shoulder, sadness and relief giving her weariness a crushing weight.

"I'm proud of you, Thomas Jennings. Old hurts don't heal themselves, we must find the courage to heal them. Your sister will weep with joy when she reads that letter, and you will welcome her with open arms."

Though very likely, Loris would not be on hand to witness the reunion. Thank God that Papa was alive and apparently well, but damn Papa's timing along with all of his other reprehensible traits.

"You will not be as impressed when you learn my motives, my dear. Fairly and his lady will return to London after the assembly on Saturday. My sister is old enough to be an adequate chaperone, and her presence will allow you to remain under my roof."

Oh, my love. "I've asked nearly everybody, Thomas, and no one has seen Chesterton in days. If he's left the area, then I have no need to bide at the manor house."

"Am I intruding?" Nicholas asked, from the French doors.

Loris sat up but remained at Thomas's side. "Of course not, Nicholas."

"Of course you are," Thomas countered, "but you did the work of six men today, so I must express myself graciously."

"That's your version of gracious?" Nick muttered, arranging a wrought iron chair to face out across the lawn.

"If I haven't said it before," Thomas went on, "thank you. You are a prodigious hard worker, as is Beckman. Miss Tanner, I am in danger of falling asleep at your side, so I will leave you in Nicholas's company, though the porter is on duty just outside the library door if you need anything. If Haddonfield makes the least improper advance, he'll be dead by morning."

Thomas brushed a kiss to her knuckles, rose, and slipped into the house.

"Sutcliffe is in love with you," Nicholas said after a moment of silence. "Unless I very much mistake the matter, you are fond of him as well."

Would this day never end? "You mistake the matter, egregiously. I am not fond of Sutcliffe, I am utterly besotted. Why that is any of your business, I do not know."

Loris bolted to her feet, unwilling to be lectured by anybody on the topic of her loyalties and affections, but Nicholas encircled her wrist in a gentle, implacable grip.

"If you will give me twenty minutes of your time, Miss Tanner, I'll explain why your situation is very much my business."

* * *

The lady resumed her place beside him.

Nicholas Haddonfield considered himself among the humbler men facing inheritance of an earldom, and yet, he'd been very proud of his scheme to hide in the wilds of Sussex. He'd planned to dodge holy matrimony for a time, give Beckman a place to find his balance, and look after a familial obligation too long neglected.

Sitting in the dark with a besotted, unhappy Loris Tanner, Nick was anything but proud of himself.

"Nicholas, do not play games," she said. "I'll kick you where it hurts, and then Thomas will finish the job, abetted by Lord Fairly."

"To provide that aid, Fairly would have to extricate himself from the arms of his viscountess, which he is unable to do except at mealtimes and for Sunday services. I'm your cousin, in a manner of speaking."

Oh, that was smoothly done of him.

"You're my *cousin*?"

"Step-cousin, actually. My step-mama and your cousin were first cousins, and Beckman is my half-brother, so you and he are cousins in truth. We have four sisters and a few more brothers too, also your cousins."

Nick had chosen his moment out of desperation, and now wished he'd at least found a time and place where he could see the lady's face.

"I have *cousins*? This has to do with Papa, doesn't it? Every single bad, hard, embarrassing thing in my life has to do with Papa."

Having cousins should not be bad, hard, or embarrassing. "Please keep your voice down, or you'll have Sutcliffe out here breathing fire."

She rose, and Loris Tanner was nearly the same height as Nick's sisters, all save little Della. Loris had their chin, their swooping brows. Haddonfield women were a striking lot, and Loris would fit in with them well.

Out of simple courtesy, Nick got to his feet.

"Thomas is too tired to breathe fire," Loris said, wandering to edge of the flagstones, "and he's worried as well. I dearly hope you have an explanation for remaining silent about your relationship to me, Nicholas. I am not pleased with you."

The fragrance of lavender wafted on the humid air, and lavender symbolized mistrust. Nick favored it in his biscuits, when ginger was in short supply.

"I am not pleased with myself," he said, making no move to approach her, "but I gave your father my word I'd keep my silence. If you'd like to hear the rest of my tale, I'll finish breaking that word."

The benefit of a conversation held in darkness was that Loris could not see Nick's expression either, could not see his self-loathing, could not assess how weary he was of keeping this and other secrets.

"Why would you break your word?" Loris asked, resuming her place on the settee where she'd been cuddled up with Sutcliffe. "You seem like an honorable fellow."

"I am honorable, mostly. When your father ran afoul of the widow, he had nowhere to turn for help except his deceased wife's family."

Nick could see enough to know Loris was resting her forehead on her updrawn knees, like a weary girl. Micah Tanner had much to answer for.

"Papa ran afoul of the bottle, Nicholas. The widow merely took advantage of that misstep."

"Micah Tanner is sober enough now," Nick said, though the statement was as much hope as fact. "As near as I can tell, that is. He came to us two years ago, nothing but a decent horse and a set of clothes to his name."

"And Mama's miniature and a Bible."

"To convince us he was truly Micah Tanner, because we hadn't seen him since you were an infant."

Nick wanted to blurt out the rest, then hop on his mare and canter away into the night, but he'd promised Beckman he wouldn't do that. For the first time, though, he understood why Beck had stayed drunk more or less for years: Sometimes, life hurt terribly, and no amount of philosophy, prayer, patience, or reason made any sense of the pain.

"I have no memory of you," Loris said. "I barely have any memory of my mother, and Papa rarely spoke of her. I wasn't even sure they were married."

Such stark loss filled those few words, Nick took the risk of appropriating the far end of the settee.

"Your mama loved Tanner awfully, and they were properly married in the Haddondale church, though her family wasn't happy about the match."

"She loved him?"

This would matter to a girl raised without her mother, and to a woman falling in love for the first time.

"My father says she did, Tanner claimed she did. She loved him enough to marry him when he'd barely a penny to his name, and only an offer of employment as an under-steward to some earl in the north."

"She must have loved him," Loris said. "She went away with him, left everybody and everything she knew to be with him. Papa expects me to do the same."

Well, hell. "How do you know that?"

"He sent me a note. Nicholas, I don't want to go, but Papa has nobody else."

Nick had caught sight of Tanner in Trieshock, and had not wanted to believe the evidence of his own eyes.

He plowed on with his story, though he could not foresee the tale ending happily. "Your mother fell ill not long after you were born. When it became apparent she would not recover, she asked Tanner to take her home to her family. He was between posts, and unable to care for her and for you adequately."

"You're making excuses for him," Loris said, simply stating a fact, not hurling an accusation. "Everybody does. I certainly did."

"He made an agreement with my father," Nick said. "We would look after your mother, Tanner would keep us informed of his whereabouts and yours at all times. We kept our part of the bargain."

Though Loris made not a sound, Nick could tell she was crying. Far off to the west, lightning flickered against pale clouds, but immediately above, stars were coming out.

"Papa took off with me, and you heard from him when he needed money, if you heard from him at all."

"Loris, I'm sorry. He changed his name, from Micah to Jeremiah, to Luke. From Tanner to Tanford, to Tranford."

Loris lifted her head. "When I was little, he did, but here he's always used his real name. His name is Micah Lucian Jeremiah Tanner. He inscribed that in the Bible."

The Bible that Tanner had taken from her when it had suited his purposes.

"His drinking is under control," Nick said. "As far as we know. My father's last arrangement with Tanner was as follows: Tanner would disclose your whereabouts to us, and for two years, leave you in peace while Beckman and I kept an eye on you. If Tanner stayed sober for those two years, then we would not interfere if he still felt the need to approach you."

A stupid bargain, though at the time, it had loomed before Nick like an answer to several different prayers—for himself and his brother. They'd believed Tanner incapable of sobriety, and he'd proved them wrong.

"Why didn't you simply introduce yourself and invite me to the family seat?" Loris asked, dabbing at her cheeks with her sleeve. "Would I have been welcome?"

"Of course you'd be welcome. Belle Maison is enormous, and my sisters would spoil you rotten, and my father has longed to meet you again." Though if Loris ran off with Micah Tanner, heaven knew if any of that would happen. "My father was insistent that Tanner leave you in peace, for knowledge of your papa's whereabouts could have become problematic for you. Tanner did not want us to take you away from all that was familiar to you. On that point, he would not budge."

Too late, Nick had realized what Micah Tanner had truly been about.

"He wanted me here to look after Linden, and he didn't want me getting ideas," Loris said. "The sort of ideas I might stumble across if I were the pampered relation of a doting earl. Ideas about new dresses, servants, or eligible young men."

The sort of ideas any proper father *should* want his daughter to get, in other words.

"More likely, he wanted you where he knew the terrain, the *dramatis personae*, the routines," Nick said. "He was not supposed to contact you until next month."

"Papa was always doing things he wasn't supposed to, Mrs. Pettigrew's allegations being a case in point. Then he'd do something else nobody should have been able to do—get rye to grow in a sour field, produce more twins by changing the breed of ram put to the ewes. Papa often said the rules were for people with no imagination."

How bitter she sounded, and how bewildered. Nick was weary too, but also relieved to have set aside at least one secret.

"Tanner claims he was nowhere near Mrs. Pettigrew," Nick said, "and that she'd been willing enough on previous occasions, if you'll forgive blunt speech."

Stars were coming out in great, pretty numbers, but off to the west, thunder rumbled in counterpoint to the lightning. This entire summer had been spent waiting for a storm to break, then enduring worse heat and humidity after it had.

"I don't know what I can and cannot forgive anymore, Nicholas," Loris said, shifting about to put her feet on the ground. "If Papa was so innocent, why did he run off? If he cared for me so much, why did he leave me here alone, when I might have been with family? Why did he keep that family from me for years?"

Nick rose and extended a hand down to her. "You'll soon be able to ask him those questions yourself."

Loris stood without benefit of Nick's assistance. Perhaps she hadn't seen his hand in the darkness, and perhaps she'd ignored it.

"I'll have time to ask Papa any number of questions," she said, preceding Nick into the house. "The more pressing issue is whether I'm still interested in his answers."

She left Nick in the darkened library and likely went above stairs to share a bed with the baron, whose household she was apparently soon to leave.

"Shite," Nick muttered to the silent books. "This was not how two years of bucolic peace and quiet were supposed to end, with broken hearts, and quite possibly, broken heads."

He resisted the urge to borrow a book without permission and instead went back out through the French doors to watch the thunder and lightning come closer, despite the stars winking above.

CHAPTER EIGHTEEN

Thomas had meant to leave Loris a note, a few words to ensure she would not be dismayed by his absence from her bed. Over the past few nights, he'd grown accustomed to her fragrance as slumber claimed him, to the feel of her in his arms.

Today had been exhausting, and tomorrow was the assembly, so Thomas had thought to leave his lady in peace. He'd found her lap desk and rummaged among the contents.

Then he'd not known what to write, so he'd blown out most of the candles and lain down on her bed. The sultry breeze had riffled the bed hangings, and fatigue had weighted Thomas's heart and soul.

He was still in Loris's bed when the door opened silently—he'd had the hinges oiled the same day Loris had moved in. She disrobed by the meager moonlight and didn't so much as glance in Thomas's direction.

Rather than come straight to bed, Loris used the wash water, first on her face. Her movements were slowed by weariness and, Thomas suspected, by worry.

"I'll do that," he said, coming off the bed and plucking the flannel from her hand. "Will it rain tonight?"

Loris made no move to retrieve the flannel or to cover herself. "What an irony that would be, if tomorrow's assembly was ruined by rain. You're still dressed."

Thomas drew off his shirt. He'd have no prayer of assessing her mood once her hands started wandering, so he left his breeches on.

"We'll remedy the rest of my oversight directly," he said, taking Loris's hand and sweeping the damp cloth from her shoulder to her wrist.

She permitted him to tend her, from her nape, to her long limbs, to the private places that Thomas refused to hurry past. The breeze gusted strongly enough to tease at the bed skirt and goose flesh rose on Loris's arms.

"You're too tired to scold me," Thomas said, lifting her against his chest. "I've let you take a chill."

"The cold feels good," she replied, scooting over when he'd set her on the bed. "I'll miss—"

Thomas paused between undoing the left side of his falls and undoing the right.

"You'll miss me when Theresa arrives," Thomas suggested, though of course, that hadn't been what Loris had nearly said. "If you think she'll bring strictest propriety with her, that won't happen, Loris. She might not come at all."

When Thomas had finished undressing, Loris held up the sheet and thin quilt and patted the mattress, a wifely courtesy that made Thomas's heart ache. If he ever did write her a love note, he'd tell her how much such simple gestures of welcome meant to him.

"Theresa will accept your invitation." Loris waited for Thomas to arrange himself among the pillows, then tucked herself against his side. "She'll accept at the first opportunity."

They fit together, Loris against Thomas's side, his arm around her shoulders. He took the space of a breath, of a silent prayer of thanks, to purely appreciate the wonder of this woman sharing a bed with him.

"Theresa and I are estranged," Thomas said, "in part because her grasp of propriety became tenuous. Long before most girls faced temptation, she embraced it wholly, though my cousins have something to answer for in that regard. They were older, they ought to have provided her a worthy example. Rather than guard her virtue, they assisted her to fling it into the sea."

Nobody else knew this story, not Fairly, not anybody.

"You hold yourself responsible," Loris said, smoothing a cool hand over Thomas's heart. "You should have protected her good name somehow when she was careless of it herself. My father—"

While the pale curtains billowed and Loris's skin warmed next to his, Thomas waited for whatever she'd say next.

Loris kissed his cheek and remained poised on her side, her mouth close to his.

"Your father?"

"I could not protect him, Thomas, not from the drink, not from his own stubbornness, and I worry. Nobody else worries about him, but I worry without ceasing. I can't seem to stop, even now."

While Thomas had been able to admit to only rage for his once-lovely sister. "What do you worry about?"

"Whose protection has Papa cast aside now? The next time he rides his horse into a church, who will plead with the magistrate not to lock him up? Who will hide his money when he's hours past sober and intent on buying gin with the coin needed for food? Who will remind the community that Micah Tanner has saved entire crops from ruin and found work for the menfolk even in the lean years?"

Thomas knew this struggle too, to recall the good, even though it made recollection of the bad more painful. He could not resolve the hurt for Loris, but he could distract her.

"Kiss me, love." He brushed her hair back from her brow. "Theresa will not judge me for sharing a bed with my intended, should she learn of it. I dare her to, in fact, when most engaged couples take the same liberties. Kiss me even though we're not engaged, simply because you and I enjoy our shared kisses, and you are entitled to have what makes you happy."

In this, though Loris had not accepted Thomas's suit, they were apparently in agreement. Loris pulled Thomas over her, and while the earth waited in vain for relief from the heat, and the sky vented futile drama in the dark, Thomas made love to his intended.

Loris's passion was at once languid and hot, relaxed and focused. She accepted Thomas into her arms and into her body with an eagerness that soothed his fears and fed his desire.

She found satisfaction easily, while Thomas held back, wondering if he'd ever hear words of love from her, words of commitment.

Insight hit him with the force of a sexual cataclysm: Loris could not give him words that had never been given to her, could not offer a commitment when none had ever been offered to her. Not a father, not a sibling, not the families who worked the tenant farms, no one had ever assured her of permanent loyalty.

But Thomas could. He could give her the words, and mean them.

"Loris Tanner, I love you." He added power to his thrusts, determined that she know satisfaction again. "I have never loved another as I love you, I never will. Marry me or not, I will always love you."

She clung to him in silence as they fell together, and clung to him still as her breathing gradually slowed.

Thomas tugged the sheets up over them both and let his lady have her dreams—or nightmares, more like.

His declaration of love had been honest, but like Loris, he'd withheld important words too. Thomas had not confessed to her that every word of her discussion with Nick on the terrace below had been audible to the man lying half-clothed among her sheets.

When Nick had asked Loris the question Thomas wrestled with moment by moment, her answer had broken his heart: She did not want to heed her father's summons, but she did not intend to refuse it.

Thomas extricated himself from Loris's embrace and dressed in silence. She was still his intended and would always be the woman he loved. His only consolation was that in heeding her father's summons, she'd likely break her own heart too.

* * *

"Are you nervous?"

Thomas's question was apparently sincere, for he posed it to Loris without a hint of levity.

"Yes, I am nervous." Anxiety had become Loris's constant companion. "I have never worn a dress so fine, and I expect to dance in public for the first time."

"With me," Thomas said, making a full circuit of her person. "You are lovely, but we must find the time to take you to London, where you will acquire finery of your own, rather than borrowed from the viscountess."

The fact that Loris would give the lovely dress back at the end of the evening was all that allowed her to wear it. Lady Fairly had found a deep blue, high-waisted silk dress edged in dark green and purple embroidery. White gloves, lavender dancing slippers, and a lavender lace fichu completed the ensemble.

Modest, but different, and so very lovely to wear. Waltzing in this dress would be like dancing through moonbeams.

"Tell everybody you borrowed this from the viscountess as well," Thomas said, holding out a small velvet-covered box.

Any minute, Nick or Lord Fairly, Loris's recently self-appointed bodyguards, would come strolling through the library door. Or perhaps they were Thomas's bodyguards—comforting thought—for he owned the stable that had been set ablaze.

"Thomas, put that box away before anybody sees it," Loris said, turning from the cheval mirror. "You must not give me gifts."

"You've given me gifts," he said, opening the box and drawing out a strand of lavender gems set in delicate silver links. "You've given me an estate that's the envy of the shire, given me your tireless hard work,"—he picked up Loris's wrist—"your loyalty."

Guilt kept Loris silent. She'd given Thomas her heart, but hadn't warned him her father lurked nearby, and might well be the author of all the harm Linden had suffered.

"I will wear it," Loris said, "but I'm giving it back at the end of the evening. A gift like this would cause talk if I admitted it came from you, and you don't deserve that."

He fastened the clasp, and the bracelet fit beautifully, a graceful weight around Loris's borrowed glove.

"Consider it a loan, then, from a friend who values you greatly."

Loris was on the point of kissing him—why must his expression be as grave as her mood?—when Lady Fairly came in with both Nicholas and the viscount.

"Miss Tanner, that dress never looked as well on me," her ladyship said. "You will be thronged with dazzled bachelors, all of them pledging undying devotion. Fairly, Nicholas, you will beat the presuming ones away, for Thomas will be too busy tripping over his own tongue."

Fairly kissed his wife's cheek. "I love it when you turn up protective, my dear."

His lordship frequently kissed his wife's cheek or her hand, and—Loris suspected—many places in between. Lady Fairly bore it all with an amused tolerance that seemed to encourage her husband to greater excesses.

"Miss Tanner," Thomas said, winging his arm. "You will save your waltzes for me, regardless of how pitifully young Pettigrew importunes you for them."

Just like that, the last private moment Loris might have had with Thomas before the evening's ordeal was over.

She took his arm and let him escort her down Linden's front steps to the waiting coach. Beckman was up on the box, looking dapper and tidy, if a bit self-conscious.

"Do you feel like a princess?" Thomas asked as he handed her up. "You look like one. My princess."

Loris felt like a fraud. If she confided to Thomas that Micah Tanner was in the area, she might feel less like a fraud and more like the woman who'd sealed her own father's doom.

Lady Fairly and her husband joined them, and the coach rocked as Nick climbed up on the box.

"Thomas, you cannot look at Miss Tanner like that in public," Lord Fairly said. "Though I can cast adoring gazes at my wife all I please."

He beamed, her ladyship preened, and Thomas smiled, while Loris felt sick. This was all wrong, and all so familiar.

The appearances were lovely—friendly people, pretty clothes, rural socializing in the offing; and yet, Micah Tanner, dear, dratted, and oblivious to the trouble he caused—cast a pall for Loris over every moment.

Papa might wait weeks to contact her again, he might accost her the very next time she was unaccompanied on the streets of Trieshock.

Not that she'd venture there on her own if she could help it.

"You're worried," Thomas said, leaning forward to brush a gloved finger between Loris's brows. "You will dance with me, the viscount, Nick, Beckman, and Belmont. Then you'll have the excuse of being too weary to dance with anybody else, and needing some air."

"A fine plan," Loris said, "though Giles Pettigrew has reminded me on at least six occasions that I also promised him a dance."

Loris would endure Giles's dancing, but how could she look Matthew—the magistrate himself—in the eye and make small talk when her silence abetted a possible felon?

"Don't plead an indisposition," her ladyship said. "People draw conclusions about indisposed women."

Fairly's lids lowered, and Thomas found something fascinating to study in the hedgerow beyond the coach window.

The viscount and his lady were in anticipation of a wondrous event. All of their gazes and kisses and the time spent closeted in their bedroom took on a glow of intimacy that transcended even what Loris had known with Thomas, and abruptly, she wanted to fling Thomas's bracelet back at him.

The end of the evening would be soon enough to return the bracelet to its rightful owner, and until then Loris would wear it as a reminder of all the dreams she'd never share with Thomas, if she chose to continue protecting her father.

* * *

Matthew Belmont had for many years hated the assemblies, especially the summer assemblies held on the village green. They'd reminded him of his late wife, who had loved the music, the flirtation, and the gossip, while Matthew had felt like a lummox on the dance floor, and a bumbling school boy next to Mathilda's bright smiles and ready wit.

Now he rather enjoyed assemblies, because somebody invariably over-imbibed, and the local magistrate was the logical resource to break up fights, sort out misunderstandings, and suggest elderly uncles be taken home before they drank themselves into a state of regrettable lechery.

Managing the assemblies appealed to Matthew. Prancing around with females half his age did not, so Matthew generally spent much of the evening by the men's punchbowl.

Tonight's brew had probably started out as a genteel blend of fruit juice with a bit of fortification, but assiduous research revealed that a bold portion of rum had found its way into the recipe, possibly accompanied by gin. Once gin joined the festivities, nobody's evening was safe from bad manners, falls on the dance floor, and words best left unsaid.

From beneath a nearby oak, Matthew monitored the patrons of the punchbowl, several of whom were already listing hard to port.

Giles Pettigrew sauntered up, his evening attire loose on his lanky frame. "Belmont, good evening."

"Pettigrew, hello. I'm watching the parade of inchoate inebriates pay their respects to the punchbowl. Summer is the worst for over-imbibing, though it's a tasty blend, at least."

"I'll stick to my flask," Pettigrew said, brandishing same. "A matter has come to my attention that rather involves you."

Matthew's enjoyment of the evening dimmed, though a magistrate was always fair game for a discussion of legal matters.

"Do we need privacy for this discussion?" Matthew asked, not that anybody noticed old Squire Belmont lurking in the shadows. If there was a male equivalent to the wallflower, Matthew would gladly embrace the term.

"We do not," Pettigrew said, in a hushed tone guaranteed to attract notice. "I thought I should let you know that I've heard rumors Mr. Micah Tanner has been seen in the vicinity of Trieshock. Out of respect for Miss Tanner, I'd appreciate it if your efforts to apprehend him were more deliberate than impetuous."

Impetuous. Matthew hadn't been impetuous since, well, perhaps on his wedding night he'd been a bit hasty, and look how that had turned out.

"Difficult to apprehend a rumor, Mr. Pettigrew."

Giles paused with his flask halfway to his mouth. The silver was embossed with a rose, though a dent marred the design.

"You'll not rush out to slap him in irons? A man suspected of multiple felonies?"

Gossip had brought Matthew some of his most useful insights, solving crimes he'd considered unsolvable. Gossip also wasted half the typical rural magistrate's waking hours.

"Firstly, irons are heavy and they clank. I defy anybody to slap them about with the desired result of shackling a criminal. Secondly, information against Tanner has not been formally laid, thus I have no warrant for the man. Thirdly, I do not arrest people on the basis of informal accusations, else I'd have to arrest you."

Pettigrew was not a bad sort, merely a young man with a difficult, headstrong female running his household. Matthew knew how that felt, and yet, Pettigrew was trying to create drama where his mother's scheme had failed to achieve that result.

"You'd arrest me?" Pettigrew asked, stuffing his flask back out of sight. "Squire, your humor eludes me, and I believe my dance with Miss Tanner comes up next."

Miss Tanner was probably wishing she'd not learned to dance. She'd stood up for every set so far, and every man within twenty yards of the green had taken notice.

"When you were sixteen years old," Matthew said, "you dipped Horatia Beam's braid into the inkwell you'd smuggled into choir practice. Her mama wanted me to have you spend an afternoon in the stocks, but alas for the wronged party, hearsay alone is no basis for a conviction."

Whatever else university had done for Pettigrew—probably left him in debt to the usurers, about which Matthew had lectured his own boys at length—Pettigrew had not grasped the basics of English law. His father, who'd been magistrate before Matthew, would have been disappointed.

While Matthew was mostly bored.

"Horatia Beam has red hair," Pettigrew said, as if this were a class of criminal offense. "I was just a boy."

Pettigrew was still just a boy, while Matthew felt positively elderly. "I'll not arrest Tanner without sworn information and due process, and if all the evidence against him is one woman's unverified accusation, then under present law, unfair though it might be, a conviction is unlikely. Now, if you don't want to dance with Miss Tanner, I'll be happy to take your place on her dance card."

Pettigrew was off as if shot from a longbow, leaving Matthew to the familiar comfort of the shadows. He hadn't long to wait before Baron Sutcliffe joined him, looking vastly more elegant—and frustrated—than the gathering called for.

"For ten years," Sutcliffe said, "Loris Tanner worked her backside off on the neighboring estate, cleaned up her father's messes, held her head up while Mrs. Pettigrew ignored a motherless young girl who might have benefited from the smallest kindness tossed in her direction. Now Giles has eyes only for that same woman?"

"While the lady has eyes only for you." Matthew passed over his flask—the good one that no horse had stepped on yet, and no foolish owner had dropped on hard ground. "Care for a nip?"

"My thanks. How long do these gatherings typically last?"

Roughly half the contents of Matthew's best flask disappeared down the baron's handsome gullet.

"They last years," Matthew said. "Each one is a small eternity, though being English, we will perpetuate the institution until not a spinster or a bachelor remains standing. Don't suppose you've seen any suspicious boot prints tonight?"

"Not since the one I spotted in the Trieshock livery. Must he hold her that closely?"

The course of true love never did run uncomplainingly, particularly when fueled with good brandy.

"It's five minutes of capering about in public, Sutcliffe. That's the only liberty Pettigrew can take, and Miss Tanner in her finery would turn any man's head."

Blazing blue eyes fixed on Matthew. "With the exception of present company, she's been ignored or worse by the entire village until tonight. What did Pettigrew want with you?"

The baron was a bright fellow—he'd have to be to keep up with Loris Tanner.

"Your report regarding Tanner's whereabouts has been confirmed. The fellows you hired to keep an eye out for him, and now Pettigrew as well, all claim to have seen Tanner in the vicinity of Trieshock."

Among the dancers, Loris Tanner smiled fixedly at Giles Pettigrew, while the viscount and his lady were a study in liberties taken in public. Beckman and Nicholas were partnering the wallflowers Matthew himself usually stood up with. But for the newlywed viscount and viscountess, the scene was typical for the Linden village. Try as he might, Matthew could find nothing to support a dull sense of unease.

"Where is Claudia Pettigrew?" Sutcliffe asked.

Damn and drat. "Excellent question," for Claudia Pettigrew liked to see and be seen, swanning about in London fashions most of the local women could only envy. "Perhaps she's grown tired of dancing with other women's husbands. Then too, sensible people don't hop about needlessly in this heat."

The musicians brought the interminable dance to a final cadence, and Matthew considered refilling his flask at the punchbowl.

"Try mine," Sutcliffe said, passing over a silver container embossed with a crest of thistles framing a rampant unicorn.

The contents were ambrosial, brandy such as a mere country squire might dream about in his old age.

"Why would Tanner use Trieshock as his base of operations?" Sutcliffe asked, tucking his flask away. "Why not hide in London or Brighton?"

Another excellent question. Matthew moved away from the temptation of the punchbowl and led Sutcliffe to a different patch of shadow.

"If I were passing through the area with intent to leave quickly, Baron, I'd stay in Trieshock. The main road to Brighton lies not two miles from the town, and yet few over that way would know Tanner because he conducted most of his business right here at Linden or in Haybrick."

Pettigrew had engaged Miss Tanner in earnest conversation, though even he had to know one did not importune a lady on the village green with all the local gossips looking on. Perhaps that's why Pettigrew took Miss Tanner by the hand and led her away to the other side of the green.

"Sutcliffe, she sees him as a boy, and you're grinding your molars to dust over nothing."

Sutcliffe checked a headlong charge to the lady's side. "Belmont, something has bothered me ever since my stable was reduced to a smoldering ruin."

"I expect much has bothered you since that unfortunate day." Having an arsonist loose in the shire certainly bothered Matthew.

"The first person on the scene, the first person to offer aid and assistance, was Giles Pettigrew, who claimed to have heard word of the fire at the posting inn two miles away from my property."

The unease in Matthew's belly coalesced into cold, miserable dread. "Neighborly of him."

"Or did Pettigrew have reason to know my stable would be put to the torch? I've had Nick make discreet inquiries, and nobody is even sure Pettigrew came to the tavern that morning. Where has that fool taken Loris?"

Sutcliffe's voice boded dismemberment for the fool in question.

"They can't have gone far. I'll fetch Nick, Beckman, and Fairly if you'd like help searching for her, but whatever you do, Sutcliffe, keep your head."

Matthew was talking to the night air, for the baron had already slipped away into the shadows.

* * *

Giles Pettigrew gave off the excited air of a boy who'd just realized he'd stumbled onto the answers to the Latin examination, but couldn't gloat about his good fortune to any of the other scholars.

His dancing was a shade too energetic, his voice a trifle too loud, his laughter forced. Loris wanted nothing so much as to get away from him, and from the entire gathering.

Though not until she'd had her waltz with Thomas. No power on earth could make her forfeit that memory.

"Miss Tanner, thank you for the dance," Giles said, bowing low enough that Loris could see his hair was already going thin on top.

He escorted her away from the area designated for dancing, while Loris tried to discreetly locate Thomas among the bystanders on the periphery.

"You dance very well, Giles, and I'm sure your next partner is looking forward to her turn with you. I'll find the viscountess and rest my feet." Or Loris would locate Thomas, who was nowhere in evidence. Nick and Beckman, tall enough to be easy to spot, had also apparently chosen that moment to visit the bushes, or wherever men went when the punch and ale caught up with them.

"If you're looking for Sutcliffe, I think I know where you'll find him," Giles said. "He and Squire Belmont were near the men's punchbowl. Shall we look for them there?"

"Yes, please. I'm sure the musicians will soon want to conclude the festivities, and I promised the final dance to the baron."

Giles linked arms with Loris, and led her off around the oak in the center of the green.

"Giles, the punchbowl is outside the tavern," Loris said.

"Well, yes, but your baron has probably gone 'round the back of the smithy. It's quiet back there, and has benches, you see."

Loris did not see, never having loitered at the smithy. "Giles, slow down. If you're seen dragging me into the darkness, I won't answer for the consequences."

She wasn't about to make a scene over what was merely forward behavior, and as to that, nobody seemed to notice her exit from the throng milling beneath the lanterns on the village square.

"You needn't worry about consequences," Giles said as they came around the corner of the blacksmith's establishment. "I'll marry you, Loris Tanner. I don't care about your past, or about your infatuation with the baron. That's to be expected when a Town man comes riding down from London, drawling fine manners and dressed to the nines."

Giles Pettigrew was daft, or perhaps giddy from an evening spent beyond his mama's watchful eye.

"That's very generous of you, Giles, but I don't think marriage will be necessary."

Behind the smithy, all was deserted. The violins sawing away so energetically back on the green were soft and distant here, the moon the only light.

"I will marry you, though," Giles said, gripping Loris by the wrist. "Have no fear on that score. That's a very pretty frock. Maybe you'll wear it on our wedding day, too. The blue goes with your eyes."

Loris's eyes were gray, not blue. "Giles, we're not getting married. Thank you for the honor you do me, but we would not suit."

Loris could not read his expression well in the moonlight, but her refusal didn't daunt him. Three months ago, she would have been grateful for his proposal, and might even have accepted it.

Three months ago, she'd been frightened, lonely, exhausted, and still waiting for her father to come riding up the drive, handing out joking apologies for his absence, and resuming the duties Loris had shouldered in his absence.

The urge to laugh at Giles's earnest condescension came from nowhere and bore a hint of grief. Fate had generously put Loris in Thomas's path, and no matter what else befell her, for a short time, she'd had the love of a good man.

Those memories were hers to keep, while Giles's proposal she could toss gently into the hedgerow.

"Giles, the baron will wonder what's become of me, and he's clearly not here. I think we've said all that need be said. Shall we return to the green?"

"I propose marriage, and you can't wait to get back to your baron? I've known you for a decade, and in a matter of weeks, you're smitten with him? He's disported with soiled doves, Loris, and don't think he humors your little masquerade as a steward for any reason other than to get under your skirts. I've seen London, I've experienced its charms. Take the word of a man of the world, Sutcliffe is toying with you."

Giles's histrionics might cost Loris a waltz with the only man to deal with her honestly.

"Perhaps Sutcliffe is toying with me, Giles, but he knows better than to take a lady somewhere private under false pretenses. Return to the green, and I'll follow in a few minutes."

Loris took the tone of voice she used on Thomas's urchins, at least three of whom had been circling in the vicinity of the dessert tables.

"I can be patient," Giles said, backing up two steps. "Up to a point. Your upbringing was unconventional, all the more reason you're dazzled by a fancy rogue. I've made inquiries about your baron, Loris, though now is not the time to reveal the results of my investigations. I'll leave you in solitude, but don't tarry long. A woman in your position can't be too careful of her reputation, and my offer of marriage presupposes your reputation remains worthy of my suit."

On that grating little sermon, Giles finally took his worldly, judgmental, condescending, arrogant young self away toward the green. Loris was tempted to sink onto one of the benches and sort anger from amusement and despair, but the bushes moved alarmingly, and a man stepped forward.

"I thought your suitor would never leave, Daughter, and I have a few questions of my own about this Baron Sutcliffe, but first, don't you have a hug and a kiss for your old papa?"

CHAPTER NINETEEN

"A grown woman in a gorgeous blue dress doesn't just disappear," Nick muttered.

"She apparently has," Beckman countered.

"A lady might need the necessary," Belmont said, though even he didn't sound convinced of his own point.

"I sent one of the boys around to watch for Loris at the ladies' convenience," Thomas said. "Nick has a point. Loris's appearance tonight was distinctive. People ought to have noticed her on Pettigrew's arm."

Thomas had gathered beneath the oaks with what help he had. To anybody milling around the punchbowl, they'd be just another group of men standing about with flasks and tankards in hand.

To Thomas, these few men were his only prayer of happiness on earth. "You gentlemen need to know something else. Micah Tanner has been seen in the area since the stable burned, and I'm confident he's come to fetch Loris before taking ship in Brighton."

Beckman left off skimming the toe of his boot through

the grass. "Brighton is a thriving port and a damned big place. I've sailed from there any number of times."

"Not much moon if Tanner wants to get there tonight," Nick said, tossing the last of his ale into the darkness. "But my mare will take me safely enough."

"Sutcliffe?" Belmont prompted. "What say you? Brighton, London, Trieshock?"

"Or none of the above," Thomas said. The violins scraped away, a simple, repetitive reel on a simple, happy tune. Inside Thomas, all was discord and misery, and yet these men expected him to think, to think logically, when the woman he loved had willingly left his side, and very likely the future he'd offered her.

"She's not at the necessary," Letty said, joining the circle with her husband. "The ladies in line said Loris hadn't been that way the entire time they'd been waiting."

Thomas's instincts had been warning him that Loris would not refuse her father's summons, that old habits didn't die that easily, not when they were habits of love and duty.

"Thomas?" Fairly said softly. "We're wasting time. Where would you like us to search?"

Everywhere, until Loris was found. Nowhere, because to find her meant Thomas might have to hear with his own ears that she'd choose the life of her father's drudge over life as his baroness. He didn't blame her, but neither did he want to watch as she threw his hopes and dreams back in his face.

And yet, Thomas needed to hear from Loris what her choice would be, needed know that she was in fact, making a choice rather than being coerced.

He need to know that rather desperately. "We widen the search. We don't stop until we've turned every—"

"Mr. Baron," a small voice called from the nearby hedge. "Mr. Baron, I found her."

"Timmie," Thomas said. "You can come out. You found Miss Tanner?"

Timmie, a leaf clinging to his sleeve, mud on the elbow of what was doubtless his Sunday jacket, dashed out of the bushes.

"Miss Tanner is behind the smithy, and she's talking with her papa. He says they have to leave right now."

"Good lad," Thomas said. "Lady Fairly will take you to the dessert table, and then you can find the other boys and quietly let them know you found Miss Tanner."

The boy skipped off at Letty's side, and Thomas still could not blame Loris for the decision she'd made, even having heard the confirmation of his worst fears. His heart broke, for her, for them, for what she'd turned her back on.

"Damn it, Thomas, either we stop her now, or you've lost her," Fairly said. "Don't be an idiot."

"I've already lost her," Thomas replied, "but let's make sure the lady's choice is an informed one. Quietly, please. Tanner mustn't know the Tenth Hussars have come to witness this touching reunion."

Five men sauntered off as if to heed nature's call.

Thomas was being an idiot—Loris had apparently left without a backward glance, had possibly even dressed for the evening with a Brighton departure in mind—but Thomas would at least get to tell her good-bye, and to deliver one stout blow to the father who'd abandoned her so cavalierly nearly two years before.

* * *

"Don't you touch me," Loris hissed.

Papa stopped mid-stride, arms outstretched as if to enfold her in a protective embrace. His expression turned predictably hurt, as it had every time Loris had refused to divulge the location of her egg money.

"I don't lay eyes on you for two years," he said. "I'm hounded from my own home, I live like a common laborer, barely keeping body and soul together, and that's your greeting for me?"

Loris smelled no gin on his breath, which meant he'd at least recall this discussion in the morning.

"I'm glad you are well, Papa, but working for a living is the fate of many, including your own daughter."

"You never shirked your duty," he said, as if Loris's sense of responsibility was his sole, cherished creation. "We can lay blame and exchange forgiveness at a later time. For now, we need to get to Brighton before anybody notices you're missing. I do hope your worldly goods are stowed in an accessible location."

Exchange forgiveness? Lay blame?

Loris was accustomed to being disappointed in her father. She *expected* to be disappointed in him, but mere disappointment didn't come close to the fury seething through her.

"You *abandoned* me," she said, moving away lest she slap him. "You simply hared off when your own stupidity once again brought trouble to our door. You never sent a note to let me know if you were alive, never sent word to join you elsewhere, and yet, you think to forgive me? You who left me without a word, no explanation, no farewell? Nobody behaves that way who has any claim to honor."

Loris could not behave that way, not to Thomas of all people. The insight was a cooling rain to her overheated sense of worry for her father, and even to her rage.

Her declaration seemed to leave Micah Tanner bewildered. He blinked at her and gripped his lapels with both hands. Loris could see him rearranging the truths he couldn't dodge and the half-truths he might get away with.

"I'm your father," he said, his tone balanced between authority and apology. "Your place is with me."

"You're a disgrace," Loris shot back, though that was a polite term for what she felt. "You were running Linden into the ground, damn you. The drinking itself wasn't the problem. You failed one of the most beautiful properties in the shire, let the sheep nearly ruin it, let profit run away with your obligation to the land because you were besotted with the bottle and with the widow. I'm ashamed of you, Papa."

Those words were so miserably, heartrendingly true, and yet, they put right a confusion Loris had lived with for too long. *The shame was his*, had always been his.

"You are out of sorts," Papa said, though at least he had sense enough not to attempt another hug. "You are wearing finery such as I never thought to see on my own daughter, and Pettigrew had to have upset you. You'll regret your words in the morning, for you should be proud of me. I haven't overimbibed since the day you last saw me."

He spoke as if Loris should burst into a rousing chorus of "God Save the King" in response, when instead she wanted to kick him.

"Papa, clearly you are proud of yourself, and I don't begrudge you that, but it's me I'm most proud of." Thomas had given her that gift. She would tell him so, too. "I've rescued Linden from your foolishness, and I'm not going anywhere with you. You must decide what to do about Mrs. Pettigrew's accusations, but I won't leave my home, my obligations, or the people who care about me. Not even for you, Papa."

She'd surprised him, and she'd relieved herself. Micah Tanner had finally, finally proved he could manage on his own, free from drink, and without a daughter to tend his household and clean up his messes.

While Loris had found a man who was worth standing by, through all of life's joys and sorrows.

"Claudia Pettigrew would have seen me hanged," Papa said. "You want to watch your own father die that way, a public spectacle, disgraced, and mocked?"

Loris had been disgraced, a laughingstock, an object of pity and gossip in the churchyard. She'd been mocked for doing a man's job, though she'd done it more conscientiously than her own father had.

Those realities left her tired and sad. She took one of the

benches where men gossiped while waiting for a horse to be shod. The wood was rough through her silk dress, and the damp of the night's dew-fall was seeping through her dancing slippers.

"Of course I don't want to see you hanged, Papa, but Nick says you're innocent of Mrs. Pettigrew's accusations, and Matthew Belmont takes the administration of justice seriously."

"Hell hath no fury," Papa muttered. "You don't know Claudia Pettigrew like I do. She will not recant her charges, and I'm bound for Lisbon."

Loris leaned her head back against the hard wall behind her and waited for something—grief, relief, surprise, anything—to wrap around her heart, and yet, nothing came. Her father had left the shire two years ago. Perhaps in all the ways that mattered, he'd abandoned his daughter long before that.

"By reputation, Lisbon is a beautiful city," she said. "I'd like to think I might one day visit you there."

Papa came down beside her on a heavy, and possibly sincere, sigh. "You break my heart, Daughter."

"You broke mine more times than I can count, but hearts can mend," Loris said. "I suggest you be on your way, before somebody gets wind that you're here, and Mrs. Pettigrew lays information."

A figure stepped out of the shadows. "Mrs. Pettigrew won't lay information. That was never the point. Miss Tanner, on your feet, please. Your dear papa must accompany us for a visit with my mama. She's stolen a fortune from me, and he knows where it is."

Giles's earlier air of suppressed excitement, his sermonizing proposal, his determination to lure Loris out of sight of the gathering now made sense. She'd underestimated him, or been too distracted by the thought of ending the night dancing in Thomas's arms.

She still wanted her dance with Thomas, wanted it badly.

"He has a gun, Loris," Papa said, shifting to stand before her. "The idiot boy has a gun."

"I am doomed to be vexed by idiot boys," Loris said, rising and stepping around her father's side. "You're no good to Giles dead, Papa, and I'd like to say a few words to Mrs. Pettigrew myself. Your drama is not appreciated, Giles, and you'll want to bear that in mind the instant you have to set that gun aside."

The noise and music from the crowd on the green meant nobody would hear Loris scream, and apparently, nobody had seen her leave the gathering with Giles.

Neither would they hear a shot fired, and while Giles might need Papa alive, Loris was absolutely expendable. That hurt, but knowing she'd miss her waltz with Thomas gave her courage.

Thomas would not abandon her, of that she was certain. Thomas would look for her, and he'd find her.

* * *

"Imminent threat of harm," Belmont muttered, "perhaps kidnapping. If we have false accusations, I can work with that, too."

Thomas held a finger to his lips, though Belmont's enthusiasm for justice was endearing. When Thomas and his men had arrived behind the smithy on Pettigrew's heels. Loris and her father had been in quiet discussion. Perhaps they'd been planning their departure.

Perhaps... not.

"We follow them," Thomas said softly. "Mrs. Pettigrew will be at home, and we'll have the advantage of numbers and surprise. We'll take my coach, though I want us to hang back a good distance. When we reach Pettigrew's place, Nicholas and Beckman will let old Johnny loose. Belmont, you're not to participate, but merely to observe."

"Might I observe with a gun in my hand?" Belmont asked.

"No, you may not," Thomas replied, "but Fairly will retrieve the pistols from my coach, and you'll stick close to him. You four take my coach, and tie the horses a quarter mile from the house, then meet me at Johnny's shed."

"You're to retrieve pistols, plural," Belmont said to Fairly. "I'm happy to carry one for you."

"Most considerate of you, Belmont," Fairly replied. "Thomas, if we're to meet you at the stable, then you're not coming with us. What do you have planned?"

Thomas had planned the rescue of the fair damsel, and possibly of his own heart. Loris had had a perfect opportunity to steal away with her father, and she'd instead remained sitting on that hard bench, looking lovely and stubborn.

"I'll borrow Squire Belmont's mare."

"My horse is temperamental," Belmont said. "The breeding stock often is."

"I'm counting on that," Thomas replied. "Be outside Johnny's stall in thirty minutes, and don't you dare let Pettigrew catch sight of you."

* * *

"Loris Tanner, you're worse than my mother," Giles said. "Why on earth can't you keep quiet?"

Because Loris clung to the inane notion that noise might make her easier for Thomas to find as she was marched down the dark lane, Giles's pistol at her back.

"Giles, you are not thinking," she said, though most men seemed to ignore her when she said that. "You might have spared everybody a lot of bother and yourself a serious thrashing simply by asking Papa where this money is."

"I don't know where any blasted money is," Papa retorted. "As much damage as Claudia Pettigrew has done to my reputation and to my life, if I'd known she'd stolen a fortune, don't you think I'd have seen her held accountable?"

A bit of grit or stone had worked its way into Loris's slipper. She stopped in the middle of the lane to get it out.

"Keep moving," Giles said, waving his pistol. He carried an ugly little piece with a short double barrel. That gun wouldn't be accurate over much distance, but it could kill if used appropriately.

"Give me a moment," Loris said, leaning on her father's shoulder for balance. She shook out her shoe and stole a glance behind her.

They were within a quarter mile of the Pettigrew lane, and nobody and nothing came along the road behind them. Loris put her slipper back on and shook out her skirts.

"Thank you, Giles," she said. "If you decide to kill me, now my corpse will at least be free of blisters."

"Daughter, don't provoke him."

Loris resumed walking, though *she* was provoked. She was exceedingly provoked, at Giles, at Papa, at the widow, at the lack of rescue.

And beneath her fury was a terror that she'd never have her waltz with Thomas, never tell him that his startling, amazing, troubling declaration the previous night was entirely reciprocated.

She loved him, she would never love another, and her prayer as she was marched at gunpoint along the dark, dusty road was that she live long enough to tell him so.

"Stop here," Giles said, when they reached the top of the Pettigrew drive. "Tanner, you know something, or Mama would not have seen you run out of the shire. Maybe you saw her forge my signature, maybe you went with her when she met with the bankers to secure a mortgage on my birthright. You know something or you saw something that would incriminate her. What is it?"

Papa gazed at the house, perhaps a house he'd expected to live in as Claudia Pettigrew's husband.

"Your mother signed all the documents relating to the estate, but I never saw whose name she was affixing to them. As for accompanying her to the bankers, I never went with her anywhere beyond the immediate surrounds. Not Brighton, not even Trieshock. She kept me in my place."

"But she entertained you frequently," Loris said. "She was a widow, so you were private with her on many occasions. What might you have seen that she didn't want you to see?"

"This gets us nowhere," Giles said. "I go to all this trouble, and you honestly know nothing?"

All this trouble?

In the pastures adjacent to the stable, the horses abruptly went into a pounding gallop. Maybe they were inspired by the cooler night air, perhaps a fox had trotted past with a bloody meal clamped in its jaws.

All those hooves thundering against the dry earth resonated with Loris's worry and anger. Where was Thomas?

"Papa, you were frequently in Mrs. Pettigrew's house. What did you see that her own son was unlikely to see?"

Papa tugged on his collar. "I'm not sure what you mean."

"Were you in her bedroom?" Giles asked. "She keeps it locked when she's away."

Loris did not want to hear this, did not want to be on this dark, deserted lane, and she did not want to die.

"Papa, you needn't protect my sensibilities. As you've reminded me, Giles has a gun, and his situation appears desperate to him." Worse, Giles was too stupid to cope with his mother's greed through sensible means, though mortgaging the estate was much worse than simply buying too many fashionable dresses.

"You were in her bedroom," Giles said. "I've let myself in there—the lock is hardly sophisticated—but it's all just a lot of pillows and gilt and cosmetics. I don't even see that she has much jewelry left, though I suspect she's pawned the good pieces."

"Two years ago, she still had a substantial collection of fine jewelry," Papa said. "She kept those in the safe."

The horses galloped off in the other direction, a tide of equine anxiety washing back and forth across the pasture.

The end of Gile's gun barrel dipped. "*What safe?*"

* * *

Linden had two safes, one in the master bedchamber, one in a second parlor where nobody would think to look for it. Thomas had memorized the combinations to both, and only Fairly and Letty knew where those combinations were written down.

Nick, Beckman, and Belmont made not a sound beside Thomas as they waited for Giles Pettigrew to act on what was clearly new information.

"You're saying my own father failed to inform me of a safe?" Giles asked. "God knows what else he didn't tell me."

"He likely trusted your mother to inform you," Loris said. "And now that you've threatened us unnecessarily, held us at gunpoint, and exonerated my father of the accusations that should never have been levied against him, we'll just be going."

Thomas held his breath, hoping Loris's bluff convinced Pettigrew he was in enough trouble. Five sizeable grown men did not fit comfortably behind a mere pair of lilac bushes.

"Unless Mama sees Tanner," Giles said. "She'll never tell me what's in that safe, much less how to open it."

"I saw jewels and papers," Tanner said, "and you don't need Loris, so you can let her go. You're being foolish, Giles, as your mother has so often been foolish."

Thomas winced, for Tanner had been too blunt.

"I need Loris to ensure you'll behave," Giles said. "Into the house with you both."

"Now what?" Nick whispered when the front door had clicked ominously closed. No footman, butler, or porter had answered the door, suggesting the Pettigrew staff was at the assembly, the same as Linden's staff would be.

"Now the evening grows interesting," Thomas said. "Thanks to the heat, we'll find open windows easily enough, but I don't think we'll need them. Nick, you take the front door. Beckman, you take the kitchen door and wait outside, in case Pettigrew or his dear mama attempt to vacate the premises.

Belmont, you're with me. Fairly, you're the rear guard, held in reserve in case Belmont and I need reinforcements."

"Take this," Nick whispered, shoving one of the coach pistols at Thomas. "It's a useful bludgeon if you're unwilling to fire it."

"No guns for me," Thomas said, stepping back. "I frankly don't care if Tanner takes a bullet, but Loris would care. Pettigrew is nervous and frustrated, and more firearms won't appeal to his minuscule store of reason."

"Then I'll have that gun back," Fairly said, snatching the pistol from Nick. "Loris will take it amiss if any harm befalls you, Thomas, as will Letty."

"I'm not too fond of the idea myself," Thomas said. "Tanner has much to answer for, as do the Pettigrews."

A mare squealed down the lane, her cry splitting the night like a trumpet blast.

"Excellent timing," Thomas muttered. "Belmont, Fairly, let's go."

They walked right in the front door and followed raised voices up the steps, to Claudia Pettigrew's personal parlor.

When Fairly had taken up a position across the corridor, Thomas dashed into the parlor as if he'd run a great distance.

"Pettigrew," he gasped, "your stud has got loose. He's at the mares right now, and I can't catch him on my own."

An equestrian could be expected to have both quick reflexes and strength, so Thomas made his one grab for Giles's gun count. In the instant Giles needed to absorb the news of the loose stallion, Thomas shoved Giles's hand up, so the gun was aimed at the ceiling.

Claudia's cries of "Don't kill my only son," and the commotion of Belmont hustling Loris from the room, were vague impressions compared to Thomas's focus on gaining control of the weapon.

The moment Thomas sensed Loris was safe, he kicked Giles in the back of the knee, had him on the ground, and passed the pistol to Tanner.

"Don't hurt him," Claudia cried again. "He's only a boy, and he hasn't done anything wrong."

"I want Nick and Beckman in here," Thomas said to Fairly, "and Loris too, if she'd like to hear what Pettigrew has to say for himself. Mrs. Pettigrew, you'll want to hold your tongue, because Belmont is present in his capacity as magistrate."

More warning than the silly woman deserved, but she took it to heart and subsided onto a pink and gilt chair.

The room became crowded, though when Thomas sought Loris's gaze, she was staring at Giles, still prone on the carpet. Her blue silk dress was dusty about the hems, and one of her white gloves bore a long dark smudge. The bracelet at her wrist was an incongruous sparkle against an otherwise wrinkled and worn outfit.

"I'll let you up," Thomas informed Pettigrew, "but the magistrate is on the premises, as are three other fellows whom no sane man would willingly cross. None of that ought to matter to you half so much as the fact that you have used Miss Tanner ill, and for that I might well kill you."

Nobody winked, nobody smirked, for Thomas was at least half in earnest.

"He's threatening murder," Giles said, getting to his feet and pointing a shaky finger at Thomas. "You all heard him."

"Sit down," Belmont snapped. "Arson is a hanging offense, and if you'd torched my stable, I'd do more than threaten murder. Mind, anything you say will bear upon how I handle this situation. Sutcliffe, you have the floor."

"Miss Tanner," Thomas said, "perhaps you'd also like a seat?" The question had come out coldly polite, when all Thomas wanted was for Loris to look at him. She sank into a chair, and her father did likewise.

"Start at the beginning, Giles," Thomas said. "From what I can see, you are likely to be charged with arson and kidnapping, at least, and that ought to be trouble enough for one young man."

Beside Thomas, Nick crossed his arms, Beckman widened his stance, and had Thomas been a betting man, he would have wagered that either Haddonfield was ready to do Giles a permanent injury.

"Mama mortgaged the estate," Giles said, which elicited a *meep* from his mother, though she didn't contradict him. "To do that she forged my signature on some documents, and she kept the proceeds of the transaction. The estate is thus in debt, and she has made no payments on the borrowed sum. She won't tell me what she's done with the money or the documents, but I reasoned that Tanner knew something about her…"

"Her fraud?" Thomas suggested. "Forgery? Misappropriation of funds?"

"Her… actions," Giles went on, "and that's why she accused him of… accused him of wrongdoing."

Giles's ears were red, while Loris was now apparently fascinated with the tips of dancing slippers that had once been blue.

"So your mother is also a felon," Fairly observed. "Sutcliffe, did you not take the quality of the neighbors into consideration when you purchased Linden?"

"Go on, Pettigrew," Thomas said, though the rest of the picture was already clear.

"Mama mortgaged the estate, she sent Tanner packing, and there I was, without funds, without authority, without a means of making Mama see reason."

Loris wiped at her cheek, and Thomas nearly ordered everybody from the room, he needed to take her in his arms that badly.

"Miss Tanner was left without funds," Thomas said, "without authority even in the position she took up to protect her father's interests, without a parent's guidance and companionship, without much of a roof over her head, and yet, I cannot recall a single felony she's committed as a result, unless working hard every day is now a crime. What am I missing here?"

Fairly passed Loris a handkerchief.

Nick growled.

Belmont had produced pencil and paper and was scribbling away at an escritoire by the window.

From outside, in the direction of the pastures, another mare was conveying her sentiments to all in the vicinity.

"Mama isn't always wise," Giles said. "She likes pretty things, and those are expensive. She'll spend all the money on millinery, when we need a new stud. She'll have fancy gowns, but we won't have hay for the horses in winter. I'd already decided I had to do something even before I learned of the mortgage. Marrying Miss Tanner was a solution to my problems—I gain control of my funds as soon as I wed. Marriage would have been a solution to Miss Tanner's predicament as well."

Such solutions would see the damned puppy bankrupt and transported.

"So you put Chesterton up to making trouble for Miss Tanner," Thomas said, "just as the new owner of Linden would have been most likely to turn her off without a character. I must commend you on the originality of your courting strategy."

Thomas paused to marshal his temper. He didn't even glance at Loris, lest the sight of her provoke him to using his fists on Pettigrew.

"Then you heard rumors Tanner had been spotted," Thomas went on, "perhaps in Brighton, perhaps closer. You learned of the mortgage, and modified your scheme. Miss Tanner would still be pressed into service as your wife, but first you'd use her for bait to draw her father to the area, so you could unravel your mother's fraud."

Claudia Pettigrew had dropped her face to her hands, but Thomas felt no compassion at the sight, not for her, not for the young man who matched her for arrogance.

Thomas lowered his voice, when he wanted to shout. "You reasoned that if Loris Tanner faced enough problems, a mutiny even, then she'd be escorted from the property, bag and baggage, and Tanner would show himself. You were right."

Tanner swore, Loris patted his knee. Thomas wanted to toss her papa out the nearest window.

"Giles, don't say anything," Mrs. Pettigrew said, lifting her face from her hands. "A mother might sign her son's name to a few documents. There's no harm in that. The money isn't all gone, but don't say a word about that fire."

"Not *all* gone?" Thomas inquired.

"Penny and Treasure nearly died in that fire," Nick said.

"*My brother* nearly died in that fire," Beckman added. "You put Miss Tanner, the baron, Fairly, and me at risk, because you and your mama acted like children."

"I didn't start the fire," Giles cried. "I would never have started a fire. I love horses, and I never told Chesterton to start the fire."

Belmont was looking very alert, his pencil poised above the foolscap.

"Did Chesterton start the fire?" Thomas asked. "Think carefully before you answer, Giles."

"Don't say anything," Mrs. Pettigrew snapped. "Keep your stupid mouth shut. Not another word."

"Claudy, hush," Tanner said. "The boy has been a fool, but he has a chance to right what he's put wrong. Your damned hats aren't worth his honor."

That rebuke silenced the widow, which was fortunate, for Thomas would not have been half so polite.

"Giles?" Thomas prompted.

"I told Chesterton to make trouble, bothersome trouble, nothing serious. Spilled oats, a gate or two left open, a stud colt in the mare's pasture, that sort of thing. He did not take direction well, though he was happy to take my coin. I gave him more money and ordered him to leave the area. The next morning, your stable burned, and I told myself it could not have been him. Stables burn, and it's not necessarily a matter of arson."

"But?" Fairly asked, sighting casually down the barrel of the coach pistol.

His lordship was a regular thespian masquerading as a viscount, and Thomas had never loved him more.

"But at the tavern that morning," Giles said, "I was assured Chesterton had been on the premises not fifteen minutes before I arrived, and acting more pleased with himself than usual. I left without ordering so much as a small pint, but I was too late."

Thomas considered options, while across the room, Loris folded and refolded a wrinkled square of white linen.

"Miss Tanner, have you any questions for Mr. Pettigrew?" Thomas asked, again simply to encourage her to look at him.

She shook her head.

"Then I suggest Mrs. Pettigrew provide Mr. Belmont the combination to the safe, and he will examine its contents as part of his investigation into the matter of the fraudulent mortgage."

"Excellent suggestion," Belmont said. "Nicholas, Beckman, if you'd accompany us. One always wants witnesses when handling valuables."

Belmont did not handle Mrs. Pettigrew, did not so much as offer her his arm as she marched from the parlor. They were back within minutes, and Mrs. Pettigrew's expression would have felled forests of stout-hearted men.

"What of the mortgage?" Thomas asked the magistrate.

Belmont read from a document, naming a sum, a bank, a series of terms. If Giles was correct, and no payments had been made against the total owed, the estate was ripe for foreclosure.

"Fairly?" Thomas asked.

"The work of an afternoon," the viscount said, "though this place needs a great deal of work, and I'd advise caution."

"Then here's what I propose," Thomas said, though that word—propose—made his heart ache. "I will bring the mortgage on the property current and take over the obligation, meaning I will hold the note on this estate. Mrs. Pettigrew, I cannot tell you what to do, but I can intimate that Belmont will pursue charges of forgery and fraud if you disregard my suggestions."

Rather than glare at Thomas, or even aim a beseeching look at Giles, Mrs. Pettigrew sought Tanner's gaze.

"You, Mrs. Pettigrew, will remove to London with a very modest allowance," Thomas said. "Miss Tanner managed well enough when you deprived her of a father and his dubious protection, and Giles will have too much work to do here to spare you much attention. You will bide on your small income and not trouble this neighborhood again. Your jewels will be turned over to Giles, in compensation for the value you robbed from his estate."

When another son might have been indignant at such treatment of his mother, Giles looked relieved.

"What of me?" he asked. "I'm not an arsonist, and I didn't forge anything."

"Kidnapping," Belmont said, pencil in hand. "Threats of bodily harm, conspiracy to commit all manner of malicious mischief through Chesterton's meddling, and now you have a loose stallion, which qualifies as permitting a common nuisance."

"I leave your fate in Miss Tanner's hands," Thomas said. "You imperiled her livelihood, held her at gunpoint when she's done you no wrong, caused harm to her horse, and threatened her only immediate family. If she says you hang, I will personally fetch the rope and wrap it around your worthless neck."

Belmont maintained a diplomatic silence in the face of that

slight exaggeration, the pencil moved across the page without stopping, and a few jewels winked near the magistrate's elbow.

A very few.

"Miss Tanner, I'm sorry," Giles said. "I'll marry you if that helps, or I'll join the cavalry, or I'll... I'm sorry. I didn't know what to do, and I never meant you any harm. Linden could afford a spilled sack of oats, a few loose sheep. I knew if I married you, you could put my land to rights and I'd have control of my funds, too. I didn't mean for all of this to happen."

"That's the problem with being foolish," Tanner said. "You only mean a little harm—a spilled sack of oats' worth—and next thing you know, you're riding your horse up the church aisle, or being accused of heinous misdeeds. If I were Sutcliffe, I'd see you transported, at least."

Loris regarded her father for a long moment. "Is that an apology, Papa?"

Say yes, Thomas wanted to bellow. *Say yes, and mean it.*

Tanner eyed the jewels. "That is an apology, Daughter. For leaving you to deal with problems I should have resolved, at least, I am sorry. The rest we can discuss in private."

For the first time, Loris met Thomas's gaze, though her expression was the unreadable, self-contained mask Thomas had first encountered in the Linden stable weeks ago.

"I did not lose my position," Loris said, "unconventional though that position has been. My horse recovered, and my father did indeed return to the area when I'd given him up for dead or long departed. I have no quarrel with Giles. Nicholas, if you'd see me home, I'll leave you lot to sort out Giles's fate. All I want is old Johnny as restitution for the harm done my horse, and for the inconvenience of this entire, misbegotten evening."

Loris swept out, dusty hems, dirty gloves, and all, head held high, leaving those responsible for creating the present situation to clean up their own messes.

Thomas didn't know whether to applaud, or to howl.

CHAPTER TWENTY

In the aftermath of the assembly, Loris slept more than usual, and for a few days, she allowed herself that indulgence. She'd resumed dwelling at Dove Cottage, while her father remained on the Pettigrew estate helping Giles sort out the effects of Claudia's mismanagement and greed.

Thomas apparently took over the Pettigrew mortgage, and whether Giles would ever have clear title to his father's property mattered to Loris not at all.

Thomas was avoiding her, and that mattered a great deal.

"You must not think you know what goes on in a man's head," Lady Fairly said, as she settled on the porch swing beside Loris. "Sometimes, they hardly know themselves, and Thomas has been closeted with solicitors and men of business all week. He reminds me of my husband, which is, of course, a compliment."

"Of course. Must you go back to London tomorrow, my lady?"

"Lord Fairly would never refuse aid to a friend, but Thomas has managed well here, and we have obligations in London.

The decision is not entirely mine to make, my dear."

Obligations... Loris had obligations, too. Since the assembly, the weather had turned to gloriously cool, sunny days and nights that bordered on crisp. The pansies that had been wilting at the base of Loris's porch steps were back in good form, and the summer seemed to have righted itself. Somebody should be keeping an eye on the fruit crops, at least.

The grain harvest was still weeks away, and Loris could not leave her post until then—assuming she still had a post.

"Nicholas and Beckman have urged me to visit Belle Maison," Loris said. "They say I have cousins who are ladies."

Lady Fairly stroke a spear of potted mint, then crushed a leaf between her fingers.

"Lovely women, they are, too, but I hope you sort matters out with the baron first. Thomas is too good at being lonely, and now he's invited that sister of his for a visit, when he has nobody to see him through such an ordeal."

Thomas needed nobody. He could sort through biblical plagues, multiple felonies, and crimes in progress, all on his own.

"I miss him," Loris said—wailed, more like. "My lady, I miss Thomas as if the heart has been torn from my body, but he hasn't come by, hasn't sent for me."

Her ladyship tucked Loris's braid back, bringing the brisk fragrance of mint with her touch.

"So you conclude, what? That your baron is disgusted with you for being embroiled in Giles Pettigrew's imbecilic machinations? You're not making sense, Loris Tanner, and you are an eminently sensible woman."

Loris was an eminently unhappy woman, and yet, she couldn't simply present herself in Thomas's library and demand that he attend her. So she sat on her swing, restless, miserable, and weepy.

Why hadn't she told him she loved him when she'd had the chance?

"Thomas knows I met my father at the assembly," Loris moaned. "Nick confirmed this—Thomas knew Papa was in the area, Thomas somehow guessed that Papa had sent for me, and then Papa met me at the assembly. I might have run away with Papa, too."

Lady Fairly got up from the swing. "How could Thomas know anything of the sort, Miss Tanner?"

"Thomas hired investigators to look for Papa, and used Squire Belmont's sketch to find him. He probably saw when I got the note from Papa, too. He'll think I was l-leaving him, and I might have. My lady, I very nearly m-might have. I h-hate to cry."

"I hate to see you cry," said a masculine voice from the path across the garden.

There he stood, not Thomas, not Loris's lover, but Baron Sutcliffe. He wore impeccable riding attire, a sapphire signet ring winked on his left small finger, and his black riding boots were polished to a high shine. Even for him, he'd troubled to look every inch the lord, which did not bode well for the lord's steward.

He came forth, his stride the same relaxed, bold gait that had first brought him to Loris's notice amid a stable full of miscreants bent on causing her mischief.

Then he stopped at the foot of the porch steps. "Lady Fairly, would you excuse us?"

"Miss Tanner," Lady Fairly said. "Do you wish a moment of privacy with our Thomas?"

Our Thomas? "Yes, please." A moment of privacy with a dyspeptic lion might pass more agreeably, so severe was Thomas's expression.

"Thomas, you will listen first," her ladyship said, descending the steps. "You will be a gentleman at all times, and you will not muck this up. Fairly accompanies me to London in the morning, and I can't spare him for any more adventures with you just now."

Lady Fairly kissed Thomas's cheek, patted his chest, and left Loris alone with the man she loved—the man she'd nearly abandoned.

"Won't you sit for a moment?" Loris asked, when Lady Fairly had disappeared down the path to the home wood.

Thomas took the place beside Loris, and the swing dipped on its chains.

"I wanted to kill him." He tapped a folded document against his palm, slowly, deliberately, in the same rhythm an annoyed cat switched its tail. "I wanted to kill him by painful inches. Generally, I abhor violence."

"I wanted to give Claudia Pettigrew a piece of my mind," Loris said. "Has she left yet?"

"You think I meant Giles? He's a puppy," Thomas said. "An overwhelmed, arrogant, helpless puppy who's lucky he rides well; and yes, his mother has been escorted to London. I've considered buying Giles a cavalry commission, but the only billets available are in India, and then I'd be left with a half-ruined horse farm to deal with."

And me. You'd have me to deal with. "Papa will put the Pettigrew estate to rights—he's the one you wanted to kill, isn't he?" Loris could admit to the same impulse. That Thomas shared her sentiments was reassuring.

He gave the swing a push with his foot. "Yes, I meant your papa. He has much to answer for, leaving you to contend with his problems, leaving you to wonder, leaving you to make explanations. And then this business with Pettigrew."

The swing was in nearly violent motion.

"Thomas, I suffered no ill effects," Loris said. "I'm angry with Giles, and I'll probably be angry with Papa for the rest of my life—we can be angry with the people we love, I know that now—but I'm fine. Nicholas has offered me the hospitality of his family's estate, and I would like to get to know my cousins."

That last was sheer fancy, for all Loris wanted to do was wrap her arms around Thomas and never leave his side.

"You'd abandon me then, after all?" His question was carefully neutral, and he let the swing slow.

"I would not want to leave you, but I can understand why you'd be upset with me." Upset was a kind word for disappointed, disgusted, furious... Loris knew them all.

"I found the note," Thomas said, leaning forward and bracing his elbows on his thighs. "The damned, conniving, sneaky note Tanner had passed to you in Trieshock. 'Be ready,' he warned, as if you were one of his raw recruits and he your commanding officer."

Worse and worse. "I did not want to leave," Loris said, though that sentiment would be paltry consolation to the man who, against every dictate of sense and convention, had given her a chance to prove her abilities. "I had decided not to go, in fact, and Papa's idea of a reunion assured me that my decision was sound."

Thomas rose and took up a position half-sitting, half-leaning on the porch railing. Loris wanted to haul him back, within kissing and cuddling range, but he was agitated, and rightly so.

"Explain yourself, Loris, for your situation has been much on my mind." He tapped the letter against his palm again, or maybe not a letter, because the paper was velum rather than foolscap. Had he written her a character? A bank draft?

Loris knew not which would be worse.

"Papa expected me to do to you exactly what he had done to me," Loris said. "To leave without explanation or notice. I know how that feels, to be abandoned, left to wonder and worry. I could not treat somebody I lo—"

Thomas ceased tapping the document. "Loris Tanner?"

Loris looked away from him, across her tidy back garden, to the overgrown home wood. A maple at the edge of the trees already had a few yellow leaves near the top, and the sight brought despair closer.

"I could not treat somebody I l-love the way Papa treated

me," Loris said. "I hadn't figured out what to say to him, how to justify my decision, but when he behaved so, so... so thoughtlessly, all proud of himself and ready to drag me away from you, from Linden... He's not a bad man, but he was a poor father. I'm grown now, and I have options I didn't have as a child."

Thomas snapped off a blue, blue pansy and held it out to her. "If you cry, I will want to break your papa's head, and because it appears Tanner will be my neighbor, Belmont would likely get involved. I beg you, madam, please do not cry."

Loris accepted the pansy, knowing she'd put it between the pages of the Bible she'd demanded back her father.

"Do you love me, Loris?"

"Yes."

"I believe you do," Thomas said, resuming his place beside her. "I read your father's presuming little epistle, though I had no overt intention to trespass against your privacy at the time. I wanted to tear his missive to bits. I still do."

The *sneaky, conniving* note. Loris stopped twirling her pansy. "When did you read that message, Thomas?"

"The night before the assembly. I wanted to leave you a note, explaining that I was being gentlemanly by letting you rest without an uninvited baron in your bed. I opened your lap desk, and there Tanner's summons sat. You were to pack immediately, leave everything you'd worked so hard for behind, and come at a dead gallop to your papa's side the instant he crooked his presuming—I'm sorry. He's your father, and he did the best he could."

Loris took Thomas's hand. He sounded mortally disgusted, though he at least grasped that Loris loved him.

"Papa's note did tell me to pack and be ready. He was just being Papa."

"He was being a self-absorbed, arrogant, high-handed... Yes, he was being your papa. Nicholas and Beckman are not in charity with him, I'll have you know. If you visit Belle Maison,

Micah Tanner will not accompany you."

Loris had dreamed Thomas would accompany her. She let her head rest on his shoulder and put aside the pansy.

"So you knew that Papa had summoned me. What you must think of me, Thomas, to have spared Papa a single instant of my attention."

"I think very highly of you," Thomas said, kissing Loris's knuckles, "but thoughts are of little moment compared to deeds. If I love you, then I will acknowledge that you have choices, and I will support your choices as best I can. Your father loves you, my sister loves me, I love her, *I love you*, you love Linden. All very lovely, but you deserve more than high-flown sentiments. You deserve to have a choice."

Did Thomas realize he'd spoken in the present tense regarding his sister? Did he realize his thumb brushing over Loris's knuckles was making her insides melt?

"Your declaration of love, Thomas, means the world to me. I understand if you can't renew it."

"I *am* renewing it, you hopeless gudgeon, but I wanted to give you time to recover your balance and make up your mind without somebody pointing a gun at you. I intend that you have options, though I warn you, I'm not playing fair."

How stern he sounded. Loris lifted Thomas's arm and settled it about her shoulders.

"If this is a further declaration of love, Thomas, you're being rather indirect."

"Oh, very well, I'll be precipitous, because my next attempt at a declaration will be made in your bed, madam." He tossed the paper into her lap. "Please marry me, and don't run off with anybody else, even your poor, helpless idiot of a father, ever."

Loris unfolded the paper and peered at it, despite her vision having gone blurry.

"I can't make it out," she said, though the words *for her sole and separate use, notwithstanding any subsequent period of coverture* leapt off the page. "Thomas, what is this?"

"It's a trust document," Thomas said. "I'm a man of business, and marriage settlements are business, but Loris, that trust goes into effect whether you marry me or not. You can choose Linden, and you can choose me, but you'll not be forced to put up with me simply as the price for biding on the estate you clearly love."

"Are you leaving me?" What did a deed of trust have to do with loving each other, if that's what Thomas was saying?

And what did *anything* matter—land, crops, harvest, *anything*—if Thomas was leaving her?

"No, I'm not leaving you, and you weren't leaving me. You hadn't packed so much as a handkerchief, madam. I realized that, as I lay among your sheets, felled by the thought of all you've dealt with. A woman eager to leave packs her treasures herself. You hadn't even a valise under your bed nor a satchel in your wardrobe."

Thomas slid off the swing and went down on his knee, though he kept Loris's hand in his.

"I'm proposing holy dratted matrimony and making a complete hash of it. That paper says you own Linden, more or less. You also own my heart, and I certainly hope I have a lifelong lease on yours. I had to get Nick and Beck involved as trustees, and your father will try to tell you what to do with land he nearly ruined, and maybe you don't—hell. Please marry me. Linden is yours, whether you marry me or not. I'm yours regardless, too. Will you be my baroness?"

Thomas was proposing, again, despite Loris's idiot father, despite notes in her lap desk, or ships leaving from Brighton. He was offering her wealth and freedom without benefit of matrimony—Linden would be hers—but he was offering her love and joy at his side, too, and that meant the world.

That meant *everything*.

Loris wrapped her arms around him, the paper crackling in her lap. "I don't care two wilted weeds for being your baroness, but I will be your wife gladly, and your lover and your friend and your adviser on all matters agricultural. I love you, Thomas Jennings, Baron Sutcliffe, and I will always, always love you, and never, ever leave you."

Thomas picked her up and carried her into the cottage, though Loris made him stop long enough for her to retrieve the pansy and set it in water. They were married within the week—Thomas had his suspicions about Loris's recent tendency toward midday naps—and Lord and Lady Fairly stood up with them.

Loris's father did not escort her up the church aisle. Loris bestowed that privilege on Nicholas, and the wedding breakfast included all of the Haddonfield sisters and brothers, Squire Belmont, and even Thomas's sister, Theresa—also his charming, if somewhat rambunctious little niece, Priscilla.

Though the difficulty that dear child endured sorting out her mama and the squire is a tale for another day.

ACKNOWLEDGEMENT:

Many years ago, I crossed paths with a man whose job was investigating all those awful transportation accidents we read about in the newspapers. While I was learning to be a child welfare attorney, and deal with families coming apart at the seams, my neighbor and friend, Dr. Merritt Birky, PhD, sorted through the wreckage of plane crashes, derailed trains, and burned out oil barges.

When Squire Belmont applies simple logic and knowledge of local conditions to get to the bottom of Linden's stable fire, he's relying indirectly on the experience of one of the world's most experienced smoke and fire toxicologists. Merritt shares Matthew's tolerant outlook toward the human condition, and his lively curiosity about the natural world, too.

Way leads on to way, and we don't always get to stay in touch with the friends we make, but I do want to thank Merritt and his fellow accident investigators. They labor for long hours under trying conditions to keep us all safer as we go on about our lives, and surely that is the work of heroes and heroines.

To my dear Readers,

I hope you enjoyed Thomas and Loris's tale! My next Regency romance, **Tremaine's True Love**, the first in the True Gentlemen trilogy, comes out in August, and features Tremaine St. Michael and Lady Nita Haddonfield.

Tremaine St. Michael is firmly in trade, and seeks only to negotiate the sale of some fancy sheep with the Earl of Bellefonte. The earl's sister, Lady Nita Haddonfield, is practical, selfless, and hard-working, though Tremaine senses she's also tired of her charitable obligations, and envious of her siblings' marital bliss.

Tremaine, having been raised among shepherds, can spot another lonely soul, no matter how easily Lady Nita fools her family. Neither Tremaine nor Nita is looking for love, but love comes looking for them!

You can order your copy of **Tremaine's True Love now**.
Or start reading an excerpt from Tremaine and Nita's story here:

* * *

Tremaine St. Michael's visit with Lady Nita's family has been cut short by illness affecting his flocks in Oxfordshire. Lady Nita knows how to treat all manner of illnesses and injuries, but she's completely at a loss when it comes to her own heartache…

"Mr. St. Michael. I gather you're leaving us."

Leaving *her.*

He took a seat on the piano bench, which left little room for Nita. "I honestly don't want to, my lady. I looked forward to turning down the room with you, learning how you cheat at chards, or singing a few verses of 'Green Grow the Rashes, o.'"

"Mr. Burns again?"

"At his philosophical best. Will you walk with me to the

stables, my dear?"

The door to the music room was open, which preserved Nita from an impulse to kiss Mr. St. Michael. She'd refrained the previous night—good manners, common sense, some inconvenient virtue had denied her a single instant of shared pleasure.

"I'll need my cloak."

Mr. St. Michael held Nita's cloak for her when they reached the kitchen door, and when Nita would have closed the frogs herself, his hands were already at her throat, competent and brisk. He did up the fastenings exactly right—snug enough to be warm, not tight enough to constrain breathing or movement.

"Have you a bonnet, Lady Nita?"

So formal. If Nita had had a bonnet, she might have smacked him with it, surely the most childish impulse she'd felt in years.

"We're only walking to the stables, Mr. St. Michael, and the sun has hardly graced the shire in the days." What would freckles on Nita's nose matter, anyway? "I take it you couldn't sleep?" she asked, by way of small talk.

His eyes looked careworn to her, like the gaze of a mother who'd been up through the night with a colicky infant.

"I did not sleep well; you're right, my lady. I'm accustomed to waking up in strange beds, but I do worry for those sheep."

Nita let him hold the door for her, though his observation was odd.

Mr. St. Michael bent near. "I meant, I travel a great deal, and spend many nights in inns, lodging houses, and the homes of acquaintances. You have a naughty imagination, Lady Nita."

She took his arm, though she was entirely capable of walking the gardens without a man's escort. Nita did have a naughty imagination, about which she'd nearly forgotten.

"Will you send word when you reach Oxfordshire, Mr. St. Michael?"

"I'll have your Mr. Belmont send a pigeon, but you mustn't worry. I'm a seasoned traveler, William is an excellent fellow under saddle, and the distance isn't that great."

The distance was endless, for Mr. St. Michael, having failed to wrangle Nicholas's sheep free, would never cross paths with Nita again.

Mr. St. Michael shifted, taking Nita's hand as they traversed the cold, dormant garden. They hadn't bothered with gloves, and his grip was warm.

"I will recall your hospitality fondly, my lady," he said, his burr once again more in evidence.

While Nita would recall his departure with bitter regret. A gust of frigid wind blew down from the north, snowflakes slanting along it.

"Must you go, Mr. St. Michael?"

"I don't like the look of those clouds either," he said as they approached the stable, "but I'll probably make London before the weather does anything serious. May I make a farewell to your Atlas, my lady?"

"Of course." Despite her heavy cloak, Nita was chilled, and the barn would be relatively warm.

They walked into the stable, out of the wind, but into near darkness. In warmer months, the hay port doors, windows, and cupola would be opened to let in light and air, but in winter, warmth was more important than light.

Atlas lifted his head over the half door, a mouthful of hay munched to oblivion as Nita and Mr. St. Michael approached.

"You need a more elegant mount, my lady," Mr. St. Michael said. "Just as you need a silly evening of cards, a waltz or two, and more poetry. I had hoped to give you that."

Nita *needed* to kiss him. Tremaine St. Michael had offered her a rare glimpse of how male understanding could comfort and please, he'd offered her poetry, and he was leaving.

"Good-bye, Mr. St. Michael."

Nita didn't have to go up on her toes to kiss him, but she

did have to stand tall. Despite the bitter wind outside, despite his lack of hat, scarf or gloves, Mr. St. Michael's lips were warm.

He tasted of peppermint with a hint of ginger biscuit. Nita hadn't planned more than to press her lips to his, but Mr. St. Michael was apparently willing to indulge her beyond those essentials.

His hands landed on her shoulders, gently but firmly, as he tucked her between himself and the wall of Atlas's stall. He slid a hand into her hair, cradling the back of her head against his palm.

Soon, he'd gallop to off Oxford, but the way he held Nita said, for the moment, *she* wasn't going anywhere.

Well, neither would he. Nita wrapped an arm around Mr. St. Michael's waist—blast all winter clothing to perdition—and sank a hand into his dark locks.

"I'll miss—" she managed before his mouth settled over hers and Nita's worldly cares, her disgruntlement with her family, her concern for the Chalmers children, all went quite… tapsalteerie-o.

Kissing Mr. St. Michael bore a resemblance to the onset of a fever. Weakness assailed Nita, from her middle outward through her limbs, and then heat welled in its wake. He held her snugly—she would not fall—but she felt as if she were falling.

Tremaine St. Michael's kiss was a marvel of contradictions: solid male strength all around Nita and feather soft caresses to her lips; dark frustration to be limited to a kiss, and soaring satisfaction to have a kiss that transcended mere friendliness; utter glee to find that her advances were enthusiastically returned; and plummeting sorrow, because Mr. St. Michael's horse awaited him in the stable yard.

He cupped Nita's jaw as he traced kisses over her eyebrows, nose, and cheeks.

"You deserve more than a stolen kiss in the stable," he

whispered near Nita's ear. "But if a stolen kiss is what you'll take, then I hope this one was memorable."

This one kiss, this one series of kisses, had banished winter from Nita's little corner of Kent in less than a minute.

She rested against him, as she had for a moment in the kitchen late at night. "You'll let us know when you've arrived safely to Kent." She was repeating herself.

"I'll let *you* know, and Nita?"

Not Lady Nita, but plain Nita. How that warmed her too. "Tremaine?"

She felt the pleasure of her familiar address reverberate through him, because he kissed her ear as he held her in the gloom of the stables.

"Please be careful. Your brother isn't wrong to worry about you. Tending to the sick is noble, but perilous. I would not want harm to befall you."

Nita added two more feelings to the bittersweet confusion in her heart. Tremaine St. Michael cared for her, and yet, he sounded as if he nearly agreed with Nicholas: the Earl of Bellefonte's oldest sister ought to spend her afternoons stitching samplers, indifferent to the suffering of others.

"I'll be careful," Nita said. "You avoid the ditches."

"I generally do, though I wish—" Mr. St. Michael stayed where he was a moment longer, peering down at Nita as a heathery fragrance sneaked beneath the stable scents to tease at Nita's nose.

Nita was penned in by the wall, the horse, and Mr. St. Michael, so she turned her face away, from him, from his wishes.

"Safe journey, Mr. St. Michael."

He stepped back, and as he tugged his gloves on, Nita could see his focus withdraw from her and affix itself to his sheep, to the journey he undertook to ensure their safety.

Nobody had *ever* tormented him with orders to stitch samplers, or plan a house party, or practice the simpler Haydn sonatas while a child suffered influenza or a maiden aunt endured a female complaint in mortified silence.

Nita was the first to move toward the stable yard, lest Mr. St. Michael ruin a delightful kiss with parting sermons and scolds.

William waited outside, a groom leading him in a plodding circle. Snowflakes graced a brisk breeze beneath a leaden sky, and Nita's resentment receded to its taproot: worry, for Mr. St. Michael, for the infirm whom she tended.

And a little bit, worry for herself.

"I have enjoyed my stay at Belle Maison," Mr. St. Michael said, taking the reins from the groom. "Every bit of it."

He led William to the mounting block, the first few steps of a distance that must widen and widen between him and Nita. She wanted to throw herself into his embrace just once more, but instead spared the sullen sky a glance.

Mr. St. Michael swung up as a flutter of white caught Nita's eye, followed by a thin, tinkling peal from the bell in the dovecote.

* * *

Order your copy of **Tremaine's True Love now**!

You can find a sneak peek of Thoma's sequel, **Matthew— The Jaded Gentlemen Book II,** at http://graceburrowes. com/books/matthew.php. The publication date will be in September, and pre-orders links should be available soon.

And to keep up with all of my releases and news, **sign up for my newsletter** by visiting http://graceburrowes.com/ contact.php.

Thanks, and happy reading!

Grace Burrowes